"YOU'LL MARRY ME WHETHER YOU LIKE IT OR NOT," said Kenric. The King of England had gifted him with Tess of Remmington, and he had every intention of keeping her. He paused to give her a brief, chilling smile of triumph. "Or do you dare defy our king's command?"

Tess struggled to recover her composure under the baron's icy glare. Ruthless power emanated from the man who stood before her. There wasn't a trace of warmth in the cold black eyes that glared down at her, nor the barest hint of gentleness in that clenched jaw. Their eyes met again and this time she didn't miss the meaning behind his fierce expression. Why, he was trying to intimidate her!

He was succeeding.

She felt a shiver run down her spine. She was snared by those eyes as surely as any trapped prey. They held her captive, the power she sensed there absolute, capable of forcing anyone to submit to his will. Surprisingly, the emotions whirling through her were the complete opposite of the fear and horror she should be experiencing. It was the strangest thing, but she had an indescribable urge to stand closer to the warlord—and to touch him. . . .

The Warlord

Elizabeth Elliott

Bantam Books

New York Toronto
London Sydney Auckland

THE WARLORD

A Bantam Fanfare Book / July 1995

ISBN-13: 978-0-553-56910-0

ISBN-10: 0-553-56910-4

Published simultaneously in the United States and Canada

Bantam Books are published by Bantam Books, a division of Random House, Inc. Its
trademark, consisting of the words "Bantam Books" and the portrayal of a rooster, is
Registered in U.S. Patent and Trademark Office and in other countries. Marca
Registrada. Random House, Inc., New York, New York.

PRINTED IN THE UNITED STATES OF AMERICA

OPM   0 9 8 7

To Nancy Fulton,
cyberfriend extraordinaire.

Special thanks to my friends in the Litforum and
RWA on-line for their invaluable advice
and encouragement.

The
Warlord

Prologue

The Holy Lands, 1278

Very little remained of the ancient city. The work of countless generations was reduced to rubble in a battle that lasted little more than three days. Skeletons of walls and buildings that had stood since the time of Christ rose in a shadow of their former glory, silhouetted against the dawn of a desert sky. Tendrils of smoke snaked upward from the smoldering ashes to join the hazy cloak that shrouded the city.

A lone knight rode through what remained of an archway, over smashed gates that had barred the enemy for a thousand years. Scattered among the tumbled stones and burnt timbers were the people who once lived there, their bodies a mute testimony to the battle that had raged through the city the day before.

With the sights and sounds of battle still fresh in

memory, the knight didn't appear disturbed by the carnage that surrounded him. His warhorse picked a careful path through the rubble, the animal alert to his footing even though his head hung low with exhaustion.

Kenric of Montague's dark face remained expressionless, the knight as unmoved by these deaths as the countless others he'd witnessed in the three years he'd been on Crusade in the Holy Lands. The people of Al' Abar had refused to surrender. Their city had been besieged until nothing remained of their defenses and no single structure stood whole that would provide any shelter. They had died. Such events had been repeated too many times over the years for Kenric to feel anything more than the bone-deep fatigue that followed a long battle.

Kenric's armor and that of his horse were covered with ashes, crusty with sweat, the leather stiff with dried blood. Another tunic ruined, he thought idly, gazing down at the once white garment with the scarlet cross emblazoned on his chest. Only the stitches that outlined the cross distinguished the holy emblem from the rest of the mutilated fabric. Luckily, this time none of the blood was his own. With an annoyed sigh, he nudged his horse forward again when the animal ambled to a weary halt.

He saw the shield first, three golden lions on a fiery red field. It lay just outside the ruins of what might have been the home of a prosperous merchant. The half-naked body of a woman lay next to the shield. The soldier Kenric was looking for lay facedown just a pace from the woman, with the body of a young Arab boy sprawled half on top of the soldier.

Kenric considered the scene with the dispassionate logic of one who can no longer be shocked by the atrocities of war. The boy was probably the woman's son or brother. He'd likely saved her from the first knight, but others had finished what the first had begun.

Kenric dismounted and nudged the knight's body with the tip of his boot, rolling the corpse onto its back. He reached inside the soldier's hauberk and removed a gold necklace with an efficient jerk. Next he took a ring from the dead man's hand and placed both items safely inside his hauberk before he remounted and turned the horse toward the edge of the city.

Normally Kenric wouldn't bother with such trinkets, but King Edward would be displeased if his nephew's signet ring or cross fell into the hands of infidels. The personal effects would also prove to the king that his nephew died in battle, rather than meeting an inglorious death from one of the many tortures inflicted on Christians by their Arab captors. He knew the bards would compose sorrowful ballads for the young man, full of brave deeds and glory, with no mention that he'd died attempting rape. Kenric doubted his own ballads would be so generous if he fell in battle. No, there were ballads aplenty about Kenric of Montague, and none could be called flattering.

A small group of knights had gathered near the outskirts of the city and one pointed toward Kenric as he emerged from the ruins. The men turned as a whole to watch the approach of their leader, each trying to guess Kenric's mood as he rode from the city. The king was sure to be upset by his favorite nephew's death, but Kenric had shown no more concern over this death than he would for a common footsoldier's. Some wondered what it would take for any emotion to cross the warlord's face.

A young squire hurried forward to hold Kenric's horse as he dismounted, and a knight named Roger Fitz Alan stepped away from the group to greet his leader. A young priest also hurried toward Kenric, the priest and Fitz Alan noticing each other at the same moment. Both men hastened their steps as they tried to be the first to reach the warrior.

"Sir Kenric," the priest called out, waving a pudgy hand in the air. "A moment of your time."

Kenric ignored the priest and tossed the horse's reins to his squire. "Make sure he has plenty of water, Evard.

And a good brushing. Be quick about his care. We leave within the hour."

"Aye, milord," the squire murmured, leading the horse away.

"He found out about the de Gravelle brothers," Fitz Alan said, jerking his head toward the priest.

Kenric acknowledged the warning with a slight nod. "Send Simon to make sure the supply carts are loaded and ready to move. The scouts returned at daybreak with word that Rashid's army is less than two days' march from here. The men are too worn to face that devil right now. With luck, we will encounter little more than skirmishes before we reach the sea."

Fitz Alan bowed slightly, then turned away to find Simon and carry out Kenric's order.

"Sir Kenric," the priest called again, coming to a halt near Kenric's elbow. His face was flushed by the early morning heat, sweat collecting already in the fleshy folds of his pale neck. Father Vachel drew himself up to his full height of five and a half feet, still looking small and insignificant next to the towering figure of the warlord. "You cannot mean to punish the de Gravelles as I have heard, Sir Kenric. No matter their crime, no Christian deserves such a death."

"Begone, priest." Kenric dismissed Father Vachel with a casual wave of his hand, as if to brush the priest away. He strode purposefully toward the group of knights, leaving the priest behind. The knights were gathered around two men who lay side by side in the sand, stripped naked and staked out spread-eagle. Kenric came to a halt at the feet of the staked men, looking slowly from one man to the other. The expressions on the bound men's faces reflected their fear. Kenric crossed his arms across his broad chest and pronounced their judgment.

"Ranulf and Dominic de Gravelle, 'tis known you conspired to murder me, but instead your poisoned wine killed four of my men. For that you will die."

Kenric gave the de Gravelle brothers a moment to come to terms with their fate. He looked toward the horizon at the rapidly rising sun then his gaze swept across the ruins of the city. "Aye, you will die by the heat of the sun, or at the hands of infidels who will be drawn from across the desert by the smoke that still rises from Al' Abar."

Ranulf de Gravelle clenched his jaw bravely, but Dominic broke down and began to sob, his pleas for mercy nearly incomprehensible. Kenric slowly drew his sword, his dark eyes devoid of emotion. "Or you can die a more honorable death than the one you intended for me."

Dominic continued to wail but Ranulf's eyes narrowed, considering his leader.

"You want to know who hired us," Ranulf stated flatly. He levered his shoulders up, struggling against his bonds to look at his brother's tear-streaked face. After a brief glance his head fell back to the sand in defeat. A quick death was the only mercy they could expect. Death from a man who should be dead. Ranulf cursed softly, refusing to reveal the name of the man behind their plot.

"We were approached at court," Dominic blurted out. "We made it known that we were mercenaries and our swords came with a price. My brother and I had no intention of becoming assassins, b-but the reward for your death was too tempting, milord. Gold, a fine keep, and rich lands. Ranulf was also promised the dowry that comes with your sister's hand in marriage."

"My father," Kenric stated quietly, his face expressionless. He'd known without being told that the old warlord was behind this scheme. Yet he'd wanted to be sure.

Dominic nodded uncertainly. "Baron Montague calls you a bastard. A spawn of the Devil. He grows old and sickly, but he is determined that your younger brother, Guy, inherit his lands and title. He hoped that you would die here in the Holy Lands, as so many others have. Indeed, 'tis known the infidels search you out on a battlefield for the glory of your death. Even they have a price on your head. Yet you will not die. When he learned that the king intended to call you home, Baron Montague arranged for us to journey here and join your army."

"Was my brother, Guy, involved in this scheme?"

"I cannot say," Dominic admitted. "The boy was at none of our meetings."

"Was anyone else involved?"

"Nay, just Ranulf and myself. But I would have you know that the plot to poison the wine was Ranulf's, not mine," Dominic confessed. "I beg you, have mercy, milord. I had no wish to involve myself in this blood feud and told Ranulf so."

"But you did not tell me, did you, Dominic?" Kenric asked mildly. "You knew of his plot yet remained silent, thus four men are dead. You will pay the same price for treachery."

"You've wasted your breath, Brother *dear*," Ranulf said sarcastically, though hatred blazed from his eyes toward Kenric of Montague.

"You should have died," Ranulf told Kenric, his voice a harsh, defeated whisper. "What keeps you alive?"

"God's will," Kenric lied. His emotionless gaze moved slowly from Ranulf to Dominic. Dominic's eyes grew round and wide with complete terror as the warlord's sword moved toward his neck. Pinned to the ground, Dominic could do nothing to escape his fate, say nothing more to sway his executioner. Ranulf's shout to face death bravely was drowned out by Dominic's screams.

Kenric turned and stalked away from the de Gravelles, his mood grim. Four men dead by treachery, now another two by his own hand. And the ruins of a city at his back, filled with corpses. Kenric mentally calculated his losses, already planning the knights and soldiers he would move into new positions to replace those who would never leave Al' Abar. His mind conjured images of the dead, men who laughed, drank, and boasted of their skills until they were silenced forever beneath the relentless sun of this hellish

place. Yet there were others just like them to take their
place. Knights and soldiers, all intent on gold and glory.
They would die the same deaths as those who went before
them.

And Ranulf de Gravelle wondered how Kenric could
survive amidst so much death? The answer was so simple,
it was laughable. There was no fear of death left in Kenric.
He'd faced the Grim Reaper each day of his life for the
past three years and had grown accustomed to the specter's
constant presence. It was that acceptance of Death that
kept Kenric alive, as much as his skill with a sword. A
warrior who fought without fear made few mistakes, his
mind intent only on tactics and strategy.

Aye, Kenric knew his worth to king and country. He
had all the characteristics of a perfect warrior; a body
molded from childhood to the art of combat, a mind edu-
cated to the military strategies of a thousand years and
countless cultures, and a heart robbed of its soul long ago.
Such a warrior left only death and destruction in his path,
an instrument of Death itself. There was no thought of
glory or honor in this warrior, no gloating or boasts, just
calm acceptance. Another battle won. Another would follow soon enough.

Kenric headed toward a blue and white striped tent,
the only tent remaining of the battle camp that had stood
outside the city for nearly a fortnight. After a quick meal
and change of clothes, he would order the army forward,
back toward the sea, back to England. And another war.

Aye, Baron Montague was right to fear his return. The
old man knew that Kenric's power would only increase
when the king sent him to join the war in Wales. As the
king's favored henchman, Kenric would not be so easy to
murder in England, or even in the mist-shrouded forests of
Wales. He just might live long enough to inherit the lands
Baron Montague fought so desperately to keep from him.

"Sir Kenric!" the priest shouted. He rushed forward
again to tug on Kenric's sleeve, trying to bring the warlord

to a halt. Kenric merely shrugged his arm away and continued without breaking stride.

"You begin to annoy me, priest. Best say your blessings over Al' Abar and find your donkey. We do not tarry here."

"You did not give the de Gravelles an opportunity to confess their sins, to meet their Maker with a clear conscience," Father Vachel said defiantly, though he seemed appeased by the justice meted out to the traitors. To leave them here alive would have been the greater sin.

"I heard their confession," Kenric replied, unconcerned.

"You speak blasphemy!"

Kenric shrugged, his attention on his army's preparations to move out. "Take a walk through the streets of the city, priest. Count how many lie dead there, none with benefit of priestly confessions to meet their deaths."

" 'Tis not the same. Those few of your knights who died gave their lives bravely in battle and had no need for confessions," Father Vachel said reasonably. "And the infidels of this city were not entitled to confession. They died by God's will."

"Nay," Kenric said slowly, turning at last to face the priest. Father Vachel backed away from the cold, unblinking gaze. His hand went to his chest, crossing himself against what he saw in those eyes.

"They died by my will."

1

Five Years Later
Northern England

The winter night was not nearly dark enough for Kenric's mission. His gaze swept over the inky silhouette of Langston Keep, scanning the shadows of the battlements for any unusual movement as he silently cursed the cloudless sky. The bright half moon turned the snow-covered ground a silvery shade of blue, making anyone who ventured into the open an easy target for guards posted within the fortress walls.

"This may yet be a trap," Fitz Alan whispered.

Kenric nodded to acknowledge that truth. He could see his breath in the faint moonlight and he stirred restlessly, trying to ward off the frigid night air and his own misgivings. The woods behind them provided little protection. They would be an easy catch, should an ambush be in order. The very fact that their plan depended on one

Scotsman betraying another nearly guaranteed a trap. But Kenric was determined to see this through and Fitz Alan wouldn't challenge the decision. Not when the king had a hand in this scheme.

"The plan seems too simple," Fitz Alan warned in a low voice. "We should have brought men to guard our backs."

Kenric didn't reply. He stared intently at a clump of large bushes that filled a gully leading to the keep. The vague outline of two cloaked figures grew more distinct as they emerged from the brush, the soft crunch of snow announcing their approach. Despite the danger they were in, Kenric nearly laughed aloud when he spotted their quarry. One was tall and broad-chested, the other short and amazingly plump. Kenric's soldiers would roll with laughter when they caught sight of this prize. A bear and a butterball were hardly fitting trophies for two of England's fiercest warriors. Five years of war in Wales, suffering every discomfort known to a soldier, and this was to be his reward?

"Perhaps her face will not be as difficult to look upon as her person," Fitz Alan whispered, his smile heard but unseen. " 'Tis the oddest-shaped woman I've ever laid eyes on."

The approaching man raised his head, as if he'd caught the scent of danger. Kenric moved silently to the edge of the brush, disappearing into the black shadows of the forest. Fitz Alan crouched low to the ground, watching the two odd shapes as they walked cautiously toward his hiding spot. They halted less than ten paces away.

"This could be a trap, Uncle Ian."

The soft, feminine voice belonged to the butterball. Her words pleased Kenric considerably. It was a good sign that their prey shared their concern. The woman drew her hood back to look around the tiny clearing, attempting to peer into the dark forest as she whispered her plea.

"I say we escape by ourselves while we can. I'll guard

your back well enough should we meet with any thieves. 'Tis obvious he is not coming. Let us be gone from here."

The woman gasped at the same instant her uncle swung around with his sword drawn.

"Put your sword on the ground, Laird Duncan. Slowly," Kenric ordered.

Ian Duncan didn't move. The moon provided enough light for Kenric to make out the Scottish laird's shape, but his expression remained obscured by the night's shadows.

"Do as I say," Kenric warned, nudging the woman's bulk with the tip of his sword. "Else she'll take my blade between her ribs."

Ian lowered the weapon to the ground, then pulled his niece to his side, away from the warrior's sword. He looked at Kenric, but nodded toward Fitz Alan. "You were to come alone."

"My man is loyal," he replied with a shrug. "Get the horses, Fitz Alan."

"Lady Remmington will ride with me," Ian said, maintaining a protective hold on the girl. "I left my horse less than a mile from here."

"We have your horse." Kenric picked up Ian's sword then sheathed his own, queerly disappointed that the lady was falling into his hands so easily. He hadn't the slightest desire to get a closer look at his prize. No matter how comely the face, it couldn't possibly make up for the package it came with. She was undoubtedly as homely as his horse or she would have shown herself by now. "The arrangements have been made at Kelso Abbey."

"You are prepared to see this through, to do what is asked of you?" Ian asked. He waited several long, silent moments for an answer.

"Aye." Kenric's reply was firm. "You can stay at Kelso Abbey until the search parties are recalled or make for your fortress immediately after—"

"I ride for Scotland tonight," Ian interrupted.

"Why are we going to Kelso Abbey?" Lady Remmington asked, her whisper nearly muffled by the cloak's heavy hood.

"Hush, Tess," Ian scolded. "Here are the horses. Be a good girl and everything will be fine. Quickly now, we must hurry."

"Yes, Uncle," Tess replied obediently.

Fitz Alan returned with the horses and the two warriors mounted. Ian placed the bulky girl on his horse then swung into the saddle behind her. The animals moved almost silently through the forest, their hooves wrapped with rags to muffle the noise. This late at night they wouldn't have to worry about patrols from Langston Keep, but the woods were home to outcasts; thieves and murderers who controlled the king's highways by preying on unprotected travelers. Kenric knew they could handle that threat, but he didn't have time to deal with such a distraction. The night was half spent already and every hour counted.

Tess Remmington gave little thought to thieves. Her worry centered on the pack of soldiers that could thunder out of the fortress at any moment. Her stepfather was going to be furious when he discovered her escape. Just the thought of Dunmore MacLeith made Tess's blood run cold. In outward appearance there was nothing to dislike about the Scot. Tall and fit, he had two wings of gray at the temples of his dark hair that gave him an air of distinction. But Tess, more than any other, knew a heart capable of cold-blooded murder lay beneath the deceptive facade. The beast had married her mother a mere week after her father's suspicious death. Even then the odd set of circumstances that put Dunmore MacLeith inside the fortress had seemed a little too convenient. A month later her mother had also been laid to rest in Remmington's cemetery after a "fall" from the tower steps. Everyone knew the baroness planned to petition the church and King Edward for an annulment. Some, including Dunmore MacLeith, had believed she might get it.

Tess wondered again how King Edward could have turned a blind eye toward MacLeith's evil deeds all these years. Could the war in Wales, problems with the church, and the endless quarrels among his barons keep the king too busy to bother with such a remote barony? Aye, he'd gone and forgotten about her and Tess had no way to bring her cause before him. Dunmore MacLeith sat as lord at Remmington Castle while Tess, the rightful heir, had stayed locked away in remote Langston Keep these past five years.

The only good fortune she could claim of late was the recent discovery of a secret passage that led from her bedchamber to the gully outside the walls. Such passages were common in border holdings of Langston's age, built to allow the family a means of escape if the keep fell to an invading army. Now it provided Tess with a different sort of freedom. Freedom from Dunmore MacLeith's plans for her life.

Two hours later, the group dismounted outside Kelso Abbey's main gate.

A small side door swung open and, as if he'd been awaiting their arrival, a cowled monk thrust a lantern through the doorway. Tess watched the taller of the two men they had met in the forest step closer to show his face. The monk nodded, turning without a word to point toward a dark path.

Tess drew her cloak closer, trying to shake a sudden chill. The monk looked like an unholy specter of death with his black robes and long, bony finger pointing them forward. She clutched the back of her uncle's cloak and walked as close behind him as the narrow path would allow.

The path led to the doors of a large chapel and the group stepped inside. Tess pulled her hood aside just enough to get a better look at the structure, but she was careful to keep her face hidden, as Uncle Ian had ordered. Ian had said he wasn't sure what kind of men they'd meet with this night and the less they knew of Tess the better. Yet once inside the chapel she couldn't help but gape in wide-eyed wonder at the fine Gothic architecture and Norman workmanship that made Kelso Abbey one of the church's prize jewels. Tess was sure she'd never seen anything so grand. Beautiful religious paintings covered the walls and ceilings, and most statues were leafed with gold. The soft glow from an uncountable number of precious beeswax candles made the place seem more fairy-tale castle than chapel. An old priest stood near the pulpit, garbed in richly embroidered red satin and gold-trimmed robes, his presence lending an air of royalty to the scene. The priest's face was wrinkled with years of wear, but his eyes twinkled with a smile that grew broader as they passed each row of kneelers.

"Greetings, my son." The priest walked stiffly toward Kenric, his gait slowed by age. He grasped Kenric's strong hands with thin, frail ones. " 'Tis been too many years, but you've grown into a fine man."

"Thank you, Father Olwen. 'Tis good to see your familiar face this eve." Kenric smiled grimly at the priest. "I'm sure you remember my friend Roger Fitz Alan. And this is Laird Duncan."

Kenric turned then to get his first good look at the giant Scot. Although Kenric stood well over six feet, Ian Duncan was nearly as tall. The Scottish laird's face was weathered and his blue eyes creased around the edges with the lines of a man who smiled often. Much as he was smiling now at Kenric.

Kenric soon spied the reason for the Scot's humor. Ian's cloak was tossed over his shoulders to reveal not only the Duncan clan's blue and green plaid, but the handle of a massive claymore that was strapped securely to his back. So much for disarming the man. Kenric acknowledged his oversight with a slight nod, then his eyes dropped to Ian's side to inspect Lady Remmington. Her back was turned to Kenric and she seemed absorbed by the doomsday paintings on one wall of the chapel. He tried to imagine a short, fat, female version of Ian Duncan and was immediately glad she had the good grace to keep herself covered. Whoever told King Edward this girl was a pleasure to gaze upon had an odd sense of humor.

The priest interrupted Kenric's thoughts by clearing his throat, a subtle hint that he was waiting for an introduction. Kenric said simply, "Father Olwen, this is Lady Remmington."

The girl's shoulders jerked. She bowed her head, then turned to meet the priest.

"I'm pleased to meet you, my dear." Father Olwen stepped forward and took hold of the girl's hands, giving them a firm squeeze. "These circumstances are a bit unusual, but I'm sure we can make your—"

"Excuse me, Father," Ian interrupted. He ignored the priest's look of surprise and pulled Tess back to his side. "Is there someplace I might speak with Lady Remmington in private?"

"Why, I believe there is a—"

"Whatever you need say to the lady can be said right here." This time it was Kenric who interrupted the priest, his expression dark.

"I'm not so sure of that," Ian said uncertainly. "My niece knows very little of this plan. I thought it best to explain the situation once we were safely away from Langston."

"She doesn't know of the marriage?" Kenric questioned sharply.

"Marriage?" the wide bundle croaked.

"Now, lass, don't get all worked up before I have a chance to explain," Ian pleaded, turning the girl toward him to take hold of her hands.

"*Marriage!*" she repeated, her voice louder. She jerked

her hands away from Ian and tried to rest them on her hips.

The knights and priest stared in amazement when Lady Remmington's wide girth suddenly sank into a lumpy mass around her feet. They continued to watch in stunned silence as she stepped closer to Ian, her cloak dragging forward to reveal two large linen sacks on the floor. It took only a moment for them to realize the sacks had been slung over her shoulders, carried beneath the cloak to keep her arms under the sleeveless garment and protected against the cold.

"You said *nothing* about a marriage!"

The men turned their heads from the floor to Lady Remmington, almost in unison.

"She isn't fat at all," Fitz Alan whispered.

Lady Remmington still had her back to the men, but Kenric smiled when the newly slimmed figure gave Laird Duncan a good poke in the stomach. Her hood fell back onto her shoulders as she glared up at the Scot, providing a pleasing glimpse of honey-blond hair.

"I wasn't sure how you would take the news," Ian began.

"You knew damned well how I would take the news! And now you've made me swear in front of a priest!" She swirled around to face Father Olwen, her hands folded demurely, eyes lowered to the floor. "Forgive me, Father. 'Tis a sinful word I spoke in anger. I will pray God realizes these are trying times for me and can forgive this transgression. It seems my uncle's plans for this evening and my own differ greatly."

Kenric didn't realize he was holding his breath until the woman turned toward her uncle. One look at those flashing violet eyes had actually weakened his knees. Now he was certain the king jested with him. Only a blind man would describe this girl as pretty. Tess of Remmington was magnificent.

"You will explain yourself," Tess ordered, a sharp nod

at her uncle emphasizing the point. She unhooked her cloak and shrugged it off, folding the garment carefully over one arm as if she had all day to hear Ian's explanation. "And it had best be good."

"I was going to tell you," Ian said. He spoke in Gaelic, his voice lowered. "But you've had your mind so set on this convent idea that I wasn't sure you would agree to leave, knowing you would be wed to a man you'd never met."

"This plan makes no sense, Uncle." Tess answered in Gaelic as well, with a sidelong glance at the mercenary knights who escorted them here. "A convent can be explained away by a religious calling. But marriage to a man of your acquaintance? Neither your king, nor mine, is like to believe you're not involved. You risk your life with this plan."

"Calm down, lass." Ian placed his big hands on Tess's shoulders. "Now you know I've your best interest at heart. Your own King Edward has named your betrothed."

"What?" Tess looked hopeful for a moment, then her expression turned suspicious. "But the king already approved my stepfather's choice of husband. How can Edward name another when he's given MacLeith his word on the matter?"

"Well now, that's the tricky part," Ian admitted, rubbing his chin. "MacLeith has kept Edward good and worried since the day he took control of Remmington. He's been a loyal subject on the surface these past five years, but Edward knows MacLeith's game well enough to see a snake in his garden. Not one Englishman remains as lord of any Remmington holding and MacLeith plaids litter every battlement. Your stepfather knew it was time to test Edward's patience with this betrothal business. By refusing MacLeith's choice, Edward would have given your stepfather an excuse to defy his overlord and start a war. And everyone knows that any war so close to the border involving the King of England would soon involve the King of Scotland. When he approved the choice, Edward avoided a war, but practically handed Remmington over to MacLeith on a platter."

"So the king doesn't intend to honor his word?" she asked, her brows drawn together in a puzzled frown. "Won't that give MacLeith another excuse to challenge Edward?"

"Not if Edward pretends ignorance of the marriage." Ian smiled over the cleverness of the plan, still amazed that an Englishman could be so shrewd. "Then it becomes a war between your husband and stepfather. Edward can provide your husband with aid, but as long as he avoids direct involvement, King Alexander will have no reason to interfere."

"Who does the king think to pit against MacLeith?"

"Your betrothed is one of the king's finest barons," Ian told her enthusiastically. "You didn't expect a baron, now did you?"

"Nay," Tess said slowly. "Before he approved Mac-Leith's choice, I thought Edward would pledge my hand to one of the landless knights who vie in his tourneys for just such a favor. 'Tis unusual to offer such a large dower to a man already landed."

"Aye, your betrothed is no pauper. His estates easily match your own. Indeed, he is a man known for protecting what he has made his own. King Edward has pledged your hand to the only warrior capable of tossing Dunmore MacLeith back over the border. You are to wed Baron Montague," he announced cautiously. "The baron is—"

"The Butcher?" She sounded as if she were being strangled. Her hands flew to her throat, her voice hoarse with fear. "You think to tie me to the Butcher of Wales?"

"Watch your tongue, lass." Ian drew himself up to his full height, the tolerant uncle transforming instantly into the powerful laird. "I'll not listen to you blaspheme the man you're to wed. You've heard one too many wild tales. Baron Montague is a man well respected by those who fight for your country, and well feared by those who do not. I couldn't have made a better choice myself, had I the opportunity. I'll rest easier with Baron Montague on my border than I do with that jackal MacLeith licking his chops over my keeps. Were you expecting MacLeith to give you a fine husband like Montague?"

"You know who I'd get from him."

"Aye, Dunmore MacLeith's own son, Gordon, is the man he chose for you. Though I have my doubts that Gordon MacLeith is much of a man."

"Is this fate any better?" Tess whispered.

She realized her hands were still on her throat and she quickly lowered them to a tight grip at her waist, wondering what she had done to her king to deserve this fate. Why, everyone from Scotland to Normandy knew of Montague's baron. The man had made a name for himself in the tourneys as an undefeatable knight, then later as a fearless warrior in the king's Crusade. His name became a legend in the war against Wales. But the stories of his deeds were never wrapped in gallantry or heroics. Nay, tales concerning the Butcher of Wales were wrapped in blood. Tess thought of Baron Montague as more of a demon than a man who actually walked the earth as a mere human. Even MacLeith's men whispered the name in awe, as if its very mention was reason enough to cross themselves against evil. Tess knew how he'd earned his name and she shuddered over the knowledge. The Butcher of Wales took no prisoners. It was said there were parts of Wales where no one of Welsh blood could be found for as far as the eye could see. He'd slaughtered them all.

Of course, some of the stories were exaggerations, but there must be some shred of truth to the foul tales. Tess had no desire to find out firsthand. She knew from the braced legs and firm tone of voice that her uncle's decision was made and any argument on her part would be a waste of time. She decided to hear Ian out, then appeal to the priest for sanctuary in the church. Surely a man of God wouldn't want to see a gentle maid forced to wed such a monster. By the time the bridegroom arrived she would be under the protection of the church, safely beyond the reach of any man.

"Edward chose Baron Montague some time ago," Ian continued. "Father Olwen here was King Edward's own confessor in his younger days. He's to perform the wedding ceremony, then send a copy of the marriage papers back to London. As for the MacLeiths, they must believe you escaped on your own. They'll be told Baron Montague caught you, thinking to collect a reward, but decided to marry you instead."

"MacLeith will go to any lengths to get me back. If I'm recaptured, the marriage could be annulled. Even the English barons would recognize that right. Then where would the king's plan be?"

Ian frowned at her logic, but continued trying to reason with her.

Kenric understood Gaelic well enough to follow the conversation, but he wasn't really listening. He let his eyes wander down the thick blond braid to its tip, past an incredibly small waist and nicely rounded hips. His fingers itched to touch the silky rope, to undo the neatly woven tresses and fill his hands with gold.

That idea held Kenric's attention until he began to wonder if he'd just imagined the color of her eyes. Rich jewels could reflect such a mesmerizing shade of violet-blue, but he'd never seen the like in a woman's eyes. Lady Remmington turned her head slightly as he pondered the unlikely color and he was given another glimpse of her face. Those fascinating eyes were hidden behind the thick fans of lowered lashes, allowing him to examine her features without distraction. Her expression was calm, composed, almost regal. But he noticed the way the corners of her mouth turned down whenever her uncle mentioned the word "marriage." That didn't distract from the lushness of her mouth. Prettily bowed on the top, full and

pouting on the bottom, he couldn't wait to feel those luscious lips beneath his. He wanted to touch her, certain her
skin would be just as powder-soft as it looked. Her lips
parted slightly to reveal the tip of her tongue as she wet
her lips. The gesture was so unconsciously innocent yet
sweetly seductive, Kenric found himself holding his breath
again. It didn't take long to realize the exquisite beauty
didn't need bewitching eyes to distract a man's attention.
Her delicate profile alone set his groin to aching.

He forced himself to look away, attempting to discipline his wandering imagination. He couldn't remember
the last time he'd reacted physically to a woman without
even touching her. Hell, he didn't even know her. What
was the matter with him? His gaze slid to Fitz Alan, and he
was pleased to realize his second-in-command appeared
just as dazed by Lady Remmington's appearance. Fitz
Alan's mouth hung open quite stupidly.

"You're drooling," Kenric informed him behind one
hand. Fitz Alan's mouth snapped shut but his eyes didn't
leave the girl.

"You were right after all," Kenric went on, a certain
smugness in his voice. "Her face is not *too* difficult to gaze
upon."

"She is an angel," Fitz Alan whispered in awe.

Smiling, Kenric looked again to Lady Remmington.
She was arguing fiercely with Ian. "Aye, an angel with a
temper."

The smile disappeared completely when he heard her
next words.

"The only solution is to take me to a convent. I'll
take the vows."

"The only vows you'll be taking are marriage vows,"
Kenric growled from his place behind her, his Gaelic almost perfect.

"I have been . . . been . . ."

Her words trailed off the moment Tess spun around
and took a good look at the knights, the mercenaries hired

to help her escape Dunmore MacLeith. Several unpleasant realizations struck at once.

They weren't mercenaries.

Mercenaries were not known to possess clothing so fine as that worn by the men who stood before her. She also recognized the worth and craftsmanship of their armor. Nay, she wouldn't gain the sanctuary of the church before the bridegroom arrived. He stood before her.

But which one?

Her gaze slid to the man on the right, and she found nothing objectionable in his appearance. In truth, he was downright handsome. He had tawny hair and deep brown eyes that had probably melted many a maid's heart. The knight's roguish grin said he knew of his appeal, but the grin soon faded and became sheepish, as if he'd been caught doing something he shouldn't. Tess felt her heart sink with her hopes. She should have known Baron Montague would not look so nice. Nay, he would look like the other one, the one who looked like the Devil.

The Devil was taller than his friend, taller even than Uncle Ian, and his bulk made him much more imposing. His cloak was thrown back, and her gaze traveled slowly over his body, studying him with open curiosity. He was clad in finely linked chain mail armor covered by a blue and white surcoat. His armor did little to disguise a powerful build and an impossibly broad chest. Her gaze lingered on one of the massive arms crossed against his chest. She wouldn't be able to wrap both hands around those bulging muscles. The man was a giant, although she had to admit there was nothing hulking or clumsy about him. Every part of his body appeared in perfect proportion to his size. He reminded her of the sleek, dangerous panther that Dunmore MacLeith kept as a pet; the coiled power magnificently fascinating, yet just as deadly.

Her gaze continued upward to his hauberk, which was pulled back to reveal hair as black as his fierce scowl. Even darker eyes glared at her from a face that was marred by a wicked-looking scar that ran the length of one cheek.

Why, his expression was all wrong.

Tess's lips parted slightly in surprise as she realized there was something intensely familiar about this man, a memory that floated just out of reach. Yet there was a difference she couldn't quite name. The eyes were too dark for one thing, Tess decided, her brows drawn together in a frown. And the lines of his face were too sharp, too vivid. She looked him over again from head to foot, trying to recall where she could have seen the man before.

Kenric knew his expression was severe enough to set friends and enemies alike on edge. It was wasted on Lady Remmington. The way she eyed him up and down like a cook inspecting a side of beef was insulting. He was about to redouble his efforts to put the bold wench in her place when their eyes met.

" 'Tis you," she whispered, looking ready to scream.

"Aye, 'tis me," he answered, his voice caustic. For a moment he'd sworn there was a look of recognition in her eyes, the same look a woman would use to greet a cherished friend. Or a lover. But the warmth in her eyes disappeared so quickly that he wondered if he'd only imagined it. The girl's lasting expression of stunned disbelief was more in keeping with a maid's normal reaction. She'd just been introduced to the Butcher of Wales, a man bearing the name mothers used to frighten their children into obedience. At least she hadn't fainted.

"You'll be marrying me whether you like it or not," he said in his own language. He was uncomfortable with the difficult Gaelic burrs and wanted the lady to understand his every word. It didn't matter if she'd rather marry a three-headed goat. The King of England had gifted him with Tess of Remmington, and Kenric had every intention of keeping her. He paused to give her a brief, chilling smile of triumph. "Or do you dare defy our king's command?"

Tess struggled to recover her composure under the baron's icy glare. It was a near impossible task, since she'd been caught so completely off guard. But who wouldn't be startled to see an image from their dreams come to life? It was too eerie. Surely that was the reason her stomach was acting queerly and she suddenly felt light-headed.

Don't be a goose, she scolded herself, shaking her head to brush away the foolish notion. So she'd seen the image of a dark-haired man while she slept, a man whose face haunted her dreams so completely that she thought she knew him. So she'd had the same dream every night for the past week. Coincidence. Aye, pure and simple co-incidence.

She risked another glance at the baron's face, just to assure herself on the matter. Chilling, ruthless power ema-nated from the man who stood before her, a man who could kill without emotion or regret. There wasn't a trace of warmth in the cold black eyes that glared down at her, nor the barest hint of gentleness in that clenched jaw. Their eyes met again and this time she didn't miss the meaning behind his fierce expression. Why, he was trying to intimidate her!

He was succeeding.

She felt a shiver run down her spine and goose bumps prick her arms. She was snared by those eyes as surely as any trapped prey. They held her captive, the power she sensed there absolute, capable of forcing anyone to submit to his will. Surprisingly, the emotions swirling through her were the complete opposite of the fear or horror she should be experiencing. It was the strangest thing, but she had an indescribable urge to stand closer to the warlord. To touch him. To—

"Do you intend to answer, Lady Remmington?" Baron Montague's voice was laced with sarcasm. "Or shall I re-peat the question? You do appear confused."

Tess bristled, her temper flaring to life. " 'Tis rude to glare at a gentle lady so evilly."

She turned to Father Olwen, missing the look of disbelief on Kenric's face. "Perhaps you can help these men see reason, Father. I would like to explain the situation, then I am sure you will see the wisdom of my decision and advise everyone accordingly."

"I will do my best," Father Olwen said uncertainly. "You should know that King Edward informed me of the reason for this marriage, Lady Remmington."

Tess nodded, then drew her braid over one shoulder and began to twist the ends.

"Tess . . ." Ian objected, her name long and drawn out, sounding almost like the hiss of a snake. Or a warning.

"I do not wish to marry." Tess saw Ian step forward and she hurried to give the priest her reasons. "My wish is to become a nun. As is customary, my estates can be divided when I take the vows. It will be as though I have died."

"You are hardly dead, Lady."

"Remmington would revert to King Edward," Tess continued, ignoring the baron's interruption. She tried not to think about the deepness of his voice, how it effortlessly filled the room, so penetrating, she could almost feel the sound vibrate through her body. *Dear God, what is happening to me?* she wondered in a panic, struggling to hold on to her argument. "If I enter a convent, Remmington will stay in English hands without bloodshed. My stepfather and King Alexander cannot object because the religious laws are the same in both countries and they would not dare defy the church in such a matter. If I marry anyone, there will be a war."

She ended her small speech by bowing her head, unable to look Father Olwen in the eye another moment. She'd lied outright to a priest! "You do see the wisdom of my plan, Father Olwen?"

The priest pursed his lips, studying the floor as he rocked back and forth on his heels. Tess finally noticed the tattered ends of her braid and smoothed the frayed tassel before letting it drop to her side. She was sure Uncle Ian knew of the lie. He could always see through her fibs. But what of Baron Montague? Did he know the truth as well? Lord help her, she had the most insane urge to marry this savage warlord!

"What say you to the lady's story?" the priest asked Kenric.

" 'Tis the truth as I know it," he agreed amiably. "Except for one part."

Tess felt her heart stop beating. She waited breathlessly for the baron to expose her deceit.

"There will be a war no matter what she does with her life."

She closed her eyes and sighed in relief. Her lie was safe from Baron Montague. She didn't hear him move silently across the room, didn't know he was anywhere near until his warm fingertips lifted her chin. Her eyes flew open in surprise. He looked deep into her eyes, his expression unreadable. Tess was sure time stood still as they stared at each other, nothing spoken, yet a certain message passing between them in that silent exchange. A warning, yes, but perhaps something more.

"She'll marry me," he said arrogantly, his eyes never leaving hers. He lifted his hand and brushed his thumb across her lower lip, sending another strange shiver down her spine. "Surely you suspected this in the woods, Lady Remmington."

He didn't give her a chance to answer. His hand dropped abruptly to his side, as if he couldn't bear to touch her another moment.

"Do not be difficult, Lady. I am not a man known for his patience with the wiles of women."

Tess frowned over his arrogance but kept silent, not about to explain that she'd thought them mercenaries, hired swords to see her safely to a nunnery. He would surely think her a fool.

"Best we get on with this," Kenric told the priest. He took hold of Tess's hand, dragging her toward the altar. "We have wasted enough time."

That was all Tess needed to spur her into action. She tried to pull her hand away from the baron's, and when that didn't work, she turned to face him.

"I have yet to hear Father Olwen's advice." She took the priest's hand with her free one, her voice pleading. "These are men of war, Father. They think only of fighting. Surely you can see the rightness of my plan and give me sanctuary."

Tess nearly winced from the baron's crushing grip on her fingers but she kept her eyes on the priest, heartened that Father Olwen seemed to consider her words. The priest was her only hope.

"The church is for those with a true calling," Father Olwen said finally. "You must obey the wishes of your king."

"But—" Tess made a strange squeaking sound when Kenric squeezed her hand so hard she thought surely the bones would break.

"The hour grows late," Kenric said in a curt tone. "Your uncle needs to be well on his way when your absence is discovered."

"This is happening so quickly!" Tess looked to her uncle for support, but Ian pushed his hands forward, suggesting she should get on with the business. She bowed her head and softly whispered her misgivings. "I have so little time to think over this new plan."

"Best you think quickly, or your stepfather will be here to witness the ceremony." Kenric sighed impatiently. "You've a choice, Lady. Either me, or MacLeith."

She seriously considered MacLeith, but only for a moment. The Butcher of Wales was hardly the best choice to her way of thinking, but she was free of her stepfather for the first time in five years and in no hurry to relinquish her freedom. But marriage? To this man? The price of her freedom was too high. Yet, perhaps if she were clever enough, she could escape the baron just as she'd escaped MacLeith. If Tess could somehow reach King Edward and explain her convent plan, he would see the wisdom of her actions and annul this hasty marriage.

Her gaze traveled slowly from the tips of Baron Montague's boots to the powerful arms, again crossed over his chest. She almost smiled at the irony of the situation. Why, Baron Montague was the only man in England whose reputation for wickedness surpassed MacLeith's. No matter how long this marriage lasted, she'd give almost anything to be in the hall when Dunmore MacLeith learned she'd wed the Butcher of Wales.

"I am ready, milord."

2

Barely an hour passed before the marriage papers were signed and the small group was shown to their horses. The ceremony was a blur to Tess, dazed as she was. Her uncle's words of good wishes were vague to her ears as he took her arm at the end of the ceremony and led her from the chapel.

"Do your duty," Ian told his niece gruffly. They stood outside the abbey gates where he engulfed the girl in a tight hug. "Make your family proud, lass."

"I will." Tess lowered her gaze guiltily. It was possible that her plan would make her family proud, she reasoned. Much as she'd like, she knew she couldn't go to Scotland with her uncle. Scotland's King Alexander was Dunmore MacLeith's ally and would only order Uncle Ian to return her to her stepfather. She couldn't allow her uncle to fall into ill favor with his king. She hugged her uncle fiercely, wondering what her reception would be if she ever saw him again. "God keep you safe."

"Try not to worry," he said lightly, his troubled expression belying his words. "You'll frown so much that the Montagues will think you related to bears."

Tess tried to give him an encouraging smile but failed. She knew her time was running out when Uncle Ian gave her hand a quick, reassuring squeeze. Baron Montague nudged his horse forward, then leaned down and lifted her effortlessly into his lap.

'Twas odd, being held so close to the stranger who was her husband. Her head barely reached his shoulders and his arms easily circled her to hold the reins. She was pressed against his hard body from the top of her head to her heels and his warmth surrounded her on every side. She decided she rather enjoyed the feeling of being protected by so much power. Scowling over her fanciful thoughts, she reminded herself that his power might be used against her someday.

"I know you will treat her well, Baron," Ian called over his shoulder. There was a clear note of warning in his voice.

"I'll keep her safe," the baron replied arrogantly, as if insulted by the implication that he wouldn't.

Safe. That was the word Tess was searching for. She hadn't felt safe in years. Wasn't it odd that the man known throughout England for his cruelty should provide the feeling so effortlessly? Her body relaxed a little, and she leaned her head back against the baron's broad shoulders.

Kenric raised one hand in farewell, then wheeled his horse around, anxious to get closer to his fortress. The sky was beginning to turn pink on the horizon, and he knew Tess would be discovered missing within the hour. Fortunately, he didn't have to cross Remmington land as Ian must. The Scot would be damned lucky to make the ride across the border to his own fortress without coming across

one of MacLeith's patrols. There was a hard two-day ride
ahead of them, but they would reach his first patrol in a
few hours. He'd stationed over two hundred men farther
ahead at intervals along the road, knowing they were less
likely to be set upon early in their flight. He wanted his
men and their horses fresh and rested if they needed to
face MacLeith in the open. He took a moment to wrap the
edges of his cloak around his wife, then spurred the stal-
lion forward.

With the plan well under way, he had no need to
worry about their journey. Kenric's thoughts turned instead to his new bride and what a pleasant surprise she'd
turned out to be. A moment later, he felt her head nod
against his chest as she drifted off to sleep. Every soft curve
seemed to melt against his hard frame, bringing an unex-
pectedly heated reaction from his loins. He was amazed
again at how easily the girl could inflame him. He couldn't
keep his groan contained when she shifted her hips and
snuggled closer to his warmth. She was arousing him
enough to make the ride painful. He pulled the horse back
to a walk and took several deep, cleansing breaths in an
effort to ease his discomfort.

"Is something amiss?" Fitz Alan questioned, pulling up
to his side.

"Nay," Kenric answered, harsher than intended.

"Are we there?" Tess asked sleepily.

"The horses need to walk for a while," Kenric lied in
a clipped voice. "Go back to sleep."

Kenric tightened his grip on Tess and pulled her back
against his chest, wanting nothing more than to lead her
into the deep woods and ease the incredible lust she stirred
in him. The reasonable side of his mind said the idea was
foolish. The sun was well in evidence and they could encounter MacLeith's men at any time. Besides which, it was
too damned cold. Still, the thought was distracting.

"I did not think I would fall asleep so easily." She
stretched and wiggled around until Kenric placed a firm

hand on her hip to stop the maddening action. "You are amazingly warm, milord."

Tess couldn't see Kenric's grimace until she turned slightly in the saddle.

"Would now be a poor time to ask a question?" She raised her eyebrows hopefully, but the baron's forbidding expression didn't change. Nor did he answer. Rudeness seemed to be his most dominant trait. Unable to meet his intimidating gaze a moment longer, she casually turned her attention to the road, ignoring his silence. "I was wondering what name I should call you by."

"I am your lord and master, Lady. You may address me as 'milord,' or 'Baron,' or . . . 'husband.' "

The man's arrogance left Tess speechless. She considered thanking him for allowing her to speak at all, but thought better of the idea. She would behave civilly for the duration of this farce, even if he did not. "What I meant to ask was your given name, *husband*. I know your titles, Baron Montague, but I do not know your Christian name."

He had the audacity to smile at her. Tess quickly dropped her gaze back to the road, half afraid she would betray her anger and smile back.

"My name is Kenric."

Though her hood was between them, Tess could almost feel his lips against her ear and his breath against her cheek. She marveled at the way his deep voice seemed to steal her breath away.

"You may call me by such whenever we are alone, *wife*."

After a moment of silence, he pulled her hood aside.

"You find some humor in my name?"

"Hm?" she inquired absently.

"Why are you smiling?"

"Your voice," Tess answered dreamily. "I can feel it. Right here." She placed her palm between her breasts, a soft laugh in her voice. "It tickles."

Kenric stared at her small hand until his body told him it was time to breathe again and he had to look away. He closed his eyes and a thousand images flashed before them. Most contained his very naked wife. He snapped his eyes open and scowled, disgusted with himself and his lack of control. This was too much. The girl was either an expert in seduction or the sweetest innocent alive. But he was determined to be safely inside Montague Castle before finding out the truth of her charms.

"You appear to enjoy my company well enough for a woman who wanted to be a nun." The guilty look on his wife's face reminded him of her reluctance at the altar. That helped cool his blood.

"I have a confession to make," she said quietly, sounding remorseful. "I have thought long on this matter and feel it best to inform you of my sin."

That announcement caught Kenric off guard. He could almost feel the blood in his veins turn to ice. *She's had a lover,* he thought grimly. How thoughtful of her to unburden her pious little soul before he discovered the truth for himself. His face became hard, his expression meant to prepare her for the rage that would follow. If she thought he would find this confession noble, she was wrong. Though he was bound to keep her even if she'd had a score of lovers, he didn't have to like it. He reined in the horse and waved Fitz Alan ahead, remaining silent until he was sure their conversation would be private.

"I'm all ears," he drawled sarcastically.

"I told a lie to the priest." She spoke so softly that Kenric had to lean forward to hear. He frowned but waited for her to continue. "I told him I did not want to marry."

"Tell me the rest of it, Tess." Kenric's voice was quiet but there was no missing the fury lurking there.

" 'Tis rare that I tell a lie, milord, and never before to a priest," she hurried to explain. "I would not blame you if you think me wicked, but I did so want this to end without bloodshed."

"Well?" he growled.

"Well, when we met in the chapel I was not displeased with the idea of marrying you, but I had to try to avert this war and the convent plan seemed like such a good one. Then again, since I was asking to become a nun, I couldn't very well admit to Father Olwen that I was taken with you right from the start and the idea of being your wife was quite appealing. Nuns do not have such earthy thoughts. Oh . . . I mean . . . I really didn't have much time to think about being your wife, but I was quite intrigued with the notion. Even though I shouldn't have thought about being a wife at all, not if I truly was of a mind to become a nun. Oh, Lord!" Tess felt her cheeks flame red, surprised at everything that had somehow fallen out of her mouth. Curse and rot her tongue! Why not just openly admit that she lusted after the man? Her poor husband looked stunned. He was certainly wondering what kind of woman he'd married. Tess looked away. Gaining his trust by admitting the lie was the stupidest idea she'd ever imagined.

"Look at me, Tess," he demanded sternly. She lifted her gaze, her eyes filled with embarrassed tears. He cupped her cheek with one hand and brushed his thumb across the creamy surface. "You are telling me the truth now?"

"Aye," she admitted. Her gaze dropped to his mouth, unable to look him in the eye another moment. "Though I did not intend to tell quite so much."

The smile she saw curve his mouth astonished Tess. She leaned back to see the rest of his face and watched in amazement as his eyes changed from a dark, steely color to a soft shade of gray.

It *was* him, she realized in stunned disbelief. Kenric of Montague was the man she saw in her dreams! The image that had suddenly come to life before her eyes stirred other realizations. Ian had once said her grandmother had the ability to catch small glimpses of the future, but Tess never knew she too possessed the strange skill until this instant.

She needed to think more on such an important revelation, but at the moment she couldn't seem to think beyond her husband's captivating smile. She lifted one hand to his cheek, fascinated by the rough growth that said he'd been a day without shaving. Kenric's smile disappeared the moment her hand touched his face.

"Your eyes are gray," she said softly, their gazes meeting.

"I'm glad you told me."

"You didn't know your eyes were gray?" she asked, her hand falling to his shoulder.

It took Kenric a moment to get his own thoughts gathered enough to follow the conversation. Those eyes of hers were enough to bewitch a saint. They actually changed color with her mood. Sapphires one moment, amethysts the next.

"I knew," he replied. He lifted Tess's hand and placed a kiss in the palm, smiling over the shiver he felt go through her. "I'm glad you told me how you felt when we first met. 'Tis no sin to appreciate your king's choice."

She blushed and tried to turn away again, but Kenric easily caught her chin, curious to see her reaction in the color of her eyes. Deep, dark blue, he mused, his lips curving into a smile.

"Are you angry that I lied to Father Olwen?" she asked hesitantly.

"Nay, Tess." Kenric couldn't resist placing a light kiss on her forehead. He immediately liked the feel of her beneath his lips, but forced himself to pull away. Her shy confession would be rewarded, settling the idea of taking her into the woods once and for all.

"The lie was a sin, but told for noble reasons," he conceded, his manner once again arrogant, his expression closed. "Women cannot always be held accountable for their actions."

Tess bit her lip, willing the sharp words to stay in her mouth. This was not the time to start an argument. Especially when she wasn't exactly armed with overwhelming proof to argue his opinion of women. Instead she nodded stiffly and turned her back to him, hoping the wretched man would be sensible enough to realize why she was angry. There were a hundred questions she wanted to ask him, to find out anything she could to make her escape easier. But the man needed a good dose of silence to think over his rude remark.

Had she actually imagined Baron Montague a fit man to judge her sin? Accountable, indeed. Any kind ideas she'd harbored about him were pushed aside. He thought her inferior, a child who could not be punished for failing to recognize the difference between right and wrong. Hah! That was a good one. As if the Butcher of Wales could distinguish between the two.

Kenric smiled over the top of his wife's head, satisfied by the stiff set of her shoulders that said he'd hit his mark. He spurred the horse forward, more anxious than he'd ever been to reach Montague Castle.

The first sign of trouble came less than an hour later. A twelve-man patrol rode straight toward them, each soldier wearing a MacLeith plaid.

Kenric and Fitz Alan quickly assessed the situation and decided the chances were good that the patrol didn't know of Tess's disappearance. The band was riding north, probably returning from a courier mission to London. Kenric guided their horses to the side of the road and slowed to a walk. He'd wrapped Tess securely beneath his cloak to shield her from the biting wind, but quickly threw the edges over his shoulders where the garment wouldn't be in the way of his sword arm.

"Wake up, Tess."

The words were softly spoken, but Tess responded to the urgency in Kenric's voice and the sudden tension in his body. She quickly pushed aside the lingering grogginess, knowing instinctively that something was wrong. Kenric leaned down to whisper in her ear.

"A MacLeith patrol is approaching but I doubt they know you are missing. They ride from the south. Keep your face covered and do not let go of my waist no matter what happens."

Before she could nod in agreement, Kenric lifted her from his lap and swung her around to seat her behind his back. She pulled her hood low, wrapped her trembling arms around her husband's waist, and began to pray.

The soldiers approached quickly, but slowed to meet the travelers. The sound of hooves, the jingle of harnesses, and creaking of leather faded until there was silence, interrupted again as a horse nickered, answered by another.

"Greetings," their leader called out. He was a coarse, insolent-looking man with a full, bushy beard that seemed an attempt to make up for his thinning hair. His gaze shifted between the two knights, his gaze plainly curious. "What brings honest men out on such a miserably cold day?"

"We travel from Revensforth to Montague," Fitz Alan lied glibly, a look of utter sincerity in his warm brown eyes. He rubbed the dark stubble of his own emerging beard. "Baron Montague has returned from the king's wars and 'tis rumored he seeks warriors to replace those lost in battle. My cousin and I have fulfilled our service to Baron Revensforth, and hope to enlist our services with Montague."

The leader's small eyes traveled slowly over the mercenary knights. His horse pawed the ground nervously, as if awaiting a decision. A bad sign, that. A skittish horse was often the sign of a nervous master. The man grunted and nodded toward the road.

"We travel to Remmington. The road is clear ahead?"

"Aye," Fitz Alan answered. "We've met with no trouble."

"Then I'll bid you good day." The soldier began to

turn his horse aside, then stopped. He leaned sideways in the saddle, trying to get a closer look at Tess. When that failed, he turned his attention to Kenric.

" 'Tis doubtful Montague will accept your sword if you are burdened with a wench. Is she valuable enough to risk your livelihood?"

"She is my wife," Kenric replied with a shrug. "She'll earn her keep."

The soldier nodded, but made no move to leave. His hooded gaze shifted from Kenric to Fitz Alan, then back again to Kenric. Both recognized the telling action. He was sizing up his opponents.

"My men and I have had a long, cold ride from London." The soldier didn't take his eyes from Kenric, but one hand flexed on the hilt of his sword. "A good week has passed since any of us had a woman to warm our loins." The soldier gave an almost imperceptible signal and his men drew their swords. Crossing his arms across the high pommel of his saddle, he leaned forward, grinning unpleasantly at Kenric. "Perhaps your woman could earn her keep on the king's road as well."

The man's grin turned evil, but then it faded when neither man moved a muscle. Kenric and Fitz Alan just stared at him.

"Of course we'd pay you for her services." His horse began to paw the ground in earnest and he straightened in the saddle.

Kenric drew his sword so fast that the soldier barely had time to flinch before the blade found his neck. The other men watched in disbelief as their leader toppled from his horse and those lost moments cost two more their lives. The soldiers quickly fell into the spirit of the battle, splitting their numbers to attack the two knights separately. Yet they soon regretted their dead leader's hasty challenge.

Kenric and his horse worked as though joined together, but Tess felt as if she'd grabbed hold of a lightning bolt. Or a warrior in battle. Keeping her grip around Kenric's waist was a near impossible task, requiring her full attention. Each time his sword lashed out she could feel the bone-jarring blows in her own body, the force nearly jolting her off the horse. She couldn't imagine what it was like to be on the receiving end of those blows.

Kenric and Fitz Alan set about their job with the methodical precision of seasoned fighters. The dense woods guarded their backs and they kept their horses' rumps close enough to provide additional protection while allowing ample room to wield their swords. Though the two warriors traveled without their heavy shields, they evened the odds by wielding a sword in each hand, one to thrust and one to parry.

" 'Tis the Remmington bitch!" one of the soldiers cried out when Tess's hood fell back. "Kill him! He has the girl!"

Kenric took advantage of the distraction to drive his sword into two more soldiers. Fitz Alan wasn't as lucky and brought down only one, but the Scots were half their original number.

One of Fitz Alan's foes tried to surprise Kenric by attacking from the right. He was unsuccessful, but kept Kenric distracted long enough for another to move past the baron's blades to his unprotected left side. Three men attacked Kenric with a vengeance while the fourth worked on separating Tess from the baron's waist. The task was made more difficult by Kenric's broadsword, falling every other blow on the man's battered shield.

The soldier became desperate when one of his comrades fell in the frontal attack. He let go of his shield and lunged forward to wrap his arm around Tess's neck, giving one mighty tug. She surprised him by going so willingly that they both fell backward off their horses. Sprawled out flat on his back with the wind knocked out of him, the soldier opened his eyes to find an enraged angel looming overhead.

"Do not move."

Tess held the blade of a needle-sharp dagger at the soldier's neck, but she didn't notice his hand inching toward the sword he'd dropped in the fall. The man kept shifting his eyes nervously to one side, so Tess turned the point of the knife to rest against his throat, intending to prick him just once to hold his attention. He brought the hilt of his sword down on her head at the same instant. The blow was ill-aimed, causing more surprise than pain, but the force of his attack knocked Tess forward. Her knife slid forward into his neck with sickening ease, right up to the hilt.

Tess threw herself off the wounded man with a pained gasp, as if she'd been burned. She scrambled backward on the cold ground to a safe distance and stared at the fallen soldier, morbidly fascinated by the sight. Blood was everywhere, gushing from his neck like a macabre fountain. Anyone who lost that much blood shouldn't be alive, but she could still hear his gasping, gurgling breaths. Strangely enough, the man didn't try to tend the injury. One hand clutched the sword to his chest, the other hand lay useless above his head, twitching every so often.

The tortured breathing finally stopped and his skin quickly turned as pale and hard as wax, his lips a vivid blue. She wouldn't have recognized him now as the same man who attacked her. Tess slowly leaned forward and pulled the bloodied plaid over the death mask, too stunned to say a prayer for his soul. She stood up and walked a few paces toward the woods, trying to block the ugly sight from memory. She didn't see the other soldiers fall, or Kenric's quick but frantic search for her.

"I told you not to let go!" Kenric bellowed as he leaped from his horse. He grabbed Tess by the shoulders and dragged her around to face him. "You let go on purpose!"

She didn't flinch or show any other emotion while her husband shouted in her face, but her eyes filled with tears.

Kenric couldn't remember the last time he'd yelled at anyone, much less a woman. His anger was always as cold and chilling as steel, his displeasure communicated in low, deadly tones that were much more effective than a raised voice. That his wife could have no idea how truly furious he was only served to make him angrier.

"He had me by the neck," Tess whispered. Her voice rose shakily as she placed her hands on Kenric's arms to steady herself. "If I'd held on he would have pulled you off balance, giving an advantage to the others attacking from the front."

"Never disobey me again!" Kenric shouted, completely ignoring her flimsy explanation. He couldn't resist the urge to shake Tess just once before wrapping her in a tight bear hug. His heart was still racing from the unfamiliar fear he'd experienced when she was pulled away from his side, knowing she was unprotected, completely vulnerable. He'd fought with a demon's rage then, quickly dispatching the fools who'd threatened to take what was his.

"Hush now," he said gruffly. Tess was weeping all over him. God, how he hated a woman's tears. But he didn't seem to mind stroking her hair, finding it just as soft and silky as he knew it would be. The scent of spring flowers drifted across his senses and he shook his head, trying to rid himself of the fanciful notion. "There's no need to cry. You're safe now."

She mumbled something against his chest. Kenric lifted her chin and waited for her to look at him. He marveled that the woman could remain so appealing through tears. "What did you say?"

"I said, I always felt safe." Tess sniffed loudly, looking disgruntled. "A fine wife I'd be if I didn't trust my husband to keep me safe."

Kenric almost smiled at the flash of fire in his little wife's eyes. A good sign, that. The tears would soon dry.

Tess began to cry with renewed gusto, her tearful vow

broken by small sobs. "But I will try . . . very hard . . . to obey your orders in the future."

"They're all dead," Fitz Alan informed them cheerfully, cleaning his bloodied sword on a fallen soldier's plaid.

"Best we ride," Kenric replied over Tess's head. "I'll feel better once we reach our first camp."

"At least there were only twelve of them," Fitz Alan commented. He tossed the plaid aside then led the horses to the road and prepared to mount.

"I am thankful for your help with the one after my lady," Kenric told his vassal as he guided Tess toward the animals. "The others kept me well occupied."

Fitz Alan halted with one foot in the stirrup, a strange expression on his face. "I did not kill him."

Both men stared at each other then slowly turned their suspicious gazes to Tess. She kept her head bowed, wiping her eyes with the cuff of one sleeve. Kenric nodded toward the soldier in question and Fitz Alan moved quickly to stand over the man, using the tip of his sword to draw the plaid away. The soldier's eyes were wide open, but they stared sightlessly at the gray sky. The plaid caught for a moment then pulled free, revealing the small dagger embedded in the man's neck. Kenric recognized the jewel-encrusted knife immediately as the one Tess wore on her belt. He'd first noticed the dagger at the abbey, impressed by the hilt's intricate workmanship. Now he was impressed with its target.

"She's killed him," Fitz Alan muttered.

Kenric pulled the knife free and shook his head, unable to imagine his delicate wife stabbing a man in the neck. Yet the evidence proved she was quite capable of defending herself.

" 'Twas an accident," Tess said earnestly. Kenric took his eyes from the dead man long enough to look at her. She could tell from the incredulous expression on his face that he wasn't about to believe her. Of course, who could blame him? A blade in the shoulder or belly, maybe. But straight through a man's throat? That did seem a bit deliberate. She turned to Fitz Alan, hoping he would be more understanding. Fitz Alan was looking at her as if she'd grown a second head.

"You two are a fine pair to give me judgment," she snapped. She crossed her arms indignantly, then swept one arm out to indicate the carnage surrounding them. "Thank goodness your own hands remain unsoiled."

Kenric and Fitz Alan exchanged a confused look.

"My lady," Fitz Alan began apologetically. "We did not think—"

"Aye, that much is obvious," she muttered. Her arms were crossed again and she scowled fiercely at the knights, even as tears threatened to spill down her cheeks. " 'Tis cruel of you both to make me feel worse than I did already about taking a man's life. One of you would have killed him sooner or later, so the result is the same. Now that I think on the matter, one of you should have taken care of the infidel before I was forced to the foul deed. Thanks to you two, I now have the sin of murder on my soul."

She turned her back on the men and walked to the baron's warhorse while Kenric motioned to Fitz Alan, warning him not to laugh. He followed the order with difficulty, but couldn't hide his broad smile.

No one said a word as Kenric lifted Tess into the saddle and mounted behind her. He pulled his heavy fur cloak forward to provide a warm cocoon and tucked her snugly against his chest before sharing an exasperated smile with Fitz Alan.

Tess sighed and closed her eyes. She didn't care what her husband thought of her. She didn't. Yet she knew this was surely the worst day of her life and it was not yet midday.

3

They rode hard and fast after leaving the scene of the skirmish.
Tess was surprised at first by the groups of Kenric's men
they met along the road. By afternoon more than one
hundred soldiers rode behind them and she was growing
accustomed to the clattering racket created by so many
horses and soldiers, all armed for battle. She no longer
worried about MacLeith. Her new concerns lay with her
husband. He grew more irritable as the day wore on, answering his soldiers' occasional questions with short, curt
replies that discouraged further conversation.

Even Tess's one attempt at talking with him ended
badly. Thinking Kenric would mistake her question for
wifely concern, she asked quietly and humbly if he was
pleased by what he'd gained through their marriage. She
hoped his affirmative answer would allow her to find out
more about his plans for Remmington.

Examining the angular lines of his face as she waited for his reply, Tess was struck again by the imposing aura of power that surrounded him. She was playing a dangerous game with a dangerous man. No one had ever made her so nervous just by looking at her, not even the MacLeiths. There wasn't a doubt in her mind that Kenric of Montague was unlike any man she'd ever met. And he was also the most uncooperative. Rather than answer the question that had but one answer, he continued to stare at her for the longest time, the thoughts behind those wintry gray eyes his alone to know. Tess met his steely gaze without flinching, a significant feat considering the fear that flowed through her.

"Nay."

Tess and her question were dismissed. She pursed her lips to release a disappointed sigh. It had been a foolish question. She realized that fact too late. Seeing matters Kenric's way, she realized that he'd gained nothing yet of any value. Marriage had brought him a wife who possessed the meager belongings contained in two sacks and an in-law who had no intention of handing over her inheritance. A warlord would find little to appreciate in such a marriage.

"Well, perhaps I did not ask that question very clearly," she conceded. "I realize my stepfather will be a bother—"

"Lady, I find both you *and* your stepfather a bother. Now cease your babbling."

"Babbling!" she echoed, incensed by the insult. "I was merely asking a polite question that—"

"Aye, you babble. 'Tis also unseemly for a wife to question her husband."

"Just what *do* you want in a wife, milord?"

The corners of Kenric's mouth tightened over the clear note of censure in her voice. "I don't want a wife at all. No more than you want a husband, Lady. We married by order of our king and I suggest you make the best of it.

You may begin by remaining silent until you are spoken to, for I dislike talkative women."

Tess wisely remained silent, seething over the unwarranted rudeness of her husband's remarks. He made her sound no more significant than a hound, a beast best appreciated when lying faithfully at its master's feet. Only this master had no wish for a pet. With that attitude, he'd probably be overjoyed when the king annulled their marriage. She certainly would be.

She was so absorbed in her own thoughts that she acted instinctively when she saw Kenric lift his hand as if to strike her. She instantly raised her arms to protect her head and turned her face toward the protection of his chest.

When the blow never came, she peeked over her arm, then quickly shielded her face again, waiting. Kenric's hand was resting on his shoulder, as if frozen in the act of adjusting his cloak. Hah. She wouldn't fall for that old ploy. Gordon and Dunmore MacLeith had both caught her with that trick, striking her the moment she let her guard down. She'd learned long ago that they would eventually lose patience if she hid her face long enough. Yet she hated the waiting.

"Look at me."

Tess wrapped her arms tighter over her ears and shook her head. Kenric resisted the urge to shake her, knowing that would do little to convince her that he intended no harm.

"I'm not going to hit you," he said impatiently. He was thankful they rode several lengths ahead of everyone else so his men wouldn't witness this scene. Some might take it into their heads that the lady was already unhappy in her marriage. That kind of trouble he didn't need. "What makes you think I would want to strike you?"

Tess was silent several moments. Her muffled explanation finally came from beneath one arm. "I annoyed you with my questions."

"You believe I will strike you each time you annoy me?" Ah, but what else would she expect from the Butcher of Wales? his conscience asked logically. He felt Tess nod her head against his chest. "You annoyed me much more at Kelso Abbey with all your foolish arguments. Yet did I strike you then?"

"My uncle might have retaliated," she countered, still hiding against his chest.

"You annoyed me when you let go of my waist during the skirmish this morning. Aye, I was good and angry with you for disobeying me. Did I strike you then?"

She remained silent, motionless.

"And it also annoyed me that you'd lied to the good priest who married us." It didn't hurt to add a lie of his own. He tried hard to think of another example, but realized it would be foolish to point out that she was annoying him mightily right now. Instead he gently pried her arm from her head. She allowed him to pull both arms away and didn't protest when he took hold of her shoulders and moved her away from his chest. But she flinched when he raised his hand to lift her chin. He frowned over her reaction but waited patiently for her to look up at him, seeing only fear and distrust in her eyes when she did.

"Did they hit you often?" he asked quietly. Her gaze slid to one side and she shrugged.

"That would depend on what you consider 'often,'" she said woodenly. "The MacLeiths find a fist handier than sharp words if someone displeases them."

"I see." He examined her face closely to see if she bore any scars but found none, no telltale marks to indicate that she'd been struck with any frequency.

"I prefer sharp words," he said tersely, allowing her to know that much of their future. He didn't want a wife who cowered and flinched each time he touched her or made a sudden move. "There will be no more beatings."

She gave him a quick, jerky nod, then bowed her head, but not before Kenric saw the surprise in her eyes.

He felt the relief flow through her body, allowing her to relax against him. A moment earlier he'd wanted her to pull up her hood and turn away from him, but now, when she did, he felt disappointed.

Still, he waited patiently for her list of complaints. Surely she would tell him how the MacLeiths had abused her, bore him with each small detail. Women loved to complain, especially to a man capable of meting out justice. It wasn't until Tess burrowed deeper beneath her cloak that Kenric realized she had no intention of telling him anything more. Aye, she remained blessedly silent. He should be pleased. Kenric scowled at the top of his bride's head.

Tess awoke hours later in a darkened room, not quite sure what startled her awake. Her gaze focused on a wall that seemed to be made of animal hides. Her eyes traveled upward and she soon realized the room was not a room at all, but a tent. She was stretched out on a fur of some sort, a bear's pelt, she decided, curling her fingers into the wiry fur. One long, blissful moment passed before she recalled the events of the day and previous evening. Her heart thudded painfully against her chest as the memories flooded back.

Tess said another silent prayer for the soul of the MacLeith soldier she'd killed, as she had each time she'd recalled the horrible incident. She doubted her husband offered as much consideration to the souls of those he'd slain. If he did, he'd do nothing *but* pray. Yet this same man had the power to make her feel safe, protected.

Tess frowned against the fur. She shifted on the pelt and cautiously peeked over her shoulder. Kenric was seated cross-legged on a pile of furs a few feet away, his elbows resting on his knees. A fat candle flickered near the opening of the tent, but as usual, his dark gaze revealed nothing. Still, there was an intensity in his eyes that unnerved her, a subtle difference in the way he watched her that sent goose bumps down her arms.

He was probably thinking about what a skilled murderess he'd married, she thought. Aye, what a fitting bride for the Butcher, a woman who slays a man mere hours after their wedding, displaying a skill that looked deceptively practiced. So much for gaining his trust. He'd never turn his back on such a talented assassin.

Fighting down her fear and uncertainty, she sat up and began to smooth her gown, brushing her hands along the worn brown fabric with exaggerated care while trying to think of something to say. The silence of the tent seemed unnatural, ominous after listening to the deafening noise of hoofbeats for so many hours.

"I fell asleep again, didn't I?"

Kenric didn't provide the obvious answer and she tried not to shiver. His eyes brought to mind a wolf stalking its prey. It was troubling how little she knew of this man and his moods. What she did know brought little comfort. He'd said he didn't want a wife. Those stares of his that lacked any trace of human warmth doubtless masked thoughts of how best to rid himself of his bride. Her heart began to beat faster as the tales she'd heard of the Butcher took shape in her mind.

Perhaps he really did drink blood with his dinner.

His eyes narrowed and she wondered if he could read her mind, if he could sense her fear. She licked her lips and tried to push her worries aside.

"I'm hungry."

Tess frowned. She'd meant to say that differently, to remind him that a full day had passed since her last meal, then to ask politely for something to eat. But his mood had affected her manners as well.

Kenric stood up and left the tent without a word. He returned a few minutes later, but she wasn't sure he'd requested food until a voice called out from the other side of the tent flap.

At Kenric's order, a young man of about thirteen or fourteen summers entered, carrying a tray laden with food and wine. At that awkward stage between youth and manhood, the boy kept a careful eye on the tray. When he raised his eyes, the tray in his hands was soon forgotten. He stared at his new baroness as if he were the one who had yet to eat, too besotted to notice the darkening scowl from his lord.

"Leave us," Kenric growled.

The anger in that voice set the squire into instant motion. He nearly dropped the tray in his haste to obey.

"Thank you," Tess murmured with a kind smile. She hoped to ease the boy's nervousness, disturbed that even the Butcher's own people seemed terrified of him. That was not encouraging.

The young man snatched his fur cap from his head and bowed at least five times as he backed out of the tent, sounding like an echo of himself as he repeated his thanks.

"Your squire?" she asked, glad for something to talk about. Kenric didn't answer her question, but she glanced up in time to see him nod. "He seemed rather . . . uneasy."

"Thomas is merely curious about his new baroness."

Tess nodded absently, none too appeased by the explanation. She was thinking Fitz Alan had likely told the boy about the Scot she'd killed, and that was the reason he'd behaved so oddly. Another thought caught her off guard, and her eyes widened with alarm. Kenric had called her his new baroness. She was Baroness Montague, his wife, and this was the closest thing to a wedding night her hasty marriage would ever allow. Tess didn't know much about marriage, but she did know that new brides were bedded on their wedding night.

Busying herself to cover her uneasy thoughts, Tess picked up a knife from the tray and sliced a wedge of cheese into bite-size pieces. Her husband wasn't acting like a man anxious to bed his new wife. Maybe he really did want to get rid of her. She knew well that a wife's death could be explained away easily enough.

The cheese Tess had popped into her mouth seemed to swell until it threatened to choke her. As if he'd guessed her distress, Kenric poured two goblets of wine, handed one to her, and settled back on his seat of furs. She gulped the wine greedily, then placed the goblet on the wooden tray, her appetite gone. Still, she'd asked for the food and he'd think it strange indeed if she ate no more than a bite of cheese. Picking up a loaf of bread, she tore off a small piece and stuffed it into her mouth. She kept the wine handy to wash it down. She glanced at Kenric, then snapped her eyes back to the food, popping a slice of dried apple into her mouth. She prayed her voice didn't sound as shaky as she felt.

"Are you going to eat s-some of this delicious food?"

"Nay. I ate less than an hour ago when we arrived."

Tess reached out to pick up the wine, but her hand shook so badly that she chose another piece of apple instead.

"I have no intent of bedding you tonight, if that is what has you so worried," he said, watching her over the rim of his goblet. "You will not become my wife in more than name until we reach the warmth and comforts of Montague. Doubtless you have heard many tales of me, but I am not a wild beast nor some coarse peasant who is unable to contain his lust."

"I—I've not heard many tales," she said unconvincingly.

"They must have been good ones to instill such fear. You looked near to fainting when your uncle told you my name at Kelso Abbey."

"I was merely startled."

"And I am next in line for sainthood."

Tess frowned. "I was merely trying to be nice. You might try it sometime."

Kenric suppressed the urge to grin. When her courage

returned, it returned with a vengeance. Of course, she'd also put away a full goblet of wine and was working on her second. He doubted she'd even noticed that he'd kept her goblet filled. "I would not want to jeopardize my reputation by turning nice at this late date."

"You are not the man of those tales."

One black brow rose. It was almost a question.

"I've heard the tales, if you must know," she said with a trace of impatience. " 'Tis obvious they are fabrications."

"Most are true," he warned, well aware of the stories. Most couldn't be denied and few needed exaggeration. He was a warrior first and foremost, a man trained to kill. And he was very, *very* good. Best she understand and accept what he was, not what she would like him to be.

She brushed an imaginary spot of dust from her gown, her eyes evasive. " 'Tis said you eat small children for your supper."

"What!"

"Plump girl babies are said to be your preference. Then you wash down your food with a mug of your enemy's blood, the one slain during the meal to provide your entertainment."

"Very well. I will allow that some have grown beyond the truth." Kenric's expression turned grim. "But I have killed many men, wife. I am ruthless and without mercy. There are reasons behind my reputation."

"Aye, but all in England know you are Edward's most powerful warlord. The other barons must respect you a great deal."

He smiled over her ignorance. "Do not harbor any thoughts of a grand life at court or acceptance among the other nobles, Tess. Most of Edward's barons are grateful that I fight for their cause, but few are willing to extend friendship to a man with so much blood on his hands. Many at court would rather see me in Hell than at their table. As my wife, you'll be as unwelcome as I."

"Perhaps they are jealous," she said thoughtfully, looking unconcerned by his prediction.

Kenric noticed she was beginning to have difficulty with any word containing the letter *s*, drawing the sound out until it was almost slurred.

"I am already accustomed to being hated for the name I bear," she went on. "So you may rest assured that my feelings will not be hurt by the opinions of others. Had I a choice, 'tis possible I would have chosen you myself for husband." She nodded, as if to assure him that at least that much was true. " 'Tis the only name my stepfather fears."

"So you bear my name gladly," he stated with a wry grin. "All this time I mistook your overwhelming joy for fear and reluctance."

"I did not say I was overjoyed. My intent was to become a nun, if you will recall. But I have accepted that my king wishes a different life for me, and I will take your advice and make the best of our marriage."

"My relief knows no bounds, Lady." Kenric had the audacity to smile at her indignant expression. He reached over to take her goblet then, and pushed the tray toward the tent flap. "You've had two full goblets of wine, Tess. 'Tis a long ride tomorrow, made no better by too much wine the night before. Best we find what rest we can before dawn."

He noticed that Tess watched his mouth very closely, as if she had trouble concentrating on their conversation.

"Will we reach Montague soon?" she asked.

"Tomorrow. Around dusk."

"A warm bed will feel good." Tess smiled as she settled into the furs.

A warm bed will feel good.

Kenric gritted his teeth. The words echoed again and again in his head until he could think of nothing else. He glared across the tent, watching Tess turn to arrange her bed of furs just so before settling under her cloak.

"Good eve, Baron." Tess ended the statement with a yawn, her shivers visible under the bulky cloak.

Kenric didn't reply. He extinguished the candle, and listened to the quiet noises Tess made as she shifted restlessly. It wasn't long before her teeth began to chatter.

Kenric lifted her cloak and slid down next to her on the bed of furs. The extra weight of his fur-lined cloak fell on top of them. She released a long, satisfied sigh and snuggled up closer to his warmth.

"Hold still," he growled, his hands pushing her hips away.

Tess obliged. "I would like to thank you, husband," she said shyly.

"For what?" Kenric asked needlessly, knowing he would be thanked for leaving her precious virginity intact.

"For taking me away from the MacLeiths," she said quietly. "For making me feel safe. You've been kind to me, even though I've brought little to this marriage other than the makings of a war. The MacLeiths will try to get me back, you know."

Kenric's sigh nearly parted her hair. "You no longer have any need to fear the MacLeiths, Tess. They will never touch you again. Now go to sleep."

She remained silent almost an entire minute.

"Milord?"

"What?"

The irritation in his voice must have changed her mind.

"Um, well, nothing. It was nothing at all."

Kenric grunted and several quiet minutes passed while Tess squirmed restlessly. She turned to her side, then onto her stomach, then rolled over to her side again, always keeping Kenric's arm as a pillow. His arm slid away so quickly that she couldn't react fast enough to prevent her head from thumping right through the fur onto the frozen ground.

"You will say what you have to say then you will go to sleep. Do you understand me?"

"Yes, well, uh . . ."

"Say it!"

"You forgot to kiss me after the wedding ceremony! I guess 'tis not required, but I thought it was, and I was rather looking forward to . . . well, it would have been my first kiss, even though you did kiss my forehead. I just didn't—"

She fell silent the moment Kenric's hand gripped her chin. His fingers covered one cheek, his thumb stretched high across the other. She was struck again by how very large he was, yet how very gentle he could be. His warm breath caressed her face and she knew he was close. An eternity seemed to pass before his lips touched hers in a kiss so tender, so exquisite, her eyes opened wide in surprise. She never would have guessed there was anything soft on this fierce warlord. He seemed to be hard all over. But his lips were incredibly soft as they moved across her own.

Kenric meant to give Tess her bride's kiss, then order her to sleep. The sweet taste of her mouth and her enthusiastic response made him crave just a bit more. She was a fast learner, quickly imitating his actions and pressing her mouth a little harder against his lips each time he thought to raise his head. It was an easy matter to open her mouth, deepening the kiss, but he was nearly undone by her low moan. Kenric couldn't resist. He used his tongue to taste her, and his loins reacted instantly to the erotic action. She didn't even try to close her mouth against the assault. She waited until he'd stroked every part of her mouth then practiced what he'd just taught her, shyly at first, but just as thoroughly.

Tess's kiss was as heady and exotic as the finest wine. Kenric's senses reeled, overcome by the wild, fierce need to possess her mouth completely. He traced the outline of her lips, then nibbled them greedily, surprised yet pleased when she did the same. He was still leaning down, one hand bracing his weight, when he became aware of Tess's hands sliding up his chest. They rested there a moment and he waited to be pushed away. This kiss had gone far beyond anything a bride would receive at her wedding. His mouth became almost frantic in a quest to enjoy as much of her sweetness as possible before she pushed him away. The slightest pressure and he would release her. He swore he would.

The grip on the front of his shirt tightened and he reluctantly lifted his head. Instead of pushing him away, Tess used all her strength to pull him back to her mouth. Kenric couldn't have been more stunned if he'd been slapped. A primitive sound emerged from his chest, and he kissed Tess as he'd never kissed a woman in his life, unable to get close enough or to taste enough of her. Yet a thin shred of sanity remained and he forced his hands to stray no lower than her neck. The sensations of touching Tess, the soft warmth of her skin, the smooth contours of her face, the silkiness of her hair, all kept him satisfied for a time. Far too short a time.

He broke away so suddenly that she didn't have a chance to catch his lips before they were gone. "You've had your kiss. Now go to sleep."

Tess lay perfectly still, then she rolled to her side and buried her face in the furs. Kenric heard her quiet sobs, knew his harsh words had hurt her feelings.

Why did he feel like comforting her?

That idea was out of the question. He was more determined than ever to wait. He'd made a vow. He was a warrior, accustomed to hardship and discomfort. One night to wait for pleasure was nothing. He wanted to savor Tess in the warmth of his bed, to see her shiver with desire instead of shivering from the cold. Aye, she would thank him one day when she understood the reasons. One day soon.

"You did not like my kiss," she accused between sobs.

He rolled his eyes and sighed, certain she was intent on making him crazed. "I liked it."

"Hah!"

"You are my bride," he said, pulling her stiff body against his chest. "I do not wish to make you my *wife* in this tent. You will remain a bride until we reach Montague and the warm bed you look forward to so much. Do you understand what I am saying, Tess? Your kisses please me greatly, but they make me want more. Much more."

She was silent, but he felt her body begin to relax.

"I liked kissing you, too," she said shyly.

"I could tell." He stroked her hair, trying to ignore the ache in his loins and the temptation to let his hands roam where they would. "Now go to sleep. We've a hard ride tomorrow and I need to rest."

She wriggled closer and sighed, a long, satisfied sound. Kenric smiled in the dark, amused by his wife's quick mood changes. She was so open and honest with her emotions, a delight to a man raised among the wiles and intrigues of courtiers. That was the reason he was so considerate of her feelings, Kenric decided. She was one of the few women who stirred his protective instinct. Tess was dependent upon him, completely trusting of the security he provided.

Aye, he would give her another day to know him better, to realize what a noble husband he was and how considerate he was being. He closed his eyes, feeling close to that sainthood he'd claimed.

Tess awoke feeling close to death. Stiff and sore, she turned to discover Kenric was gone, relieved that he wouldn't see her in this condition. The cold ground had done its job on sore muscles during the night, and she tried twice before she could stand upright in anything less than excruciating agony. But the cold ground was not the real cause of her pain.

Nearly a fortnight had passed since Gordon Mac-

Leith's last visit to Langston, but the marks of his latest beating were taking longer than usual to heal. And rightly so. She'd received her worst lashing yet for the insults she'd hurled at him that day. Luckily, she'd been wearing her thickest wool dress, else he'd have marked her for life. She said another prayer of thanks that Gordon carried a slim riding crop rather than a true whip that would slice through any gown. As it was, he'd only drawn blood on a few lashes, and those not too deep. The long ride had done little to help the healing process, but in another fortnight or so the welts would fade. Though she'd left her sickbed only a week before her escape, she was growing accustomed to the dull pain, aware that it faded some each day.

She wondered if she could escape her husband before he discovered her injuries. He'd tasted enough of her temper to know she'd courted the beating. Not that she'd accused Gordon of anything but the truth. The man was a catamite and everyone in the MacLeith clan knew of his preference for males in his bed. She was just the first to accuse Gordon to his face. And in front of his soldiers, no less. Aye, she'd asked for the beating. But how could she have known she'd have a husband so soon? A husband sure to see her naked sooner or later. She had to figure out a way to make it later. Much later.

" 'Tis time to ride," Kenric announced.

Tess nearly jumped out of her skin. Her husband was standing right behind her.

"I did not intend to startle you," he said in a quieter voice. "Didn't you hear me enter?"

"Shadows have been known to make more noise, milord." She turned to face Kenric, feeling recovered from the surprise. The sight of him made her rethink that notion. Why, he'd grown quite handsome over the night! She stared openly at his face, wondering how she'd ever thought him akin to the Devil. The color of his eyes was much too soft for a Devil, the chiseled lines of his face far too pleasing. His bemused smile was heavenly.

"Is something wrong?"

"Wrong?" she repeated dumbly.

"You've a most peculiar look on your face."

"Oh." Tess made herself look away from the tall warlord, a difficult task since he took up so much of the tent. She stumbled for a quick explanation. "Perhaps I always look peculiar in the morning."

Tess groaned inwardly as soon as the words left her mouth. *Perhaps I am the most dull-witted woman alive,* she added to herself.

"I hope so." Kenric grinned. "That look somehow reminds me of the lie you told Father Olwen."

"I believe I am ready to depart," Tess announced in a clipped voice, a blatant attempt to change the subject.

Kenric picked up Tess's cloak and draped it around her shoulders, missing her wince of pain. He pulled the hood up to protect her from the cold. " 'Tis colder today. Let us hope we don't get snowed on before we sight Montague."

Kenric hoped in vain. The snow started less than an hour into their journey. Fluffy white flakes drifted in lazy circles from the sky before the winds picked up and the soft flakes turned into hard, driven pellets. Tess was covered under two warm layers of cloaks but she worried for Kenric and his men. The soldiers donned fur caps and those who owned them wore gloves, but they were surely miserable. She was the best protected yet she seemed plagued by chills that set her teeth to chattering, only to become warm, almost hot, each time the bout of chills passed.

A fever, she finally realized with a shudder. Please God, let it be a mild one, she prayed. Fevers were feared by rich and poor alike. Though most were not fatal, one could never tell until it was too late. She slipped her arms around Kenric's waist and decided God would not be so cruel.

Kenric shifted Tess in his arms, feeling much like a well-used bed. He couldn't blame her for using sleep to escape the dull ride and harsh weather, but as the day grew longer, he began to wonder how anyone could sleep so much. At least she'd be well rested, he thought with a grin. She would need her strength for the evening he had planned.

The weather broke near noon and Kenric was relieved to discover the snow had scarcely touched the road ahead. They made good time in the afternoon and were within sight of his castle when the dying sun broke through the lingering gray clouds.

Kenric drew his cloak back and spoke softly in Tess's ear. "You are home, wife."

4

Castle Montague rose dark and forbidding against the fading twilight, an uninviting place made gloomier by scores of fire-charred trees. Their lifeless limbs rose from the snow like specters, silent guards standing on all sides of the massive stone fortress. The bleak sight was enough to make Tess shiver.

" 'Tis little better on the inside," Kenric warned. "Best prepare for the worst, then perhaps it will not seem so bad."

"What happened to the trees?" she asked, deciding to ignore the warning. No need to let her imagination run wild, wondering what the "worst" might be inside the Butcher of Wales's fortress. She'd find out soon enough.

"I had them burned. They would provide too much shelter should an army lay siege to the castle."

Tess nodded then glanced around his shoulder. His soldiers rode forward silently, their faces grim. Odd, she thought, pondering this strange reaction. MacLeith's men would be riding into the bailey amidst their own loud cheers if they'd kidnapped an heiress for their laird. Their solemn stares increased her dread.

The baron pulled his horse aside and allowed the men to file past him through the outer gates. She could feel the somber mood increase as they rode through the outer bailey of their bleak home. They passed the inner gates without so much as a word of greeting called down from the walls. The baron's men were still mounted, lined up by rank on each side of the road that led from the inner gates to a set of massive stone steps. The steps led to Montague's great hall. Not one servant was in evidence, a situation unheard of even in a small, poorly staffed keep, much less a sprawling castle the size of Montague. Tess was too curious about this strange reception to be insulted by the cold welcome to her new home. To be sure, Kenric's men acted as if they didn't expect to see a living soul within the walls.

Kenric rode up to the stone steps and dismounted, pulling Tess down to his side. Every pair of eyes followed their progress up the steps. Tess had never been the focus of so much attention. She was Baroness to these strangers, wife to their leader. Did they know Kenric didn't want her? Did they know they'd soon be going to war over her, risking their lives for an unwanted bride, a stranger, a murderess?

Her grip on Kenric's arm tightened, and he laid one hand over hers. The effect was immediate. She could almost feel his strength surrounding her, calming, giving her a burgeoning strength of her own. Just as she was thinking the gesture was unintentional on his part, that he couldn't know how frightened she was, Kenric leaned down to whisper in her ear.

"Calm yourself, Tess. These steps lead to the great

hall, not a sacrificial altar." He turned then to face his men, saving Tess the embarrassment of a reply.

"I have taken Tess Remmington to wife," he began. His voice rang out through the courtyard, the deep sound reverberating off the stone walls. "All of you know the challenge laid down to Dunmore MacLeith when I made her my bride. As of the night 'ere last, Dunmore MacLeith is a trespasser on my land."

Tess glanced up at Kenric, then wished she hadn't. The look on her husband's face was frightening. He smiled, yes, but it was a smile that didn't reach his cold eyes.

"The MacLeiths will challenge this marriage, but I intend to take Remmington Castle and all her good English keeps from the Scottish squatters by any means necessary."

The men cheered at the end of that declaration. But they really weren't cheers, Tess decided. Nay, they were roars of battle cries. The sound was nearly deafening, making the feverish ache in her head even worse. The awful noise continued as Kenric drew her forward, unfastened her hood, and pulled the cloak from her shoulders. He placed his hands on her shoulders in a blatant display of ownership. Tess locked her knees so they wouldn't buckle beneath her.

"You will protect my lady's life with your own. The loyalty you owe me now extends to my wife."

Fitz Alan drew his long battlesword, an act followed by each man until the entire bailey glittered with swords, each lifted in a silent pledge of fealty. Tess thought she should say something, but found herself speechless for the first time in her life. The fiercest army in England had just given her their loyalty. Nay, Kenric gave her their loyalty. And she intended to betray them all.

"Come, Tess," Kenric said quietly, turning her toward the doors.

Tess tried not to dwell on the issue of allegiance as he led her inside, then up another set of stone steps to the hall. She focused all her attention on the strangeness of her new home. Inside the great hall, Montague was a mixture of wealth and squalor. The wealth was well evident. She found her eyes drawn to intricate carvings of faces, flowers, and miniature scenes on each end or crossing of the massive rib beams that supported the structure. The windows were cased with glass in a myriad of colors and the casings were as intricately carved as the beams. Not one, but two massive fireplaces flanked the hall, and well-vented ones at that. Each had its own chimney instead of a simple hole cut through the ceiling, as was the case at Langston Keep. Rich, colorful tapestries covered several walls, and Montague banners hung from the huge, round pillars supporting the roof.

Yet the squalor was just as apparent. Filthy, broken reeds littered the floor, their stench no doubt worsened by the remnants of more than one meal and the pack of hounds running loose through the hall. The dining tables, set up to form a U-shape in the middle of the room, were uncovered and fashioned of the crudest lumber. Long benches and simple stools were the only available seats.

Whatever hard times had befallen this hall, they were recent ones, she decided, completing her inventory of the place. If she had any intention of staying here, a good cleaning and a visit to the carpenter would have been the first order of business. Kenric's hall was in sore need of a lady to see to such things. A lady much like the one walking toward them.

The woman was dressed in the kind of finery Tess had only dreamed of in her days at Langston. Her gown was made of richly trimmed blue velvet embroidered with white stags. Sapphires sparkled at her throat and wrists. Waves of jet-black hair framed a delicate face with high, exotic cheekbones and eyes perfectly matched to her gown. She seemed a bit older than Tess, but perhaps that was because she walked with such stiff dignity. Her gaze narrowed with ill-concealed hate as she came to a halt before Kenric.

"Welcome home, *brother*." The woman's greeting was so cold, Tess expected icicles to form in the air.

"Good eve, Helen," Kenric responded curtly. He pulled Tess closer and introduced her to his sister.

"I am very pleased to meet you," Tess said sincerely. This woman could be an ally, someone who might be able to aid in her escape. She clasped Helen's hands and smiled at her sister-in-law, hoping to melt some of the ice in Helen's eyes. "I hope we shall become good friends."

Helen's composed expression faltered for a moment before the cool mask of indifference slipped back into place. She pulled her hands away and folded them at her waist.

"We shall see," she replied with a regal nod.

"My men are in need of food," Kenric told his sister, his face as disinterested as hers. "Make arrangements to serve a meal as soon as possible."

"The kitchen is ill prepared to serve a meal at this hour," Helen informed him. She turned and walked toward the kitchens, then called over her shoulder, "I shall see what is available."

Kenric's face didn't show any emotion. Tess was amazed by her husband's control. The MacLeiths would have bloodied Helen's lip the first time she uttered a word.

"Helen did not know you would arrive this eve?" she asked, unable to contain her curiosity.

"She knew."

Kenric's tone said the subject was closed. He took his position at the head table, then motioned for Tess to sit next to him. The servants finally appeared, each bearing flagons of wine and ale to the groups of men near the tables and fireplaces. Some of the men's faces were familiar from the courtyard, but many were present in the hall when they arrived. Montague's vassals, Tess supposed, eyeing their rich, colorful clothes. These would be the knights who ruled at Montague's keeps or smaller fortresses. It wasn't unusual for them to gather at their lord's main fortress, although their ladies were conspicuous by their absence. Aside from some of the servants, Tess was the only woman in the hall.

Several men seemed eager for Kenric's audience and they soon had him deep in conversation. Though Tess tried to find something to do other than eavesdrop, the task was not easy. Helen had disappeared and Fitz Alan was talking to several men she didn't know. She didn't think it good manners to start a conversation with anyone she hadn't been properly introduced to.

Bored by her own company, she gave up all pretense of disinterest and listened avidly to Kenric's conversation, discovering some intriguing details about her husband's past. Most curious was the fact that, until recently, Kenric had not set foot on Montague land since his departure for the Crusades, nine years earlier. Being far away in the Holy Lands was excuse enough to stay away from home, but in the five years of war with Wales, Kenric hadn't found or made the time to visit his family. Not even when his father died three years earlier and Kenric assumed the title.

Kenric's vassals droned on and on while Tess struggled to remain alert. The excitement of their arrival was wearing off and the conversation had turned to mundane matters that didn't interest her. Nearly an hour passed before the meal was served, if the slops laid before them could be called such. Every dish was either undercooked, overcooked, or unrecognizable. All were awful. If she were of a mind to stay married to Kenric, a trip to the kitchens would have topped her list of tasks to accomplish, right after a tour of the castle. Not that she'd be staying at Montague long enough to concern herself with those wifely duties. She was leaving at the first opportunity.

No one lingered over the tasteless meal. Kenric rose immediately after eating what he could to join a group gathered near one of the fireplaces. Tess remained seated, unsure what she was expected to do. She tried to keep herself occupied by thinking over the chores that would be necessary to right the place. Habit, she told herself. She'd been trained from birth to run an estate the size of Montague. Helen's training must have been lacking, indeed. The conditions at Montague were disgusting. The rushes were filthy, the hounds showed no signs of being housebroken, and the remainders of the meal still lay upon the table. God only knew what the rest of the fortress looked like. Thank goodness she wouldn't be staying long.

Tess stretched from one side to the other, trying to relieve the cramped pain in her back and ignore the thought of how wonderful a bed would feel. There was the slight worry over Kenric's promise to make her a wife in more than name, but she doubted he meant that night. He'd been in a saddle for at least four days, with little enough rest the last two. Surely the man wasn't up to such vigorous activity.

A moment later Tess snapped her head up in alarm, shocked to realize she'd actually nodded off at the table. Right in front of Kenric and all his men! She didn't relax until a quick glance around the hall satisfied her that none had witnessed the slip.

Relaxing was a mistake.

Her eyelids seemed weighted with lead. She desperately searched the hall for something that would hold her interest enough to stay awake. Kenric was extremely interesting to look at, but staring at her husband would surely be considered rude. Her attention turned instead to the vast array of weapons that hung on one wall. She began to study the diverse designs. She was concentrating on keeping the wall in focus when true panic set in. No matter how hard she fought the urge, her eyes were determined to close. She propped her elbows on the table, chin in hand, and reserved every bit of strength for the mighty effort of keeping her eyes open. A moment later they slid shut.

Why did I fight this? she asked herself. Just a few more minutes and she'd open her eyes feeling good as new.

On the other side of the hall, one of the servants dropped a tray and the loud clatter brought Tess awake with a start. Disoriented, she lifted her head then raised one hand to her forehead, wishing the room would stop tilting back and forth. Kenric was at her side in an instant.

"What is wrong with you?" he demanded. He took the stool next to Tess and put a steadying arm around her shoulders. A hand placed against her forehead made him swear foully under his breath. "You burn with fever, Tess. Why didn't you tell me you were ill?"

"Ill?" Tess tried to shake her head but the sudden movement made her dizzy. She put one hand on Kenric's knee to steady herself. "Am I ill?" Realizing the truth of his observation, she said, "Doubtless 'tis just a slight fever, milord. I am sure it shall pass by morn."

Kenric didn't reply. He lifted Tess in his arms, unaware that she winced in pain, and walked toward the steps leading to the upper chambers. He stopped long enough to give orders to Fitz Alan.

"Tell the men my wife is exhausted from her journey and bid them enjoy my hospitality. She has a fever," he went on, lowering his voice. "Send someone for the old healing woman in the village. She can administer her foul brews if this does not pass by morning."

Tess tried to protest the order, but Kenric's glare was fierce enough to keep her silent until they reached his chamber. She still didn't say a word as he walked into the room and laid her on the bed. It wasn't the aches and pains of her fever that kept Tess silent. She was simply too awed by her surroundings to speak.

Kenric's bedchamber was a study in exotic luxury. Handsomely wrought candlesticks, plates, and foreign-looking objects crammed the mantel above the fireplace, and most were made of gold. Two chalices were so encrusted with jewels that the metal beneath was difficult to determine. There were no dirty rushes to litter the floor in this room. Plush Persian rugs covered the cold stones, probably brought back from the Crusades. The bed was covered with a heavy blue brocade and the canopy draped with shimmering midnight-blue silk shot through with gold thread to form the bed curtains.

"You are rich!" she exclaimed, brushing away the lingering effects of her short sleep to examine the room. "This chamber is finer than the king's!"

"My efforts have their rewards," Kenric acknowledged dryly. He pushed her against the pillows, then turned away to lay more logs on the fire. "And what would you know of the king's bedchamber?"

"Nothing," she admitted. "But I am sure it could not be so nice."

"I am glad you are pleased." He returned to stand by the bed, arms crossed, feet braced as if ready for battle. "Now you will please me by staying in this bed until your fever passes." He pointed to the linen bundles near the foot of the bed. "Thomas brought your bags up earlier. I will help you out of those clothes and into your nightshift."

"I . . . I would sleep in my gown, milord."

"You need to rest. That heavy gown cannot possibly be comfortable."

"You will not look while I change?"

"I am your husband," he told her arrogantly. "You may be too ill to fulfill your wifely duties this eve, but there is no reason why I should not see what I cannot have." His look was determined. "Yet."

"I am quite comfortable in my gown," she assured him, folding her hands across her chest as she closed her eyes. "Truly, I find myself too fatigued for such a chore. Please allow me to rest now, milord."

She waited for Kenric's argument. When he remained silent, she peeked under her lashes. Her eyes widened when he began undressing.

"Unlike you, I prefer comfort over modesty when I sleep."

He was only going to sleep beside her. Tess caught herself before she sighed her relief aloud. She'd grown accustomed to his solid warmth the last two days in the saddle and actually found herself looking forward to sharing his heat through the night. After all, there was no sin in enjoying the comfort of her husband's arms.

Kenric ignored her completely as he undressed, and she couldn't resist stealing brave glances. Tess soon stared boldly at her husband's body. The wonder of it nearly took her breath away. The power and strength she'd only guessed at were displayed in all their male glory as the trappings of civilization fell away, revealing the primitive warrior lurking beneath the surface. This was the dangerous man of the tales, she decided, watching the way his muscles flexed and rippled at this simple task. She could only imagine what those muscles would look like when he wielded a weapon, calling forth the incredible power of his body.

There was that feeling again, the strange fluttering that began in her stomach and spread quickly through her limbs. She now recognized it for what it was. Desire. Carnal desire. She wanted to touch him, to know what that strength felt like.

Kenric turned to shed his breeches and Tess snapped her eyes shut. They popped wide open when she felt him slide into bed next to her.

"Go to sleep, Tess. I am too exhausted to argue with you."

Sleep? Not likely, Tess thought. Sleeping next to him in a tent, fully clothed, was one thing. This was quite another, sleeping in bed next to a naked man. Next to her husband! The thought sent a shiver of excitement through her body. Yet there was a more pressing worry to keep her occupied. She knew Kenric well enough already to know he'd agreed too easily with her request to remain in her gown. What was his game? She was too tired for this trial, too ill to think clearly. Her teeth worried at her lip until she decided to close her eyes and pretend to sleep, just to see what he would do. Moments later, she was asleep in truth.

Kenric waited until his bride was resting soundly before he began undressing her. Talking Tess into undressing on her own was a waste of time and he'd been in too many battles to pursue a useless tactic. This was a much quicker way to accomplish the same task. Kenric was so pleased with himself that he felt like whistling. He gave up all pretense of stealth when she slept through the gown being tugged over her head.

"Sleeps like the dead," he muttered.

She moaned in her sleep as he removed the garment, the small cry of pain reminding him that he could look but not touch. And he looked his fill. The fire provided just enough light to view her perfection, turning her skin to liquid gold. His gaze lingered on full, luscious breasts before traveling lower, across a trim waist and flat belly to a thick triangle of dark blond curls. A long, lusty moment passed before his eyes were finally able to leave that tempting sight to take in the sleek beauty of the longest, shapeliest legs he'd ever laid eyes on.

"Beautiful."

He breathed the word reverently, his gaze traveling the length of her again. She was small, yes, but there was nothing childlike about her body. Her womanly curves were made for a man's hands. His hands. He ached to touch her, but the even greater ache in his loins told him one touch would be impossible. He'd never lain with such a beautiful woman, never thought he'd be gifted with such perfection given his brutish size and scarred body.

One more night, he promised himself, startled to realize the depths of his own disappointment. He'd set out to teach Tess a lesson, but was learning one of his own: do not start what cannot be finished. He was tired, she was fevered, and now was not the time. He growled in frustration, lying down stiffly beside his virgin bride. He yanked the covers up to hide the temptation and locked his hands behind his head. Fully aroused, he had to concentrate hard to ignore his needs. He decided he must be insane, torturing himself this way.

"You had best be healthy as my horse come morn," he ordered his sleeping bride.

"Ummm," Tess sighed. She rolled onto her stomach, her head nearly buried beneath the covers, unconcerned and unaware of her husband's discomfort.

God was testing his endurance, Kenric decided, turning to his side to watch her sleep. He got a wife he didn't want, then wanted a wife he couldn't have. The irony of the situation was not lost on him.

Tess stirred in her sleep, and the cover slipped lower on her shoulders. Kenric gave up the fight, unable to resist tracing his fingers along the soft curve of one shoulder, then lower to stroke . . .

His hand stopped. He moved his fingertips slowly over the strange ridges covering his bride's shoulderblade. His brows drew together in confusion. He slipped out of bed and went to the mantel for a candle, wanting more than dim firelight to examine this strange discovery.

Holding the candle with one hand, he pulled the covers off her shoulders with the other, unable to believe what was revealed. Kenric stared at the maze of welts and angry red stripes in stunned silence. Someone had taken a whip to his tiny wife and beat her like an animal.

Tess awoke with her heart in her throat, the roar of some wild beast still ringing in her ears. It took a few frightening moments to get her bearings. The sudden realization that she was in Kenric's bed, naked, didn't ease her fears a bit. Her eyes widened in panic when she heard his question.

"Who did this?" His voice was a low whisper, almost emotionless.

"It doesn't hurt much anymore," she said quickly, knowing exactly what he was talking about. She tried to meet her husband's gaze, but she'd forgotten he was naked. Her gaze dropped quickly to the pillow. " 'Tis ugly now, but truly not as bad as it looks. Why, it hardly bothers me. Even Mag, the baker's wife, said I won't have any scars this time."

"This time?" He spoke slowly, carefully pronouncing each word. "Give me the name."

"Gordon MacLeith," she murmured, not even pretending to misunderstand the question. She waited in dread for him to ask why, knowing she'd have to tell the truth. She was simply too shaken to think up a good lie.

Kenric remained silent, his face emotionless as he stared at her back. There were bruises from her neck to her waist, most yellowed enough to tell him many days had passed since she'd suffered this savagery. Looking at the results, Kenric knew she was lucky to be alive. But Gordon MacLeith was a dead man. The sickening realization that the son wouldn't do anything the father hadn't sanctioned wrenched at his gut, honing his rage. Never, Kenric vowed, would he underestimate his new enemies. Such animals were too unpredictable. This was not a punishment meted out to a girl with a quick temper. This was hatred in the form of a whip.

At last he left the bed and walked to the chamber door, opening it so quietly that Tess nearly leaped from the bed when he bellowed into the hall.

"Fitz Alan!"

He waited a moment, listening to the answering silence, then swore under his breath. He stepped back into the room long enough to don a pair of breeches, then he was gone.

Tess turned over on the bed and pulled the covers up to her chin. The knot of shame in her belly quickly turned into something more sickening. Fear. That Kenric was angry there was little doubt. But why didn't he ask more questions? And what could he want with Fitz Alan?

Kenric appeared again in the doorway, followed almost immediately by Fitz Alan and two other men. Their drawn swords said Kenric hadn't explained the summons. They skidded to a halt just inside the room, silently turning their eyes toward the baron, waiting for him to explain the situation. Kenric looked at Tess. His icy gaze made her shiver.

"Get on your stomach."

The words sent a knife of dread down her spine. She knew his intent then. A man could reject a flawed wife. She shook her head vigorously, not trusting herself to speak. Kenric flatly rejected her refusal.

"Now!"

His roar had the desired effect. Tess dove under the covers, but she was on her stomach. He took hold of the bedding and easily pried her fingers away before carefully pulling the covers down to her waist. Drawing her elbows tighter against her sides, she covered her face as tears of humiliation trickled silently through her fingers.

"Tell me again who did this," Kenric demanded. She remained silent until he pulled one of her hands away from her face.

"Gordon MacLeith!" Tess wailed. She buried her face in the pillow, hoping she would be lucky enough to suffocate.

"The king will take an interest in this marriage at some point," he told his men, his voice cold and exact. "You will each bear witness that she came to me this way. Gather your weapons and wait for me in the hall. I feel the need to work off some of this . . ."

"Aye, milord," Fitz Alan said quietly. "We will await you in the hall."

Kenric nodded and the men departed. He gently pulled the covers over his wife's trembling shoulders, then dressed quickly.

"Do not torment yourself, Tess," he said as he gently stroked her hair. She was still sobbing into the pillow. "This is not your fault."

Tess tried to nod, but how could she agree with such a lie? It *was* her fault. She had provoked Gordon deliberately. But this was the cruelest, meanest punishment of all, to let her believe she'd escaped her tormentors, only to be sent back to them, found lacking because of what they'd done to her in the first place. She cried harder into the pillow, unaware that Kenric had left the room until she finally lifted her head. She sat up slowly, trying to calm down enough to think clearly.

"What to do," she whispered, hugging her knees. Mag had told her a story once, about a bride rejected by her husband because she stuttered. The girl and her betrothed had not met before the wedding and she was instructed to remain silent until after the ceremony. A full day passed before her husband discovered the flaw, but she was returned to her family, the marriage annulled.

Tess knew she should be happy. She'd wanted an annulment from the moment she married. That Kenric wanted it as well would only make the formalities that much simpler. But to be returned to the MacLeiths after spiting them with an escape? She would not live through that punishment. Knowing Gordon, he would make sure she suffered long and hard for her folly.

Tess let her forehead drop to her knees. Suddenly she believed every story she'd ever heard of her husband. He truly was the Butcher of Wales, a man unburdened by any feelings or conscience. He had to know as well as she did what her fate would be at the hands of the MacLeiths. He'd sentenced her to death as surely as if he'd taken his sword and done the deed himself.

Her chin trembled and fresh tears formed in her eyes. She angrily swiped them away. Crying wasn't going to change anything. She slid from the bed and found her clothes, wondering why Kenric had bothered undressing her in the first place. Had he guessed she was hiding something? Aye, she decided, Kenric barely knew her, yet he could spot her lies and deceits already.

A plan began to take shape as she dressed. Whatever happened, she would not willingly return to the Mac-Leiths. She had to reach the king.

Getting out of Montague was the first and biggest problem. Even if she managed to get through the gates of the castle, she had no food or horse. Her gaze was drawn to the chalices on the mantel. Just one would see to her needs for at least a year. She stared at the gems a long time before shaking her head.

There was a small bow and quiver of arrows in one of her bundles. She was good at hunting small game and she would rather rob the king's forests than rob her husband. The king would never miss an occasional rabbit, but Kenric would surely miss one of his beautiful chalices. Nay, she would not have him think any less of her, if such were possible.

Tess finished dressing, then strapped on the cloth bundles and donned her cloak. At the door she paused for one last look at the beautiful chamber, memorizing each detail so she could always savor the thought that she once belonged in such a fine room.

5

The great hall was strangely silent. Only a handful of soldiers were gathered near one massive fireplace. No one noticed when the new baroness made her way down the stairs at their back, the sound of the outer door being opened dismissed as a servant returning from some duty.

Tess drew her hood low against the brisk wind, trying to remember the direction of the main gates. The place looked so much different from when they'd ridden in amidst Kenric's men. The courtyard was deserted now and she hurried across the empty yard, staying close to the shadows. Montague's main gates appeared on the other side of the stables but Tess nearly cried at the sight that greeted her.

The drawbridge was up.

How could she have overlooked this problem? There

wasn't a gatekeeper in all of England foolish enough to lower a bridge at this time of night, not for any reason. Even if she managed to talk the guards into lowering this bridge, Montague had a second drawbridge at the outer bailey's gatehouse. She would never succeed.

Tess leaned against the stable wall in defeat. She couldn't wait for dawn when the bridges would be lowered for the villagers. Her escape must be made in darkness when she would have a chance of getting far enough away to hide in the woods, just in case Kenric sent out a search party.

There had to be another way out. Tess closed her eyes and thought back to the days spent at Remmington Castle. Though laid out differently, her childhood home was about the same size as Montague. How would she get out of Remmington if the gates were closed? The answer came in a flash.

The postern! Almost every large fortress had a postern gate cut high into the castle wall. The small gates were built to prevent enemy soldiers or spies from entering the castle in wagonloads of supplies. Goods were unloaded at the bottom of the wall and hauled up a wooden ramp. A ramp that led directly through the outside walls! Surely Montague Castle possessed such a gate, but could she find it by dawn?

Tess inched her way along the wall, careful to avoid being spotted by guards on the battlements above her. Luck was on her side and her search was rewarded less than an hour later. She hid in the shadows and took stock of the gate before venturing forward.

Montague's postern was a simple affair of a large door barricaded with two crossbars; one high overhead near the top, the other at chest height toward the bottom. The gatekeeper stood watch over the ramp from his post on the battlements. A flickering rush torch outlined his axe, kept at the ready to sever the main supports and collapse the ramp should the castle come under attack.

Gathering her courage, Tess called up to the gatekeep, startling him from his watch. Leaning over the wall, he squinted against the dim torchlight as if trying to decide her identity.

"What ye be wantin, Mary?"

"To leave," Tess replied, wondering who Mary was.

"To leave," he repeated with a snort. "Not at this time o' night."

"My . . . my husband has rejected me." It was a poor excuse, yet the only one she could think up.

"Find a bed with the kitchen wenches, then go in the morn," he ordered. "Cook will be sober by then and like as not take you back. You should know better than to listen to anything that man says when he's in his cups."

"My husband insists I leave the fortress tonight," Tess argued, beginning to understand her mistaken identity. The gatekeep's confusion might be used to her advantage. "I must abide by his wishes."

"Thinks he's master of Montague," he muttered. "Ye be going to yer family in the village then?"

"Aye." Tess held her breath.

The gatekeeper cursed all troublesome females then poked a foot against a boy sleeping at his feet. "Climb down and see to the lower bar."

"Someone is bringing supplies?" the boy asked, rubbing the sleep from his eyes. " 'Tis dark. Why would—"

"Cook's wife needs to go to her family in the village." The gatekeep ruffled the boy's hair affectionately. "See to the lower bar then go on home to yer warm bed, son. I'll not be needin' yer help the rest o' this night."

Tess released her breath as the bars were pushed aside. She couldn't believe she was actually being allowed to leave until the gates swung open. What a good liar she was becoming! She did allow that being mistaken for the cook's wife certainly helped.

The gates shut behind her and she started uncertainly down the dark ramp, the treacherous walk lit only by faint moonlight. It appeared steeper than the one at Remmington, though she'd never actually set foot on the thing. The gatekeeper called to her over the wall, as if he read her mind.

"Watch yer step. One tumble and ye'll break yer neck."

"Thank you for the warning," she mumbled.

Tess picked her way down the steep ramp, tempted to kiss the ground when she finally reached the bottom. She hurried down the castle lane, pausing a moment where the lane met the king's road. She quickly took the direction opposite the one they'd ridden in from Kelso Abbey, and at the edge of the forest she turned around for a last look at the forbidding castle. She still couldn't believe she'd escaped so easily. She didn't feel very satisfied over the accomplishment. If the truth were known, she would almost face being returned to the MacLeiths someday if she could stay in Kenric's beautiful room until she felt better. Every bone in her body ached.

Tess turned and walked away from the castle before self-pity could interfere with her plan. Walk until dawn, she told herself, then find a hiding place to rest during the day. That plan seemed reasonable. Staying warm while she slept would be a challenge, but she could face that problem later. Her immediate concern was getting as far away from Kenric as possible, before he discovered she was missing. She'd escaped once from Langston Keep, so why couldn't she escape again? Of course she lacked a horse and a knight's protection, but as long as the impossible odds were ignored, that bit of logic made some sense.

The sun was well over the horizon when John shuffled toward the kitchens to take his morning meal. He noticed the baron's men running in all directions on his way from the postern and learned the reason for the commotion from a passing soldier.

"The new baroness has disappeared," the soldier told

him, shaking his head in disbelief. "You didn't see anything on your watch?"

"Nay," John replied, perplexed by the news. "Cook's
wife was the only female at the postern gate last eve."
John scratched his beard. "At least . . . Nay, I'm sure
'twas Cook's wife. The master's lady is a pretty thing, I'm
told. Small and dainty, ain't that the way of it?"

"Aye. The baron is half crazed thinking someone
snatched her. As if any would dare risk that one's wrath."

" 'Tis unlikely," John agreed. The soldier hurried away
to search the buttery, leaving John deep in thought.

"Nay, it could not be," John told himself, grinning at
his foolishness. Still, it wouldn't hurt to double-check.
Cook would probably think him strange indeed, but he'd
rest easier once he knew for sure.

The kitchen was in as much chaos as the rest of the
castle, the servants busy searching every barrel and store
for the new mistress. John thought it laughable, the tiny
crevices being searched for a grown woman. 'Twas unlikely
any lady could fit in the small turnip barrels, yet their lids
lay scattered about the room. He finally located Cook near
the flour bins, but the gatekeeper's face turned as pasty as
the flour when he spied the big woman standing nearby.

"Where did you go last eve?" John grabbed the
woman's arm and spun her around.

"Nowhere," Cook's wife gasped, stunned by the sudden attack.

"What goes here?" Cook bellowed. He jerked John's
hand from his wife's arm. "What . . ." He steadied the
pale gatekeeper by the shoulders. "Are you aright? Ye're
the color of wax, man."

"Your wife did not leave the castle last eve?" John
whispered hopefully. Cook shook his head. "Is there another of her size in the castle?"

"Me wife's one of a kind. A man in my position can
afford a well-fed woman. She's—"

"Oh, God," John wailed. "I am a dead man."

"What are you talking about? Why—"

"The b-baron," John stuttered. "Where is the baron?"

"The stables, last I heard."

The gatekeeper disappeared through the kitchen door faster than he had ever moved before.

John searched frantically for his overlord, and finally spotted him near the gate to the outer bailey. He rushed forward, but the soldiers surrounding their baron acted instinctively to protect the warlord from this unknown threat. John soon found himself facedown in the dirt with three swords at his neck.

"The mistress," John croaked. "I must tell the baron—"

He was suddenly hauled up by the collar, his feet dangling in the air.

"Where is she?" Kenric roared.

"I swore it was Cook's wife," John blurted out, inspired to new terror by the look on Baron Montague's face. "Huge as a horse, she was—"

"Answer!"

John tried twice before he could get the words past the baron's new hold on his throat. "Family," he gasped. "Said she was going back—"

Kenric tossed the man aside like an old rag, already turning toward the stables. Fury hastened his steps, for his worst fears were confirmed. Tess was outside the walls. The chit could be frozen already, or the meal of any number of dangerous creatures who lurked in the woods. A woman alone would not last a day in the frigid wilderness, especially a woman weakened by a fever. If he found her alive, she would wish for death before he was done with her.

Less than a quarter hour later, Kenric's warhorse thundered through the gates with fifty others, their riders hastily armed yet ready to face any danger. The group stayed on the main road until they entered the forest, then Kenric began dispatching men every quarter mile to search the woods. A half hour later they drew to a halt.

"She is on foot," Kenric told Fitz Alan, though he spoke more to himself than to his friend. "She could not have journeyed this far."

" 'Tis unlikely," Fitz Alan agreed.

"Tess knew that Ian Duncan could not give her sanctuary. And she had no wish to return to the MacLeiths." Kenric frowned, realizing his thinking was clear for the first time since discovering Tess had left the castle. He cursed himself again for sleeping in the hall last night, for thinking he could face his wife's injuries with a calmer head in the morning.

"Where else would she go?" Fitz Alan asked. "A convent?"

"The king." Kenric wheeled his horse around, his expression grim. "There is nowhere else for her to turn. She's taken the road to London."

The men backtracked to the castle, then began searching to the south. The lane was frozen solid, rutted and packed down by carts and horses, which made tracking nearly impossible. They kept their eyes to the sides of the road instead, searching for any unusual tracks in the light cover of snow.

"There!" Kenric pointed to a break in the frozen brush to one side of the road. Following the small set of footprints into the forest, they eventually came to a small clearing bordered on three sides by steep hills and littered with enormous boulders. Kenric scanned the open field, then nudged his horse forward to follow the tracks to a rocky outcropping flanked by two boulders.

"Stay where you are," a small voice called out. Tess slipped from her hiding place behind one of the huge rocks to face her husband. The arrow aimed at Kenric's chest added enough weight to her command that his men heeded the order and pulled their mounts to a halt. Kenric ignored the threat and continued to advance.

Tess looked close to frozen. Her face was the color of wax, her lips nearly as blue as her glassy eyes. The dark smudges of exhaustion surrounding her eyes gave his bride a hollow, haunted look. As near as Kenric could tell, she could collapse at any moment.

"Stop, I say!"

There was a frantic note in her voice, but Kenric just shook his head and allowed his horse to move steadily forward.

"I'll put an arrow in you. I swear I will."

Tess sounded nearly hysterical, but Kenric's voice was determined.

"I will still take you back."

"I won't go back to MacLeith," Tess shouted. That announcement finally made Kenric pull in his mount.

"I would rather die by your hand or your man's," she vowed, nodding toward Fitz Alan. Kenric stared at her as if she'd lost her mind. She drew the bowstring tighter. "I mean what I say."

"What are you talking about, you little fool? I am taking you home with me."

"Why?"

"*Why?*" Kenric's horse skitted nervously and he took a moment to calm the animal. He resisted the urge to gallop forward and claim his errant wife. Her bow was pulled tauter than he'd believed her capable. If she had any skill at all with the thing, her arrow would slice through his chest if she decided to skewer him. How was he to know that retrieving a wife would require full armor?

"Stop this nonsense, Tess." He tried to keep the anger from his voice. The arrow aimed at his chest did call for some diplomacy. But he couldn't help adding, "You will come home with me this instant!"

"You rejected me," Tess accused, tears spilling freely down her cheeks. "You do not want me for wife. You even brought your men to see my flaw so they can justify your claim when you petition for an annulment. I will not live a fortnight beyond my return to Remmington. The MacLeiths are not known for their forgiving nature. If I am lucky, I will not live a day. How can you send me back, knowing my fate?"

"Only yesterday I promised you would never return to Dunmore MacLeith," he reminded her, allowing Tess to see some of his anger. Did she really think him such a monster? "I did not reject you. My men will only testify to the king that my reasons for killing Gordon MacLeith are justified."

Tess didn't respond to that enlightening statement, but her eyes grew wider and her bow arm began to tremble noticeably.

"If you do not lower that bow soon, you will shoot me by accident." Kenric's horse pawed the ground and snorted, as if echoing the impatience of his master. Tess still hesitated. "A flesh wound will not improve my mood, wife."

"You . . . you would not trick me?" she asked, even as she slowly dropped her weapon.

Kenric spurred his horse forward. He leaped off the warhorse and grabbed his wife in one motion, his grip on her shoulders painful.

"You are *never* to run from me again," he shouted, so loud that Tess winced. "Is that clear enough for you?"

"Aye, husband," she said quietly. She wrapped her arms around his neck, pulling his head down to whisper in his ear. Kenric was so surprised by the unexpected action that he let her. " 'Tis a fact I have never swooned, but there is the oddest . . . ringing in my ears and . . ."

Her voice faded and she went limp. Kenric shook his head and lifted her into his arms.

"Sick with fever and you think to journey alone to London," he muttered. "You are incredibly bold or incredibly ignorant. I do not think I have decided just yet."

"Have someone gather her things," he told Fitz Alan, nodding to the bundles still lying on the ground. "I am curious to see what other surprises she's packed."

Kenric mounted with little difficulty, shifting his limp burden to one shoulder as he gained the saddle.

"The mistake is understandable," Fitz Alan said.

"The mistake was idiotic," Kenric snapped. "She should have known I wouldn't send her back to those bastards."

"They've had five years to terrorize her," Fitz Alan said cautiously. " 'Tis doubtful she will forget that fear overnight."

Kenric didn't give any indication that he'd heard the words, but he took them to heart. He felt Tess stir in his arms and he pulled aside the cloak. Her eyes were still glassy, her face deathly pale. They stared at each other, each trying to read the other's thoughts. Tess finally broke the silence.

"Have you decided my punishment?" Her voice was flat, without emotion.

"Nay," Kenric replied. Tess looked as if she'd been through quite enough at the moment. An hour ago, he would have cheerfully beaten her. But now? Now he wasn't so sure. "What punishments have you received in the past for disobedience?"

"A week locked in my room," she said, her voice pitifully weak. "On a diet of bread and water. Sometimes a week to work in the kitchens, or the stables, or in the fields, or—"

"I understand," Kenric drawled. His mouth quirked downward at the edges. "These are the punishments you usually received from the MacLeiths?"

First she nodded, then she shook her head. "Mostly the whip."

She closed her eyes, simply too tired to keep them open any longer. Tess felt a little guilty about relating such trivial punishments. She wouldn't mind any one of them. Given the way she was feeling, a week in her room . . . Nay, in Kenric's room . . . That sounded like heaven.

6

The next time Tess awoke she was surrounded by billowing golden clouds that floated in the deepest, truest blue sky she'd ever laid eyes on.

"Beautiful," she breathed in awe. " 'Tis just as I imagined."

"What is?" a deep voice asked.

She raised her arms, trying to embrace the lovely clouds. "Heaven!"

Something cold and wet was slapped over her eyes, blinding her to the beautiful scene. She frowned and cried out "No!" as strong hands pushed her down, down, down, into a deep, black hole. She clutched at the air, trying to slow the fall, but she landed painlessly on something soft. Her eyes opened slowly to the blackness of the pit surrounding her. One by one flames flickered and rose up around her in a complete circle, so high and hot that she was certain her skin was on fire. Her body seemed made of stone, unable to rouse enough strength to attempt an escape from the inferno.

The faces of fiery demons took shape in the flames, demons exactly like the ones painted in the doomsday scenes in Kelso Abbey's chapel. With horned heads, bulbous eyes, and razor-sharp teeth, the creatures held Tess's full, horrified attention. The head of one monster curled away from the fire to loom over her, laughing down at her helplessness while his breath blasted her face with molten heat. Tess squeezed her eyes shut and screamed in mindless terror.

A pair of strong arms suddenly reached down and snatched her up and out of the pit. She feared the demon had her until she found enough courage to open her eyes, amazed to find herself in Kenric's arms.

Now where had he come from?

"Don't let me fall," she pleaded. She clutched at Kenric's arms and looked past his shoulder into the fiery pit looming below them, shuddering over the flames licking at the heels of Kenric's boots. "It was *awful* down there."

"I have you."

He kept talking, but his words seemed to blur and run together until they became a low hum, drifting to nothingness. Snatches of murmured conversations sometimes penetrated the edge of the silence, but the sounds evaporated again before they could leave a lasting impression. Time became as distant as reality. No past, no present, just the swirling colors of an unknown dream that lacked shape or substance. The void didn't fade away until the humming sound began again, growing louder and louder until Tess was forced to leave the empty dream. The hum became a voice, a bit familiar, yet she couldn't put a face to the sound as it droned on and on. Was that Latin he was speaking?

"A priest," she whispered, thinking she recognized his forlorn chant. A priest had been sent for, which meant someone was dying. She tried to open her eyes but couldn't accomplish the simple task. It took a moment to make the connection, to realize that *she* was the one dying! She began to cry, but stopped when she heard Kenric's voice bellow through the haze, his words perfectly clear.

"I'll not send for a priest!"

"But you must honor her request," someone answered. "She is dying."

"Tess is *not* dying. I will not allow it!"

Tess closed her eyes and let herself float away into the fog again, greatly relieved to know she wouldn't die. Aye, that was certainly a nice worry to set aside. Kenric would keep her safe. He would protect her. With her thoughts on Kenric, another strange dream began to take shape in her mind. She saw Kenric not as a grown man, but as a lad of no more than fifteen summers. He stood among a group of boys about the same age, yet he towered above them, his body already developing into the powerful warrior he would become. Standing in the center of the group, he faced a pock-faced boy with mousy brown hair. The two were arguing fiercely, and Tess strained to hear their words.

"You are a bastard," the boy sneered. "Your mother was nothing more than a whore who spread her legs for the king."

Kenric's fists were balled at his side, rage hardening the lines of his face, yet he made no move toward the taunting boy. The strain of his anger could be heard in the crack of lingering youth in his voice.

"You will take back those words and declare yourself a foul liar," Kenric demanded loudly. "Or I will kill you, Royce of Northton."

"Oh, ho," Royce laughed, his lip curling in disgust. "So the king's bastard would kill a man for speaking the truth. Well, I have news for you, Kenric of the King's

Whore. You could not do it." Royce turned confidently to his companions, looking for support. "Have you never wondered why seasoned warriors fall so easily against him in tourney? I trow the king's gold eases their falls, making his bastard look the better man."

"For God's sake, Royce," a boy called from the crowd. "You talk treason. Do not—"

"Shut up." Royce's eyes narrowed on Kenric. "I have waited a long time to see this bastard's blood soak my blade. He mocks us with every tournament he wins, making us look like foolish boys. Explain how we can beat him in practice when seasoned knights fall to him like old women in tourney?"

"Have you considered," Kenric asked between clenched teeth, "that I let you win?"

"Hah! You are the liar!" Royce shoved one hand against Kenric's shoulder, but Kenric turned his body to let the blow brush by. "You have shamed every honest knight with your cheating ways and need to die!"

Royce drew his sword, but Kenric was quicker, easily deflecting the ill-planned blow. The circle of boys widened, some yelling encouragement to Royce, others shouting in favor of Kenric.

Less than a dozen blows were exchanged before everyone realized the match was uneven. Royce fought like a demon while Kenric exerted little effort in his own defense. There was no need when holding Royce at arms' length proved such easy work. The knowledge that he was being toyed with and his inability to dent Kenric's easy defense drove Royce into a screaming fury, his sweaty face twisted now with hatred. Kenric wasn't even breathing hard.

The grating ring of metal striking metal continued until Kenric finally tired of the lesson and easily struck the sword from Royce's hand. The flat of his sword fell next against the boy's chest, knocking him to the ground, then the point of Kenric's sword was at Royce's throat.

"Thus it is proven." Kenric's voice was calm, his face devoid of emotion. "The matches won against me were to spare you this humiliation, Royce. Honor is everything to a knight, something I would never sacrifice to become one. My spurs were earned fairly this day and I have done nothing to deserve your foul slurs against my family." He pressed his sword a little harder against the boy's throat, all traces of indifference gone from his voice. "Now you will apologize."

"Go to hell, bastard."

Kenric stared at the fallen boy for a long moment, the disgust and temptation easily read in his expression. The sword finally lowered.

"Get up, you worthless worm." He slammed his sword into its sheath. "I'll not foul my blade with your blood."

Kenric turned on his heel and stalked away, the silent crowd moving aside to let him pass. He didn't realize he was in danger until someone called out a warning at the last moment. Kenric swung around an instant before Royce's sword would have found the back of his neck. Driven by instinct alone, Kenric's blade was drawn and driven upward into the chest of his attacker in one blur of movement. Royce was dead before he hit the ground.

The fog began to roll in and Tess struggled to keep Kenric in sight. He was looking around now, searching vainly for the woman who had called his name in warning.

"I am here, Kenric. Do you see me?"

"I see you just fine."

Tess struggled to brush away the fog, surprised to find herself in bed. Kenric was seated in a chair at her side, but this Kenric was older, the man she'd married.

"I saw you kill him," she whispered. Her hand found his in the twisted bedcovers, unconsciously seeking comfort. "I was so afraid."

Kenric's brows drew together in confusion as he absently squeezed her hand then straightened the sheets. "Who did you see me kill?"

"The boy who said those awful things." Tess reached out to touch her husband's cheek, needing to reassure herself. His face was so familiar, comforting, as if she'd known him always. "You called him Royce."

Kenric's expression turned from surprise to anger. He stiffened noticeably. "Who told you of that?"

"No one. I saw it in my dream just now. When Royce attacked your back, I called out your name to warn you. I was sure you heard me call to you."

Oh, he'd heard all right, Kenric thought grimly, remembering the day well. But Tess hadn't been there. One of the bystanders had called out the warning, his voice breaking in the excitement of the moment into a high, womanly screech. Yet Kenric also recalled how everyone had looked around in confusion when he wished to give thanks for the warning, each boy insisting he'd heard nothing. Aye, the excitement of the moment, Kenric had told himself. Everything had happened so quickly. He'd thought little more of the odd matter until this moment.

How did Tess know he'd heard a woman's voice?

He racked his memory, trying to remember what the voice had sounded like. The realization of what he was doing suddenly struck and he shook his head in disbelief. The very idea that Tess had called out a warning in her sleep just now to be heard nearly ten years ago was ludicrous. How could he even entertain such a notion?

Her delusions were the catching kind, he decided, frowning. The tale had probably spread like all the others Tess seemed to have knowledge of. Aye, that was all there was to the mystery. Another tale she'd heard somewhere, twisted by the fever into reality.

He lifted her hand from his knee and tucked it under the covers. She was asleep again, her brow still hot with fever. It had been two days since he'd carried her home and still there was no sign of a recovery. Sometimes she rested quietly, more often than not the delirium of her fever kept her in a tormented state somewhere between sleep and reality. At least she didn't appear to be getting any worse.

He still couldn't believe she'd tried to escape on foot, without even food for a journey of several weeks. She wouldn't have lasted the day. If he'd been thinking clearly that night, he wouldn't have left her alone. It was his responsibility to protect his wife, even from herself. He'd seriously underestimated Tess, expected instant loyalty and trust from a woman who'd known little of either in her own home. Still, she'd betrayed his trust and he would never give her an opportunity to do so again.

Kenric stood up and stretched muscles cramped by the long hours of his vigil. Trust was also the reason he refused to leave his wife's side during this ordeal. Tess was a threat to many at Montague, and there wasn't a servant within the fortress he'd trust with her life. More than one would rejoice if she succumbed to this fever.

Hoping he'd be able to sleep a few hours before her next nightmare took hold, he lay down next to Tess and wearily rubbed his eyes. She tried to move closer, and when she whimpered softly in her sleep, Kenric gently pulled her to his side. She felt right there. He couldn't seem to stop himself from trailing his fingertips along the smooth curve of her cheek, marveling at its softness. Her content expression didn't betray a hint of fear or hate, or the quick temper he didn't seem to mind. She looked so innocent and vulnerable when she slept, the urge to protect her was nearly overwhelming. Kenric didn't question that urge. Nay, it was his duty to protect those under his care. It was the tightness in his chest he found worrisome.

The rim of a cup pressed against Tess's lips, but she was allowed only a small sip before the cool water was pulled away. She opened her eyes to protest this latest cruelty, but instead gasped in wonder at the sight she beheld. An angel was sitting next to her bed!

Golden clouds surrounded the angel and a bright light

shimmered all around, so bright that Tess couldn't see his face clearly. There was no need to ask the angel's identity, for that much seemed obvious. This was surely Saint Peter, and the bright light came from the gates of Heaven.

"I am not supposed to be here," she told the angel, smiling over his mistake.

"And why is that?" the angel asked.

"Because I am not going to die. Kenric said so himself."

The angel didn't answer immediately. He was probably surprised by her knowledge. His next words confirmed her suspicion. "You were not supposed to hear that."

"Do not be so sad." Tess reached over to pat his hand sympathetically. "Friar Bennet says even angels are allowed to make mistakes."

"You think me an angel?" He sounded shocked by the idea.

"Well, of course," Tess said, pleased with her cleverness. "You are Saint Peter, and I am to tell you all about my life, then you will decide if I can pass through the gates of Heaven." She frowned. "But I don't think I should be here. I heard Kenric say quite clearly that I would not need a priest because I was not dying." Her eyes filled with tears and she began to cry again. "Perhaps I just imagined Kenric saying those words."

"You will not die." The angel brushed the tears from her cheeks and lifted her onto his lap. Her fears were soothed instantly within his safe embrace. "Why don't you tell me about your life while we wait for this mistake to be corrected? I would like to know more about you."

Tess couldn't refuse a request from an angel. She told him everything she could think of, the good and the bad, knowing the kind angel wouldn't judge her too harshly for her human failings. She fell asleep often during the telling but would awake to find the angel waiting patiently near her bed. His question then was always the same. Each time she awoke, he would ask her to say his name. He seemed to think she would forget him.

The angel seemed especially interested in her life at Langston Keep. Even though Tess admitted she didn't like to talk of that time, she dutifully answered his questions. The questions turned next to the few days of her married life.

"Kenric frightens me sometimes," she admitted thoughtfully. "I've never met a man like him. The tales are so savage, yet I don't see the cruelness in his eyes that I see in the MacLeiths. Perhaps he is just better at hiding it. 'Tis worrisome to never know what he is thinking."

"Is that why you fear him?"

She shook her head. "I fear his size. 'Tis doubtful I will survive many of his beatings."

"Your husband promised not to beat you. Do you doubt his word?"

"Men forget their promises when they are angry," she answered matter-of-factly. The angel didn't argue that point, and Tess fiddled with the bedsheets a while before admitting her other reason for fearing Kenric. "He doesn't want me, you know. 'Tis easy enough for a man to rid himself of an unwanted bride."

"Do you really believe your husband capable of murder, simply to escape marriage?"

Tess thought that over for a moment, then shrugged. "Gordon MacLeith promised to put me to death, just as soon as I'd borne a healthy heir. He said it would look as if I'd died in childbirth. It was a foolish taunt, for he only strengthened my resolve to escape. But Kenric is much more clever and cunning than either of the MacLeiths. If he intended the same fate for me, I doubt I would be sure of his plan until I felt a blade against my throat. 'Tis not an easy fear to live with."

" 'Tis a foolish fear. Your husband intends you no harm."

"Are you sure?" Tess asked hopefully. "He really

doesn't seem to like me very much, even though I can understand his disappointment. Kenric surely had his pick of all the beautiful ladies at court, but the king stuck him with me."

"You do not think yourself appealing?"

"Oh, my parents called me pretty, but all parents think their children are handsome. Nay, I do not appeal to a man's eye like the queen or Kenric's sister. Dark hair and pale complexions are the fashion these days. I felt like a limp old rag when I stood next to Helen." Tess sighed in resignation. "Perhaps Kenric will grow accustomed to my looks."

"And will you grow accustomed to your husband's looks?"

"I doubt that will ever happen." She gave an un-ladylike snort over the improbability of such an occurrence. "My legs tremble and my stomach acts queerly each time I look upon him."

"That bad, is he?"

"Oh, no," she breathed dreamily. She yawned again, hoping the angel wouldn't mind if she closed her eyes for just a moment. "That good."

Kenric raked a hand through his dark hair, feeling just as exhausted as his bride. He'd slept in snatches the past four days, occasionally stretching out beside Tess in her more restful moments, but usually sleeping in the chair he'd pulled up next to the bed. If nothing else, her fever was proving enlightening. He yawned again and tried to clear his mind of all thoughts but sleep, awaking with a start a short time later.

Tess was sitting up in bed and smiling quite prettily. He smiled back uncertainly, wondering who he would be this time. She appeared as though she might almost be recovered, but there was something odd about her expression, something elusive in her appearance that made her seem several years older, the look in her eyes somehow wiser. Yet the color had returned to her face and she was, if possible, more beautiful than ever.

"Kenric!" Her smile was nearly blinding. She held out her arms, hugging him fiercely when he moved to sit on the bed. "I have missed you so!"

Her warm greeting stunned Kenric. "You are feeling better?"

"I feel wonderful now that you have returned. It seems like a year has passed instead of a month. What think you of your new son?"

"Son?" Kenric asked, truly dumbfounded by this turn in the conversation.

"Your son," Tess chided, playfully nudging his arm. "You left only a week after his birth. Surely you have not forgotten the babe already? Or are you still pouting that I have yet to produce a daughter?"

"I . . . I am not sure what to say," Kenric said honestly.

"Then say you are happy to have three fine boys." She rubbed up against his chest. " 'Tis been long enough since the birthing to start working on your girl," she purred seductively. Tess traced little kisses along his throat until Kenric pulled her away.

"Now is not the time," he chastised, annoyed to hear desire thicken his voice. "You must rest."

"I have rested nie a month now." Her pout turned up at the edges as she trailed her fingers along the inside of his leg. Kenric caught her hand, unable to believe she would have carried through with the direction her actions were leading. The playful smile faded from her face. "You do not want me?"

"This is not the time," he told her again, wondering how on earth to handle this situation. He knew the fever was ruling her mind, but something in her look and the certainty of her words made the hair at the nape of his neck stand on end. "How long have we been married?"

"What an odd question. Have you forgotten the celebration of our fifth year of marriage already?" She looked worried by his reaction, and placed a gentle hand against his forehead. "Are you feeling quite well, milord? You are acting rather strangely."

Kenric stood up, reminding himself of Old Martha's words about the fever's delusions, but he couldn't rid himself of the odd sense of reality this one stirred.

"What is it? Is something wrong with the babe?"

"Nay, 'tis you who's been ill, Tess. Ill with a fever these past four days, ever since I found you in the woods aiming an arrow at my chest."

"That was years ago," she argued. "What on earth would make you say such a thing?"

"Because it is true. I have not left this room these last days, much less been on a month-long journey."

"I think you are the one who should be in bed," Tess teased halfheartedly. She patted the covers. "Come rest with me a while. You have had a very long journey, love."

Kenric slid into the bed against his better judgment. He wasn't at all surprised when Tess tried to kiss him.

"Just one kiss," she promised. "Then we will rest. Agreed?"

Kenric smiled at the hopeful tilt of her eyebrows. He leaned down and kissed her softly, feeling the raging heat of fever through that slightest touch. Tess was asleep before he lifted his head. Kenric lay back on his pillow and sighed, wondering what to make of this latest hallucination.

7

Tess opened her eyes slowly, her senses disoriented and groggy
with sleep. The dim light coming through the window said
the day was just beginning or just ending. Dawn, she decided. She knew without looking up that it was Kenric's
chest beneath her head, his strong arm around her waist to
hold her securely in place. His deep, even breathing made
her believe he was asleep.

Her eyes slid along a sideways view of his bare chest,
one eyelash fluttering against the crisp mat of black hair.
The bedcovers were pushed to his waist, and Tess knew
from the way her leg lay draped around his that he wore
little or nothing below the covers. She'd never lain with a
naked man before, never touched one so intimately. The
clear, steady sound of his heartbeat was comforting somehow, his scent familiar as she drew a deep breath.

Tess shifted her leg higher. She'd only meant to get more comfortable, but her eyes widened in alarm when her knee brushed against the most intimate part of him. Even if Kenric wasn't awake, his body certainly was. Before she could collect her thoughts enough to be shocked by that discovery, Kenric gripped her chin and forced her to look up at him.

"How do you feel?"

Her answer was a hoarse whisper, startled out of her by the fact that he was not only awake, but looked as if he had been for some time. "Awful."

Kenric reached past her for a goblet that sat on a bedside table. He slipped his arm around her shoulders to prop her up, then held the cup to her lips. "Drink this."

Tess drained the contents in greedy gulps. Kenric took the empty goblet, then his gaze came back to her face and he eyed her dispassionately. "The fever has passed."

"I did say it would pass by morning," she said defensively, pulling the covers higher. Waking up in bed with a naked man definitely required one to be on her toes, especially when the man seemed to be in a far from pleasant mood, but Tess could barely collect her thoughts. She pressed her fingertips against her temples, trying to concentrate. Her head ached fiercely and her eyes didn't seem capable of focusing properly when she moved her head. "You see? It was nothing to worry over."

Kenric jerked the covers back then rose from the bed with a barely muffled curse. "Aye, 'tis morning, wife. And time to face the reckoning."

"What reckoning?" Tess asked, trying to sort out her thoughts. She glanced around the room, surprised to find it messy. A tray of half-eaten food lay on one table and some of Kenric's clothes were strewn about the floor. She didn't recall the room being so cluttered last night.

"Do you really think you can defy me without punishment?" he asked as he pulled on a pair of breeches.

"I defied you by coming down with a fever? I am to be punished for falling ill?"

"You will be punished for sending me on a wild-goose chase," Kenric said through clenched teeth. "You will be punished for nearly putting me in the extremely awkward position of having to explain away your death mere days after our wedding. You nearly died, you little fool."

" 'Twas just a fever," she whispered.

He studied her face, searching for an answer he apparently did not find. "What do you recall of your illness?"

"I recall you carrying me to this room last night. We had a short conversation and retired for the evening."

"Allow me to refresh your memory, Lady." Kenric locked his hands behind his back and frowned down at her. "Not two hours after I carried you to this room, you fled like a thief in the night. Not only from my bed, but from the castle itself. And 'twas not last night, but five days ago."

The look of dawning horror on Tess's face said her memory was indeed refreshed. She pressed her hands against her forehead, as if trying to stop the rush of returning memories.

"Then imagine my delight when I found my wife, only to have her aim an arrow at my chest. Compared to that, wondering for five days if she would live or die was only slightly more pleasant."

"Oh, nooo . . ." The moan was long and drawn out. Tess kept her hands over her face, but she began to rock slightly.

"I assume that means you have recalled your idiocy. Are there any details that need clarifying? Any small points you cannot recall clearly? Do let me know, wife. I will be happy to recount your every deed."

"I cannot remember my illness," Tess said helplessly, trying to piece the puzzle together. "What came before, aye, but nothing after we left the woods."

"You became a raving lunatic," he answered in an almost bored tone. "The very first day you took one look at Old Martha, the healing woman I'd sent to tend you, and flattened the woman with your fist."

"Nay!"

"Aye. The servants thought you possessed by demons. You do realize that most believe hot coals laid against the skin is the only way to exorcise demons?"

Tess paled and shook her head.

"Rather than allow my terrified servants to tend a woman they clearly thought crazed, I took over the duty myself. You should be well pleased with yourself, Lady. Many would be impressed to learn that you turned the Butcher of Wales into little more than a sickmaid."

"I—I find this very difficult to believe," Tess whispered, her mind still unable to accept everything he'd told her.

"The night we married, I would have said the same," Kenric replied evenly. "Yet since our marriage, you've slit a man's throat, betrayed me, and put me to more trouble than any female on the face of the earth. If you were trying to make me regret this marriage, you have succeeded. I should have taken you to a convent when I had the chance."

"Aye, you should have," she answered softly. "In a convent I would never know the burden of taking another man's life, or risking my own to flee what I thought was certain death. And whispering during vespers is surely the most trouble I would have been like to cause."

The wintry expression that settled over his features made Tess regret her rash outburst. She knew before he spoke that she should have remained silent.

"Do not twist my words, Tess. Your small attempt to stir my pity is pointless. It tells me that you are trying to shift the blame for your actions rather than accept responsibility. And accept it you shall. Aye, wife. 'Tis time for the reckoning. By your own misdeeds, you have lost any rights to husbandly consideration. I will judge you today as your lord. Stand before me, Tess."

The cool finality of his words struck terror in her heart. Tess stared at him in silence, paralyzed by fear, trying desperately to think of some argument in her defense. She had betrayed him. She would be punished the same as any other traitor. The punishments that came to mind made her thoughts spin dizzily.

Although she tried to comply with his order, fear combined with her lengthy illness made obedience impossible. She managed to get her legs over the side of the bed, but her knees gave out and she crumpled to the floor. Humiliated by her defeat and terrified by her helplessness, she remained there. Waiting.

"Stand before me," he repeated, his voice lacking any trace of compassion.

She shook her head and whispered, "I cannot."

The silence lasted so long that Tess felt the sweat on her palms grow cold and clammy. Then her hands began to tremble.

"So, you are unfit to receive your punishment," he said finally. "Just as you are unfit to be my wife anytime soon."

Tess felt herself nod. Her chemise was tangled about her legs and one sleeve had slipped low on her shoulder, but she was too numb to care about something so trivial as her modesty. Her worst fears were coming true. She'd tried to escape the Butcher, and she'd been caught. And just like the MacLeiths, he wanted her alive. Yet the fact that they all had an interest in her life didn't make the living of it any easier. She would be made to pay for her deceit, and pay dearly.

Tess closed her eyes, beyond tears or crying, beyond pleas for mercy. She'd known the consequences and could do nothing now but accept them. There was no compassion in the man she'd lain with so intimately this morning, no tenderness or feelings for her that would temper his judgment. He'd made it clear that he disliked her intensely. She had plenty of experience with men who hated her.

Kenric grasped her arms and hauled her to her feet, intending to vent more of his anger. He had known all along that she was too weak to stand before him. He'd given the order simply to prove a point. Making that point was the only thing he was likely to find satisfying for quite some time. From the deathly white pallor of her face, he guessed what was happening a moment before her eyes rolled back and she went limp in his arms.

"I will be gone exactly seven days. She will not leave this room for any reason while I am away. Is that clear?"

The sound of Kenric's deep voice stirred Tess from her sleep, but she opened her eyes only a crack and didn't stir from her cocoon of blankets. From beneath her lashes, she spied two soldiers near the doorway. Both nodded and echoed, "Aye, milord."

"That goes for you as well," Kenric added, turning toward a woman who stood near the bed. "If she talks any one of you into disobeying my order, I will see all three of you in the dungeon. Miriam, you will see that she heals as quickly as possible. I want her healthy when I return. *Completely* healthy."

"Aye, milord," Miriam answered.

"Other than Old Martha, she is to have no visitors. Tell my wife she is to do nothing that might jeopardize her health and that she should use this time to prepare herself to greet me properly upon my return."

Tess closed her eyes, afraid someone would sense her fear if she kept them open. She had seven days to prepare for his punishment.

After he left, Tess tormented herself by trying to imagine what horrible punishment she would receive. Then she tried to cheer herself up with thoughts of what it might not be. If Kenric had spoken truthfully that day in the woods, he did not intend to return her to the MacLeiths. That would have been the worst punishment she could imagine. He also said he wouldn't beat her, but she didn't put any stock in those words. Not now. He'd given her a promise, and she'd betrayed him. She had no right to expect him to keep any promise.

She didn't realize she'd sighed aloud until Miriam looked up from her sewing. The two guards had left with Kenric, but the servant remained.

"You are awake, milady?" Miriam asked needlessly. Tess nodded glumly. "My name is Miriam, milady. The baron left on a journey not long ago. He will be—"

"I heard his every word. You've no need to repeat them."

Miriam bowed her head, making Tess feel guilty about the curt answer. It wasn't Miriam's fault that she'd been ordered to guard her baroness. The servant had a friendly face, kindly blue eyes, and soft waves of gray hair that gave her a motherly air. The quality of her fawn-colored gown said she held a position of some importance at Montague, probably that of lady's maid to Helen. Tess tried a more congenial tone. "It seems we are to be companions for a time, Miriam."

"Aye, milady."

A long, uncomfortable silence passed between the two women. Tess gazed steadily at the servant, trying to guess her loyalty to Kenric, wondering if she might be bribed while trying to think of something to bribe her with. Even if the servant could be persuaded to her camp, there were two of Kenric's guards just outside the door, the same two who had rushed into the room the night Kenric discovered her injuries. That meant they were probably two of Kenric's most trusted soldiers. She would never make it past the door. Miriam's gaze finally dropped to her lap and she resumed her sewing.

"I would like you to tell me everything you know

about Montague Castle," Tess said abruptly. The servant looked up warily from her work.

"Mistress Helen does not allow gossip about the family, milady."

It was telling that Miriam's concern was with Helen, not Kenric, but Tess had to dismiss that oddity for the moment.

"I am not asking you to gossip about the family," Tess said. "I am your baroness, Miriam. I have a right to know about those who live here. You may begin by telling me the names of those who hold positions of importance within the castle, the duties of the servants, and any trades or craftsmen living within the walls or in the village."

"Milady! There are well over three hundred living within the walls, and as many in the village."

"Then we may need to review the list twice, to make sure I forget none."

Miriam's list took two days to recite, even though Tess didn't ask the woman to repeat the names as she'd threatened. Much to Tess's delight, Miriam was a natural gossip and couldn't help but interject opinions and hearsay with the facts. One thing she learned was that Kenric refused to involve himself with anything related to running the castle. He made sure of the castle's defenses, but it was Helen's duty to oversee the daily operations of the place. As near as Tess could tell, Helen had performed her duties quite adequately until Kenric's return from Wales. She'd done little or nothing since then. And time was measured strangely at Montague. Anything of importance happened either Before the Old Baron Died, or After the Old Baron Died. After would have been when Kenric assumed the title. That seemed to be when things at Montague began to decline, and Tess sensed an undercurrent of resentment against her husband because of it. So much the better, she decided, even as she pushed aside the nagging thought that Kenric was being judged unfairly by his people. Not that they had any right to judge him in the first place.

Old Martha, the woman Tess had unknowingly attacked in her fever, also paid a visit and proved a most forgiving sort. Especially after Tess promised to ask Kenric about finding an assistant for the spry old woman. She needed someone to help gather herbs on her trips into the woods and Tess secretly hoped to be that assistant. A trip outside the walls to gather herbs might present another opportunity for escape. Although her first attempt was a dismal failure, she still hadn't given up her plan to reach the king. It just might take longer, now that she'd put Kenric on his guard.

After only three days, she was pacing the room like a caged animal. The gradual return of her health had resulted in a full-blown case of boredom, interrupted only by her dread of what would happen when that boredom came to an end.

Although Miriam tried her best to be good company, the forced confinement made Tess more restless than ever. Knowing she was not the most pleasant person to be around in this frame of mind, Tess took pity on the maid and gave Miriam permission to return to most of her usual duties.

Robbed of Miriam's company, Tess had only the distraction of exploring Kenric's plush room. The handsomely carved trunks that lined the walls of the room were locked tight against prying fingers, frustrating her to no end. Only the trunk cleared for her use and Kenric's clothes chest could be opened. But a discovery at the bottom of Kenric's chest eased her confinement considerably.

Kenric owned three books.

Tess was amazed to find books, of all things, kept in an unlocked chest. If such priceless treasures were so easily accessible, then the riches kept under lock and key must be fabulous, indeed. The king himself possessed only four books, and everyone knew those were locked away in the royal treasury. She began to wonder at the extent of Kenric's wealth.

She handled the precious objects with great care. Though no one could possibly see her, Tess looked around guiltily before opening the first finely tooled, leather-bound cover. Few men outside the priesthood could read, and the skill was unheard of in a woman. Friar Bennet had indulged Tess's thirst for knowledge shamelessly. Kenric would probably be scandalized if her unusual skills were discovered. At the moment, Tess was too excited about the unexpected entertainment to care.

The first book was in Latin, an introductory page explaining its translation from a group of Greek stories collectively named Aesop's Fables. The first letter of each page took up nearly a fourth of the space, drawn in beautifully vivid colors. The characters described in the story were artfully intertwined with the letter to depict their actions on that page. One almost didn't need the ability to read with such delightful drawings to accompany the text. Tess curled up in the center of Kenric's big bed and began to turn the pages. The sunlight stretched across the room with amazing speed, quickly slanting to long golden streamers of light. Miriam was at her door all too soon with her meal, driving Tess mad with her endless chatter. The riveting tale of a vain fox awaited Tess, half read under the pillow. An hour passed before the woman could be politely dismissed. That Miriam remained so long with the good intentions of relieving the boredom made Tess feel slightly guilty, but even Miriam's gossipy tales could not compare with Aesop's. By the end of the week, Tess had read Aesop's Fables four times, and the two dull books on military strategies twice.

Only one more night, she reminded herself for the hundredth time as she settled into bed for the evening. Kenric would return the next day and her confinement would be at a blessed end. She was almost ready to face the gallows if it meant leaving this room at last. She'd never liked being locked away in her room when the MacLeiths did it, but at least she'd known her punishment would be finished when her time was over. Being locked away to await a punishment was crueler yet.

If nothing else, her disastrous escape was proving that she'd been right to try in the first place. Everything she'd learned that week told her that she'd married a man no more fair or just than the MacLeiths, one who would exact his vengeance just as thoroughly. Still, she needed to regain a measure of his confidence if she ever hoped to leave this castle. Any thoughts of begging his forgiveness were immediately dismissed. She'd never been able to play that role very convincingly. But perhaps he would appreciate an apology. That might make him believe she was sorry enough to obey him in the future. It certainly couldn't hurt matters.

The candle on the bedside table finally flickered and died in a puddle of tallow, telling her the hour had grown late. She left the bed long enough to roll more logs into the fire, then curled up in the big bed and practiced her apology in quiet whispers. It was something to do other than dread her husband's return.

8   ❦

*Another hour passed before Kenric entered the gates of Monta-
gue,* surprising everyone with his early return, including
himself. Returning early was a mistake, he decided. Tess
would probably think he couldn't wait another day to see
her. He went immediately to his chamber, intent on making sure his bride was where she was supposed to be. At
least, that was the excuse he gave Fitz Alan. He didn't
realize how anxious he was until he opened the door to his
chamber and sighed in relief. Tess was fast asleep in his
bed.

She'd kicked the covers off and her chemise was
pushed up high on her hips to reveal long, shapely legs.
The light from the fire cast a warm glow to her skin and
made her hair shimmer with a golden fire all its own. This
was the vision, the sight of her in his bed, that had enticed

him from the moment he'd laid eyes on the woman. Well, almost, he decided with a frown. Her mouth should be curved with the satisfied smile of a wife well bedded.

A grim smile touched his lips and he almost laughed at his own fantasy. How could he believe that a woman who flinched from his most innocent touch would enjoy herself in his bed? Rather than mooning about smiles he would never see, he should be wondering if she would come to him willingly, or if he would have to take her as he took everything else in life. By force.

Kenric shook himself from his musings long enough to slam the door shut behind him, purposely waking his bride. He had no intention of allowing her to sleep through *this* night.

"I thought you would be asleep by now," he lied, keeping his expression stern when a pair of sleepy eyes widened with recognition.

"Kenric!" The careful speech Tess had planned flew out of her head the moment she spied him. She'd forgotten the strange effect his presence had on her senses, something she could never quite anticipate, much less prevent. Her eyes drank in the sight of him, and she felt the same flood of confusing emotions that had assailed her that first night in the abbey. Fear, desire, and an overwhelming sense of familiarity, the disturbing feeling that she knew him better than any other.

He still wore his armor, his helm tucked under one arm, his other hand resting on the hilt of his broadsword. Her eyes drifted across what seemed to be acres of chain mail, idly wondering what vast amount of yardage was required to fashion his surcoat. Most men looked stiff and unwieldy in armor, the effort required to carry so much extra weight telling in their stilted movements. Kenric wore at least a hundred pounds of weapons and armor, yet moved as if he were clad in nothing more cumbersome than silk. In fact, it was his garments that seemed to strain under the effort of keeping so much strength contained.

The large room was suddenly smaller, yet Tess knew it was not only his big body, but his very presence that filled so much of the chamber.

"Come, wife. Help remove my armor," he ordered, already unbuckling his swords.

He released the breath he'd been holding when she drew back the covers and rose from the bed, walking toward him. She was as beautiful as he'd remembered, more so now that her health had returned. The thin chemise she wore left little to his imagination, and he turned away before he gave in to the urge to crush her against his chest, to tear away that dainty garment and feast his eyes on what belonged to him alone.

No, he would not take what was his just yet, not until he knew if it would be offered. That would make the taking all the more sweet, well worth the wait. *Best not hold your breath,* his conscience warned. *Better to prepare yourself for tears and pleading.*

With his back to her, Kenric placed his helmet on a clothes chest, then ordered her to unfasten his leggings while he worked on removing his hauberk. Her touch was disturbingly gentle, nothing like the efficiency he was accustomed to. She didn't work as quickly as his squire, for she had to search for the hidden buckles. Kenric ignored the feelings her hands roused, concentrating instead on the fastenings of his hauberk.

"Did you have a good journey?" she asked.

"Aye." An excellent journey, Kenric mused, placing the mass of chain mail in a chest. Just what he needed to regain his rigid control. He would prove to her that she'd married a man, not some wild beast driven to ravage her. "You may await me in bed, Tess."

Kenric had removed his armor with care, but his tunic, shirt, and breeches were shed with abandon as his mind raced forward to the moment when he would climb into bed with his bride. He hesitated for just a moment, then decided his loincloth should stay. Even though he usually slept in the nude, he didn't want to make his intent too obvious. But the loincloth was hardly sufficient to protect him from his wife's assessing gaze.

When he turned to face her, it took less than a heartbeat for the look in her violet eyes to turn his bones to jelly, his flesh to tempered steel. Her gaze traveled boldly over every bit of exposed flesh, and his skin soon burned to feel her hands travel those same paths. His breath came out in a rush when her attention finally returned to his face.

His eyes never left Tess as he walked toward her. He stretched out on top of her on the bed, his hands braced on either side of her head. "Have you no kiss to welcome your husband home?"

Her eyes widened with uncertainty even as she nodded. Kenric lowered his head, savoring the warmth of her breath against his lips, then he covered her mouth completely. He lingered over the kiss, nipping and tugging almost playfully at Tess's lips before his mouth settled firmly against hers. He was pleased to discover she'd not forgotten his first lesson in kissing. He finally moved to the smooth column of her neck. He was hungry for her, as if he'd been without a woman for years. She would be his wife, his *willing* wife, he decided with a dark, hidden smile. His hands slid across her shoulders and down her arms, then up to her shoulders again to repeat the motion, as if to assure himself that she wasn't going anywhere. His hand wrapped around her wrist and he stretched out her arm, leaning over to kiss the throbbing pulse at her wrist. His lips grazed a path to the soft skin at the crook of her elbow, lingering there to savor the spot.

"I would like to—"

"You would like to become my wife."

"I am already your wife," she reminded him, tilting her head slightly to bare her neck as his lips skimmed over the capped sleeves of her chemise.

"You are my bride," he murmured, kissing the outline

of her ear. His warm breath made Tess's own breath grow short. "But that will change soon enough, little one."

"I meant . . . I meant to say—" Tess gave up when she felt Kenric's tongue against her ear. Her whole body stiffened and there was nothing soft or sighing about the groan she gave him then.

"That you like what I'm doing," Kenric finished again.

"Aye," she whispered, curling her toes when she felt his tongue once more. He lingered there a moment, then used his mouth to trace the line of her jaw, moving higher until his lips were just touching hers.

He drew back abruptly and his gaze searched her face, as if looking for the answer to some question. "I want to see your back."

" 'Tis healed." The injuries to her back were the least of her concerns at the moment. Her skin tingled so much that she felt nearly numb. She felt light-headed but not at all ill, and her heart ached but it didn't hurt. The feeling was a warmth that seemed to spread through every part of her body, a strange sensation that made her want to arch up against Kenric's body. Her arms slipped around his neck, pulling him without resistance to her lips.

Kenric ended the kiss by rolling to Tess's side, determined to see her back before he was too far gone with lust to care what his passion would do to her. His desire was ready to burst into flame, but he knew this first time was too important to let the fire burn out of control, to burn her carelessly beyond healing. He would treat her gently, show her his patience and skill by fanning the flames of her own desire slowly and carefully. But not until he knew how much her injured body could handle.

"Show me your back," he demanded simply. She blushed and lowered her gaze. He nudged her chin up, trying to show her that patience he'd silently promised. " 'Tis only natural to be shy about letting me see your body. Yet you must know I gazed upon you often while you were ill. I even bathed you."

She gasped. "You didn't."

"I did." He couldn't decide if Tess looked more outraged or humiliated, or an equal measure of both. He liked her shyness, but needed to think of a way to make her more at ease with this situation, a way that would demonstrate his patience. An idea came almost immediately. "If you'd prefer, I could wait until after my bath to look at your back."

" 'Tis rather late for a bath, is it not, milord?" she questioned uncertainly. "The servants are sure to be abed."

"The servants have not been in a saddle all day and most of the night," he scoffed, already moving away from her. "I doubt they shall suffer overmuch by heating water and filling a tub for a man who has. Don't you agree?"

He almost smiled over Tess's reaction to the reprieve. Her head bobbed in quick agreement. "The ride from Marshall seems to have stiffened my muscles," he lied. "A bath sounds like just the thing."

"An excellent idea, milord."

"I thought so." He smiled over his cleverness. With his own clothes shed, it wouldn't be long before Tess's followed. She would soon be as comfortable about his nudity as he was about her . . . Well, that wasn't quite it, but what better way to acquaint Tess with his body? Every inch of it.

Kenric walked briskly to the door and gave several orders to one of the soldiers standing guard in the hallway. He busied himself by shaving away several days' growth of beard as a small army of servants began arriving in a steady stream. Most lugged buckets of steaming water to fill the tub that was hauled into place before the fire, but one carried a tray of food. He picked up the tray when he'd finished shaving and placed it at the foot of the bed, taking a seat next to Tess.

"Hungry?" he asked. When she nodded, he handed her a thick slab of buttered bread and a mug of thin ale.

"Do you always parade around your servants near naked?" Tess whispered. Her gaze dropped conspicuously to the loincloth he wore.

Kenric shrugged indifferently. "They do not seem to mind."

Tess's look said she did.

"You believe I should wear a robe?"

She nodded, her gaze wandering over his broad shoulders and chest. She stared so intently that he began to wonder if she was trying to count the scars that covered his body. He'd never given them much thought in the past, but he was suddenly aware of each ugly mark.

" 'Twas forward of me to make suggestions, milord," she said a little breathlessly. "You must not wear a robe simply for my sake."

Kenric hid his smile behind the mug and downed its contents, his confidence in his ability to seduce his wife reinforced. She was practically devouring him with her eyes. The tray was pushed aside when the last servant departed, and he stood by the bed, watching Tess expectantly.

"Milord?" she questioned.

"I am waiting for your offer to assist with my bath."

"Oh!" Tess slipped from the bed and walked hesitantly toward the trunk where soap and bath linens were laid out. Her gaze lowered to study the carpet pattern while Kenric stripped off his loincloth and stepped into the water.

"Have you done this before?" he asked.

"Nay," she admitted. She was trying hard not to look below his chest. His big body nearly filled the tub that had looked so huge just a moment ago.

"Good," he replied smugly. "I would not like to think of you bathing those Scots."

He gripped the sides of the tub, closed his eyes, and leaned back to dunk his head under the water. He lifted his head a moment later and smoothed the wet hair back with his hands. Tess stood rooted to the spot, those simple movements more erotic than anything she'd ever seen in her life. The water made Kenric's skin glisten like molten bronze and the unstudied gestures displayed his physique to perfection. The warmth in her cheeks spread down her arms and into her belly.

Unaware of the effect on his bride, Kenric motioned her forward with one hand. "Start by washing my hair."

She stepped closer and began working the soap into his dark hair, enjoying the feel of the thick mane slipping through her fingers. He wore his hair longer than most knights, cut away into shorter lengths in front but flowing well past his shoulders in the back. She twisted her fingers through the longer strands, liking the way the ends curled around her fingertips.

Now would be a good time to apologize, a silent voice reminded her, now while he is not scowling at you. A seduction was surely planned tonight, but would the punishment come later? The thought made her hands still abruptly in his hair.

"I would like to apologize for what happened before I fell ill," she said hesitantly, forcing her hands to continue their work.

"As well you should. You would do well to remind me of that later. There will be a better time."

"Aye," she whispered, feeling the fear snake its way around her heart.

Kenric patiently allowed her to play with his hair, thinking this would surely be the longest bath on record. He finally leaned back to duck under the water again when it became obvious that she would happily massage his head all day.

"I've had seven long days to dwell on what punishment I will receive," she began, when his head emerged from the water. "Though you may wish to hear my apology at another time, milord, I wish to learn my punishment now."

Since she was standing behind him, Kenric knew she

couldn't see his smile. Lord, she was bold. After he'd left for Marshall, it had occurred to him that she would spend every day of his absence worrying over what his return would bring. He'd even laughed aloud on occasion at the image it brought to mind. Served her right for putting him to such trouble. He'd lost four precious days of training with his soldiers while he played sickmaid. Her escape had simply made him look foolish. Aye, she deserved every single moment that she'd terrorized herself. "So you want to know what punishment I deem fitting for trying to escape me?"

"Aye," she said firmly.

Kenric took his time wiping the water from his face. "You want to learn the payment I will exact for returning to my chamber, only to discover that my new bride had fled? For rousing an entire castle at dawn to search every square inch of the place? For inconveniencing myself and fifty other men who rode after you? And for refusing to return with your husband after you were found?" He shook stray drops of water off his hand with a flick of his wrist. "At the point of an arrow, I might add. Is that about the whole of it?"

"Aye," she answered, hesitantly this time.

"I would imagine you had many long hours to think over your foolishness this past week," he mused. "Have you come to regret your actions, Tess?"

"I have." This answer was firm again.

"And do I have your promise that you will never attempt to escape me again, no matter what you think I might have planned for you?"

Tess hesitated as one hand reached for her braid, the silence just long enough for Kenric's suspicions to be aroused. "Aye, you have my promise."

She was lying and Kenric knew it. She didn't trust him, no more than he trusted her. Still, he could ensure that she kept her promise even if she didn't want to. If Tess needed a keeper, then she'd have one.

"I have little doubt that the tortures you dreamed up for yourself this past week were quite colorful. It pleases me that you dwelt on them often, for you surely deserved one of them. Yet I am willing to consider that your fevered state contributed greatly to your folly. No woman in her right mind would have attempted such a foolhardy venture, knowing there could be naught but dire consequences with success or failure. Therefore I have decided that the week's confinement will suffice for this offense." Kenric watched her face closely; he looked for some sign of gratefulness. He supposed she was too overcome with gratitude to express her feelings. She simply stared at him, her face blank with shock. "Do not mistake me, Tess. If you do anything so foolish again, the punishment will be carried out. It will be one you remember not for a week, but forever. Something so vile that no gently bred lady could conjure it up in her wildest imaginings. Remember that if you ever again consider defying me."

Satisfied with his speech, Kenric began to splash water on his arms and shoulders, eager to finish a much more pleasant task.

"That's it? I am to be punished no further?"

"You have some wish to change my mind?" he asked mildly.

"Nay," she answered quickly, looking bewildered.

"You may proceed with my back," he said, when she made no move to continue the bath. She picked up a linen cloth, but he snatched it away and casually tossed it aside. "I want you to use your hands to bathe me."

Tess didn't reply, but he felt her soapy fingers glide across his shoulders. She was soon doing just as thorough a job as she'd done with his hair, working her way down his back muscle by muscle. The smooth, erotic strokes made his breath quicken and his heart beat harder. A shadow of doubt began to form in Kenric's mind about the wisdom of this bath.

Tess was too caught up in her own thoughts to realize

the effect of her ministrations. Kenric was a puzzle, to be sure, a man known for cruelty who could kiss her with such sweet poignancy that she could scarce remember her name, a man who didn't want a wife yet spent four days nursing her back to health. Even when she betrayed him, he seemed to forgive her without so much as a slap. How on earth had this man gained a reputation for being the most bloodthirsty warlord in England? Was the Butcher of Wales truly capable of justice tempered by compassion? That was something to think about.

The longer Tess smoothed the soap over Kenric's back, the less she feared him. He truly intended her no harm. Not now, anyway. But he did intend to bed her. She was not so naive to be fooled by this bath business for an instant. This was surely his means of working up to a seduction. Yet she was the one doing all the caressing. She stared at his back with new awareness, watching his shoulders and muscles flex to follow the path of her hands. He was enjoying this. Thoroughly.

"Will you want me to do this for your other knights?" she asked, absently experimenting with a circular stroke.

"Nay!" Kenric growled. "If you are ever asked to assist a knight at his bath, you will politely refuse. Tell them your husband forbids such and they must gain permission from me." The thought of his wife's hands on another man's body resulted in a scowl. "I will not give it."

"Oh, good. 'Tis not that I mind assisting you, milord. I just don't think I would like to touch another man so . . ." Tess glanced down at her hands. They looked so small against his broad shoulders. His skin was much darker than hers, tanned by the sun, golden brown even now in the dead of winter. She wondered if he took his tunic off in the summertime on the practice field. What would he look like then? How would she react to seeing him bare-chested in public, knowing she'd caressed him so intimately in private? "So . . ."

"I know what you mean," he said, and urged her on to

his arms. His muscles seemed to contract wherever she touched him. Tess was soon fascinated by the reaction. Her fingers traced each ridge and contour. She became enthralled when she washed his chest, swirling her fingers around the light covering of hair, tracing small circles around his hardened nipples. She spread her fingers wide across his chest and drew her hands down until they reached the water that lapped against his flat stomach, too caught up in her exploration of his body to notice her husband's gasp.

"My legs," he said hoarsely, raising one and propping it on the edge of the tub.

Tess washed his leg in long, languorous strokes. She couldn't resist wrapping her hands around his ankle then pushing her hands upward, unconsciously massaging rather than washing, finally stopping where the water met his upper thigh. She had the strangest desire to press her lips against the places her hands touched, to see what his skin would taste like.

Kenric wasn't at all sure he had the control required to carry out this plan. He closed his eyes and tried to ignore what she was doing to him, but he was aroused beyond belief. The feel of her hands on his body was fast becoming unbearable. She made his skin burn and his body ache to touch her in the same delightfully tormenting ways. It took every ounce of willpower he possessed to remain still. He tried to brace himself for the most exquisite torture yet to come.

"Now the rest," he said abruptly. He gripped the sides of the tub and stood up, closing his eyes when he heard Tess draw in her breath. He could almost feel her gaze travel boldly over his body.

Patience, Kenric told himself, repeating the litany over and over again in his mind.

Tess stared at her husband in wonder, her gaze drawn unwillingly to the hard proof of his desire for her. She was mesmerized by the sight of his manhood, unable to stop herself from thoroughly exploring that part of him with her eyes. His hardness uncoiled the knot of heat in her belly and it spread like a fire through her body.

She raised her eyes reluctantly, embarrassed at having stared so openly for so long, but was relieved to realize that Kenric probably didn't know. His eyes were squeezed shut, the expression on his face one of pain. His whole body was tensed, hard, each muscle standing out in rigid relief, his fists clenched tightly at his sides.

"You are in pain?" she asked, amazed by the possibility.

"Aye." His answer was half groan, half laugh.

"Am I doing something wrong?"

He opened his eyes to look down at her. The fierce, raw desire in his gaze made her retreat a step. "You are doing something very right."

He took another deep breath. "I want you to know my body, Tess. I would not have your fear just now."

Tess let her gaze rake boldly over Kenric's body again. He was a giant, his chest at least twice the width of hers, arms bulging with muscles that could crush her in their grip. His legs were as sturdy as tree trunks and just as solidly muscled as the rest of his body. The sight of so much naked strength and power was nearly overwhelming. And there was still a trace of fear, uncertainty in not knowing if he would ever use his great strength against her.

This is my husband, she tried telling herself. This magnificent male animal was hers to touch, to kiss, to caress . . .

Her eyes returned to the forgotten soap still clutched in one hand. She moved to his back and slid her hands over his buttocks, certain the smooth, firm skin encased steel. Her hands trembled, lingering at the sides of his hips, trying to work up enough courage to discover him completely.

"Enough," he said hoarsely, pushing her hands away

as he turned to face her. "I can stand no more, Tess. Take off your chemise."

Tess's fingers trembled as she worked at the laces, her eyes locked with Kenric's as the garment fell in a soft pool at her feet. She didn't start to blush until his gaze slid downward. Her skin seemed to catch fire wherever his eyes rested. He lingered over her breasts and she felt her nipples tighten in response to the fiery look. He studied her legs and her knees began to tremble.

My body belongs to Kenric now, she told herself, determined to please him by being as open about her body as he was about his. She forced her arms to stay at her sides, fighting the urge to drape them across her body to shield her nudity.

He stepped from the tub and lifted her into his arms. They both gasped at the feel of so much warm, damp skin touching together. There wasn't time to savor the feeling. He carried her to the bed and lowered her slowly to the floor, sliding her intimately against the length of his body. With one hand braced against the bed, he laid her down and covered her body with his own.

"I don't . . . I don't know . . . ."

Tess tried to tell him between drugging kisses that she didn't know what to do. She gave up when his lips slid to her ear, his hot breath heating her senses to the boiling point.

"I know, sweet," he murmured. His mouth burned a trail down her neck and across her chest. "I want to touch you everywhere, Tess."

His hands caressed her hips, moving closer to her heat until his fingers slipped between the hot, slick petals. His finger slipped inside her tight sheath, and he captured her moan with his mouth, matching it with his own. The kiss was long, demanding, his tongue mimicking the action of his fingers as he began to move inside her, stroking, caressing, preparing her for what would come.

"I will be inside you soon," he told her, raining kisses

across her face, his words coming in short, harsh gasps. "But I have to hurt you once before I can give you pleasure. More pleasure than you've ever dreamed of, little one."

Tess didn't think such was possible. How much more pleasure could exist? His mouth burned another fiery trail to her breasts where he used his tongue to caress sensitive, swollen nipples. His hands searched hers out, insistently encouraging them to explore. Caught up in her own desire, Tess had almost forgotten the pleasure that could be gained by touching him. She let her hands roam where they would, delighted by the feel of him, the warmth, the strength, the need that had his body as taut with anticipation as he was making hers.

Kenric accustomed Tess slowly to his touch and the fierceness of his desire. The more he aroused her passion, the stronger his own grew, the raw sensuality of her response a potent drug to his senses as she writhed beneath him, her hips arching to meet his caresses. Finally he found her lips at the same time he positioned himself to enter her.

"Easy, love." He gripped Tess's hips to keep her still, then pushed forward carefully. He was trying his damnedest to go slowly, to open her to his desire as gently as possible. He kept her head tucked under his chin, every part of his body straining to keep her pinned beneath him and motionless. The urge to let go, to abandon his precious control and take her with all the sweet savagery he felt was an incredible temptation.

He drew back, but Tess urged him to return, drawing him closer. "Please. Don't stop."

Her whispered plea drove Kenric forward, shuddering as he sank deeper into her body. The proof of her virginity slowed his progress and he hesitated to savor the feeling, the final moment before complete possession. Until that instant there had been the small but lingering doubt that no virgin could possibly respond so openly, so lustily. He could only wonder what she would be like with experience. A wave of molten heat ran through his blood, and he squeezed his eyes closed, trying to shut out that thought in a desperate battle to maintain his control.

He lost.

Kenric drew back and thrust forward into her soft body, powerfully, forcefully, unable to stop until he was completely buried in her tight sheath, his growl of pleasure muffled by Tess's cry of pain. He groaned in defeat and stilled his body immediately, hoping he could allow her time to recover from the shock of his invasion.

"Hush, love," he said, frowning over the ragged sound of his voice. The blood surged wildly through his body, pounding an urgent message in his ears to complete the act. "The hurting part is over, sweet."

She trembled violently beneath him, and he felt hot tears mar her cheeks. He lifted his head to place light kisses across her face, whispering comforting words, trying to be gentle as he stroked her face and hair. But she gripped his throbbing shaft in convulsive waves, the sensation too powerful to ignore. His hips moved instinctively against her. Tess whimpered and squeezed her eyes tightly shut.

Kenric summoned forth the dwindling reserves of his willpower, steeling himself against the fantastic sensation of being buried deep within her body, of holding her so close that she felt a part of him. He took a ragged breath and turned his attention to arousing her again, praying her pain would fade quickly. "You will know only pleasure from now on, sweetheart."

"S-something is wrong," she gasped, turning her head to avoid his lips. "Please let me up. I want to stop now."

"Hush, sweet. It's too late to stop."

Her body stiffened and she pushed against him until he raised up on his elbows. Her voice was edged with fear and the frightened, trapped look in her eyes made Kenric hesitate. "Something is wrong with me. I can't do this!"

Urgency was swiftly replaced by a strange desire to comfort. He cupped her face in his hands and brushed the tears away with his thumbs, annoyed to realize his hands were trembling. He'd never trembled in his life.

"There is nothing wrong with you, Tess." His voice didn't sound as calm or steady as he'd like, but Tess seemed to hear him. "A virgin's maidenhead can be breached only once. I will not hurt you again."

"You are hurting me now," she whispered tearfully.

Damn. Now he wished he'd paid more attention to his soldiers' bawdy talk of the best ways to bed a virgin. He'd probably done this all wrong. He hadn't been very gentle, and really had no idea how long it took a woman to recover from her body's first taste of a man. "Does it hurt as much as when I first entered you?"

She shook her head uncertainly.

"You see?" He smiled to cover his uncertainty. "Your body is adjusting to me already."

His smile disappeared when she instinctively tightened around him, as if to test his words. "You must trust me in this matter, Tess." His voice was ragged again, his desire returning full force. "I want to give you pleasure, make you forget the pain. Let me kiss you again, sweetheart."

She hesitated only a moment before raising her lips, returning his kiss. He didn't force her passion to return, but let her set the pace until she allowed her senses to surrender to his kisses. He knew the importance of this moment. Forcing her now would mean forcing her each time he took her to his bed. She would never trust him again. This she must finish willingly.

The tension in Tess's body seemed to ease, and she gave his kisses her full attention. She shifted restlessly beneath his hips, and moaned with pleasure at the simple movement.

"God, Tess," he gritted out between clenched teeth. "Don't move if . . ." He couldn't finish the thought. He buried his face against her neck, his body braced, struggling to remain still.

"You feel wonderful," Tess sighed.

Kenric withdrew until he felt her arch beneath him. Then he began to thrust within her. Wave after wave of pure, sensual pleasure washed through them both with each delicious, measured stroke he gave her. Her body moved, stretched in ways she seemed to have no control over. He knew where to touch her, to kiss, to move in just the right way to increase the sensations and make her strain for more.

Her low, breathless moans told Kenric how fully she was responding and he whispered seductive words of encouragement in her ear. His strokes became more powerful, driving them both to more primitive instincts.

He felt her tremors begin, saw the look of awe and wonder widen her eyes before they closed against the drowning waves of fulfillment that washed over her body for the first time. A roar of completion unleashed his own shattering climax.

Kenric was slow to return to reality, feeling as though Tess had drained every ounce of life from his muscles. He was probably crushing her, but he couldn't seem to find the strength or inclination to move. He didn't want to move until he was forced to let her breathe. This strange feeling of utter contentment was unique. He'd never experienced the like. His usual habit was to roll away from a woman once his need was satisfied, which made the desire to languish in his wife's arms a completely new emotion. And an unsettling one.

He forced himself to shift his weight to his elbows, to see Tess's reaction to this experience. Her violet eyes were soft and sultry, her hair, undone at some point by his hand, fanned in a bright golden wave across his pillows. Her steady gaze still reflected her innocence, her wonder.

Suddenly uncomfortable, he looked away. What

they'd done had nothing to do with innocence, everything to do with lust. He wanted her desire, her body, nothing more. His eyes drifted back to her, seeing several marks of his passion, bruises that marred the creamy skin of her neck and breasts. The scowl on his face grew darker as he tried to recall when that had happened, disturbed that he couldn't remember. He'd never lost control so completely. What had she done to him? When his eyes returned to her face, the sleepy, satisfied expression was gone. She looked worried.

"I did not please you?"

Kenric didn't ease her fears. In fact, he didn't even hear her question as he frowned over his reluctance to separate their bodies then forced himself to roll away. Locking his hands beneath his head, he stared sightlessly at the ceiling. So much for his well-vaunted control, he thought in disgust, his mighty vow to keep his lust for her tightly reined. She'd turned him into a mindless beast.

Never again, he promised himself solemnly. He would never give her that much power over his body ever again. He would never give *anyone* that much of his control. The next time he would perform the duty as just that, a duty. She would not look at him again with eyes that made him feel all at once like a savage conqueror and the most tender of lovers.

Tess rolled away from Kenric, a cold knot of shame building in her heart. She flipped back the covers, intending to rise, but was stopped by his grip on her wrist.

"Where are you going?"

"To bathe," she answered bravely, not quite able to meet his eyes.

"Not yet." His voice brooked no argument, but he coaxed her back to bed by kissing the palm of her hand. The kiss did nothing to relax her rigid body, and she turned away, artlessly draping a thick swatch of hair over her face.

"Look at me, Tess."

She shook her head, mumbling that she'd rather not.

His mouth drew to a thin, tight line. "Did I hurt you so badly?"

Tess lowered her gaze and answered him quietly. "Nay, I just wanted to bathe."

She wanted to wash away her humiliation, to scrub away the memory of what had foolishly meant so much to her, and nothing to him.

"You will not wash away my seed," he said callously. "This marriage has brought me little but trouble. If nothing else, I will have an heir of you."

"Am I to be a brood mare, then?"

"Your ability to give me legal heirs is your greatest asset at the moment," he said tersely. "Any common wench can satisfy my other needs."

Tess resisted the urge to slap him. "You believe that my ability to give you children legally is the only thing that sets me apart from your serfs and servants?"

He shrugged, looking unconcerned. Tess fumed in silence, not about to voice an argument. If he was truly so ignorant that he thought wives were good for nothing more than children, she certainly wasn't going to correct his opinion. She could prove him wrong, of course. Given the state of Montague, she could prove him wrong in short order. Not that she'd do anything to make his life any easier, the heartless beast. He was—

"Be satisfied that I found pleasure with you."

She narrowed her eyes to angry slits, infuriated that he had the gall to scowl at her while telling such a huge lie, hurt that he truly thought her so worthless. "Now that I know frowns are an indication of your pleasure, I will not mistake them again for disgust, milord."

"Disgust?" Kenric began to chuckle then he laughed outright. He brushed a stray lock of hair behind her ear, then traced the curve of her cheek. "Aye, the taste of your lips disgusted me greatly, Tess. Perhaps I need remind myself just how awful it was."

"I don't—"

He covered her mouth before she could object further, holding her chin firmly when she tried to turn away. Yet he didn't force the kiss upon her, lifting his head before she could respond.

"Nay, I find nothing disgusting in your kisses. Perhaps it was the sight of your body," he said with mock concern, his gaze sweeping the length of her. Tess blushed and tried to cover her nakedness, but he pulled her hands away.

"Nay, I see nothing that displeases me," he said, his disappointment exaggerated. "It must have been the feel of your skin against my lips, or your body beneath mine." He placed light kisses against her shoulder, traveling higher until he was nibbling at her ear and his body covered hers once again.

"I think we need try this again, just to make certain," he whispered in her ear.

Tess tried to stay mad, to use her anger as a weapon against his steady seduction. But he was a conqueror at heart, relentless until she surrendered completely. She was lost when he murmured his desire for her, told her how he would make love to her, murmuring sweet words she'd never imagined. Whatever reasons he'd had for scowling, he convinced her that they had nothing to do with the physical side of their marriage.

Yet afterward he stared down at her with the same fierce expression, his frown as black as ever. He swore softly and rolled away, presenting her with his back. Tess sighed in resignation, wondering if she would ever understand this man.

9

Nearly three hours had passed since Kenric's departure to lead an afternoon patrol, but Tess could almost feel his presence in the room even now. She held her mirror at a new angle, deciding she didn't look any different. It wasn't fair. There should be some noticeable change when a maid became a woman. She should look older, wiser somehow.

Kenric certainly hadn't changed, inside or out. This morning he'd frowned his usual frown then risen from the bed the emotionless stranger she'd married. Not one word was spoken as he dressed. He left with the brief explanation that he'd be out on patrol and would see her at evening meal. He'd asked no questions about what she intended to do with her day, offered no suggestions about how to begin her duties as the new mistress of Montague, telling her without words that he meant what he said the night before. Her worth was limited to the duties she would perform in their bedchamber.

Tess was sorely tempted to do exactly what he expected, which was exactly nothing, just to spite him. She could blissfully ignore her duties and let the man wallow in the filth of his house. She could sit back and watch everything within the fortress slowly crumble while she waited for her husband to join her each night to perform the only duty he expected of her. Yet her mind rebelled against the thought of allowing herself to be used so lightly. Besides, he would never know what he was missing if she didn't show him. Doing the opposite of what Kenric expected was the only way to keep any shred of self-respect, and to prove how foolish his ideas were about the usefulness of a wife.

His behavior reminded her that she must allow their newfound intimacy to mean nothing, to change nothing. She must do whatever she could to escape again, this time for good. In the meantime, she would not only run Kenric's home as efficiently as he ran his army, she would act the perfect wife as well. What better way to regain his trust and that of his people? What better way to plot an escape than to act as if the thought would never occur? They would let down their guard eventually. An opportunity would arise sooner or later. Then Kenric would realize how valuable she was, how much she'd brought to his life, not in lands or coin, but with riches that couldn't be counted.

The shadows on the wall had grown long and she knew dinner would begin in little more than an hour. The thought of seeing Kenric again made her pulse quicken, fear mixed equally with excitement. Aside from spending the afternoon plotting to betray him, how would she be able to calmly eat her meal seated next to a man who'd seen her naked mere hours before? Heavens! She did much more than lie naked with Kenric.

Tess tugged the ribbon from her hair and frowned over

her failure with her braid. She picked up her brush and headed toward the door. It was past time to become better acquainted with her sister-in-law, and this was the excuse she needed to pay Helen a visit. She threw open the door but stopped abruptly, startled by what she found there. The guards outside her door looked almost as surprised as she did.

"You are still here?" Tess asked. It was a statement really, and her expression said as much. "I assumed I was free to leave my room now that my husband has returned. He did ask me to meet him in the great hall for evening meal."

"You are free to go wherever you wish, milady." The older of the two gave her a small bow, adjusting his dark blue tunic with a firm tug. "I am Sir Simon Delacort, and this is Sir Evard of Cordray," he said, indicating the younger man on his right. Shifting her gaze from the grizzled warrior, Tess noticed that Evard wore the same dark blue uniform as Simon. His dark hair stood slightly on end, as if he'd just been running his hands through it, and his bright green eyes were still wide with surprise at seeing her. It seemed nearly all of Kenric's men had this odd habit of staring at ladies.

"The baron wishes us to accompany you whenever you leave these chambers," he continued. "He worried you might become lost, being new to the castle. We are here to escort you wherever you wish."

"You must sleep at my door to do this?" Tess asked pointedly, eyeing the pallets spread along the wall in the hallway. Hah, new to the castle, indeed.

"We are ever at your service, milady." Simon bowed again. " 'Tis as the baron wishes."

"I was just on my way to find Lady Helen," Tess said hesitantly. This was her chance to make certain they were under orders to follow her everywhere. "There are a few questions I wish to ask Lady Helen, but 'tis not such an errand as needs an escort. I shall be quite fine should you just point the way to her chamber."

"The nature of your errands are not my business, milady," Simon said patiently. He forced a smile, as if he enjoyed his duty. "Whether the errand be large or small, we are at your service."

"Very well, then," Tess muttered, her question answered.

When Tess hesitated, Simon gestured toward the south passage, then fell into step behind the baroness. She chanced to look over her shoulder and spied Evard, rooted to the spot, still looking as startled as he had when she opened the door. Simon took several quick steps backward and grabbed Evard's arm, hissing a warning under his breath. "Shake out of it, boy. Shall I tell the baron you neglect your responsibilities to gaze cow-eyed after his wife?"

Evard's eyes widened and he snapped to attention, his steps brisk with military precision.

Tess hesitated for a moment when they reached Helen's chamber, uncertain now if her visit was such a wise idea. She took a deep breath and knocked on the door. To her surprise, Simon reached around and opened the door, telling her in a low voice that a baroness had no need to knock at her own doors. Simon eased his way around her and announced stiffly, "The baroness seeks your company, Lady Helen."

Simon bowed slightly to Helen. Kenric's sister was seated at a small table with her hand frozen in midair, caught reaching for one of many small jars laid out in front of her. Simon turned and gave a more formal bow to Tess before backing out of the room.

Helen ignored Tess completely, returning her attention to the toiletries. The woman was obviously vain enough to pay close attention to her personal appearance, but Tess wondered where that vanity disappeared to when it came to the state of her home. Helen's room was also as spotless as Kenric's, though not as richly appointed. A warm, hand-knotted rug covered the area before the hearth and the rest of the floor was covered with woven rushes. But they were clean and sprinkled with herbs to scent the air. In fact, everything in the room was as neat and tidy as its owner. Either Helen didn't care how the rest of the castle looked, or it looked that way on purpose.

"Hurry with that sewing," Helen ordered.

"Aye, milady," Miriam murmured. The servant was seated on plush blue-velvet pillows that lined the window well in Helen's room. The cozy seat looked so inviting that Tess decided to make the same sort of seat in her room. The light streaming in would make reading much easier. Miriam, however, was using the light to sew by, a rose-colored gown spread across her lap.

"Your man is too rude by half, Lady," Helen announced, turning her attention for the first time to her new sister-in-law. The glance she gave Tess was brief, no more than one would give a bothersome fly.

"He does seem a bit formal for a casual meeting between family," Tess said hesitantly, taken aback by the woman's cold tone. "Even though we are not well acquainted."

Tess waited for a reply, wondering why Helen was being so hateful. She'd also noted the brief flicker of distaste on Helen's face when she pointed out their new relationship. Did Helen truly hate her brother so much that she would extend that hatred to his wife? And why did she hate Kenric in the first place? Tess gave up her idea of asking Helen to help braid her hair and decided to come straight to the point.

"I came to ask your assistance on a matter that might help us become better acquainted. Being new to Montague, I happened to notice a few changes that could be made to improve the place. The castle is large, and I can understand how one woman would have difficulty managing such an estate, but we could accomplish much by working together."

Helen looked at Tess without a hint of emotion. It unnerved Tess the way these Montagues could look one over so impersonally. She lifted her chin and stood her ground. The smile Helen finally gave her was chilling.

"I wish you luck with the improvements you wish to make, Lady Tess." Helen turned again to the table, removing the lid of one jar and dabbing her fingers inside. She tilted her head back and rubbed the cream onto her throat, speaking to Tess as one would to a child. "But you will find the servants resentful of interference from an outsider. It will take time for them to accept you as their mistress."

"I suspected as much," Tess allowed. "However, I was not asking for the servants' assistance just yet, I was asking for yours. For instance, the hall would benefit by the addition of sturdy chairs and finely stitched cushions such as these," Tess said, brushing her hand along Helen's blue window cushions. "The carpenters will need to make the chairs, but I would appreciate your help with the cushions. Did you stitch these yourself?"

"I do not sew." Helen's lips were pressed together so tightly they were nearly white, her expression as stony as ever.

"You do not sew," Tess repeated slowly. She let her gaze travel around the room, examining numerous wall tapestries and the embroidery work that festooned a vast pile of pillows on Helen's bed. "Or perhaps you do not sew when the project is not of your liking. Who fashioned the pillows on your bed, Lady Helen?"

"I do not seem to recall." Helen shrugged. Tess was silent a moment before shrugging her own shoulders.

"Given time, I believe we shall see great improvements in your sewing skills, Lady Helen." Tess stood up and walked leisurely toward the door, turning to face Helen once more. "In fact, I believe you shall be skilled enough to begin stitching seat cushions within a fortnight."

Tess closed the door on that prediction and Helen's mutinous expression. It was a beginning, she decided with a grim smile. Not a very positive beginning, but a beginning all the same.

Kenric did his best not to pace the great hall as he waited for his wife's arrival. Fitz Alan was droning on about some stupid horse in his stables, but Kenric's thoughts were occupied elsewhere. The candle that marked the time, burning from one red ring to the next each hour, told him Tess was late. Kenric hated tardiness. It bespoke a lack of discipline. He'd have to have a talk with her on the subject.

Maybe she was keeping him waiting on purpose, just to annoy him. He wondered if she was angry with him for some reason, perhaps because he'd left her to lead the afternoon patrol. She didn't seem angry when he left. Not that she should be. It was his duty to patrol the perimeters of the castle whenever he was in residence. The task showed his men how seriously he took his obligations. He was no lax lord to wallow in wine and a soft castle bed while others saw to his protection. Riding out with his men showed his concern for their safety. Surely Tess understood that.

Aye, of course she understood, Kenric decided. He relaxed against the mantel of the fireplace, one arm stretched out negligently along the polished oak beam. A moment later, he caught sight of Tess out of the corner of one eye and bolted upright, his senses suddenly alert. He edged away from the fireplace to keep her in his line of vision. The pretense of speaking with Fitz Alan was a convenient way to observe her without revealing his interest as he watched her take a seat at the head table.

"Aye, this colt is the most amazing shade of pink I have ever laid eyes on," Fitz Alan declared.

"Hmm," Kenric murmured absently, his eyes glued to

Tess. He thought her eyes sparkled like jewels, her hair had a sheen to it that gold could not match. God, she was beautiful, like a splash of sunshine in his dreary hall. In that moment, Kenric knew he would never tire of looking at her.

"And imagine my astonishment when the beast suddenly sprouted wings and flew from the stable, right over my head."

"Aye, amazing," Kenric agreed seriously. Tess turned to thank Simon when he poured her a cup of wine, but she kept her gaze glued to the table. Why wouldn't she look at her husband? Kenric frowned as he tried to recall what he might have said to upset her.

"Of course, one would expect such a feat. The colt's sire was bright green with big blue wings."

"What the devil are you babbling about?" Kenric asked, annoyed that he was finally being drawn into Fitz Alan's conversation. "Nay, do not explain," he continued, certain the explanation wouldn't be to his liking. " 'Tis mealtime and I am hungry. Save your tales for some gullible squire."

Fitz Alan bowed low to cover his smile and outright laughter. He strolled over to the table and took the seat at Kenric's left. Kenric spoke quietly with Evard before gaining his own chair, sparing a quick glare for Simon who seemed to be telling Tess a most amusing tale. She had yet to turn and look at him. By accident or design? Kenric wondered.

"You may take your seat next to Fitz Alan," he ordered Simon, displeased with the attention his vassal showed his wife. It wasn't proper. Was it? And he didn't like the way Tess's back stiffened at the sound of his voice. Simon removed himself and Tess turned in her chair, one hand reaching for her goblet of wine. She took a delicate sip then finally, finally, turned toward him.

"Good eve, husband."

Kenric thought her voice sounded delightfully husky.

She wore no adornment in her hair and it framed her face in a soft, golden cloud. Her eyes were the color of spring violets. He studied them intently and saw no traces of anger. Kenric sighed, realizing he'd been holding his breath again, a bit surprised at the relief he felt.

"Good eve, *wife*." Kenric stressed the word "wife" to remind her that they were well and truly married as of last night. He even smiled to show his pleasure over the fact. Tess bowed her head and stared intently at her hands.

The meal began in strained silence, Tess looking anywhere but at her husband, Kenric frowning over being ignored so thoroughly. After trying three times, Fitz Alan gave up his attempt to speak with Kenric and turned to start a decent conversation with Simon. Their loud talk soon covered the quieter conversation between the baron and baroness.

"Your hair is not braided," Kenric commented, feeling foolish for sounding so awkward and stilted. Why did he feel so ill at ease? Next he would be talking of the weather.

"You do not like it this way?"

"On the contrary. I find it most appealing."

"Then I shall wear it this way often." Tess blushed and tucked her chin against her chest, concentrating on the most unappealing food she had ever laid eyes on.

"Good." Kenric also returned his attention to the food, wondering what might have changed her manner so drastically. She seemed embarrassed about something, but what?

He attempted to expand the conversation. "Evard tells me you visited Helen earlier."

"Aye," Tess replied evasively.

"Did you have a . . . nice visit?" Kenric had never experienced a nice visit with Helen in his life. It was a foolish question.

"Aye, most pleasant."

"Did you speak of anything in particular?" he asked, truly curious now.

Tess shrugged her shoulders, intent on pushing a soggy turnip around her trencher. "This and that, milord."

"Such as?"

"Lady Helen agrees that the stools in your hall need replacing with sturdy chairs and benches." Tess used the point of her knife to flip the turnip over and over. Her other hand dropped to her lap and began to twist a stray lock of hair. "She graciously offered to stitch nice, soft cushions for these new seats."

Kenric nearly laughed in her face. Helen had yet to "graciously" offer anything that might benefit her brother. Tess was lying through her teeth. "I see," he said. "Did you discuss anything else? Our recent marriage, perhaps?"

"Oh, nay, milord!" Tess was clearly appalled. She lowered her head and leaned closer to whisper behind her hand. "I would never discuss what we . . . I mean, our . . . I would never discuss that with anyone but you."

Kenric looked puzzled. It took him a moment to realize she was thinking of the physical side of their marriage. "Are you certain there is nothing you wish to discuss? Something of a personal nature perhaps?"

"Nay, milord!" Tess was already fanning her face with one hand before she caught the telling action and dropped the hand to her lap.

"Ah, but I think there is," he said smugly, smiling over her distress.

Tess shook her head and began to spear her food in random patterns, doing her best to ignore him again. He could hardly believe this blushing maid was the same passionate woman he'd bedded only hours before. The reason for her shyness suddenly crystallized in his mind. Kenric wanted to laugh aloud with his pleasure. It was her maidenly modesty that had returned full force. He'd expected Tess to act like his other women, wenches who pawed at him and hung on his arm after he'd bedded them, working their wiles to extract pretty compliments or gifts. But not Tess. She'd probably faint from shock if he so much as touched her. With a wolfish grin, he slipped his hand behind her back and gently caressed the curve of her hip.

She didn't faint.

Aye, he'd give her that much. Tess leaped a good foot into the air, knocking over her stool in the process. She would have fallen off the back of the platform if Kenric hadn't grabbed her. He quickly righted the stool and reseated Tess before turning to their audience. Every pair of eyes in the hall stared at them.

"A rat," Kenric drawled, to no one in particular. He sat down and leaned over to whisper in Tess's ear. "You are certain there is nothing on your mind, sweet?"

Tess rubbed her ear.

"Nothing of importance," she replied stonily. He reached across the table to cover her hand, his thumb idly stroking her fingers. She snatched her hand away as if he'd burned her. "Please do not do that, milord!"

"Why not?"

"Why not?" Tess repeated, looking up to meet his gaze. Her eyes turned soft and sultry. The sight of her tongue darting out to wet her lips sent heat snaking to his belly. She stared at his mouth and he clenched his hands into fists so they wouldn't pull her up against his chest for a long, deep, kiss.

"You should not look at me this way in public," Kenric whispered, the objection lacking any conviction. In truth, he loved the way she was devouring him with her eyes. But not here, for all to see. "Go upstairs, Tess. To our chamber. I shall join you soon."

"The meal is not ended," she pointed out, her voice still a whisper. " 'Tis a rudeness if I leave the table before you have finished your meal. Your men will talk."

"Imagine what they will say if I bed you here."

Tess's mouth dropped open. It took a moment for her to recover, but she gave him a small, shy nod, her eyes still locked with his.

Fitz Alan waited until the baroness disappeared above the stairs before addressing Kenric.

"Perhaps now would be a good time to give any orders you wish carried out on the morrow, milord." Fitz Alan reached forward and picked up a pitcher of ale, filling both their mugs. "Then none would need disturb you for much of the day."

Kenric turned and eyed Fitz Alan a long, silent moment as the meaning of his words sank into his dazed senses. His wife was making him daft, lowering him to the point of acting like a smitten squire in front of his men. "Am I that obvious?"

"Aye," Fitz Alan replied genially. "That you are, milord."

Kenric scowled. "She is a distraction. She occupies my thoughts far too often."

" 'Tis not exactly a curse to have a beautiful wife," Fitz Alan pointed out. "Many a man would cherish a lady such as yours."

"I will not care for her," Kenric said quietly. "You know as well as I the dangers that involves. The Welsh baron . . . Welton was his name. You remember how we used his wife against him?"

Fitz Alan's expression hardened, Kenric's meaning clear. A man with enemies did not need a weapon that could be used against him. Lady Tess would be safer if the baron's enemies believed she held no special place in his affections.

" 'Tis likely no more than an infatuation," Fitz Alan predicted.

"Aye, one that needs end soon. I intend to keep her in my bed till I've had my fill of her charms. The attraction always wears off," he added confidently, tossing down a healthy portion of ale. "Ofttimes after a night or two, I have trouble remembering why I found a wench comely in the first place."

Fitz Alan nodded. "You wish me to oversee the train-ing on the morrow?"

Kenric gladly put the subject of his wife behind them. Yet he couldn't deny the haste with which he gave Fitz Alan his orders, or his anticipation of the night ahead.

10 ❧══════════════❧

Sometimes a man had to set his worries aside and simply enjoy the moment. An unusual piece of logic for a man who filled his days with rigid discipline. But Kenric decided to set aside an entire day of duties and responsibilities in favor of his wife's company. He might as well. The day was already half spent and they were still abed, Tess draped across his chest like a warm blanket.

His mighty vow to regain his self-control when he made love to Tess had proved impossible. He would begin her seduction with the right intentions and they would last all of two minutes. A touch, her scent, the softness of her hair brushing against his chest, her eyes changing color as desire took hold. Kenric had lost track of what sent him over the edge. There was no one thing he could watch for or guard against. He wanted to blame Tess for whatever it was that made him senseless with lust until he lay sated in her arms, cursing his traitorous body. Yet she gazed up at him with such innocent confusion that he could do no more than frown over the power she held unknowingly. He knew she still wondered about his moods, yet she said nothing. Let her worry, he thought with some satisfaction. He'd certainly done his share.

The cure would work eventually, he told himself optimistically. None would think it strange that a newly married man spent an entire day with his bride. He'd never spent more than two full days with a woman before he grew heartily sick of her. He would tire of her chatter, or grow bored with her silence. Her beauty would fade until he saw only her flaws. He would sate himself to the point that a Roman orgy could not rouse his interest. Aye, everything would work itself out, so this worrying was pointless. He was simply acting like a child with a new toy, fascinated for the moment. It wouldn't be long before she ceased to amuse him, to capture his attention so thoroughly. Why not enjoy her while it lasted?

Kenric let his gaze travel across the room, looking for a distraction. He smiled when he spied an overturned bucket near the tub. Last night he'd returned to his chamber to find a hot bath and warm wife awaiting his pleasure. The memory of her wet, soapy hands moving across his body made him arch his hips against Tess, one arm around her waist to keep her in place. Aye, he'd taught her to bathe a man a bit too well.

"Mm," Tess sighed. Her eyes fluttered open to reveal sleepy, satisfied pools of violet and she stretched lazily against him. "Good morning."

" 'Tis afternoon, wench. You sleep more than any creature I have ever known."

" 'Tis not my usual habit," she admitted. Her smile became mischievous and her hips wriggled seductively. "But I do feel much rested."

Kenric gripped her hips to stop her game, grimacing. "I have unleashed a wanton."

"Are you sorry?" she asked innocently, continuing to move against him in ways that could never be called innocent.

"Perhaps. Stop that," Kenric growled. Tess rubbed against his chest once more before obeying the order. "You may not need sleep, but you do need rest."

"Hah," she scoffed, her grin still teasing. "My husband is obviously exhausted by his wife's . . ."

Tess paused to search for just the right word. Her eyes rolled up toward the ceiling, as if she would find the answer there.

"Enthusiasm?" Kenric suggested blandly.

"Aye. Enthusiasm." Tess nodded. "Perhaps a nice nap would do you some good as well, husband?"

"Your words ring false to me, wife. 'Tis not I who will be unable to walk the rest of this day." He stroked the back of her legs, still spread wide across his hips. "I vow you will barely be able to stand now."

Tess's smile faded when she tried to shift one leg and her muscles refused to respond. Kenric assisted the effort, but her moans erased his smile as well.

"You should not have slept that way." His voice echoed concern, but it was also tinged with perverse male pride. He whispered seductively in her ear. "At least, not until you become accustomed to the position."

Tess smiled at the wicked suggestion despite her aches and began to inch her knees up. There was no sin in enjoying her husband, she told herself reasonably, pushing aside the thought that he would not be her husband for very long. At the moment, they were no different than any other married couple. "I will look forward to the practice, milord."

"No more," Kenric groaned, his fingers digging into her hips to hold them still. "You will be the death of me yet."

"Surely you cannot die from this," Tess murmured, her voice teasing. She struggled some to sit up, still straddled across Kenric's hips, and began running her fingers through the soft mat of hair covering his chest. There was no part of him that failed to fascinate her. This plan to act the perfect wife was rewarding in ways she hadn't imagined, the role played so effortlessly that she wondered already how much of it was an act. She smiled triumphantly over the expression on his face when she shifted her hips again. "I was just getting comfortable."

"Do not get too comfortable, little cat." Kenric caught a few stray locks of her hair and arranged the silky tresses around her shoulders. "Else I'll change my mind about taking you on a tour of the castle."

"A tour?" Tess asked, delighted by the possibility. She couldn't believe he would accommodate her plans so thoroughly. "Really?"

"Really," Kenric chuckled.

"I cannot wait! Can we leave now? Will you show me everything?"

"Aye, everything," he assured her. "Best be careful, sweet, or your enthusiasm will injure my feelings. Not a moment ago, you seemed in no hurry to leave my bed."

A soft smile curved Tess's lips and her manner became seductive once more. "Do you wish it, I will not leave your bed all day, milord."

"You are a liar, wife." Kenric's rakish smile faded as he lifted her from his hips, his eyes lingering intimately on her body. His voice was edged with roughness when he ordered her to get dressed.

Tess rolled from the bed then took a moment to rub mobility back into her legs. She quickly sponged herself off then rummaged haphazardly through her clothes, the prospect of touring the castle with her husband hastening her steps.

Tess was dressed in little time but her hair slowed her progress to an annoying degree. She was amazed when

Kenric lifted the brush from her hands and began to gently work the tangles from the long tresses. The odd expression on his face made her wonder over his actions.

"You don't mind brushing my hair?" she asked softly. Only a lady or her maid should be bothered with such tasks. It hadn't occurred to her that a man would demean himself with such a duty.

"I love the feel of your hair," he answered, allowing several strands to spill from his hands. " 'Tis like spun gold, Tess. It reminds me of the story of the old miser who loves to run his hands through piles of gold coins, though I know they could not feel so silky."

Tess smiled over the fanciful words, surprised by this unexpected side of his personality. Butcher, indeed, she scoffed to herself. How different her husband was from the man of tales.

Think of Remmington, Tess told herself firmly, knowing she was softening again. It didn't matter if Kenric had a gentle side. He was still a warrior intent on putting her lands to the sword. Only an idiot would allow herself to be fooled by her own act. Kenric's next words only strengthened her resolve.

"Come, Tess," he said gruffly, extending one hand. "You have tarried long enough. I have no wish to waste the entire day in this chamber."

Three hours later they were high atop the battlements overlooking the inner courtyards of the castle. The view from such a height was breathtaking, but Tess had eyes only for the outbuildings and structures within the fortress walls, memorizing the information Kenric shared about each part of Montague. He'd shown her the major rooms of the castle and the defenses of Montague, but hadn't taken her to the places she wanted to see most. To play the part of mistress, she would need to know the workings of the kitchens, tannery, smith, and all other places with activities vital to the daily operations of the castle. Knowing those tasks held little interest for a man such as

Kenric, she decided to wait and ask Miriam for the tour she really needed. She would assume her duties soon enough, but she wanted this time with Kenric too much to risk chasing him off.

A message from Fitz Alan disrupted the couple anyway and Kenric departed with Simon, promising to return soon. Tess leaned over the battlement walls and gazed out over the charred landscape, glad of a few minutes alone to absorb everything she'd seen of the castle. The plans to make sweeping changes at Montague were pushed aside hours ago, due mostly to the attitude of Montague's servants. They were an obedient bunch, she would give them that much. But their insolence was a barely veiled mask on every face. With the example Helen set as their mistress, she should have expected as much. She just didn't expect Kenric to be so tolerant of that behavior.

Tess propped her arms atop the cold stone wall and rested her chin on her folded hands, watching the flash of steel as Kenric's men practiced on the training grounds below. The attitude of the servants was worrisome, but Kenric's soldiers were another matter entirely. All activity on the training grounds had ceased when she and Kenric arrived for an inspection. The men waited in respectful silence for Kenric to address them then they greeted her politely. Aye, Kenric tolerated nothing short of absolute obedience from his men. A simple frown at a knight he thought a bit too eager to impress her sent the man into a fit of stammered apologies.

How the MacLeiths would laugh if Tess asked for the same measure of respect from Gordon and his men. The MacLeiths insulted her openly. At least they had respected Dunmore's order to keep their distance from Tess. It was the one show of kindness, albeit a selfish one, that Tess could thank him for. Dunmore simply didn't want her producing a bastard before she could be married off to Gordon and present a legal heir. Hah. As if Gordon were capable of such a feat! Kenric, on the other hand, was more than capable of getting an heir on her. At the rate they were going, it wouldn't be long before she found herself with child. So many problems, she thought with a soft sigh. So many decisions she didn't want to make.

Kenric stood silently in the tower doorway, captivated for the moment by the picture Tess presented as she gazed over the battlement walls. With her chin resting on her hands, her face was profiled perfectly against the cloudless blue sky, the breeze occasionally ruffling the cloak of sunshine that was her hair. Beautiful, yet sad. She looked no happier to be within Montague's walls than he was.

No, she'd not annoyed him with hollow flattery of his home. She'd walked silently by his side as he showed her the fortress, her brows often drawn together in a frown, asking few questions. He'd had a ridiculous urge to haul her back to their chamber then search Helen out and order her to make their home presentable. But, no, he would do nothing to make anyone believe he had any pride in Montague, that it represented anything more to him than a worthless, unwanted mess. Instead he'd taken Tess to the training grounds to show her the one thing in his life he did take pride in; his army.

He'd expected her to be appalled. Gentle ladies had little appreciation or interest in the workings of an army. The women he'd known at court would be insulted if he exposed their delicate sensibilities to the coarseness of the training grounds, deeply offended if he thought to introduce them to the common soldiers there. Tess had greeted his men warmly, conversed with the sweaty soldiers as if they were finely dressed courtiers.

His men had acted like idiots. He'd been so concerned with his wife's reaction to his soldiers that he hadn't considered his soldiers' reaction to his wife. Some simply stared slack-jawed while others did all but juggle their swords to impress her. The effect one slight woman had on the brawny, battle-hardened soldiers would have been laughable if the woman had been any but Tess. Kenric

knew that, knew also that he'd approached a state of pos-
sessive jealousy when he'd snapped at any man who succeeded in capturing her attention for more than a moment
or two. He'd left his soldiers much quicker than he intended, suddenly in no mood to share his new toy.

She'd started smiling again after they left the training
grounds, as if that had been the most pleasant part of their
tour. For some reason, Kenric found himself absurdly
pleased by those smiles. Yet now she looked near tears.
Given her behavior so far that day, she was probably recalling some amusing jest. Her moods were impossible to
outguess. She frowned over a home any woman would appreciate despite its filth, and smiled over an army that had
terrorized half the civilized world.

Turning fanciful for the moment, Kenric imagined
Tess standing here alone, awaiting his return from some
war or battle, her heart burdened by the worry that he
wouldn't. That was a pleasant fantasy, the thought that a
woman as beautiful as Tess would pine for him. Being tied
for life to the Butcher of Wales would be enough to make
any woman cry. Most likely she was indulging in a bit of
self-pity, feeling sorry for herself because she was trapped
in this hellish place as surely as he was. Would she admit
as much?

"What are you thinking?"

Tess was so caught up in her thoughts that she didn't
hear Kenric's return. His quiet words startled her.

"That you should not creep up on people," she chastised, smiling to soften the admonishment. Kenric
shrugged and turned his attention to the view beyond the
walls. Though he didn't move, Tess felt as if he'd suddenly
stepped away from her, placed a wall between them as
solid as the one she leaned against. "You finished your
business with Fitz Alan?"

"A minor matter. You still haven't answered my question. Why the serious expression on such a fine day?"

Tess thought about lying for a moment then decided the truth could do no harm.

"Less than two fortnights have passed since I believed myself destined to be Gordon MacLeith's bride. I was thinking how different my life would have been with Gordon." She tilted her head back, her gaze uncertain as she looked into his eyes. "I would tell you the reason he last beat me."

"I know already." Kenric gave her a roguish smile. "You told me when you were fevered."

"What did I tell you?" Tess asked in a worried tone.

"That you called Gordon a catamite."

" 'Tis true," Tess whispered. "He came to my chamber after he beat me and sent everyone from the room. I thought he meant to murder me, but he was there only to revile me with threats. He said I disgusted him and promised to give me to his men once we were married. They were all MacLeiths, he said, so it wouldn't matter where my bairn came from as long as I produced a child. He made other promises, but they are . . . they are obscene, vile beyond repeating."

Kenric moved closer and cupped her face between his hands. "I cannot take away the pain of your past, but I can guarantee that you will never have to fear Gordon or his father, ever again. You are mine now, Tess, and I protect what is mine."

A wave of tenderness swept over her, so sweet and fierce that it finally succeeded in bringing the hidden tears to her eyes. She moved into his arms and laid her cheek against his soft fur cloak. He was telling her the truth. In her heart, Tess knew he would protect her with his life. And she intended to repay him by running away. Guilt, Tess decided, was the most unpleasant of emotions. Her decision would be so much easier to live with if only Kenric were cruel, a man no better than the MacLeiths. He deserved more than a bride who would pretend to be his wife, then leave him at the first opportunity.

"The MacLeiths are jackals, not to be trusted," she said hesitantly, deciding he should be warned in case he ever did face her stepfather. "Do not expect a fair fight if you face those traitors."

"You, ah, told me that as well when you were ill."

"It seems I was very talkative," Tess said guardedly. "What else did I tell you?"

"What else?" he repeated, reaching over her head to scratch his chin. "Well, let me see. There is probably very little you did not tell me. At least, very little of importance. You do tend to babble, wife."

She frowned at his wolfish grin. " 'Twas rude of you to listen to such ravings."

"You like my eyes."

"I talked about you?" Tess was horrified by the thought. Almost anything she said about Kenric would be humiliating. His next words proved that thought correct.

"I remind you of a knight you dreamed of the sennight before we wed."

"Oh, God," Tess groaned. She recovered quickly and tried to school her features into an expression of disbelief. "You see? I was obviously talking nonsense. You must put little stock in the truth of anything I said while I was ill."

Kenric nodded, but his expression said he didn't believe a word of that. Thankfully, he changed the subject. " 'Tis near time for dinner. Would you like to continue this discussion in our chamber? We can take our meal there."

Much to Tess's dismay, Kenric was as good as his word. He told her the events of her illness in great detail. Tess denied everything, scowling when Kenric laughed aloud at her ridiculous objections. But his laughter disappeared when Tess asked about *his* life before they met. He claimed there was little to tell. Tess took her turn laughing at that bold lie. She kept after him until he finally relented, telling her fascinating tales about the lands of the Crusades.

Tess didn't remember falling asleep in her chair, or being carried to the bed a short time later. When she woke up during the night, Kenric was lying next to her, his head propped up on one elbow. The glowing embers shadowed his expression, but she was sure he was watching her as he rubbed her arm in a soothing motion. She couldn't quite recall his reply when she sleepily asked if anything was wrong. She thought she heard him say he wasn't sure. That answer was odd enough to convince her that she'd dreamed the whole thing.

The days that followed fell into a comfortable routine. Kenric rose early to train with his men or to ride out on patrol. Tess kept busy exploring the castle. He joined her occasionally in the hall for the midday meal, but often as not, his time there was spent with the bailiff or steward, or any number of his men with problems to be solved. Evening meals went much the same, though Kenric never tarried afterward and neither Kenric nor Tess actually ate in the great hall. Each waited until they reached their chamber to share a meal and conversation.

" 'Tis no wonder you've managed to lure me here for meals," Kenric remarked one night, eyeing a spoonful of thick stew. Though their meal was simple, it was considerably better fare than that served in the great hall. "How do you manage to find such good food in this place?"

"I am tempted to take the credit," Tess replied with a smile, pleased that her plan to appear the perfect wife was progressing so nicely. "But 'tis Miriam who arranges our meals each evening."

"You will thank her for me." He took a bite of the stew, then washed it down with a gulp of cider and reached for a loaf of fresh bread.

"I have thanked her often, but she acts nervous and brushes the compliments aside. If I didn't know better, I would say she is afraid someone will find out what she is doing."

Helen was the someone Miriam feared. The servant

had as much as told Tess that Helen would see an end to
their fine fare if she found out that Miriam was being so
accommodating. She'd wanted to ask Kenric about Helen's
obvious hatred ever since they arrived at Montague.

"I saw your sister in the solar today," she began. "Is it
your mother or your father that you both resemble so
closely?"

Kenric looked up slowly from his trencher and the
cold blast of his gaze made Tess swallow nervously. What
on earth had she said to stir up that much anger?

"My family is none of your concern."

"Why not?" she asked defiantly. "Whenever I ask
Helen about your family, she says I must ask you. Whenever I ask you, the subject is conveniently changed or I am
told it is none of my concern. Am I so unworthy of the
Montague name that I am to be told nothing to help me
find my place within it?"

The anger faded from Kenric's eyes until he looked
little more than annoyed. The soft tone of his voice was
surprising. " 'Tis the Montague name that is unworthy of
you, Tess. You are curious and that is natural, but I do not
discuss my family with anyone. Perhaps I will tell you
more after I take Remmington, but that will not happen
anytime soon unless you can tell me what you know of her
defenses. 'Tis said Remmington is impregnable, which
means a lengthy siege is likely in order. Are there any
boltholes under the walls?"

"None that I know of," Tess answered, still shocked
by the revelation that he thought his name unworthy of
her. Amazing. He'd certainly fooled her into thinking just
the opposite. "My father wouldn't allow any escape tun-
nels to be built. He was very proud of the fact that Remmington could withstand any army and said there was no
need."

"Yet Remmington fell to MacLeith," Kenric said
softly.

"My father was lured outside the walls by trickery on

the grandest scale," Tess said tersely. Her grip on a goblet of wine tightened until her knuckles were white. "Dunmore MacLeith will doubtless stay safe and snug behind Remmington's walls unless he gets me back."

Kenric pushed away from the table then strode over to her chair, startling Tess when he pulled her up against his chest.

"You're mine," he reminded her. "I will deal with your stepfather."

Tess wanted to tell him that he was wrong, that she didn't want him to deal with MacLeith, knowing Kenric's methods would destroy everything her family had built, everything it represented. She wanted to weep for the unfairness of it all, because his words tempted her beyond reason, stirred a sadness so great it hurt. She could do neither, for his mouth captured hers for a kiss that was all fierce possessiveness. Tess kissed him back just as hungrily, desperate for his possession, knowing he would make her forget for a while that she belonged anywhere else but here.

A visitor arrived at the beginning of the next week and the news he carried brought the couple's tranquil interlude to an end. One of Kenric's vassals had died at Penhaligon Keep and the knight's bastard son immediately took control, denying the rightful heir. Everyone was gathered for the evening meal when the news arrived and Tess couldn't help but wonder at the strange silence this announcement caused. Was Penhaligon's bastard such a dangerous man, then? She looked to Kenric and her fears were calmed by his expression. He wasn't worried.

Nearly an hour later, one hundred of Kenric's soldiers were mounted and ready to leave the fortress. Tess knew it was Kenric's responsibility to ride with his men. Aye, she understood and agreed with his decision to see to this matter personally. But she didn't understand her strange reluctance to see him leave.

" 'Tis a long ride to Penhaligon," Kenric told her. They were standing in the main courtyard, the reins of Kenric's warhorse looped over his arm as he bid his wife farewell. "I might be gone a month or more, but Simon and Evard will remain behind to look after you."

"I shall be fine, milord." Tess gave him an encouraging smile, pleased that she wasn't crying. Why she felt like crying was a mystery. She should be delighted that he was leaving, giving her the perfect opportunity to begin setting her plans into motion. "I do worry that this might be a trick to get you out of the fortress."

Where on earth did that come from? Tess frowned. It was a nice touch, though. She'd been acting the perfect wife for so long that it was becoming second nature.

"Darvell has caused trouble before," he said reassuringly. "Most of my men will remain at Montague, as well as the regular castle guards. This is nothing more than it seems, wife." He reached out to gently stroke her cheek. "Do you need for anything, just ask Simon."

"If you have no objection, I would like to assume my place as mistress while you are away," she said quickly. Kenric looked puzzled and she hurried to explain. "There are some changes I would like to make, mostly in the kitchens and great hall. Surely you have noticed the food could be better."

"Aye." He chuckled. "The meals would be considerably better could any of my men digest them. I will speak to Simon before I leave. He will make sure you get any help you need."

His expression turned serious. "Come give me a kiss, wife. 'Tis time to send me on my way."

The kiss was sweet yet brief, both aware of their audience. He turned away first, calling Simon over to walk with him.

"My lady wishes to make some changes as Montague's new mistress. You will see that she encounters no difficulties," Kenric informed his man. He waited until they were beyond Tess's hearing before giving the seasoned knight the rest of his instructions. "Do not let her from your sight unless she is in our chamber. She goes nowhere without you. I am counting on you to see to her safety, Simon."

"Aye, milord," Simon replied. "I will keep her safe for you. No harm shall befall the baroness while she is under my care."

11

It took just three days for Simon to know that he'd lied to his overlord. Given the chance, almost anyone within Montague's walls would gladly murder their new baroness. Aye, there wasn't a doubt remaining in Simon's mind that the Butcher of Wales had married a female intent on overshadowing her husband's reputation. At the close of the second week he admitted defeat as Tess's keeper and sent word to Baron Montague. The baron's anger at being summoned home to tend his wayward wife would surely be less than being summoned home to attend her funeral. Several days later at Penhaligon Keep, the messenger wasn't as sure of Simon's opinion when he gave his report to Baron Montague.

"She *what?*"

"Aye, milord," the messenger said, taking several steps

back. She threatened to hobble Cook by cutting off his toes. Actually, Lady Tess threatened Cook's entire staff with that punishment, should they displease her."

Kenric clasped his hands behind his back and gazed over the battlement walls, hoping the peaceful view of the surrounding forest would lighten his mood. It didn't work. His voice was edged with anger when he ordered the soldier to continue with Simon's message.

"On the very day you left, a patrol was dispatched to each of your holdings at Lady Montague's order. She sent word that each holding was to provide one-tenth of their stores to Montague Castle at certain intervals. When Derry Town refused, she ordered their tithing barn torched. The mayor changed his mind before your wife condemned their alehouse to the same fate. Sir Simon bids you know that Lady Montague had your hounds impounded and she expects you to pay the pinder his due to release them. Lady Montague has also set a large number of soldiers to weaving reeds for the great hall's floor." The messenger's tone clearly indicated his disgust with that insulting punishment. "And Sir Simon is most concerned about your lady's decision to accompany the village healing woman into the woods to gather cures. Sir Simon tried to discourage her from this idea, but the baroness was most determined, claiming you gave her permission to name the old woman an assistant and that she is the most qualified. Though Sir Simon and a score of men accompanied the baroness, he worries for her safety because she intends to help the old woman each week."

Kenric unclenched his fists and leaned over the battlement walls. Retaking the keep from Darvell had been an easy task, yet in that time Tess had created an even greater challenge. Aye, this was the trouble that came with being too fond of a wife. Women grew bold when they thought themselves above punishment. "Is that all?"

"Nay, milord," the messenger reported. "There have been many other incidents, mostly with the craftsmen and villagers, but Sir Simon wishes to speak with you personally concerning those matters and would have you know he believes them less serious in nature. He also sends his apologies for troubling you with these problems but feels his powers to control the situation are limited. Lady Tess claims to have your permission to act as mistress of Montague, therefore Sir Simon is bound to honor her wishes even when he feels you would object. Sir Simon says he would be most grateful did you set matters aright before a tragedy befalls your lady."

Kenric would have laughed at Simon's dilemma if not for his anger over Tess's acts. He shook his head in disbelief, wondering if Tess had a wish to die, or if she was too simpleminded to realize how she placed herself in jeopardy.

"Find Roger Fitz Alan," he ordered the messenger. "Tell him we ride for Montague within the hour."

"Skill with a needle is gained through practice and patience," Helen advised, watching Tess begin the hated task of undoing several rows of new stitches to correct her error. She had to admire Tess's determination to create such a complex pattern of Montague's standard with so little experience to ease the task.

"This project may yet prove too ambitious for my talents," Tess admitted.

The two women were seated in chairs that flanked the fireplace in Helen's room and she leaned forward to inspect Tess's tapestry. "You are doing well enough for someone who hasn't stitched in five years. For a novice, your work is very good."

Tess nodded to acknowledge the compliment. Helen leaned back to observe the progress of her sister-in-law's handiwork, wondering at her reluctance to dampen Tess's spirits. She should hate her brother's wife. In fact, she'd been most determined about the matter. But Tess had come into Helen's room a few days after Kenric's departure and announced that she wasn't moving from the spot until seat cushions were started for the great hall. Almost an entire bolt of fabric lay in ruins when Helen discovered she would dine on bread and water until the task was performed correctly. Two more days dragged by while Helen stabbed her needle into cushion fabric and silently gloated over her sister-in-law's lack of sewing talent. Tess chattered on endlessly, telling stories as if Helen were truly interested in what she had to say. Watching Tess yank out the same stitches over and over finally proved too much for Helen. On the third day, Helen grudgingly demonstrated the correct stitch and the undeclared war became an uneasy truce of sorts. Two weeks later, Helen no longer considered Tess her enemy, but she wasn't her friend, either.

"I should still be angry with you for blackmailing me into this task," Helen said, bending over her tapestry to pretend interest in the work.

"Aye," Tess agreed, not bothering to look up. "You have a most forgiving soul, Lady Helen. I thought you would hold out much longer before agreeing to help stitch these cushions. And I was not at all sure you would ever talk to me." Tess laid her needle down and gazed into the fire, her expression reflective. "'Tis been a long while since I had someone to talk with."

"You near talked my ears off those first few days," Helen admitted with a genuine smile. "You asked so many questions that at first I thought it some sort of punishment. What was my favorite color? Did I have any pets? Where did I get the cloths for my gowns? I finally began answering, hoping for a bit of silence. Yet once I started talking, I realized how much I too have missed having company." Helen lowered her gaze and returned to her stitching. "Before my father died I took my friends for granted, not knowing they would soon be called home."

"Your friends do not visit anymore?"

"Oh, they still visit occasionally," Helen said. "At

least, they did before Kenric returned. But they used to live here. Young men were sent to train as squires for knighthood. The young women came to learn the workings of a large household, although most were more concerned with finding a husband."

"But why were they called home?" Tess asked. Helen worked diligently over her tapestry, so engrossed in the task that Tess all but gave up on an answer.

"Because their parents did not want them in Kenric's household. Within a month, all were gone. Even my younger brother, Guy, was called away to serve the king."

"You have another brother?" Tess asked sharply, startled by that revelation.

"Guy turned sixteen last summer." Helen's eyes grew misty and she turned away. "I have not seen him for almost a year. Guy's training keeps him very busy and he is allowed to visit just once each summer."

"Now that Kenric has returned, perhaps the king could be persuaded to let Guy come home. Kenric is more than qualified to see that Guy is well trained."

Helen stiffened noticeably and her practiced mask of indifference slipped into place. Tess wished again that she was half as good as the Montagues were at disguising their emotions. No show of temper. No hint of anger. Just a cold, emotionless stare. What a handy talent that would have been in her dealings with the MacLeiths!

"Guy will never return to live at Montague. Not while Kenric is here."

"But this is Guy's home," Tess argued. "If Kenric truly believes Guy should not return, then you should make him see the wrongness in his thinking."

"There is much you do not know about the Montagues," Helen said bitterly, shaking her head.

"I know practically nothing about the Montagues. There is no question that something is wrong in this household. Even a blind man would sense it the moment he walked through the gates. Yet I will never know what is wrong if no one tells me."

"How naive you are." Helen sneered. "Don't you know who you've married? The *real* reason they call him the Butcher of Wales? He slaughters for sport. Not only enemy soldiers, but defenseless women and children."

"Kenric does not kill for sport," Tess said staunchly. "He is a knight and a warrior. Knights slay their enemies, but they do not kill innocents."

"The Butcher of Wales does. Ask anyone. Four years ago, Kenric and his army came across a rebel camp in the forests of Wales. The Welsh soldiers were off fighting somewhere else, so Kenric put their women and children to the sword." Helen's eyes narrowed, her tone venomous. *"That* is the reason they call him the Butcher. The knight's code of honor means nothing to a man who lacks honor entirely. He kills anyone who gets in his way. Think of the women he raped as he holds you in his arms at night, how he slit their throats afterward. Think of the children he hacked to pieces when yours gather round your skirts someday. Try to—"

"Stop!" Tess wailed, covering her ears.

"Do you think a monster like that would hesitate to kill the boy whose rightful place he has taken as Montague's baron? Whose heritage he has stolen? You want to know the truth? The truth is he has deceived you, Lady. He made you believe he is the rightful Baron of Montague, fit to marry a woman of noble blood, when in fact he is no more than a bastard."

"I don't believe it," Tess whispered, still thinking about the Welsh tale. No honorable knight would kill defenseless women and children. Then again, none other was called Butcher. She wrapped her arms around her stomach and began to rock back and forth.

" 'Tis true enough. You have *married* a bastard," Helen added dramatically. "Your children will be tainted with a bastard's blood. Your own soul is stained beyond heaven's acceptance, even though you were tied to Kenric without knowledge of his sin. Father Bronson says bastards are the evil seed of man come to life. Spawns of the Devil, put on earth to punish men for their sinful ways."

Tess wanted to escape to her chamber, to hide from the truths she'd so foolishly demanded of Helen. But now that she was finally getting what she wanted, it would be foolish to leave. Knowledge was a useful weapon. She forced herself to respond to Helen's ridiculous beliefs.

"You and Kenric bear a strong resemblance," Tess began, but Helen interrupted her to explain.

"He is my mother's son," Helen admitted. "My mother was a lady-in-waiting to King Edward's mother. Our king was as handsome in his youth as he is now in his prime. And the Plantaganet males have always had an eye for beautiful women. My mother was very beautiful," Helen said with a shrug. "Her marriage to my father was arranged as soon as the pregnancy was discovered."

"The *king* is Kenric's father?" Tess whispered, truly shocked by that news. Oh, Lord. This changed everything.

"Aye, 'tis the sorry truth." Helen stood up and turned toward the fire. Tess remained seated, stunned into silence.

"My father was married once before but his first wife died childless. He was near two score years and the last of his line. Without an heir, Montague would revert to the crown upon my father's death. Old King Henry saw a way to avoid the problems involved with naming a new baron and to avoid the scandal of his son's pregnant mistress. He gave my father a ready-made heir to claim as his own and my mother a name for her bastard. No one expected they would have more children. Yet I was born four years after they wed, Guy, three years after that. My mother had a calming influence on Father, but his hatred of Kenric was obvious to all by the time Guy was born. In the last years of his life, my father did everything within his power to drive the king's evil seed from our home. But there was nothing he could do to change the fact that Kenric was his legal heir."

And Tess thought to petition the king for an annulment from this son? He would laugh in her face. Her elaborate plan to gain the king's support went up in a puff of smoke.

"You must—"

"I must think," Tess interrupted, waving a hand for silence. Perhaps a priest would annul the marriage because Kenric was a bastard. If she could find a priest with no wish for a long life, Tess thought gloomily. And what would her own life be worth if she exposed a secret the king himself had gone to such lengths to hide? It would never work. There would be no annulment.

"Those within Montague know the truth," Helen said, seeming determined to interrupt Tess's thoughts. "'Tis the reason they will not accept Kenric as their baron."

"You have done nothing to ease the situation," Tess said irritably. Helen's hatred of Kenric was the least of her concerns at the moment. Yet Helen's next comment drew her back to the conversation.

"That is the reason my younger brother cannot come home. If Guy returns to Montague, Kenric will kill him. Guy is the true Baron of Montague," she said haughtily, earning a raised brow from Tess. "Given the opportunity, I believe my father would have killed Kenric to see matters set straight."

"But your father was not given the opportunity to harm Kenric?"

"Nay, the king must have suspected Kenric's danger," Helen said. "Kenric was called away to train at court soon after Mother died giving birth to Guy."

Helen fell silent and began to pace. Tess leaned against the cold wall, her senses numbed by Helen's tale. No wonder Kenric was so ruthless. She felt a moment of intense sorrow for the child forced to grow up resented and hated by the only family he could call his own. How could a man show compassion when he'd known none in his own life? Tess shook her head in defeat. What was she thinking? It didn't matter if she pitied him or not. That lack of compassion would be the death of her people when he seized Remmington.

She thought of the gentle way Kenric could kiss and caress her, then imagined his blade at her neck instead. *Think of the women he raped as he holds you in his arms at night, how he slit their throats afterward.* He would return soon, would doubtless want her in his bed soon after. How would she be able to bear his touch when every time she closed her eyes her mind was filled with the picture of innocent babes falling beneath his sword?

Tess shuddered, remembering how she'd welcomed his caresses, how she'd reveled in their lovemaking. The man she'd made love to was one of her creation, one she'd only imagined. In truth, she'd lain with a murderer. The Montagues had created this vile monster, the man who might one day be called the Butcher of Remmington. Her rage focused on the man responsible for her husband's upbringing, the one who had turned an innocent child into a soulless devil.

Tess rose and caught Helen by the elbow, gently but insistently pushing her down onto the chair. She clasped her hands behind her back and took up Helen's task of pacing, her voice amazingly calm considering the chaos of her thoughts.

"You must despise Kenric for causing your father such heartache and preventing Guy from assuming his rightful title."

"Why, I believe I do," Helen agreed readily. "The king placed his evil seed in our home and—"

"Enough!" Tess bellowed. Helen scooted as far back as the chair would allow, her eyes wide. Tess resumed her pacing. "The words 'evil seed' will *never* be spoken in my presence again. It is wrong to blame a child for the sins of

his parents. It is wrong to seek revenge on the man who had no control of his destiny, for a sin he didn't commit. *That* is what your priest should have taught you, Helen, though it sounds as if he had not a drop of Christian charity in his pious blood. Doubtless your father greatly influenced his thinking."

Tears began to cloud Tess's eyes as she imagined the cold, lonely childhood Kenric had surely endured. She swiped them away angrily, knowing she could never allow herself to pity him.

"The sin does not lie on Kenric's shoulders," she said, hating Helen's father more than she'd hated anyone in her life. "And his blood is no more tainted than yours or mine."

Tess stopped her pacing and stood directly in front of Helen, though Helen continued to stare off into space, her face pale. Tess leaned forward, trying to regain her attention. "Are you listening to me, Helen?"

Several moments passed in silence. Tess was about to repeat her question when it was answered by another voice.

"I do not believe she is."

"Oh, dear Lord," Tess groaned. Swaying slightly, she prayed that her ears deceived her. She closed her eyes, unable to find the courage to turn around and face her husband.

12

"I wish to speak with you in our chamber, wife." Kenric's voice was strained, as if he knew he'd be yelling if he talked any louder. Tess knew that was not a good sign. She bowed her head, clasping her hands behind her back to hide the way they shook.

"Now, Tess!"

Kenric turned on his heel and stalked out, slamming the door shut behind him. Both women jumped several inches at the sharp sound then Helen began to sob.

"He heard everything!" Helen wailed, wringing her hands in terror. "He will beat me for telling, I just know he will."

Tess stared blankly at the door. If she'd tried to imagine the worst end to her conversation with Helen, this would surpass it. What else could possibly go wrong? A strange calm settled over her, a numbing sense of peace too welcome to resist. Gazing down at Helen's tear-streaked face, she managed to give her an encouraging smile.

"Do not worry, Helen. He is sure to spend his anger on me."

Helen looked horrified, her eyes reflecting her pity. Tess patted her hand reassuringly, then walked toward the door. She was just reaching for the latch when the door shot open. Kenric reached inside the room to grab her wrist and yank her into the hallway.

"You are hurting me," Tess said breathlessly, tugging against his painful grip. She was nearly running to avoid being dragged down the tower steps. Kenric's long, angry strides and her own quick, choppy steps nearly set her teeth to rattling.

Kenric stopped so abruptly at the foot of the steps that Tess crashed into his back. So did the two soldiers trailing close on her heels. Kenric reached over her shoulder and shoved the guards away.

"You have not learned the meaning of the word. Yet." Tess's guards retreated several steps when she opened her mouth to reply. Fortunately an interruption turned the baron's attention away from Tess.

"Milord!"

Kenric spun around to face Simon.

"Just where have you been?" Kenric bellowed. He pulled Tess forward, as if the sight of her was sufficient excuse for his charge. "You dare let her out of your sight?"

"Milord, there was an urgent matter requiring my attention in the lower bailey," Simon explained.

"There was an urgent matter requiring your attention in my sister's chamber," he roared. Simon winced and bowed his apology. Kenric brushed by him with Tess towed in his wake. "I will deal with you later, Simon."

"Baron, please," Simon pleaded, scurrying to keep up

with Kenric. "I must speak with you concerning my message. Most urgently."

Kenric threw open his chamber door then slammed it shut in Simon's face. "Later!"

Tess nearly stumbled to her knees from the force propelling her into the room. Trying to put space between them, she moved closer to the fireplace. He was going to hurt her. He'd just promised as much. Tess clenched her jaw and tried to calm her racing heart. No matter what, she would not shame herself by pleading for mercy. This man had none.

"If you kill me, the MacLeiths will have grounds to annul the marriage and you will lose all claim to Remmington." Pointing out the truth was not begging. Considering Kenric's strength and size, surviving his beating was unlikely. She tried to meet his gaze but instead caught sight of his hands. Her gaze remained locked there, watching them flex. "The MacLeiths needed me alive too, though Gordon forgot that fact when he was angered. You would do well to remember it, milord."

Tess refused to look higher than his shoulders, afraid of what she might see in his face. He'd taken the time to remove his armor, but he still wore the quilted black tunic that acted as padding beneath the heavy chain mail. He'd not tarried long before seeking her out. The faint aroma of leather and horses drifted across her senses, a reminder that he'd probably ridden hard to reach Montague before nightfall. She wondered if he could smell her fear.

"You want to die, don't you?"

"By your hand?" she asked tonelessly. "A quicker end, I trow, than the one Gordon planned for me. I stood up for my people when he would abuse them and turned his anger toward me instead. The price was to be my death. You would beat me senseless or to death for gossiping with your sister. There seems little honor in that end."

"Gossiping?" Kenric's snort sounded like a growl of

impotent rage. "You idiot. I don't give a damn what my sister told you."

"I find that hard to believe," Tess said boldly, incensed by his lie. Why else would he be so angry? She decided she had nothing left to lose by asking for the truth. "Did Helen speak the truth? Did you really slaughter women and children in Wales?"

"I did not bring you here to talk about what I did in Wales. You are here to explain your own actions."

An innocent man would have denied the charges to his last dying breath. She was sure of it. Avoiding the question was almost the same as answering it.

"I did nothing but ask your sister a few questions," Tess said quietly. He'd never denied what he was. She did that for him, convinced herself that he was worthy of her affections. He was no less handsome now that she knew the truth. Aside from his anger, she still couldn't see the darkness in his soul. He was, indeed, unlike any evil man she'd ever known. She'd married the Devil himself.

"I am talking about the trouble you caused in my absence," he corrected. "What Helen told you is of no significance."

She shook her head, unable to let him change the subject so easily. "You think it insignificant that your sister accuses you of murder?"

"What I did in Wales or anywhere else is none of Helen's concern. Nor yours," he added tersely. "You will tell me why three of my soldiers are busy weaving reeds in the great hall."

"They were being stubborn. Those three—"

"Silence!" The word cracked across the room like a whip. He pointed to a chair near the fire. "Sit down!"

Tess decided it would be best to obey. She slid into the chair and absently rearranged her skirts, wondering how on earth she could manage to get an annulment. Uncle Ian never should have allowed this marriage to take place. It was doubtful he would have agreed, had he

known more about the Baron of Montague. Tess's brows
rose as a new idea took shape. An English priest would not
annul her marriage, but a Scottish priest might be persuaded to see things her way.

Kenric took a step forward but stopped abruptly, turning to stare sightlessly out the chamber's narrow window
with his hands clasped tightly behind his back. "You will
never take it upon yourself to punish any of my men, ever
again, for any reason. Is this clear?"

"But I—"

He turned to glare at her. *"Is this clear?"*

Tess nodded, dismissing the matter as she unconsciously rubbed her chin. Escaping Montague would be
even easier, now that she knew the lay of the castle and its
routines. Yet Uncle Ian's lands were more than a week's
journey away and the shortest route would take her within
half a mile of Remmington Castle. It would be a journey as
dangerous as the one to London.

"My hounds are missing from the hall. Are you responsible?"

Tess nodded again, thinking she would have little
problem with a horse and supplies. She'd already figured
out how to make her way from the fortress with both.

"Did you threaten to cut off the toes of the kitchen
staff?"

Another distracted nod. After the annulment, a convent would be the perfect place to repent for the sins she'd
committed these past few months. And the ones she had
yet to commit in order to end this marriage. In a convent
she would never again be gulled by a handsome face that
hid a black heart. She would be safe. Her people would be
safe. Relieved that she had a new plan to bolster her
hopes, she turned her attention to the conversation at
hand.

"Did you requisition one-tenth of my holdings' provender without my permission?"

Tess's eyes widened, wondering how he'd found out about that so quickly. She nodded uncertainly.

"Are you responsible for the fire at Derry Town's tithing barn?"

"Aye, but—"

"Yea, or nay!"

"Yea," she whispered, a sense of dread gathering in the pit of her stomach.

"Did you charge one of my soldiers to carry out your orders when, in fact, I left Simon in charge of you?"

Tess looked surprised, her nod not quite as certain.

"And did you disobey Simon's charge by wandering off into the woods, knowing it was possible to stumble across a band of MacLeiths who are surely waiting for such a golden opportunity?"

"I am guilty of defying Simon about going to the woods, for I knew the risks," Tess admitted, absently twisting a fold of her skirt. "Yet I also know that Martha is old and may not live through the winter. No one has shown an interest in learning her healing skills, and no one knew where she gathered her herbs and medicines. I can take her place and tend the ills and injuries at Montague, should Old Martha fall ill, but I had to know where she finds the ingredients for her potions."

"So you risked your life and that of my men on the chance that a woman might die?" Kenric's tone was condescending and he rolled his eyes. "There were others who could have gone with Martha. I received word that you have maimed some of the servants," he continued briskly. "You will give me the names of those so punished and your reasons."

"None of the servants have been maimed or harmed in any way," Tess said defensively. "I would not actually inflict such a punishment, but after the fire at Derry Town, the kitchen staff readily believed my threat to remove their toes. That gave them an incentive to serve up the fresh provender as edible meals instead of disgusting slops."

"You never threaten a punishment unless you are ready to carry it out," he told her in a clipped voice. "Did you order my soldiers to strip the buttery to the walls, simply to make a cleaning easier for the servants, knowing you took my men away from their duties on the training grounds?"

"You make it sound so—"

The reason for his anger suddenly crystallized in Tess's mind. He'd learned of everything she'd done in his absence and, amazingly, he was angry.

"Answer!"

"Aye!" Tess's angry bellow surprised Kenric. He was astonished when she stood up and took a bold step forward, planting her hands defiantly on her hips. "And I would hear some word of praise rather than listen to my accomplishments being shouted out as criminal charges!"

"Praise?" Kenric sputtered. He pointed again to the chair. "I did not give you permission to stand!"

"I did not ask it." Tess tossed her braid over one shoulder with a sharp nod to defy him openly, her temper ignited beyond caution. "Had I guessed what was going on at Montague, known that you were ignoring your duties as lord for a reason, I would not have worked my fingers to the bone these past weeks trying to regain ground that was lost through your neglect. Aye, I will never again interfere in your household, milord. Your soldiers can go back to living like pigs and sleeping amidst their own garbage in the great hall, right alongside the rats who come to feed on the remainders of their meals."

"You dare accuse me of neglecting my duty then refuse your own?" he asked ominously. "I think not. 'Tis your duty to see to my household, and well you know it. 'Tis not your duty to interfere with my soldiers or to overstep your authority. You will indeed continue the duties that are yours as my wife, without complaint."

Tess opened her mouth to disagree but realized just in time that she needed to continue overseeing the household affairs to gain another opportunity to escape. Her short nod of agreement was mutinous.

"If you have any other explanations for what you've done in my absence, I would hear them now."

Explanations he would tear apart to make her look the culprit? Not likely. Tess shook her head, glaring at the floor so he would not see her anger.

"You have done nothing but defy me from the moment we wed," Kenric said quietly. "Look at me, Tess."

She met his gaze boldly. His eyes were almost black, the lines of his face etched by a harsh scowl. Aye, he clearly intended to punish her for working like a draft horse, for doing things he should have done himself long ago. The thought was infuriating. Yet she knew the anger would give her the strength she'd need to withstand the punishment. He needed her alive, she reminded herself.

"Had any one of my men endangered so many lives, or done half what you have done these past weeks, I would see him tied to a post and flogged. If any had died as a result of his foolishness, he would die as well. By luck alone, none have suffered harm by your actions." He gave her a moment to consider his words. The smooth, utterly calm expression on his face was more frightening than any harsh look or word. "I will not order you flogged, or even do the deed myself. Your back was laid open by a whip only weeks ago and another flogging would surely kill you. But this time I cannot ignore what you have done. This time you will be punished."

A knife of dread went through Tess and she swayed slightly. Dear God, he meant to use his fists on her! She closed her eyes so she couldn't see his hands, but remembered their size just as clearly. She'd been cuffed by Dunmore and Gordon, but never when they were in a true fury, only when she'd annoyed them in some way and was unfortunate enough to be within striking distance. Despite Kenric's outward calm, she knew he was furious.

"On the whole, I have found your skill at performing the duties of a wife sadly lacking. Yet there is one duty you seem to have a talent for." His voice was as cold as she felt. "Take off your clothes, Tess."

Tess felt the blood drain from her face. He wasn't going to beat her, but she felt no relief over the knowledge. What he intended was far worse.

"You would humiliate me further by demanding I perform that duty against my will?"

"There is little you can do to avoid it. You have agreed to perform your wifely duties without complaint. Are you telling me you lied?"

Tess bowed her head, glad he couldn't see her face. She'd agreed to continue her household duties, and those would likely be threatened if she balked at anything he demanded of her now. As long as she remained his wife, it was not within her power to deny him. She vowed that he would soon learn the difference between what was given willingly, and what was taken. "I did not lie."

She hesitated a moment, then her fingers began to fumble at the laces of her gown, fear making her tremble.

"Get into bed."

Dropping the chemise that she'd been clutching to her chest, Tess obeyed. She slipped into the bed and pulled the covers to her chin. Squeezing her eyes shut, she waited for him to tear the covers back and begin ravishing her. The minutes dragged by. Rather than pounce on her, Kenric barely disturbed her when he slipped under the covers. He didn't grab her and use her roughly, but instead pulled her almost gently to his side. He was naked.

She felt his hand brush across her hips and she held her body taut. When his hand moved to her legs, she clamped her knees together as tightly as she could. He began to stroke her, coaxing her to respond, his fingertips lightly tracing the line between her legs. Tess refused to obey the unspoken command, yet she felt her muscles relax slightly. He continued caressing her from her neck to her knees. She tried to concentrate on everything Helen told her, tried to picture the bloodshed of innocents. It was impossible. His hands were too much of a distraction. The tautness in her body no longer had much to do with denial, and everything to do with the desire he was stirring to life. Her body could not change its ways so easily. She'd craved his touch too often during the weeks of their separation.

Her breath quickened even as she tried to deny what was happening. He wasn't going to force her to do her wifely duty. He was going to seduce her into being his lover, shame her with her own needs. He had control of her life, and would control her body as well.

"How many women have you raped, milord?" she asked between clenched teeth. "Did you kill them after you were through, or did you allow a few to live? Killing is what you are best at, is it not? How long will you allow me to live after you gain control of Remmington?"

Kenric shifted his weight abruptly. Before she could lock her knees together, he forced his leg between hers. One hand grabbed hold of her braid, the pressure steady until she opened her eyes to meet his dark gaze. "Does the thought of coming willingly to my bed repulse you so much? Is the thought of being seduced by a bastard too disgusting for your delicate sensibilities?"

"Nay!" she said honestly, realizing he did indeed care what Helen told her. But he seemed most concerned about the part that mattered least.

"*Liar!*"

"Nay, I—"

"Silence!"

He released her braid and his hands covered her breasts. Contrary to the harsh words, his hands caressed her until she was biting her lip to keep from responding to him.

"You like what I do to you," he murmured in her ear. "Even if you deny it, your body cannot."

He shifted slightly and slipped his hand lower, trailing down across her belly to her legs, then up again to find her soft core.

"Nay," Tess said hoarsely, hoping the word would disguise her groan. It was pointless. There was no disguising the sound she made when he caressed her, no denying her arousal.

"Aye, wife. Your body is ready for mine. You want me. Admit it."

Tess closed her eyes and shook her head. His fingers parted her, exploring until he found the most sensitive part of her womanhood. Then he stroked her, gently and thoroughly. She kept shaking her head, struggling to keep the low moans locked in her throat.

"Tell me that you want me, Tess."

It was pointless to deny the truth. She was only delaying the inevitable. Her voice was a harsh, defeated whisper. "I want you."

He withdrew his hand and she moaned again, but he ignored her wordless plea to continue the pleasure. She felt him caress her legs then her hips, lifting her to receive him. Her hands stretched out to grip the bed as he surged into her, crying out in pleasure when he filled her completely.

Tess couldn't picture the horrible images his touch was supposed to make her remember, couldn't think of anything but the urgent cravings that had been too long denied. She felt her body begin to tremble beneath his and she gave herself over completely to his possession, unwilling to examine the wrongness of what felt so right.

13

Kenric readjusted his clothing with quick, angry jerks. A willing wife was about the only thing he'd wanted of marriage, and Tess tried to deny him even that. He should have taken her by force, he thought darkly, shown her exactly the kind of animal she'd married. She was still lying on the bed with her back to him. He wondered if she was crying.

He raked a hand through his hair then turned and stalked to the door. Making his way back to the hall, he was pleased to find Fitz Alan still in attendance. He needed the company of a friend to distract his thoughts. His soldiers took one look at his scowl and the room emptied as fast as it would if a plague had been announced. Only Fitz Alan and Simon remained.

"I did not expect to see you again until morn," Fitz Alan greeted, his smile uncertain.

Simon approached hesitantly from one side and touched Kenric's shoulder, then backed up a step when Kenric turned to glare at him.

"Milord, I would speak with you about Lady Tess."

Kenric relished the opportunity to vent some of his anger. "Aye, I would hear why you did not lock her in my chamber the *first* time she caused trouble, so she could cause no more."

"She is your wife, milord." Simon's startled tone said he hadn't thought of such a drastic measure.

"She is a meddlesome troublemaker." Kenric took his seat and poured a mug of ale. "Did it not occur to you that one of my men or the servants might have felt justified in rebelling against her? Your own message said you feared for her safety."

"That message was sent before I knew what the mistress was about. Her actions appeared foolish at first, yet I came to understand her reasons. Everything Lady Tess did was for the good of Montague and your men, Baron."

"She set my soldiers to women's work," Kenric shouted. "Think you any of those warriors will be quick to forgive the woman responsible for such humiliation? I've seen men killed for lesser insults."

"They would not dare harm your lady." Simon shook his head several times to emphasize the fact.

"You think not? I am probably the only reason it did not happen. They knew it was my right and responsibility to see to her punishment myself."

"They have come to appreciate her ways," Simon argued quietly.

Kenric wondered why the soldier was so determined to defend Tess when no defense existed. "She has set them against her. You've been bewitched, old man. Made gullible by innocent eyes that mask a mind constantly plotting mischief."

Simon's face flushed a dull red with the effort of keeping in a retort contained.

"Tell me the reason she robbed my holdings," Kenric demanded.

"Lady Tess did not tell me the true reasons until the bailiff turned up missing," Simon answered evasively, tugging nervously at his collar. "Your bailiff was plotting against you. Lady Tess sought to end his treachery before anyone else discovered that he had weakened Montague's defenses."

"Explain!"

Simon backed up half a step. "The story is long, milord."

"Then best you get started!"

The soldier nodded. "You will recall that there was some concern when we arrived here from Wales. 'Twas known that Montague stores were rich and well stocked, yet feeding five hundred extra mouths in the middle of winter would place a strain on any fortress."

"You assured me that my army would not deplete the castle's supplies," Kenric reminded him.

"Aye, milord. Yet that information came directly from the bailiff. Shortly after you left for Penhaligon, Lady Tess discovered the truth. She spent several days inspecting the storehouses and found all were nearly empty. In truth, the villagers here were near starving and food for your army and the castle servants nearly spent."

"What?" Kenric rose halfway from his stool. Fitz Alan was already on his feet beside him, one hand on his sword.

"Where is the bailiff now?" Fitz Alan asked.

"He fled almost a fortnight ago," Simon answered, his frustration over the fact reflected on Kenric's and Fitz Alan's faces.

"Find him," Kenric ordered flatly.

"I dispatched a dozen men to search him out, but they've had little luck flushing their prey. He's been hiding in the villages that are scattered between Montague keeps, but has managed to stay one step ahead of us. Lady Tess believes he may be headed for Remmington, to gain the protection of her stepfather. I took her advice and sent men to patrol the northern roads."

"You trust a woman's judgment more than your own?" A muscle flexed dangerously along the taut line of Kenric's jaw.

"The advice made sense."

"You will order those soldiers to continue searching the villages." Kenric gritted his teeth, realizing that the man he'd left in charge of his army was taking orders from his wife. "The bailiff has not set foot from Montague lands in his lifetime. He will not flee them now, but will seek refuge in familiar territory."

"Aye, milord."

"Why didn't someone come forward sooner with this news?" Kenric asked, determined to get to the bottom of this treachery.

"Lady Tess wondered the same," Simon answered, frowning when that remark earned him another glare. "Each person she asked about the stores told her that she must speak with the bailiff. Rather than go to the person who was assuring everyone that there wasn't a problem, Lady Tess approached your steward. He admitted the extent of the situation then told her that many had brought their concerns to the bailiff but they were told to keep silent, that you were aware of the situation but could not be convinced to order the provender from your holdings. The bailiff also said that you promised to punish anyone who mentioned the matter again before springtime. Lady Tess learned from the steward that your fiefs are rich in grain and cattle because the provender they owe you each year had not been collected for three. The vassal in charge of collections died shortly after the old baron, and the bailiff never appointed another. The steward was powerless to make the requisitions himself, though he was certain you would put a blade to his throat either way. He put himself at your lady's mercy and she promised he would be spared retribution in exchange for his help collecting the provender. Your lady handled the situation cleverly, milord. Rather than alert anyone to the dire situation and risk more treachery, she issued orders to each of your holdings, demanding a tenth of their winter stores to replenish Montague's supplies. She made sure all thought it was her own greed behind the orders, that she was anxious to collect the coins the supplies would fetch at market. That was the reason Derry Town refused her request and she ordered their tithing barn torched to gain their cooperation. Derry Town built a new tithing barn last year and the old one was empty and near collapsing with age, but well able to provide a most spectacular tale of your lady's ruthlessness to be carried to your other holdings. The example was all that was needed and Montague's stores were quickly replenished."

"What is the situation now?" Kenric suddenly wished he'd never asked for an explanation of his wife's activities, and longed for the battlefield where none could ever accuse him of neglect. *I would hear some word of praise* . . . Tess's words came back to haunt him. She was right. He'd neglected his duty to Montague, ignored it completely. He'd allowed his hatred of the place to cloud his judgment, to miss warning signs that she'd seen clearly. And he'd punished her for it.

"The storehouses are restocked, milord. There is more than enough food and grain to last until summer and the first harvest."

"What about you, Simon? Do you have an excuse for withholding this news from me until now?"

Simon stared guiltily at the floor. "I was certain my first message would bring you home, milord. Lady Tess already had the situation in hand before a second message could have reached you at Penhaligon, and I knew it would not bring you home any faster. If such a message fell into the wrong hands, it would have meant—"

"You report to me, not my wife! I don't care if the message reached me a stone's throw from Montague's walls. You will never again keep me ignorant of what I should be the first to know!"

"Aye, Baron," Simon murmured, bowing his apology. "I made a mistake."

"See that you make no more." Kenric dismissed the soldier with a curt wave. "Get to your post at my lady's door before I decide to give you the punishment you deserve."

Simon bowed again then made a hasty exit, not waiting to be told twice.

"Christ!" Fitz Alan swore, settling onto his stool again. He grabbed his mug of ale so abruptly that it sloshed over the rim, spilling onto his leather tunic. He brushed at the damp spot with the billowy sleeve of his shirt. *"Damn."*

"A colorful vocabulary," Kenric remarked, refilling his own mug.

Fitz Alan ignored the jibe. "Had your vassals to the north learned the truth behind your lady's 'greed,' that Montague was in fact on the brink of starvation, they would have descended like a cloud of locusts. Especially since most knew you were a good week's journey away at Penhaligon. The fortress would have fallen."

"Aye," Kenric agreed tautly. "But I would have retaken the castle just as quickly."

"Anyone who took the castle would have found themselves short of supplies as well," Fitz Alan reasoned.

"They would have found themselves dead."

Aye, killing is what you're best at . . . Kenric scowled and pushed away the memory of his wife's taunt, drowning her words by washing down the entire mug of ale.

Fitz Alan's gaze grew speculative as he eyed the empty mug. "Your wife—"

The blast of the baron's icy gaze cut the sentence short.

"You punished her before you knew about the bailiff," Fitz Alan deduced, his expression sympathetic.

"Whatever good came of Tess's meddling matters little," Kenric snapped, growing angrier. He'd come here to take his mind off his wife, but so far she'd been the only topic of conversation. "She placed herself and others in danger by—" Kenric stopped abruptly, his grip tightening on his mug as he glared at Fitz Alan. "You think to question the methods I use to discipline my wife?"

"Nay, of course not, milord. She is like to forgive you in time."

"Forgive me?" Kenric slammed his mug down on the table. "What the hell must I be forgiven for? She should have sent for me the moment she discovered the bailiff's treachery. Tess shouldn't have meddled in things that were none of her business. She defied me and she knows it."

Fitz Alan wisely said nothing. They each consumed two more mugs of ale in silence.

"Have you ever had to discipline a female?" Kenric asked, staring into his mug to avoid Fitz Alan's gaze.

"Once. I caught a wench trying to steal my purse and beat her soundly for the offense." Fitz Alan shrugged. "She got off lightly. The sheriff in that shire would have hung her for the crime."

" 'Tis not the same," Kenric decided, draining the contents of his mug once more. His hand was amazingly steady as he poured yet another drink. "A wife is a different matter entirely."

"Did you beat her?" Fitz Alan asked bluntly.

"Think you I would make myself so like the MacLeiths in her eyes?" Kenric made a sound of disgust deep in his throat. "Believe me, she did not suffer long."

Fitz Alan nodded but continued to look at him expectantly, no doubt waiting to hear what manner of punishment he'd used. Kenric sighed in defeat.

"I merely bedded her, if you must know." Kenric ignored the fact that Fitz Alan hadn't actually asked the question. "Not that it is any of your business."

Fitz Alan surprised him with a snort of laughter but quickly hid his expression behind his mug.

"You find some humor in this?" Kenric asked, a dangerous gleam in his eye.

"Aye, milord," Fitz Alan said recklessly. "I am picturing your lady trembling in her slippers when she heard those dire consequences."

"She also heard that I am a bastard."

That news wiped the humor from Fitz Alan's expression. He set his mug on the table and waited in silence for the explanation.

"I found her in Helen's chamber, my sister regaling her with the details of my parentage, along with the reason I am called Butcher."

"How did she take the news?" Fitz Alan asked hesitantly.

"I disgust her. She tried to refuse me."

Fitz Alan looked thoughtful for a moment. "Most likely she tried to refuse you because her pride was involved. She was likely disappointed over your failure to appreciate her efforts."

I would hear some word of praise . . . How many women have you raped, milord? Kenric scowled, wondering how many more mugs of ale it would take to silence the voice in his head.

"Nay, she hates me," he said surely.

"You should try seducing your wife rather than ordering her to your bed," Fitz Alan suggested, with a lewd wink.

"Take care, my friend. I am in no mood for teasing this eve." Kenric lifted his mug and gave Fitz Alan a dark frown over the rim, but the other man shrugged the threat aside.

"Perhaps you need a distraction to take your mind off the troubles with your wife. There are many pleasing wenches at Montague who would willingly share their favors."

"I do not want a wench," Kenric muttered, downing the contents of his mug. He reached out for the jug of ale and poured another round. "I want at least one more pitcher of this ale and to sleep undisturbed until morn."

Fitz Alan nodded sympathetically then continued to get drunk with his overlord.

Tess awoke hours later when the sturdy oak door to her room was thrown open with a resounding crack against the wall, followed by a loud, *"Shhhh!"*

She bolted upright in bed, clutching the blankets to her chest as she peered toward the doorway, shadowed now in the dying firelight.

"You'f waken her, you clumsy oaf!"

Tess recognized the sound of Kenric's voice, and gathered the covers closer when she realized her husband was not alone.

"My deepess apologies, Lady Tess."

Fitz Alan moved close enough to the fireplace for Tess to make out his identity. He made the mistake of trying to give her a courtly bow, forgetting that much of Kenric's weight rested on the arm draped across his shoulders. Thrown off balance by the sudden move, both men tumbled to the floor amidst great shouts.

Tess flew from the bed to Kenric's side, certain one of them had to be injured by the fall. "Milord, you are too close to the hearth!"

Both men were laughing like naughty boys by this time, but Kenric struggled to sit up first. The sight of Tess, clad only in her chemise, wiped the smile from his face. He clapped a hand over her eyes and yelled over one shoulder.

"Cover your eyes, Fitz Alan!"

"Milord," Tess sighed, tugging at Kenric's hand. "You have covered the wrong eyes."

Kenric lowered his hand slightly. He peered into Tess's face to confirm the fact then swung an arm around to cover Fitz Alan's eyes. His fist caught Fitz Alan in the chest, knocking the man back to the floor.

"You should be in bed," he accused, forgetting Fitz Alan.

"I was. Perhaps that would be a good place for you too, milord." Tess eyed the fireplace nervously, aware that both men were well in their cups. She waved her hand in front of her face. "You both smell as if you've bathed in ale."

"Is that insolence, wife?" The potent fumes of Kenric's breath nearly knocked Tess over. "I'll not tolerate such."

She gave him her most innocent gaze, knowing there was no use arguing with a besotted man. "Why, no, milord. I would never be so disrespectful to my husband."

"You lie," Kenric accused halfheartedly, struggling to his feet. He pointed toward the bed, his arm swaying slightly in the air. "You are near naked, lady. Get into bed before my man sees you."

"I do not think he will see anything for some time," she countered, nodding at the floor. Kenric's gaze followed and locked unsteadily on Fitz Alan. The sound of steady snoring confirmed the man was out cold.

"You cannot sleep here," he bellowed, using one foot to prod Fitz Alan's ribs. "Get up, man."

"He will rest fine there," she said firmly, tugging on Kenric's arm. This was just what she needed, a belligerent drunk. At least Fitz Alan had had the courtesy to pass out. Wary of turning a quarrelsome drunk into an ugly one, she used her most coaxing tone. "Why don't we all get some rest? 'Tis been a long day, milord."

"Cease this 'milord,' nonsense." He swatted Tess's hands away, then shook one long finger dangerously close to her nose. "I prefer to hear my given name on your lips."

" 'Tis time for bed," Tess amended, refusing to speak his name. She was convinced that he would sleep as soundly as Fitz Alan the moment his head touched the pillow. Then she could slip away and find a bed that didn't reek of an ale keg.

Tess crawled into bed, expecting he would soon follow, but the chore of undressing was taking him longer than usual. The task could be accomplished much quicker if he took one leg completely from his breeches before attempting to remove the other. Tess smothered a startled giggle behind her hand. His clumsy efforts were vaguely similar to those of the dancing bear she saw last year at the spring fair.

"In future, I would rather you hold your laughter while I disrobe." Kenric gave her an intimidating scowl then climbed into bed. He propped his head on one elbow and grinned lopsidedly, his mood suddenly playful. "You think me drunk?"

She lifted one brow in challenge. "I know you are."

He slipped his arm beneath her and pulled her closer to rest her head on his shoulder. "Good. That was my intent."

Tess stiffened, thankful that her body wasn't having its usual traitorous response to his nearness. The fumes that seemed to encase him kept her from any baser thoughts. "What was your intent?"

"To get drunk." He tucked her head beneath his chin and sighed. " 'Tis your fault, wife. You are driving me mad."

There was some justice to this day at last, Tess thought. She would have told him he deserved all the trouble she was going to give him, but Kenric was sleeping already. Thinking she'd give him another few minutes to fall deeper asleep before she crept out of the room, she settled her head on his shoulder again and closed her eyes. She had to escape Montague. Soon.

14

The bright shaft of sunlight moved steadily across the room until it reached the bed. Kenric rolled away from the light, trapping Tess beneath his great weight. She'd been having a pleasant dream, a dream about swimming in a pond warmed by the summer sun. The dream turned menacing as her legs tangled in unseen weeds beneath the dark waters and she was dragged so deep below the surface that her lungs felt ready to burst. She fought against the long tendrils that snaked around her like steel bands, her struggles only encasing her more firmly in their deathly grip.

"Be still!"

The words whispered harshly in her ear made her struggle harder. With her arms and legs pinned uselessly, her mouth was the only means of freeing herself. She sank her teeth into something that didn't feel at all like pond weeds.

"*Ouch!*"

Her eyes flew open at last. She gave a small, startled shriek at the sight of Kenric looming above her, his expression far from pleasant as he rubbed a suspicious-looking mark on his shoulder. He glared down at her accusingly.

It took but a moment for Tess to realize what had happened. She blushed furiously.

That show of embarrassment didn't seem to do anything to ease Kenric's temper. His red-rimmed eyes narrowed dangerously.

"You flatter yourself, Tess. I am in no mood for you this morn."

The faint scent of stale ale drifted across her senses and Tess wrinkled her nose as she sat up. Misinterpreting her expression, his scowl darkened. "I can see you are in no mood for me, either."

"My head." Fitz Alan sat on the floor with his elbows resting on bent knees, one hand massaging his skull.

Kenric pulled the covers to Tess's shoulders, then sat up to glare at the interruption.

Tess tucked the covers under her arms and looked from Fitz Alan's slightly greenish complexion to Kenric's healthy one, amazed that one could look so much worse than the other. Spitefully, she hoped Kenric felt as bad as Fitz Alan looked.

"Good *morn*, Fiz Alan," she called out sarcastically.

Fitz Alan winced, as if she'd shouted the greeting. His head came up slowly, his gaze moving to her husband's black scowl. "I do not think it will be so, milady. The day does not look so good from here."

Tess agreed completely. She risked a glance at Kenric and found him gazing steadily at her, the look in his eyes saying they had unfinished business to attend to. She had no wish to find out what it might be. Cursing herself for falling asleep when she could have slipped away the night before, she tucked the covers more firmly beneath her arms. The chemise she wore was nearly transparent.

"A dutiful wife would have a hearty breakfast awaiting her husband," Kenric goaded, his eyes never leaving her.

"A dutiful husband would not drink himself into a stupor." Tess bit her tongue. A man suffering from the effects of ale was not one to bait.

"I would have performed my husbandly duty willingly last eve, had I known you would be so snappish for lack of my attention. Was the attention I gave you earlier in the evening not enough to keep you sated?"

Noting the dangerous undercurrents in his eyes, she decided not to provoke him with her opinion or an answer. "You seem much healthier this morn than your man."

Kenric shrugged. "Ale does not affect me."

Tess snorted as she recalled his antics of the night past. Finding difficulty undressing was hardly what she would call unaffected.

"He's better than I at hiding it," Fitz Alan muttered, rising unsteadily.

"Are you still here?" Kenric drawled, his eyes still locked on his wife's.

"I am trying, milord." Fitz Alan leaned against the mantel. "I must beg your indulgence a moment."

Kenric sighed and leaned back on one elbow. Tess tried to scoot away from him but he caught the end of her braid with one hand, trapping her. When she turned to glare at him, he brushed the silky tassel back and forth against his chin.

"My apologies, Lady Tess," Fitz Alan said with a slight nod. He turned and tried to walk straight to the door, but had to stop several times to place a steadying hand against the wall.

When the door closed behind him, Tess waited in tense silence for Kenric to release her. Holding her braid in one hand, he scratched his chest with the other, yawning lazily. "I think I shall want a bath after my breakfast."

Tess's urge to flee was so instinctive that she forgot about his hold on her braid. She lurched forward, only to land on her back against the pillows. She'd reached the end of her rope of hair rather abruptly.

"Tired again so soon?" He shook his head, the sarcastic tone belying his considerate words. "I will send one of your guards to the kitchens to fetch my breakfast and have them order my bath made ready. You, my poor exhausted wife, may rest here until I require your assistance at my bath."

He walked to the door and gave his orders, with no care for his nakedness. Tess threw the covers over her head and hid beneath them, wishing she could turn into a snake and slither away.

A few hushed footsteps and the sound of water being poured into the tub were the only indications that the servants had arrived. After she was sure they had left, she waited to hear Kenric lower himself into the water, hoping beyond hope that he would think her asleep and leave her be. He removed the covers with one quick jerk.

Kenric gazed down at his wife with a grim expression. Her face was buried in the pillows, her arms and legs curled protectively to her body. Not exactly the picture of a wife willing to do her husband's bidding. Any lingering guilt he felt over Simon's explanation was dispelled by his wife's reluctance. Before leaving for Penhaligon, she assisted him willingly with his baths, indeed, most eagerly. It had become something he looked forward to at the end of each day, yet she would take away that small pleasure as well.

" 'Tis time for my bath."

Tess slid from the bed, her gaze lingering wistfully on the door.

"You would not make it," he warned, reading her

thoughts. "Do not think my lack of clothing will stop me from going after you."

Tess nodded and walked toward the tub, her head bowed as she waited for him.

Kenric lowered himself slowly into the steaming water, certain every muscle in his body ached. At the moment, he was pleased by the state of his health. He knew from experience that too much ale the night before would render him incapable of responding to any woman, even his wife.

Ducking beneath the water to drench his head, Kenric fought down a wave of dizziness, determined to hide how ill he felt. He was about to teach the little witch another lesson. He knew that she liked to touch him. He'd watched her expression often enough when she ran her hands across his body. She'd wanted him in her bed readily enough before learning the truth of his parentage. By the time this bath was finished, she would want him again.

Kenric imagined her expression when Tess realized he wouldn't ease her need. Then she would learn exactly how it felt to be unwanted. This one small lesson would give her but a taste of what he'd experienced all his life. He sucked in his breath with a long hiss. She was scrubbing his back with hellish efficiency.

"Sheathe your claws!"

Tess obliged and he leaned forward with his elbows on his knees, cupping his hands to scoop water up and over his head to wash away the soap. He wasn't entirely sure he'd make it back up if he submerged his head again. The pressure of one hand against his shoulder made him lean forward more so she could reach his lower back. His stomach protested violently. He'd wolfed down half a loaf of buttered bread and a mug of cider while waiting for his bath to be filled. Now he was regretting every mouthful.

Kenric concentrated on deep breaths while Tess bathed his arms, though he didn't need the kind of self-control that he usually did in his wife's presence. He suspected she'd draw ale rather than blood if she succeeded in slicing him open with those sharp nails of hers.

"Stop scratching me," he snapped, swallowing down the effort of that statement. "I am not a horse who needs be curried down."

Tess rinsed his arms with more soothing motions then moved around the tub to begin on his chest. She kept her head bowed, but he noticed the way she worried at her lower lip with her teeth. Good, he thought, realizing she was beginning to be affected. It wouldn't be long and he would have her where he wanted. He noticed her expression soften when she laid her hands against his chest and he managed an inward smile that lasted all of one second.

Panicking, Kenric grabbed her hands when they slid toward his stomach. Tess started at the quick movement but didn't flinch, her gaze uncertain. The moment he released her hands she made a grab for an empty water bucket, handing it over just in time.

The sounds of her husband's retching was gratifying. He'd earned every moment of the misery. Tess frowned, hurrying to the table to pour a mug of cider left over from his breakfast. She picked up a linen cloth and walked back to the tub to wait.

When he finally finished, he set the bucket on the floor and leaned back against the tub, his eyes closed, his face a deathly shade of gray. Holding the bucket as far away as possible, Tess carried it to the door and handed it over to one of the unfortunate guards. Returning to the tub, she dipped the cloth in a bucket of fresh water and gently sponged his face.

"Would you like a drink of cider?" she asked, holding up the mug. Kenric nodded but didn't lift his head or open his eyes. She lifted the rim to his lips, cradling the back of his head with her arm as he drank little more than a mouthful.

Kenric thanked her in a hoarse voice. Tess chewed on

her lip, trying to decide the best way to get him back into bed. Even if he brought this illness on himself, it wasn't in her nature to ignore anyone this sick. She wondered fleetingly how Fitz Alan fared then decided that was someone else's problem. This one was bound to keep her hands full most of the day.

"Can you make it to the bed?"

He opened one bloodshot eye, looking suspicious of the offer. "Not yet."

Tess wondered what she should do now. Scooping the water from the tub so he wouldn't drown was probably a safe bet, but then he might take a chill. That she didn't need. Instead she took the mug of cider to the table and dumped all but a small amount back into the pitcher. Rummaging through her trunk, she found the packets of powdered herbs she needed and pinched a few of each into the mug, stirring the mixture until most of the specks dissolved.

"Drink this," she ordered, holding the mug to Kenric's lips again.

"Poison?"

"The cure for it." She poured the tonic into his mouth. He gagged twice but managed to keep it down.

" 'Tis awful!"

"Aye." She was glad to see his eyes open again, even if he was glaring at her. The effect was greatly diminished by eyes that were watery, red-rimmed, and bloodshot. She set the mug aside and picked up a linen towel. "You'll catch a chill if you sit in that water much longer. Surely a warm bed sounds more appealing?"

"The only thing appealing at the moment is a quick death."

Ignoring his complaints, she dried his head and shoulders, hoping to give him the time he needed to gather his strength. When he rose on unsteady legs and climbed from the tub, she finished drying him then took his elbow to lead him to the bed. Kenric pulled his arm away unsteadily.

"I am not an invalid," he said between clenched teeth, even as he swayed on his feet. "I can make it to my bed without your help."

Tess kept her mouth shut, deciding that pride and a sore head made men stupid beyond telling. When he was finally in the bed, she began picking up the clothes he'd discarded the night before.

"You will feel better soon. A few more hours of rest will see you healthy again." She glanced over her shoulder to see his response but realized he was asleep already. His face was still pale and there were dark circles under his eyes, but he looked more comfortable in bed than he did in the tub. Perhaps he would appreciate her assistance.

Tess rolled her eyes, thinking herself gullible beyond compare that she considered receiving gratitude from the Butcher. Doubtless he would find some way to blame her for this illness, accuse her of serving poisoned ale or some such nonsense. He was bound to be foul tempered for the entire day. She should go about her business and leave him here to suffer alone. Tess looked longingly at the door then at Kenric. The door looked much more appealing. Still, he might become ill again. If she wasn't here to hold a bucket, he might very well be sick all over the bed or the carpet. Tess shuddered over the mental image of that mess, deciding she'd better stay.

After straightening the room, she found one of her gowns with a loose hem that needed repair. The dress was her ugliest and Tess had been putting the task off for some time, not really eager to mend a gown that looked more like a patchwork puzzle. It was actually a combination of several dresses that Mag had cleverly sewed into one. The bodice came from a saffron-colored gown, the skirt was made from strips of a pumpkin-colored gown and a forest-green one, both of which she'd outgrown years ago. Mag called the result "festive." Compared to any one of

Helen's, it was comical. Still, it was one of precious few dresses and she'd learned to make do. Two hours later, the torn hem and other small tears were nearly repaired when Kenric began to stir, with a long, low groan.

"Are you going to be sick again?"

"Nay." He sounded tired, but his eyes weren't so badly bloodshot anymore as he looked her over, his gaze coming to rest on the dress spread across her lap. "You have godawful taste in clothing, wife. That gown nearly hurts my eyes."

Tess pressed her lips together in a tight line, refusing to respond to the insult, wishing she had left him the moment he started retching. Ungrateful cur.

Kenric closed his eyes again and took several deep breaths, testing the state of his stomach. Queasy but controllable, he decided as he sat up. The dizziness wasn't so bad but it was still annoying. A bad brew, he decided, conveniently forgetting the number of pitchers he and Fitz Alan shared. His gaze moved to Tess, still seated by the bed, and he eyed her speculatively. If learning he was a bastard hadn't disgusted her completely, this surely had. So much for teaching her a lesson.

"I would have thought you long gone by now. You stayed to watch me sleep?"

"I thought you might become ill again."

"Ah, you were hoping for more entertainment." Kenric missed her disgusted scowl. "What was in the tonic you gave me?"

"Chamomile, mint, and several other herbs meant to calm your stomach and ease the ache in your head."

Kenric realized his headache had indeed disappeared. Even his stomach was beginning to feel better. Sore, but better. "Why?"

Tess looked up at the ceiling, as if at the end of her patience. "I daresay because you drank enough ale to souse half an army."

"Nay, I meant why would you give me the potion? It

must have pleased you to see me suffering. Why would you do anything to ease my pains?"

"It does not please me to see anyone suffer, though you and Fitz Alan surely earned your sore heads. The two of you could scarce stand up last night. In fact, you both landed in a heap by the fireplace. I would have left you there, had I not worried your hair would catch fire."

"I did nothing of the sort." Kenric's brows drew together in a puzzled frown.

Tess smiled. "Then you do not remember apologizing to me?"

"For what?" Kenric was appalled by the possibility. The question sparked a memory of Fitz Alan asking something along the same lines the night before. He ran a hand through his hair, silently cursing the ale, all men who brewed it, and most especially, their ancestors.

"Why, for failing to appreciate everything I did in your absence."

Kenric eyed the hand that was busy twisting her braid and his mouth drew to a grim line. "You are a poor liar, wife."

Tess sighed in defeat. "I know."

"Now that you have brought up the subject, I might as well tell you that I have learned more since we last spoke. Simon sought me out last night, determined that I know the full extent of your meddling with the bailiff." Kenric tossed back the covers and rose carefully from the bed to get dressed. "I told him, and I will tell you. If ever you encounter a situation that serious, I will be the first to be notified. Through luck alone, a tragedy was avoided at Montague."

Kenric looked up from the laces he'd been tying when he heard Tess's snort of disagreement; yet she sat quietly with her head bowed.

"If you thought I would be pleased to learn the full story, you were wrong," he continued, donning a clean linen shirt. He refused to give her the satisfaction of knowing he was secretly pleased she had so skillfully averted a disaster. "You took foolish risks and involved yourself in concerns that were none of your business. In future you will confine yourself to the duties required of you by this household and your husband. Is everything I have told you clear in your mind, Tess? Do you understand exactly what I require of you, and what I will not tolerate?"

"Aye, but there is one more thing I should warn you of," she began hesitantly, bowing her head again. "I asked Cook to prepare a feast the day after your return. He was instructed to have everything ready by midday. I realize you will not feel like celebrating today, yet the food is surely near ready and will only go to waste if you do not put in an appearance in the hall and encourage your men to enjoy the festivities."

Kenric sighed his relief, realizing he'd been prepared for far worse news. He was actually starting to feel hungry again. Whatever Tess put in her tonic was effective.

"My men are doubtless ready to celebrate the fact that their lord has returned and put an end to his wife's reign of terror. I am not such a weakling that I will fail to attend a feast in my honor. Come, wife. We will go down together."

Kenric held out his hand, but as she walked toward him, he held it up to stop her. "Before joining me in the great hall, you will go to my sister's chamber and request her presence at this feast as well. You may tell her that I have a few words for her that will be best spoken in the company of others, where I will not be tempted to give her the beating she deserves."

Tess swallowed nervously, then nodded.

15

The sight that met Kenric in the great hall soured his mood. The meal was already in progress, though the servants should not have placed food on the tables until the lord and lady were present. Several of his men called out their greeting even as they tossed greasy bones and scraps over their shoulders. Kenric hadn't thought it possible, but the food actually looked worse than it did before he left for Penhaligon.

His men were testing him, appearing very certain their leader would not support his wife's new rules. If the food was any indication, the kitchen staff was also looking to find their limits with the new lord. He had no doubt that one and all knew the reason for his early return and of his anger with Tess. Very little to do with the lord and lady of a castle escaped notice. Now all of Montague waited to see how the wind blew.

If Tess saw this mess, Kenric was certain she would lay the blame at his feet. She'd doubtless hurl another insult about duty and neglect in his face. Frowning over that thought, Kenric motioned Evard forward with a crook of his finger. "Tell Cook I wish to see him immediately."

Cook appeared and hurried forward to stand before the baron, looking around nervously as he came to a halt. The noise in the hall disappeared as each man strained to listen to the conversation, their curiosity evident in their expressions.

"Remove your shoes." Kenric's voice was deceptively calm. When the cook complied, Kenric removed a small dagger from his belt and began toying with the weapon, flipping it over and over in one hand. "I see your toes remain in their proper numbers."

Cook swayed. "Aye, milord."

Kenric's gaze came to rest on a platter of food so congealed with grease as to be unrecognizable. "I suggest that will not be the case when my wife discovers you have served my men pig swill."

"A-aye, milord."

"Being a fair man, I would give you and your staff a choice," Kenric drawled, turning the point of the dagger into one of the table's knotholes.

"A choice, milord?"

"Of which toes to remove."

Cook's face drained of color.

"On the other hand, my lady has been delayed for a short time." Kenric tapped the point of his dagger against his lips, as if pondering a weighty decision. "Your staff may yet be able to clear away this mess before she arrives."

Cook nearly stumbled to his knees, whispering his gratitude in a hoarse voice as he bowed low to his lord. "It shall be done, milord. The dishes Baroness Montague requested for your arrival are near ready."

Cook looked ready to offer an excuse for the slops on the table, then seemed to decide against the idea. Kenric waved his dismissal, waiting until Cook was nearly out of the hall before halting the man's flight with another disturbing question.

"Did you agree to prepare this feast my wife ordered?"

"Ah . . . Aye, milord."

"Then you would be well advised that my wife's punishments are those devised by a gently bred lady. I cut out the tongues of liars so they will lie no more. You have half an hour to keep your promise."

Cook's mouth dropped open but snapped shut a moment later, as if to protect his tongue behind his teeth. Kenric turned then to address his men.

"Each of you would do well to heed my advice to Cook," he said, looking pointedly at several piles of bones. The men dropped their food almost in unison, scrambling to retrieve their garbage from the floor. He crooked his finger at Evard.

"Find and delay my lady for at least half of an hour."

"What shall I tell her?" Evard asked.

"That is your problem," Kenric snapped.

"Aye, milord," Evard groaned, bowing to Kenric before hurrying away.

The allotted time had nearly passed when Tess entered the hall, a pale-faced Helen to her right, a red-faced Evard to her left. Simon trailed behind the trio, his grin stretched from ear to ear.

"Are you sure you are feeling better?" she asked Evard. "You still appear quite flushed."

"I am fine, milady." Evard's answer was terse, his lips tightly compressed.

"What's this about not feeling well?" Kenric gave Tess a barely civil nod of greeting and had her seated before returning his attention to Evard. "Evard, you have not answered my question."

"He fainted!" Simon coughed loudly to cover his laughter.

"How unfortunate." Kenric gave Evard a sympathetic look. "But you are feeling better now?"

"I am in perfect health," Evard said through clenched teeth, his glare directed at Simon. He gave Kenric a stilted bow then walked stiffly to his seat.

Simon claimed a stool next to Evard, whistling a tuneless ditty. Fitz Alan's chair remained conspicuously empty.

Cook entered the hall leading a parade of kitchen servants, each bearing steaming dishes, platters, or bowls. Tess worked hard to contain the urge to clap her hands in delight. She had suspected Cook was talented, but the food laid before them surpassed her expectations. A platter of fowl nestled in a delicate cream sauce was followed by glazed beets, roasted corn, spiced apples, and thick slabs of roast beef. Two servants placed a table in the center of the hall, then six servants came in bearing an entire roast pig.

The squires entered the hall next, each dressed in their finest garments, most recently repaired or stitched by Lady Helen's seamstresses. The young men waited until Thomas filled a trencher for Kenric and Tess before they began filling trenchers for the knights they served.

Kenric carved a portion of roast beef and gallantly offered the choice morsel to his lady. Tess's eyes sparkled with suspicion, but she accepted the offering graciously.

"Did you think I lacked courtly manners?" he asked sardonically. "Even bastards can be taught to dine with kings."

Tess's pleasure over the meal evaporated. She leaned forward so none other would overhear her remark. "As you are a king's bastard, that hardly seems surprising."

They glared at each other until Fitz Alan settled onto the stool next to Kenric, murmuring an excuse for his tardiness.

"My apologies, Baron. I was delayed by an unavoidable . . . inconvenience." Fitz Alan gave the food a dubious glance while one of the squires hurried forward to fill his trencher with the hearty fare and his goblet with wine. Fitz Alan stared at the goblet as if it contained a serpent.

"My wife is possessed of a potion that will cure what ails you," Kenric told him. Fitz Alan looked hopeful over the possibility. "See that you take it after this meal has ended. You have duties today that do not involve chamber pots."

"Aye, milord," Fitz Alan murmured, continuing to stare dolefully at the food.

Kenric turned his attention to his sister. "Helen, you will stand before me."

Helen kept her gaze lowered as she walked around the tables to stand before her brother.

" 'Tis obvious that you have been too long without a firm hand to guide you," Kenric began. "You were given plenty of time to prove your worth to Montague and to your overlord, yet I see little evidence that Montague would suffer for lack of your presence. I have no use for worthless females."

Helen's eyes grew round with fright and she shook her head.

"There are two solutions to this problem," he continued. "The promise of your dowry is enough to convince a man to find some use for you. In fact, my vassal, Roger Fitz Alan, is well known for his ability to deal with stubborn, troublesome women."

Fitz Alan choked on the sip of wine he'd finally steeled himself to taste. Simon pounded his back sympathetically. Helen's horrified gaze locked on Fitz Alan, eyeing him as if he'd turned into a repulsive toad. Kenric smiled. Fitz Alan was also a bastard, and Kenric knew his sister was aware of the fact. He recalled her every word about evil seeds and stained souls, hoping Helen's memory was just as sound. It was the perfect punishment.

"The other solution?" she whispered, her terrorized gaze returning to Kenric.

"You have managed Montague's household for many

years. You are familiar with the duties required by the mistress of this place, yet my wife seems to have little knowledge of which duties belong to the chatelaine and which ones belong to her overlord. Your other choice is to make yourself useful to my wife. You will work alongside her to teach the duties of this place, accepting whatever tasks she would give you."

"I will do whatever Lady Tess requires of me," Helen said quickly.

"Know that you will have but one choice remaining if you fail in these duties." Kenric turned to Fitz Alan. "You will court my sister until she has proven herself more useful to my wife than she has been to me. You may yet find her your bride."

Fitz Alan simply nodded, looking beyond words.

Kenric dismissed Helen with a slight movement of his hand. "You may retire to your chamber until tomorrow morning to consider your new duties."

Helen stood motionless for a moment, then she picked up her skirts and walked slowly from the hall, her chin held at a tight, regal angle.

Tess's sympathy went out to her. Kenric had humiliated his sister as thoroughly as he'd just humiliated his wife. She pushed her trencher away, her appetite gone.

"If you have finished your meal, you may be excused to go mix a potion for Fitz Alan," Kenric told her. " 'Tis doubtful his taste for food will return anytime soon without it."

Tess left the great hall gladly, Fitz Alan trailing behind. Heartless, muleheaded, arrogant, insulting. She listed off her complaints silently as they made their way to her chamber, vowing to remain just as silent in her husband's presence from this moment on. The churl deserved it. Aye, she would never speak to him again.

Fitz Alan followed her into the bedchamber but stayed her action when she would have closed the door behind them, pushing the door wide open. "I would not have your husband suspect anything needed hiding behind this door, should he decide to join us."

Tess shrugged. She didn't care what Kenric's thoughts were one way or another. Rummaging through her trunk, she found the herbs and spread them on the table. A small caldron hung from a spit over the fireplace and she filled the pot with water. After sprinkling the herbs in the water, she used a poker to push the caldron over the flames.

"The potion works best when warmed," she told him, turning from the fire. "Though it wouldn't be needed at all if some men knew how to curb their thirst."

Fitz Alan clasped his hands behind his back and stared at the floor. " 'Tis rare I have need of an ale cure. The baron does not approve of those who overindulge."

"I should never have guessed."

"Well, I suppose it does not exactly appear that way after last night," he conceded. "In truth, I have never seen your husband consume so much drink in one sitting."

"I daresay you felt obliged to match his amazing pace?"

"Aye, Lady. I had no great desire to keep his company sober." Fitz Alan's grin was disarming but his gaze turned speculative. "Not after Simon related the events that took place in our absence."

Tess began packing away the herbs, hoping Fitz Alan wouldn't notice her sudden tenseness. "I take it he was furious?"

"He seemed more concerned with something else he heard that day. More precisely, your reaction to it."

"Kenric heard many things yesterday that he had little liking for," Tess replied over one shoulder. "Do be more specific, sir."

"He seemed concerned by what Helen told you."

Tess shrugged. "If you think to deny the truth, do not bother. He as much as admitted his unspeakable crimes."

"Crimes?" Fitz Alan echoed.

"I know he murdered innocent women and children in Wales."

"As did I," he admitted, shaking his head. "Yet they were not the innocents Helen would doubtless have you believe."

Tess's eyes narrowed. "What do you mean?"

"There was not a child less than fourteen years in that pack of heathens and they did their own fair share of slaughtering before Kenric put an end to their savagery. That there were three women in that group as bloodthirsty as any man I've met was not your husband's doing. They decided to kill or be killed and paid the price of their decision. When word spread that women had been slain, the full story behind the deed did not spread with it." Fitz Alan's slight frown was as admonishing as any of Kenric's scowls. "That is what I mean, Lady."

"I see." Tess's relief was tempered with caution. "Your explanation does not change the fact that Kenric will slaughter my loyal retainers along with MacLeith's men when you lay siege to Remmington."

It was almost a question, though she knew Fitz Alan couldn't give her the answer she wanted. He shrugged again, without apology. " 'Tis a fact of war. The innocent perish with the guilty. You should take comfort from the fact that your husband will restore your lands."

"I should take comfort, *knowing* Remmington lands will run red with the blood of my people?" Tess shook her head, feeling secure again in her decisions. "I know too well what happens when an army lays siege. Those within the keeps and fortresses will be slowly starved until they are forced to fight or die. With Kenric's army outside the walls, they will die anyway. My vassals and retainers will have MacLeith swords at their backs, and Kenric's swords at their throats. They will be the first to die."

Fitz Alan remained silent, unable to deny what he had doubtless witnessed times beyond counting. Tess knew she was not far wrong in her summation. That Remmington was Kenric's by law would only make the warlord more ruthless in his methods.

Steam drifted from the small pot over the fireplace and Tess pulled the caldron from the fire. She used her skirt to protect her hands as she poured the mixture into the mug Fitz Alan held.

" 'Tis hot," she warned, as he sniffed the brew with a wrinkled nose.

"You have said naught about the other things Lady Helen told you," Fitz Alan murmured, blowing lightly across the top of his potion. "Most ladies would be aggrieved to learn their husband was not the result of a marriage."

Tess supposed that was Fitz Alan's delicate way of avoiding the word "bastard." He seemed the only one at Montague with any such aversion this past day. " 'Tis of little consequence. Why should that fact change my opinion of Kenric at this late date?"

"Why, indeed?" he said, smiling again. His smile dimmed as he sniffed the potion again, looking tempted to hold his nose as he swallowed the foul brew. His complexion took a turn for the worse as he handed back the empty mug. "God, 'tis awful!"

"Your lord's opinion exactly." Tess smiled, thinking both men would likely gag if they learned the true contents of the mixture. Her smile faded at the sound of a commotion in the hallway. Kenric appeared in the doorway, Simon and Evard close behind. He eyed the open door then gave Fitz Alan a pointed look, nodding approvingly.

"I thought you might join us," Fitz Alan said with a shrug.

"It took you half of an hour to drink a damned potion?" Kenric demanded. Even knowing the state of Fitz Alan's health, he'd started to rethink the order that sent him off alone with Tess to a room that conveniently contained a bed. Fitz Alan had been known to take advantage of a lady in much more precarious situations.

"Lady Tess said the potion must be warmed first," Fitz Alan explained.

Kenric gave Tess an accusing look. "You did not warm my potion."

"I thought it best to pour the cure down your gullet as soon as possible."

He stalked across the room and pulled out a quilted leather tunic, armbands, chauses, and other clothing he wore beneath his armor, his comments addressed to Fitz Alan. "Collect what you need for a ride to Derry Town. Simon tells me the bailiff hid in that village first. We shall see if the mayor can be convinced to tell me more of the traitor's flight. I will meet you in the armory in a quarter hour."

Fitz Alan gave Kenric a quick bow then left. Kenric's gaze brushed by Tess, quickly passing her over.

"You two will stay with my wife," he told Simon and Evard. "Stay outside her door when she is in this chamber, within her sight when she is not."

With that, Kenric departed. Tess closed the door behind him, trying to ignore the two soldiers who took up their positions in the hallway. It was humiliating for them to know how little Kenric thought of her, that he would not bother to give her a word of farewell or even a notion of when he'd return. Not that it mattered. The whole castle knew what little regard he had for her. Tess released a long sigh, realizing that Kenric's latest order for her keepers to remain within her sight would only make her escape more difficult. Nearly impossible, as a matter of fact, if she failed to trick them into relaxing their guard.

Afraid of feeling sorry for herself if she remained in her room any longer, Tess donned her cloak and made her way to the battlements. Evard and Simon followed dutifully. The crisp, fresh air was exhilarating, but Tess noticed that her guards watched her nervously, looking half afraid of her intent when she leaned far over the wall to peer down into the bailey. Simon was at her elbow before she gained a clear view of the area.

"Please, milady," he said quietly. "Should you fall, the baron will see that we meet your fate."

Tess doubted either event, but she took a step back from the wall. "Do not fret, Simon. The ground holds little appeal from this height."

She leaned more cautiously against the wall and Simon nodded his approval. She didn't have a long wait before she spied Kenric riding out from the main gates with a score of his men. Even in full armor, she knew him immediately. Aside from his blue and white surcoat, he was simply the tallest and largest of the men, his black warhorse sized on the same massive scale. He was an impressive sight. She pitied Derry Town's mayor. That man was sure to be frightened witless by the sight of his overlord bearing down on his town, dressed for war.

"He is a fool to ride out this late with so few men," Tess remarked, gauging the angle of the sun over the tree-tops to the west.

"Only a fool would challenge the baron," Evard stated, his voice filled with pride in his overlord's prowess. "Night *or* day."

Tess was ready to retort that wild beasts cared little for a man's reputation, but at that moment Kenric turned in his saddle to gaze back at Montague. She quelled the ridiculous urge to lift her hand in a gesture of farewell. He'd granted her no such sign of consideration. He turned forward but his head suddenly jerked back around and Tess knew he'd caught sight of her. She could almost feel his gaze though his eyes were shielded behind his helm and she was too far away to see them anyway. She was certain he was waiting for that wave. He wasn't going to get it. At last he turned around again as the group rode over the crest of a hill and disappeared from sight. Tess turned away from the wall, her smile meant to hide the curious sheen of tears in her eyes.

"What say you we visit the kitchens?" she suggested with forced cheerfulness. "I would like to compliment Cook on the fine meal we enjoyed this day."

The two soldiers exchanged an odd look then nodded their agreement.

The kitchens were still abuzz with activity, the servants busy cleaning up the remnants of the feast and turning the leftovers into new meals for the next day. Everyone came to a sudden halt when they spied the baroness, the silence that descended over the group befitting a church service until a tray slipped from someone's grip and the bowls that were stacked on top clattered to the floor. It was almost a signal of some sort, for everyone suddenly returned to their duties, looking busier than they had a few moments before. The low hum of hushed conversations filled the room again.

"Milady," Cook murmured, rushing forward. He bowed, then stepped back a pace and eyed her nervously. "Is . . . is anything amiss, Baroness?"

"I wanted to thank you personally for producing such a fine feast," Tess said warmly, mistaking the Cook's uncomfortable flush for modest pride. "The food surpassed my expectations. You and your staff have talents worthy of the king's table."

Cook twisted his apron strings, avoiding the baroness's clear gaze as he mumbled a reply. "Thank you, milady. 'Tis an honor to serve our lord and lady."

Tess glanced around at the flurry of activity, knowing the effort the meal had cost. "After working so hard, you and your assistants deserve a day less strenuous. You will be excused from your duties on the morrow with your lady's blessing. I will instruct the chamber servants to serve a simple nooning meal from the remainders of the feast."

Cook looked embarrassed by the reward. Holidays were a rarity when a castle had to be fed on a daily basis, no matter what. Tess was a little surprised by his lack of enthusiasm.

Knowing her presence disturbed their work, Tess didn't linger in the kitchens. It was too late to begin any worthwhile projects, yet too early to go to bed. She paused in the great hall long enough to pour a mug of cider and mull over her options for the next few hours. Surprisingly, she met a silence in the great hall that nearly matched the one in the kitchens. Nearly three score of Kenric's men were gathered near the fireplaces, yet they turned from their groups and watched her expectantly. Uncomfortable with the scrutiny, Tess gulped down the cider then made her way to the castle's chapel. Never far behind, Simon and Evard took positions on either side of the door inside the large, vaulted chamber. Rather than take her place on a kneeler, Tess walked forward to the nave where tall candles were kept burning day and night. Prying a taper from its holder, she began walking along the walls of the chapel, stopping at the evenly spaced wall sconces to light the rush torches they contained.

"My prayers were said this morning," Tess told her two guards over one shoulder, her arm raised to light another torch. "We have business of a more earthly order here tonight. The servants will be scrubbing this chamber down on the morrow." She wrapped her fingers around an impressive cobweb that hung from one sconce then removed it with a flick of her wrist. "Father Gilard is on retreat at Roeston Abbey for three more days and I would surprise him with a clean place of worship on his return. The cleaning will be made easier if the kneelers and altar pieces are removed to the antechamber before the servants arrive."

Both soldiers sighed long and loud, but they dutifully began moving the kneelers. Tess removed the altar pieces, stacking them carefully in a corner of the antechamber.

"Did you notice how everyone in the kitchens acted so oddly?" she asked, concentrating on wrapping a delicately carved Madonna. She didn't see the wry smiles that were exchanged. "In the great hall, as well. Do you think something is amiss?"

"Amiss, milady?" Simon asked, hefting another kneeler onto his hip to carry it to the antechamber. He gazed despondently at the other fifty or so kneelers that had yet to be moved.

"Everyone seemed rather quiet," she said finally, not quite able to describe her uneasiness any other way.

"They were simply showing you respect, Baroness. Servants and soldiers alike should be expected to await your bidding when you enter a room."

"They did not seem quite so respectful before today," Tess said, following Simon into the antechamber with a statuette. Evard was there already, arranging the kneelers in a compact row.

"The baron put the fear of—" Evard paused long enough to eye the holy objects that filled the room, apparently rethinking his words. "He put the fear of himself in them."

"How so?" Tess asked, curious. She set the statue aside and waited for Evard's answer. Evard's gaze shifted to Simon.

"You might as well tell her, now that you've stuck your foot in it," Simon told him.

"They meant to defy you, Lady. Both servants and soldiers. They were testing the baron, seeing if he would enforce the rules you laid down in his absence."

"They complained of me?" Tess asked in a quiet voice that bespoke injured pride. "To my husband?"

"Nay, milady. They simply ignored your rules. Blatantly so. I don't think—"

"The baron does not like being tested," Simon interrupted. "Your husband made it clear to all that your rules would be followed else he would enforce them."

"I see," Tess said quietly. She turned and went back to

the altar to wrap another statuette. Simon and Evard followed, exchanging an uneasy glance.

"He showed his support of you, milady," Simon ventured, lifting another kneeler.

"Aye," she responded simply. She had no idea that her actions had forced such a confrontation. No wonder Kenric was so rude at the feast. He was doubtless blaming that dissension on her as well. It was galling to know it was truth. "Perhaps we could begin sweeping down some of the cobwebs after the kneelers are moved. I think I saw some brooms in the antechamber."

Both soldiers balked at that suggestion. Evard claimed he would rather face a flogging than wield a broom. Noting the stubborn expression on the baroness's face, Simon used reason to talk her out of the demeaning chore, telling her it was late already and her bath would be waiting by the time they were done with the kneelers. Much to their relief, Tess agreed.

It was late the next day when Kenric returned from Derry Town. As Tess prepared to go down to the hall to greet him, a servant arrived at her door with a tray of food and word that the baron had business to discuss with his men that night in the hall. Tess interpreted the message as an order to remain in their room. It was well past midnight when he finally entered the bedchamber. Tess feigned sleep as she listened to the quiet sounds he made as he undressed for the night, tensing when she felt the bed give beneath his weight. She waited for him to pull her to his side, as was his custom. Several long, silent minutes passed before she realized he wasn't going to touch her.

Just as well, she decided, telling herself that the soft sigh she released was one of relief. Tess was ready to give him a good piece of her mind if he thought to demand another duty of her this night. She'd thought a long time about what she would say to him when he returned. At the moment, she was simply too tired to start a decent argument.

Kenric's warmth beckoned to her beneath the covers but Tess resisted the urge to move closer to his heat. She would do nothing to make him think she wanted him in this bed. As long as he glared at her during the day, Tess knew she could remain firm in her resolve to flee for Scotland. If he turned to her at night with soft words and gentle caresses, how long would it be before she began filling her head with her own lies? Before she began making more excuses to delay her escape? Nay, she must remain strong. The lives of her people were at stake.

16

"*I have no idea how you manage to play that thing with quills,*" Tess declared, nodding to the psaltery in Helen's lap. She plucked another string of her lute, trying to tune it to Helen's instrument.

The two women were seated at a table near the hearth in the great hall, using the time following evening meal to practice their instruments. It gave them both something to do when the men gathered to gamble or tell stories. Helen looked resplendent in a cream-colored gown trimmed with gold braiding. Tess's gown was a light color as well, the result of countless washings. Still, the fabric was made of sturdy linen and didn't look quite as dowdy as her other gowns when compared to her sister-in-law's. Kenric and a large group of his men were involved in a loud game of dice that was taking place at the opposite end of the hall.

In the five days that had passed since Kenric's return from Derry Town, Simon and Evard had proved such diligent guards that Tess began to wonder if she would ever find an opportunity to make her escape. She no longer had much cause to worry about Kenric while waiting for that opportunity. He'd scarcely spoken more than a handful of words to her the whole time. That suited her just fine the entire first day of his silence. She was still angry with him over the way he'd humiliated her in the hall then left for Derry Town without so much as a by your leave. If he wanted silence, he was going to get it. As the days dragged on, she became warier of his dark mood. He spoke to her only when absolutely necessary, and then only a word or two, as if he'd decided they had nothing more of importance to say to each other. She risked a quick peek at her husband, wondering if he would remain in the hall until all hours as he had every other night this week. It was becoming obvious to all that he was avoiding her. He rose near dawn each day to train with his men but didn't retire until well past midnight. Each night he followed the same simple routine. After joining her in bed, he would turn his back to her and go to sleep.

Tess tried to tell herself that it was all for the best. It didn't matter if he no longer found her desirable. She should delight in the fact that he didn't show the slightest interest in kissing or caressing her. She shouldn't feel a twinge of regret if he flinched away whenever he touched her accidentally, as if he found the slightest contact with her repulsive. The thought of Kenric with another woman should not consume her with jealousy to the point that she kept a careful eye on every female at Montague, watching for some sign that one was enjoying the kind of attention their lord should show to none other but his wife. She was fast becoming consumed by her suspicions.

"I could not play a psaltery using my fingers to pluck the strings, much less quills," Tess said evenly, determined to turn her thoughts from Kenric. "There are just too many and I never find the right strings quickly enough to carry a song."

"I am sorry for the trouble I caused us both that day in my chamber," Helen said suddenly, startling Tess with the unexpected apology. "I was so angry with Kenric for breaking his oath that I spoke without thought of the consequences."

"What oath?" Tess asked, the lute forgotten in her lap.

Helen's gaze traveled cautiously around the room to make sure none were within hearing. "Many years ago, Kenric made a vow never to marry. We were all very young at the time, yet he swore this oath on our mother's grave with Guy and I as witnesses. After my father died, Kenric promised Guy that Montague would someday be his. Kenric swore he would have no legal heirs of his own to challenge Guy's right to inherit." Helen's mouth drew to a thin line and her eyes narrowed. "Yet he conveniently forgot his vow when Remmington fell into his lap like a ripe apple. Now he will have two fine estates while Guy has nothing."

Tess stared at Helen with her mouth wide open. She recalled the first few days of their marriage, his unreasonable anger at the time suddenly making sense. He told her he didn't want a wife and he'd meant every word.

"Do close your mouth," Helen chastised. "You look like a carp."

Tess pressed her lips together but shook her head. "Helen, your brother did not want to marry me. Kenric was forced into this marriage as surely as I was. He meant to keep his word to Guy."

Helen waved her hand to dismiss the matter. " 'Twas foolish to believe him in the first place. He knew what his marriage would mean to Guy, yet he wed you anyway. No man can force Kenric to do anything against his will."

"There is one," Tess said cryptically.

She remained silent, her gaze steady. Helen's eyes widened, guessing the truth. "The king?"

Tess looked indecisive for a moment then slowly nodded. "I can tell you no more. If you breathe one word to another living soul of what you know already, I will kill you myself, Helen."

Helen bobbed her head.

"Do not think I am bluffing," Tess warned in a low voice. "The future of my people depends on this secret being kept. Do you understand me?"

"You have my word," Helen whispered, glancing around the hall again. "Your secret is safe. I will tell no one."

"Good," Tess answered, turning her attention to the lute. "And I accept your apology for the nasty things you said to me that day."

"I didn't know you were forced into the marriage," Helen mused. "Most of the things I said about Kenric that day were simply meant to hurt you."

"I realize that now." Tess sighed. She was beginning to realize a great many things. "You don't hate your brother, do you?"

Helen squirmed uncomfortably on her stool. "He's done little enough to make himself endearing." Her brows drew together in a frown. "But I do not think I truly hate him. Kenric was kind to me when we were children, he even protected me when my father would seek me out for some punishment. My father was not an endearing man, either," she confessed sullenly.

Tess left that admission alone, glad she never had the misfortune to meet the man Kenric was forced to call his father.

"Everyone has noticed that something is wrong between the two of you." Helen nodded toward Kenric. "Is it because of what I told you that day?"

"Nay," Tess admitted, sounding more miserable than she'd meant. She was supposed to be glad that Kenric had lost interest in her. "As you said, Kenric has done little of late to make himself endearing. I fear he feels the same of me."

"He looks at you when he thinks no one is watching."

Tess looked surprised for a moment, but her expression soured. "Doubtless he is thinking of the best ways to rid himself of his wife."

Helen shrugged, as though she didn't think the look in her brother's eyes suggested anything of the sort.

"Good evening, Lady Helen, Baroness."

Tess glanced up, meeting Roger Fitz Alan's gaze. She set her lute aside as he took a seat opposite Helen on the other side of the table.

"Why, good evening, Sir Roger," Tess said, her tone curious. "What brings you to our table this eve?"

"Your husband suggests I begin my courtship of his sister," he replied, looking unenthused at the prospect. "He also requests your company, Baroness."

Tess didn't take time to wonder over her summons. She hurried to take the seat next to Kenric's as he returned from the dice game.

"You wished to speak with me, milord?"

"I wish you to leave Fitz Alan alone while he does his courting," he said curtly, thinking that a good excuse to request her presence. He didn't want to give the idea that he'd missed having her at his side these past days. "Would you like a goblet of wine?"

Tess glanced up, looking surprised. He knew it was the nicest thing he'd said to her all week. The trip to Derry Town had proved useless, but it did give him time to think over the best way to deal with his wife. This time he was determined to stick with his decisions. Forced seductions would differ little from begging. He would not beg. She would come to him willingly, or not at all. Eyeing the stiff angle of his wife's back, Kenric was beginning to suspect it would be not at all. He wondered how many more nights he could lie beside her, waiting for her to reach out for him, his senses aroused beyond bearing by the simple fact that she lay within reach. Bastard or not, he knew she would submit to him, she would even respond once she had her guilt-easing protests out of the way. He was insane to continue torturing himself. Yet now it had become almost a test of wills.

"You seem to be enjoying my sister's company of late," he ventured. He twisted the stem of his goblet between his fingers, acting as if it were commonplace for them to make idle table talk.

"Aye, milord."

Tess bowed her head and stared at her hands. She'd been too quiet this week, sitting beside him each night in silence during their meals. She rarely looked at him and joined Helen somewhere else in the hall as soon as the meals ended. She was avoiding him, trying to stay as far from him as possible. Kenric knew it would strain his endurance sorely, but he made a mental note to seek her out more often. He wasn't going to make her capitulation any easier by wooing her with words, but this torture had to end soon. "She is being helpful?"

Tess shifted restlessly on her stool, rubbing her palms against her thighs before placing her hands on the table. "Aye, milord."

He placed his hand a few inches away. One small move was all that was needed. She had but to pick up her hand and place it on his and he would have her. Kenric stared down at her hand, willing it to move. A bolt of heat rushed through him when it actually did, his hopes sinking even lower as he watched the hand move to her lap.

Perhaps he was going about this the wrong way. These deathly silences were getting him nowhere.

"What have the two of you been doing this week?" he asked tersely, wondering if she would somehow manage the same answer for this question.

Tess looked down at her hands and began to pick nervously at her nails. "The hearths have been scrubbed in all but the buttery and the old solar, the panes washed in all windows that contain them, the holding pens have been moved farther from the kitchens to reduce the odors, the gardens have been plotted for spring planting, soap and a new supply of candles have been laid in for the coming month."

Tess drew another breath and continued her list for several minutes. Kenric rested his chin in his hand and listened in amazement. Not only was the sheer volume impressive, but it was amazing that she could remember it all. He had no idea that she'd been keeping herself so busy. Little wonder her hands were calloused. She'd earned each one. His gaze drifted to her hands, wondering when he would feel them against his skin again. His eyes traveled upward, lingering on the swell of her breasts, wondering when he would feel *his* hands on her again.

"The smokehouse was moved closer to the butcher's hut, and part of the armory roof was rotting so that was repaired with new beams and shingles." Tess glanced up hesitantly. "I assume you have no objection to that?"

"Objection to what?" Kenric had been studying the curve of her hip. He found nothing to object to there.

Tess's eyes narrowed. "Have you listened to anything I just said?"

"Most of it," he admitted with a grin, pleased to see a spark in her eyes that had been missing of late. "Did you truly do all that in so few days, or is that everything you've been doing since I left for Penhaligon?"

"I . . . ah, those duties were done these past days." Tess dropped her gaze to the table again when he smiled. "Would you like to hear the duties I carried out while you were at Penhaligon? The household duties, that is. The . . . the others you know about."

"I will take your word that the list is longer than the last one." His smile grew broader. Aye, he'd been all wrong about remaining silent. Simply talking to Tess was having much more of an effect than allowing her to slink off without a word each evening. "Why don't you tell me what you plan to do next?"

"There are several children in the village who have fallen ill with a chest ailment and I thought to take more medicine to their mothers and—"

"You will not tend sick children," Kenric interrupted. "Old Martha tends the ills of the villagers."

"Old Martha fell last week on the south tower steps and twisted her ankle. She will be abed at least another week."

"Then you will send another with your potions." Kenric was tempted to reach out and tilt her chin up as he had so often in the past. Staring at the top of her head was becoming irritating, but he refused to touch her. He had broken their silence, but he would not be the first to extend his hand. That was the most important part of this test of his endurance. She must reach for him first, prove to him that she could overcome her disgust of his birthright. He used words rather than his hand to get what he wanted. "I would have you look at me when we are talking."

Tess lifted her head slowly to meet his gaze. He nodded his approval and gave her a another smile. Her eyes were pale violet now, the color of her fear. She was afraid of the effect he was having on her. He was sure of it.

"Send one of my men with the medicine," he told her, his tone considerate. "I would not have you expose yourself to some disease and fall ill."

"Hah—I, ah, ahem." Tess cleared her throat several times. "Perhaps a sip of your wine might help this odd tickle in my throat," she said weakly.

Kenric held out his cup, his hand wrapped around it near the rim. Tess took hold of the goblet by the stem but Kenric didn't want to let go. He stared intently at their hands. She had to tug once before he released his grip. After taking a small sip she handed it back, but he was careful to avoid touching her hand.

"I will ask one of your men to take the medicine," she finally conceded. Looking across the hall, she saw Fitz Alan returning a chess board to its place on the mantel.

"Ah, I see the game has ended," Tess declared, earning a startled look from Kenric. His gaze followed hers for the explanation. "Would you like me to stay, or would you mind if I retire for the evening, milord?"

I would like you to place your hand in mine. "You may retire, Tess."

Kenric watched the sway of his wife's hips as she left the hall, pleased that he'd made progress, yet frustrated that it seemed so little. Still, she had her lower lip between her teeth when she left. That was a sure sign. Perhaps tonight she'd reach out to him.

Tess didn't reach for him that night or the next. Even so, Kenric knew he was making more progress. The wall she'd built between them was crumbling a little each day. Though she might not be touching him yet, she was all but caressing him with her eyes. A simple polite word or two when she tried to avoid looking at him and he was soon devoured by a violet gaze. She watched him constantly and he no longer avoided her gaze but met it steadily, often smiling to encourage her attention. It didn't take long to realize that his smiles had a curious effect on his wife. Each one made her blush becomingly, though often as not she became tongue-tied and flustered. Kenric began to smile more than he had in his life.

Though they were both busy during the days, he used the excuse of Helen's and Fitz Alan's courtship to keep her by his side each night after dinner. He was amazed by the variety of subjects they found to talk about. She was genuinely interested in everything he had to say and Kenric found himself talkative for the first time in his life. At times their discussions were serious, but often as not, their conversations concerned subjects as trivial as the color of the moon and what made it change shape through the year, or their likes and dislikes of everything from food, to pets, to people. It might have been his imagination, but Kenric felt certain her chair moved closer to his each evening, that she leaned nearer to him during their quiet discussions, the longing he sensed in her growing deeper. Yet every night in their chamber, silence fell heavy between them and the routine didn't vary.

Kenric continued to rise early, his willpower at its lowest when he awoke, often as not with his wife in his arms. That didn't count. She must consciously give herself to him, be fully aware of what she was doing. Oddly enough, his resolve seemed to grow stronger each day, his body past the point where it could be aroused any further, tortured any more thoroughly. Rather than grow irritable over his lack of sleep and near constant state of arousal, Kenric was fairly basking in the glow of his wife's banked desires. She would soon be on fire. Kenric couldn't wait to be consumed by the flames.

17

"Please stop scowling. You will give Thomas the wrong impression."

Kenric lifted a mug of ale and used it to shield the look of exasperation he gave Tess before he downed a healthy portion. The hall was nearly empty, but Kenric held little doubt about the urgency of the tasks that called most of his men away just after dinner. They fled soon after the announcement of the evening's entertainment. Aye, there were certain unpleasant prices to be paid as lord of the manor. Suffering through his squire's latest attempt at epic poetry was surely one of them.

" 'Tis impossible. How much longer can this continue?" Kenric whispered back to Tess.

"Shhh."

Kenric grimaced and leaned back in his chair, the new

one delivered just this morn by the carpenter. The wobbly tables were gone already, exchanged for a score of sturdy tables discovered in storage. Another piece of Helen's work, no doubt. Yet she'd volunteered their location and that of matching tablecloths without prompting. Kenric smiled with satisfaction. Tess was getting to Helen, just as Tess got to everyone.

"That was a delightful poem," Tess exclaimed, clapping her hands enthusiastically when Thomas wound down at last. Kenric suspected she was more delighted to hear it end. "Don't you think so, husband?"

"Aye, most delightful," Kenric agreed wryly. "Now off to bed with you, lad. 'Tis a long day you will be putting in on the morrow."

Tess waited until Thomas left the hall before addressing Kenric, a frown creasing her brow. "Do you intend to punish the boy with extra work tomorrow, just because his epics tend to be a bit windy?"

"I would not dream of such a thing," Kenric claimed innocently. "But perhaps some hard work will leave my squire too exhausted to dream up these torturous poems."

Helen's soft laughter drifted across the hall and his attention was drawn again to the couple playing chess. Nearly a week had passed since Fitz Alan started his courtship, and the two had barely been apart since then. If he didn't know better, Kenric would swear that Fitz Alan was truly snared by Helen's charms. Helen appeared just as smitten. Both stared at each other like lovestruck fools.

"He is going to bed her beneath my nose," he muttered, glaring at Fitz Alan.

"Pardon me?" Tess asked, following the direction of Kenric's scowl.

Kenric watched Helen contemplate her next move while Fitz Alan contemplated his sister. He spoke to Tess without taking his eyes off his friend. "Go tell Fitz Alan that I wish to speak with him. You will stay with Helen."

Tess left to do his bidding and he frowned at her back,

already angry with Fitz Alan for denying him his wife's company.

"How fared the poetry?" Fitz Alan asked when he joined Kenric. He poured a mug of ale and settled on a nearby stool.

"Thomas has no ear for poetry and well you know it," Kenric replied, irritated with Fitz Alan for escaping the "entertainment" by entertaining Helen. "You seem to have found one diversion or another to excuse yourself from most of the evening amusements of late."

"Aye, 'tis true. Your sister has amazed me with her quick mastery of the chess game. I fear she may beat me one day soon," Fitz Alan admitted with a smile, his eyes on Helen. "I have found her just as talented with music. Quite an amazing woman, really."

"Amazingly devious," Kenric snorted.

Fitz Alan's expression turned sheepish. "She asks often if I know your plans for Montague, and mentions Guy's name more frequent of late."

" 'Tis the only reason for her sudden infatuation. You were right to suspect as much."

Fitz Alan smiled and inclined his head. "She truly thinks to gull me to the point that I will use my influence to gain a position for Guy. Yesterday I finally promised to broach the subject with you."

"She plays you well."

"Aye, that she does. She has been the sweetest, most biddable of maids. I am having great fun with her game."

"Best you keep in mind that it is only a game," Kenric warned. "One I will not see played too far. I intend to find a husband for Helen when we go to court and the task will be no easier if she is fat with your bastard."

Fitz Alan nearly dropped his mug. His head pivoted stiffly as he turned to stare at Kenric.

"I've seen the way you look at her," Kenric went on. "And I have not forgotten what a smooth tongue you have with women. As I see it, 'tis only a matter of time before you have her talked into your bed."

Fitz Alan flushed guiltily and stared down at his mug, unable to meet Kenric's steady gaze. "I had not intended it to go that far."

"But it will," Kenric stated without question.

Fitz Alan sighed. "She is much different than I thought. More tempting than I imagined."

"You see what she wants you to see. She is using you, man!"

"Aye," Fitz Alan said glumly. "But I think she is coming to care for me as well."

"You cannot be serious! Once she learns my true plans for Montague, she will treat you as a leper."

"Perhaps."

"Perhaps?" Kenric's expression turned grim. " 'Tis time to bring this farce to an end. Helen's plot is no different than we thought and no purpose is served to keep her ignorant of our knowledge. Her punishment will be marriage to a man of my choosing. 'Tis my belief that she will realize it is in her best interest to remain biddable, in hopes of improving my choice. I'll give you an hour to tell her this game is at an end, then I intend to inform her of her punishment."

Fitz Alan listened quietly to Kenric's decision, his expression thoughtful. Several silent moments passed before he responded.

"You allowed me to court your sister with no other purpose than to discover her plottings and make sure they were not harmful. This I have done. But I have grown fond of the lady, despite her scheming, and have no wish to see her wed another. I do humbly ask your permission for your sister's hand in marriage, milord."

Kenric stared at Fitz Alan as if he'd suddenly turned into a troll. He finally found his voice but it was a bare, disbelieving whisper.

"You have lost your mind."

"You may be right," Fitz Alan agreed with a humorless smile. "My heart is gone already, though I know not how. I knew that little witch's game from the start, yet I have still managed to fall under her spell. I have few illusions that her feelings are the same, but in time I believe I could gain her affections."

"You are actually serious!" Kenric shook his head in disbelief. "More likely, you will gain her dagger in your gullet some eve as you sleep."

"I thought to wait a few weeks before asking your permission," Fitz Alan continued, ignoring Kenric's comment. "But your decision forces me to hasten my offer. Though you know me to be landless, the riches I acquired in our campaigns are ample to support a wife in any style she desires. Your sister will surely object, but she cannot deny your right to name her husband. If you wish to punish Helen for her scheming, I ask that you do so by naming me as that husband. She is sure to be miserable as many months in our marriage as she would be dreading marriage to another."

"She would make you miserable as well. Hell, Fitz Alan, she would make you twice as miserable. Are you so smitten that you would punish yourself?"

"Aye," Fitz Alan murmured solemnly, without a trace of his usual humor. Kenric had never seen such a serious expression on Fitz Alan. "But I would not make the offer if I believed she could not come to tolerate me as a husband. If you accept my suit, I have no intentions of telling her of my affections until they can be returned. I would have her believe the marriage is simply a punishment for her scheming, that perhaps I agreed to the marriage simply to gain her dowry. I think she'll find that believable, as she has no means of knowing the true extent of my wealth."

"You've put some thought into this," Kenric mused. "What happened to the man who agreed that bedding a wench was the best way to get her out of his system? If that is what it takes for you to reconsider this insane notion, I would actually consider turning a blind eye to the matter."

"Nay," Fitz Alan said. "Since your marriage I have thought often of a wife and family, and have decided that I want children at my hearth before I am too old to enjoy them. I would want that their mother be Helen."

"Good God, Fitz Alan. You've grown poetic." Kenric found himself smiling over Fitz Alan's lovestruck words. He was also greatly reassured that he'd not made a fool of himself with his musings about Tess earlier in their marriage. The example of true foolishness over a woman sat before him.

Fitz Alan shrugged. "You will consider my offer?"

"You have no doubts about this?" Kenric shot back.

"Plenty." Fitz Alan grinned, the sparkle of good humor returning to his eye. "But none I fear, or cannot put to rest."

Kenric mulled over the implications of Fitz Alan's request. He'd be seeing his sister far more often than he'd like in the years to come. He sighed and spread his hands in defeat. "Consider yourself betrothed."

Fitz Alan acted as if he'd just been handed a great treasure. Kenric wondered if his friend would still thank him a year from now. The two men spent the next hour working out the details, each agreeing to let Helen believe herself caught in her own game. When Kenric finally called the women forward, he motioned for Tess to take the seat Fitz Alan occupied, and Fitz Alan rose to take his place at Helen's side.

"I've just had a most interesting discussion with Fitz Alan," Kenric began, addressing Helen. "He believes you would have me consider Guy as lord of Montague, when my position at Remmington is secure. He also believes that to be the only reason you have encouraged his attentions these past days."

"Nay, 'tis not true," Helen protested. "I have become quite fond of Sir Roger, and do enjoy his company."

"You are certain of that?"

"Aye, most certain, milord."

Kenric remained silent for a moment, as if weighing Helen's words. "Then I see no reason you should question my decision to see you wed to Roger Fitz Alan."

"What?" Helen shouted. Her trapped gaze flew from Kenric to Fitz Alan, then back to Kenric. "You cannot do this, milord. Please, I beseech you."

"Beseech me with the truth," Kenric ordered, his voice booming across the hall. "Tell me the reasons you accepted his courtship so readily and I shall reconsider my agreement with Fitz Alan."

Tess's expression faded from surprised delight to a worried frown. She'd spent few evenings with Helen these past days, for Fitz Alan seemed to be with her constantly. But during the day, when they worked together at some task, Helen could speak of little but Roger Fitz Alan. If Helen had been acting, she'd been most convincing.

"All right," Helen said bitterly, every line of her scowl echoing her resentment. "I encouraged him only to put the idea of Guy as your vassal at Montague into his head and see that he encouraged you in the matter. When that was done, I meant to break off the courtship gently." She turned to glare at Fitz Alan, not looking very contrite. "I am sorry I misled you, Roger, but I felt my reasons justified."

"I was not misled at all," Fitz Alan informed her, grinning cheerfully. "I guessed your game right enough from the very start."

"Why . . . why, you black-hearted miscreant! You've been laughing at me all this time?"

Fitz Alan's nod set off a steady stream of curses, the likes of which Tess had never heard from a lady's mouth. Many she'd not heard at all.

"Enough!" The bellowed word gained the silence Kenric wanted and he nodded to Fitz Alan. "It seems you were right after all, Fitz Alan. I do double her dowry, as we agreed."

"You wagered on me?" Helen screeched, turning on Fitz Alan. She looked ready to claw his eyes out. But a look of dawning horror soon covered her face and she paled noticeably. "You still intend to marry me?"

Kenric answered the question for her.

"And glad you should be, sister. You are in need of a husband to guide you. My tolerance of your meddling has reached its limits. I'd intended to find you a husband among my acquaintances at court, but our wager and the size of your dowry finally convinced Fitz Alan to take you off my hands himself. You will have many long years to show him your gratitude, for the men I thought of as candidates would be far less to your liking."

Helen swayed slightly, opened her mouth to protest, but fainted instead, caught effortlessly in Fitz Alan's arms.

"I believe my bride is overcome with happiness," he declared with a chuckle. "If you will excuse us, milord, Lady Tess, I will take her someplace more comfortable to contemplate our nuptials."

Kenric started laughing before Fitz Alan even left the hall. God's truth, he had to sit down and wipe the tears from his face, he found the scene so funny.

"Ah, I have not laughed that hard in years," Kenric gasped. "Did you see the look on Helen's face? She was as pasty as a flour bag." Turning to his wife, his smile faded. "You are not laughing."

"I cannot believe I was taken in so completely by Helen's mooning," Tess sputtered. "I truly thought she was falling in love with the man."

"People are not always what you think they are," he said quietly, his expression growing serious. Gazing into the depths of his smoky eyes, Tess knew he was no longer talking about Helen. "Sometimes you must look beneath the surface to discover a person's true character."

He'd been showing her what was beneath the surface

for nearly a fortnight, Tess realized, struck by the sudden insight. He probably wasn't even aware that he'd shown her the man beneath the mantle of a fierce warlord. She liked what she saw, liked it so much that it terrified her. She had been so concerned with controlling her reactions to what she saw on the surface, that she didn't take time to guard against what went much deeper. Her eyes widened over the knowledge. Kenric didn't find her disgusting. He hadn't lost the least bit of interest. He was waiting for her to tell him that she felt the same.

"I have looked beneath the surface, milord."

Kenric's hand rested on the table and she reached out to stroke her fingertips across the dark skin. He didn't move. His gaze dropped to their hands, his expression never changing as she shyly withdrew her hand.

"Touch me again," he whispered hoarsely.

Tess hesitated. She knew what he was asking, knew it went far beyond a simple touch. Her hand moved of its own accord, coming to rest on his. As if he were afraid of startling her, his other hand reached out to cover hers, holding her. His eyes were closed, an expression on his face she'd never seen before.

He finally turned her hand over and pressed a lingering kiss in the palm, never letting go of her hand as he stood up and led her from the hall. He remained silent until they reached their chamber. After closing the door behind them, he leaned against the heavy oak panels and finally released her. His gaze began at her slippers and traveled slowly upward, lingering on her breasts, even longer on her mouth.

"Show me," he said simply, waiting for her to come to him.

Tess took one step, then another, then she rested her hands lightly on his shoulders and leaned up on her tiptoes to press a kiss against the cleft of his chin. His hands moved up to his chest, covering hers, as if he treasured the feel of them against his body. Then he caught her in his arms, drawing her up against the length of his body as his lips descended to hers. It was a slow, drugging kiss, urgent yet patient at the same time. He kissed her mouth, the curve of her cheek, her temples, then back to her mouth again for a full taste of her. His hands moved carefully, loosening her braid to let her hair spill over her shoulders.

"Spun gold," he murmured against her lips, sifting the golden strands through his fingers. One hand cupped her cheek, stroking the smooth contours, trailing lightly down the pale column of her throat then moving beneath her chin, holding her to receive his next kiss. He used his lips to trace the outline of hers, touching rather than kissing, finally covering her mouth to take what she offered.

His arms slipped beneath her legs and he lifted her into his arms, never breaking the kiss as he carried her to the bed. Tess thought he meant to lay her down but he turned at the last moment and sat on the edge, cradling her in his lap. He used his mouth then to show her what it meant to be tormented, thrusting deep with his tongue then slowly withdrawing, giving then taking away, teasing, tantalizing, stroking her again and again, drawing her into his mouth to let her taste his power then dominating once more. His arms tightened around her, holding her completely, one hand beneath her head to keep their lips firmly joined.

One of his legs slipped out from under her, moving slowly over her legs to trap them between his, pulling her closer until her thigh was pressed firmly against his hard arousal. Tremors shook Tess's body and her groan was matched by his, joining in the soft song of love. Vaguely aware that her arms were twined around his neck, her hands fisted tightly in his hair, she reluctantly loosened her grip to slide the flats of her palms over the corded strength of his neck, cupping his face between her hands. The sandy roughness of his cheeks, the way he moved beneath her hands while pleasuring her mouth engulfed her in waves of dizziness. She was falling, deeper and deeper, but Kenric was holding her, protecting her from the fall, making sure there was no end to her tumbling emotions, no end to the sheer delight and exhilarating terror. Tess finally pushed against him, the feeble, gentle pressure the only effort she could summon up to save herself.

His kiss became less erotic, drawing away from her until their lips were just joined and he could look into her eyes. He deepened the kiss once more when he saw their color, unable to resist the lure. Drawing back again, he reluctantly parted from her when he saw a dim light of panic in the amethyst depths.

"What is wrong, sweet?" he murmured, pressing tiny kisses against her dewy lips. Until now, Kenric had had no idea that making love to a woman's mouth could be every bit as pleasurable as making love to her body. He was anxious to enrich his knowledge. "Tell me, and I will make it better."

"I . . . I think I'm going to faint," she whispered weakly.

Kenric smiled, tracing the outline of her lips with the tip of his tongue. She shuddered against him. He lowered his head and whispered seductively in her ear, his mouth exploring that part of her just as thoroughly. "Should you swoon, I will hold you safe and pleasure you with caresses until you arouse to me once more."

Her eyes fluttered closed.

"Tess?" he asked hesitantly, thinking she might be playing out his teasing. She didn't respond. Kenric leaned back to take a better look. Her body was completely relaxed against his, her breathing deep and steady. He shook her gently. Nothing. Good God, she'd actually fainted.

Kenric smiled hugely, suddenly feeling like the most powerful man on earth. The wait had been worth every single second. He trailed the backs of his fingers against one powder-soft cheek then used his fingertip to trace every line of her face. He hadn't even made love to her yet, but he knew he'd already won the battle. Tess accepted

him, knowing what he was, knowing he could never
change the circumstances of his birth. Her surrender was
sweet beyond bearing, arousing feelings he'd never guessed
were lying dormant. He'd never dreamed that this test of
willpower would have such remarkable results. Tess began
to stir in his arms and he smoothed her hair away from her
face.

"Welcome back," he murmured softly, watching her
eyes drift open. Deep purple, laden with passion. His body
responded unconsciously to the knowledge that she was
still aroused.

Tess lifted one limp hand to her forehead. "I don't
know what happened."

"I do," he answered, his smile growing broader.
"Though I'll admit, I thought it an exaggeration until
now." He leaned down and pressed a gentle kiss against
her forehead. "You have proven it truth, Tess; a woman
can indeed be overcome completely by her passions."

"I . . . I'm sorry," she apologized, blushing as she
struggled to sit up in his lap.

"I'm not." He loosened his grip and allowed her to
rise, brushing her hair over her shoulders as he bragged of
his prowess. "I know of none other who can claim such
skill. This must surely make me the most potent of lovers."

Tess smiled over his arrogance, even as her heart grew
heavy. Kenric might have won their silent war, but he
didn't know yet what it cost. This would be the last time
she allowed herself to turn traitor, but tonight she would
turn traitor completely. She deserved that much for what
she would be forced to sacrifice tomorrow. A wave of sorrow swept over her, and self-pity, too. It seemed her whole
life had been filled with sacrifices, all for the sake of the
cold-stone towers that were her home. Her parents had
died for Remmington. Tess had kept herself alive at Langston Keep for the sake of Remmington. She'd even considered marrying Gordon MacLeith, knowing her child would

eventually inherit. Now Remmington would force her to forsake her husband.

"There's no need to cry over a simple exaggeration," he admonished, frowning at the tears that spilled silently from his wife's eyes. He brushed them away with his thumbs. "Was it so hard to come to me?"

"Nay," she answered, trying to smile through her tears. Her plan was still the best. Truly, she told herself, even as she buried her face against Kenric's shoulder to cry in earnest. "I'm sorry!"

"I thought you knew I was waiting for a sign from you," he said hesitantly, trying to guess the source of her tears. The weeks of separation had certainly been trying. He supposed Tess could be moved to tears by what he simply found frustrating. "Didn't you know?"

She shook her head, using the sleeve of her gown to wipe away the tears as she lifted her head. "I thought you didn't want me anymore. I thought you'd taken a mistress."

Kenric mentally kicked himself for not being more obvious. "You needed time to become more accustomed to the notion."

"What notion?" she asked, sniffing away the last of her tears.

"The notion that you'd married a bastard," he said quietly.

Tess scowled. "I told you the truth that day. I don't care."

"Every noblewoman cares," he answered harshly, waiting for the telltale sign that would say she was lying. His frown faded to confusion. " 'Tis the reason I've rarely been pursued for marriage. Most at court know or suspect the truth, and none would dare mingle their highborn blood with that of a bastard."

"Good Lord. Your father is the King of England. You have more royal blood than any other nobleman, save the royal family itself. Do you honestly think yourself lacking because of it?"

"Nay," he admitted, giving her a pointed look. "But most do."

"Well, I don't," she said simply.

"Then why did you try to deny me after learning the truth? Why did you spend the last weeks avoiding me?"

Tess's eyes narrowed. "I tried to deny you because Helen had me convinced that you made a habit of slaughtering women and babies. I was furious with you for thinking you could demand your husbandly rights after treating me like a wayward child."

Kenric regretted asking the question. "All right, I will admit that my timing left something to be desired that day. What about all that followed?"

Tess eyed him warily, as if she didn't believe he'd dismissed her argument so easily. "When a man is finding pleasure elsewhere, he has no need of it from his wife."

One brow rose over the challenging tone of her answer. She was asking a question of her own. Tess really had no idea that he'd lain awake for hours on end, tormenting himself into an agony while she stewed with jealousy over an imagined mistress. It was almost laughable. Almost.

"You have lost time to make up for." He decided to let her wonder about the mistress. No need to let her become complacent. He stood up with Tess still in his arms then let her slide slowly down the length of his body, his eyes still locked with hers. "This night you will make up for all the nights of pleasure you have denied me."

"You are—"

Kenric placed his fingers over her mouth. "This is not open for discussion."

Tess nodded slowly.

"I will make up for your lost time as well."

Tess smiled.

Within the strong circle of his arms, Tess found thoughts of anything but her husband amazingly easy to push aside. She allowed herself to think only of Kenric, only of giving herself to him completely. And she was greedy, the sure knowledge that this was their last night together pushing aside any temptation to sleep once they both lay sated. She used her hands to memorize his body, committing every part of him to memory. She started on his back, still marveling at the power she held over him, watching his muscles flex instinctively in response to her soft, exploring caresses. By the time he turned over, his desire had already stirred to life again and her explorations came to an abrupt end. At last the sleepless nights caught up with him and he rolled to his back, cradling her at his side. He was asleep within minutes. As the cold gray light of dawn pushed away the darkness, Tess felt her tears begin to fall again in a steady, silent stream.

A weaker woman would stay within the circle of these strong arms. She wouldn't think of the consequences of her selfishness. Tess forced herself to picture the battle that would result if she remained with Kenric, images of people she'd known all her life falling beneath his sword, villagers and serfs dying the slower, crueler death of starvation. Hers was one life, theirs were many. Her father told her often that it was her responsibility to do whatever was necessary to protect the people of Remmington, that the burden she would bear as his only heir would be both blessing and curse. Turning to place a gentle kiss in the center of Kenric's chest, tasting her own tears, Tess decided that her father had been wrong about the blessing part. It was time to leave.

18

Tess stayed within the circle of Kenric's arms as long as she dared, glad of his exhaustion as she slipped from the bed without disturbing him. She pulled out the dress with the saffron bodice and colorful skirt, knowing what she had to do today would likely see a gown damaged beyond repair. After dressing and quickly braiding her hair, she tucked her cloak under one arm and crept quietly from the room.

There were two young soldiers asleep in the hall, the guards who relieved Simon and Evard at night when she was with Kenric. She stepped soundlessly over the guards and made her way down the tower steps. An hour was all she needed to get away from the castle. She would gain an even greater lead when the fortress was searched to no avail. If her luck held, Kenric wouldn't know anything was amiss for hours. She didn't want to think of his reaction when he opened their chamber door and discovered her guards still waiting for her to emerge for the day. She would never allow herself to picture that image.

The great hall was still quiet, but Tess could hear the muted sounds of servants beginning their day in the kitchens. The sun had peeked over the horizon by the time Tess slipped through a small door and hurried down the path that led to the gardens.

Missing Tess's warmth, Kenric reached across the bed to pull her closer. His hand swept over the sheets, his search not finding even the lingering warmth of her body. He opened one eye then the other, his gaze moving from the bed across the empty room. She was probably off to one of her projects already, he decided, closing his eyes again. She should have stayed with him this morning, knowing he'd not want to part from her company soon this day. Hell, she should have known he'd want to spend the entire day with her. Disgruntled, he opened his eyes again, deciding to seek her out and make his wishes known. No more beating about the bush.

The warmth of his bed lulled him into remaining there a few minutes longer. He stretched his arms and legs out as far as he could and yawned hugely, wondering if Tess might have gone to the kitchens for his breakfast. What a treat that would be. Knowing Tess, he supposed it more likely that she was already up to her elbows in some scrub bucket, yet he decided to give her a few more minutes in case she was doing what she should this morning: returning with his breakfast.

He was very good at waiting. He crossed one ankle over the other and propped his hands behind his head again. Hadn't he waited nearly an entire fortnight to bed his wife, handily resisting temptation every single night? Aye, everyone knew he had the patience of Job when it came to waiting. Tess was probably making her way down the hall right now. He uncrossed his legs then switched positions, propping the other leg on top. Patience was definitely a virtue he possessed in great quantity. Any minute now the door would open. The foot that was propped in the air began to wiggle back and forth in a steady, irritated rhythm. Where the hell was his breakfast?

With a snort of disgust he rose from the bed. He would give her a few more minutes, he decided, walking toward the window. The days were growing warmer and he pushed aside the shutter that kept out drafts at night. The sun was already peeking over the horizon and it promised to be a fine day.

A movement far below caught his eye and his gaze swept over the gardens that were still shadowed from the morning sun by the battlements. A servant woman was making her way through the maze of rose arbors. He would have dismissed it as a lover's tryst if she wasn't making her way so determinedly toward the south wall. It was the most remote part of the gardens and well suited to rendezvous, but the prickly vines that covered the wall also concealed the castle's only bolthole.

The servant's cloak caught on one of the thorny hedges and she was forced to back up a step to untangle the garment. After tugging twice to free the cloak, the woman tossed the edges over her shoulders to avoid further entanglements and Kenric caught sight of her gown. Only one woman at Montague owned a gown that ugly.

She was simply going for a morning stroll. Kenric had repeated that silent litany five times when she reached the shrubs that concealed the bolthole. His blood turned to ice as he watched her bend toward the shrubs. Even from this distance he could make out the shape of a linen sack as it was pulled from its hiding place. From the way she was tugging away the vines, it would only be a matter of minutes before she was in the tunnel that led underneath the walls. She truly intended to run from him. Again.

Liar! his mind shouted, recalling every word she spoke the night before. Everything she'd done and said had been a lie. How she must have laughed at her besotted husband. She was good at playacting, he'd give her that much. Something inside he'd never known was there began to die, its dust blown away in a gale of mounting fury.

"TESS!"

Kenric watched the distant figure freeze and he knew she heard his bellow. She frantically stuffed the linen sack back into its hiding place and hastily rearranged the vines. Satisfied that she wasn't going to make a run for it, he stalked across the room to the chamber door, flinging it open just short of the force required to remove it from its hinges. His wife's two guards were already stumbling to their feet, one with a drawn sword.

"If either of you wish to live long enough to see the sun set, you will get to the gardens and bring my *wife* back here immediately!"

He slammed the door shut then marched over to a trunk, jerking out a handful of clothing. This time he was going to kill her. He was certain of it. Last night had been an act. Tess hadn't meant one word. She'd avoided him as long as she could, submitted when she thought he would tolerate no more, then fled after making certain he slept in the sated exhaustion of her lies. *Deceitful little bitch.*

His fingers flew over his laces, dressing with military precision, tugging on his boots with one vicious jerk each. He needed her alive. That thought made him livid. He needed her alive and she knew it. If she said one word to him, one lie, he would take her slim throat between his hands and choke the life from her. He'd enjoy doing it.

Kenric left his chamber and made his way through the great hall to the barracks. A few soldiers had already risen but more remained in their beds. Kenric marched down the long room until he found one of the two he was looking for. One booted foot shoved Evard from his bunk to the stone floor. Simon was there already when Kenric turned on his heel to start searching for him.

"Both of you come with me," he told them in a deadly voice. "Now!"

Simon was dressed, but Evard had to make a hasty grab for his breeches, pulling them on beneath the linen shirt he'd worn to bed the night before. The baron led them back through the great hall to the castle's solar, where he simply paced the room for a good quarter hour.

"Evard," he finally said. "My wife will be in my bedchamber by now. If she is not, you will return here immediately and tell me so. If she is, you will make certain she remains there. The two guards who were on duty there last night will be confined to their quarters to await my judgment. Go now."

Evard didn't even bow in his haste to leave the room. Kenric continued to pace. Simon wisely remained silent.

Kenric tormented himself by remembering every single moment of the night, how he'd treasured the touch of her hand on his, feeling as if she'd just bestowed the greatest gift in the world. It meant nothing to Tess. He'd treated her with near reverence, cherished her. She had cried her eyes out, doubtless aggrieved because she faced an entire night of his unwanted lovemaking. Her sweet surrender in their chamber had been nothing but a duty she could no longer avoid. Their chamber. His jaw tightened, the muscle there working spasmodically. It was not *their* chamber, it was his. He'd not share it with her again.

Another hour passed before he felt ready to face her. His bedchamber held too many memories. He would summon her to the solar where he would be less tempted to violence. He continued to pace, knowing it mattered little if he faced her here or in his chamber. He wanted to see her suffer and it didn't matter where.

"Send her."

The two words were all Simon needed to make his exit from the room.

Tess was doing her own share of pacing at that moment. She knew without being told that Kenric had guessed the reason for her absence. She just wasn't sure how much he knew. From the look on Simon's face when he arrived at her door, Tess knew the answer was not far off. By the time they reached the solar, her knees were nearly knocking together. Simon rapped once on the door then pushed it aside, giving her a reassuring nod as he whispered under his breath. "I will be just outside the door, milady."

Tess returned his nod but didn't think it very encouraging that he would be outside the door. Her trouble lay on the other side. She took a few quiet steps into the room and bowed her head to wait. Kenric's back was to her as he stared out the long, mullioned window, directly into the harsh morning sunlight that streamed into the room. He was dressed all in black. Tess supposed that was fitting enough. She could feel nothing but malice in the air.

"Who told you about the bolthole?"

She couldn't detect a trace of emotion in his voice. She hadn't expected any. Her heart sank as she realized he'd likely watched her from their chamber window and knew all.

"The steward," she said quietly. "He told me that the bailiff must have used it for his escape."

"What did you plan, once you reached the other side?"

Tess remained silent.

"Answer the question!"

"I meant to go to my uncle in Scotland."

"His king would have ordered him to send you to MacLeith. Do try again."

Tess wished he would turn around and face her, then decided she liked his back better. She'd rather remember the way he looked at her last night, the warmth in his eyes as she laid her heart at his feet. Today he would crush it beneath his boot. She should have fled the instant she heard him shout her name, should have known that he was not simply angry over her absence when he awoke.

Thinking she could conjure a lie to explain away her absence, then escape later was a huge mistake. She had thrown away her last hope.

"I meant to appeal to his priest," Tess began, knowing he would have the truth sooner or later. "I have known since our marriage that there is but one way to avoid bloodshed at Remmington. The church is the only law MacLeith would dare not defy. Even his own men would not follow a leader who lost the sanctions of the church."

"You meant to annul the marriage," Kenric stated flatly.

Tess could admit anything but that. She couldn't bring herself to speak the truth.

"I will assume your silence is an admittance of guilt."

She heard the finality in those words, knew he'd made a decision about what she'd done. Yet he knew none of her reasons. "It seemed best, milord. My lands would revert to King Edward. 'Tis a certainty he would name you lord, yet you would not have to war for the estates. Without a wife, you could keep the oath you made to your brother, Guy, although—"

"*Silence!* You will never again speak to your lord unless you are spoken to."

The room fell silent. Tess had no idea what he planned to do with her. Something unpleasant, she was sure. It didn't matter. Nothing mattered anymore. She'd done what she could to save Remmington and she'd failed. With failure came a defeat greater than any she'd ever known. Remmington would not be the only thing she lost today. She'd also lost her husband.

"Go to my chamber and collect everything that is yours. You have a quarter of an hour to pack your belongings. I will not be fouled again with your presence."

Somehow Tess made her way from the solar, so numb that she could barely feel her legs beneath her. Packing her belongings meant she was leaving. He would no longer live with her; he made it brutally clear that he never wanted to see her again. Whether he sent her from the fortress or kept her somewhere within it, what did it matter? Nothing mattered. There was no point left to anything, no purpose. She'd done all she would be allowed to do. Remmington would fall in a sea of blood.

She moved around the room in an unconscious haze, packing the remainder of her clothing in one of the linen sacks she'd brought from Langston Keep. Half her belongings were already in the sack hidden in the garden. She no longer had any use for them.

Having packed her bags in half the time allotted, Tess sat down on the edge of the bed and waited, staring sightlessly into the fireplace. No troublesome thoughts ran through her head, only peaceful silence. The minutes drifted by quietly. Her gaze moved from the fireplace to her hands held limply in her lap, watching the pulse that beat almost imperceptibly in her wrist to mark off the seconds of her life.

"Milady?" Simon asked hesitantly from the doorway. He turned to Evard and two other soldiers who lingered curiously in the hallway. "Evard, you will go on ahead. You two go back to the great hall."

Simon waited until his orders were obeyed then took another step into the bedchamber. "Milady, you are to return with me to the solar."

Tess stood up like a puppet and followed Simon from the room, barely aware of his guiding hand on her elbow as they walked the long hallways back to the solar. Kenric was gone by the time they arrived.

"I received word that the baron wishes to speak with me," Simon told her quietly, after seating Tess in one of the chairs near the fireplace. He avoided the blank stare in the baroness's eyes. "Evard will be outside, should you need anything while I am gone. I will leave the door open so he will hear should you call for him. Is there anything you need before I leave?"

Simon waited patiently for an answer. The baroness

simply stared unblinking across the bright chamber. With a silent curse he left the room and hurried away to find the baron. He finally tracked Kenric down in the armory. Thomas was busy helping the warlord into the light armor he wore for morning practices with his men. It seemed he intended to go about his business as usual. Simon walked forward and Kenric dismissed his squire with a curt nod.

"My sister will resume her duties as chatelaine. Fitz Alan will ensure that she performs them adequately. My wife is to remain in the solar," Kenric told the soldier bluntly, his attention on the fastenings of a metal armband. "She will not leave that chamber for any reason. No one will be allowed to see her other than those who bring her food and those who guard her. As of now, you and Evard will return to your duties on the practice fields where there is greater need for your talents. You will assign others to guard the solar door and no one man will receive the duty more than two days in a row. Any soldier who enters that room without my permission will be flogged. Any soldier who allows her to set foot from that room will be put to death. The ones who slept outside my door last night may sleep all they want in the dungeons. They will remain there three nights without sustenance. Those are my orders. See that they are obeyed."

The baroness did not fall into a fit of hysterics, as Simon half expected when he delivered the news. She remained seated in the chair, her expression empty, exactly as Simon left her before receiving these hellish commands. The look in her eyes remained startlingly vacant when he recited the orders in his own words, trying impossibly to make them sound less harsh than they were. He tried prodding her with questions to get some response but she remained silent. He told her he'd arranged for Miriam to deliver the lady's meals, but still no response.

Simon had a bed moved in from one of the unused chambers, but he received no thanks for that kindness. He found a clothes trunk, but her pitiful bag of belongings only seemed to emphasize the fact that she had little to put in it. Other pieces of furniture and comforts were brought to the room, none of it drawing a response from Lady Tess, each piece as unappreciated as the last. Knowing his absence would soon be noted on the practice field, Simon finally departed.

Miriam arrived at noon with a tempting meal of stew and cider. It remained untouched on the table that Simon had placed near the hearth. Giving up after a few cajoling words about the tastiness of the meal, Miriam made up the bed with linens and a coverlet she'd brought along, doing her best to keep up a one-sided conversation.

"Lady Helen's tapestry is half started, milady," Miriam said, her tone cheerful. She nodded toward the loom in one corner that contained the tapestry, but the baroness's blank gaze didn't follow. "She would surely appreciate your help with the piece. I often find comfort when plying a needle, the results of my work the reward of the effort."

The bed made, Miriam began fluffing the pillows, taking longer at the task than required. "Old Martha is still in her bed, but she intends to deliver a few of your meals when she's able to get around again. She wants to thank you for your help with the village children. The weekly medicines you meant for their mothers are ready and she wonders if she should send them ahead." Miriam waited a moment for an answer. "Would you like Old Martha to send the medicines to the village, milady?"

Miriam shivered at the lack of expression in Lady Tess's eyes. She asked the baroness a few more questions then finally shook her head in defeat. Hours later, she had no better luck at dinner. Nothing had the slightest effect on the woman who sat as still and mute as a statue.

Sometime after Miriam left, Tess felt the need to relieve herself. Her head finally turned toward the door that led to the garderobe, an unexpected twinge of stiffness in the movement. She stood but stumbled to her knees, the muscles in her legs having locked after so many hours of absolute stillness. Moving slowly, she gained her feet again and walked stiffly to the door, performing the necessary task then returning to the main room. Miriam had stoked the fire before leaving and Tess walked toward its warmth. She sat cross-legged on the fur that was spread before the hearth and stared into the flames, the sight of the fire just as hypnotic as staring at the wall.

Miriam found her in that same position the next morning, staring sightlessly into the cold hearth. She laid a new fire, but could not coax the baroness to the bed, or even back to the chair. Tess's muscles stiffened of their own accord when Miriam boldly tried to pull her to her feet. Gazing down at the lady's empty eyes, Miriam crossed herself against evil then quickly left the chamber.

The warmth from the new fire seeped slowly into Tess's bones, as if awakening her from a deep sleep. She watched the flames dance along the oak logs yet the fire didn't hold the same strange fascination that it had the night before. The sound of voices returned with the warmth, as if carried in the heat of the flames. Tess didn't want to hear them, but they would not be silenced.

Closing out the world and retreating within herself was not the answer. Trying to shake off the strange lethargy, she straightened her legs and rubbed them to get the blood moving. When she felt reasonably certain they would not falter, she rose and made her way to the table, taking a seat in front of the breakfast Miriam had left behind. The smell of the food made her stomach lurch violently, but Tess forced herself to eat, one small biteful at a time. A fat tear splashed onto her hand and Tess idly wiped it away. The food roiled in her stomach and she clapped her hand over her mouth, barely making the garderobe before losing her meal.

When Miriam arrived at midday with her meal, Tess used Kenric's trick and stared silently out the window with her back to the room, discouraging any conversation. She wasn't ready to face anyone, to see the questions or condemnation in their eyes.

The ploy worked well and Tess was left alone with her meals. Keeping food in her stomach was proving more of a challenge than she'd imagined. By the third day of her confinement, she had learned to avoid anything with even a hint of spice or strong flavors. So far bread was her most successful food. Her meals contained little else to help her keep even that down. The sickness would pass, she told herself, trying not to dwell on the problem.

19

Kenric ate more from habit than hunger, barely tasting the delicious food. The bounty from the kitchen had continued in his wife's absence and the great hall was as quiet tonight as it had been every other night this week. His men ate in respectful silence, no longer fouling the hall with the remnants of their meals. No one within Montague would be so lacking in sense as to test him. They knew the days of his leniency were gone.

"Simon still absents himself from my table," he remarked to Fitz Alan, nodding toward an empty chair. Simon had found one excuse or another to make himself scarce at meals for the past week.

"Aye," Fitz Alan answered. "He said there were duties that would keep him busy in the armory until late this night."

"There is no more word of the bailiff?" Kenric asked.

"Nay, every village has been searched and most of the countryside. No one has seen him for more than a fort-night. 'Tis as if he disappeared into thin air."

Kenric nodded and returned to his meal. Fitz Alan frowned, realizing the discussion was over. The baron spoke rarely since his wife's aborted escape, only to give orders or to make an idle remark such as the last that invited little conversation. Fitz Alan was the only person at Montague who had not actively avoided his company this past week. He'd mistakenly believed that Kenric might want a sympathetic ear to vent his anger, yet he kept it to himself instead. No one doubted its existence. Each day he pushed his men to the limits of their endur-ance, often taking the field himself to test their mettle. The smallest mistakes were punished ruthlessly.

Fitz Alan knew Kenric had good reason to be furious, but he was beginning to wonder who was being punished the most. He also wondered what would happen when they were called to court. The baron would be expected to produce a wife who stood willingly by his side. It seemed an unlikely event if he didn't change his mind about keep-ing her locked up. Although Fitz Alan wasn't foolish enough to question Kenric about his intentions where Lady Tess was concerned, Simon had confided all. Fitz Alan still had trouble understanding the severity of the punishment. The lady hadn't actually escaped after all, and no one had been hurt or even worked up a good sweat in detaining her. Confining her for a week or two would be a fitting way to show her the errors of her ways, but locked away for the rest of her life? It was unreasonable. Everyone but Kenric seemed to realize that fact.

"Helen has been extremely cooperative of late," Fitz Alan ventured, bolstering his courage. The subject he in-tended to broach would likely earn him a black eye or sore jaw. No one yet had had the nerve to mention Lady Tess's name in the baron's presence. He foolishly decided to be the first. "She tells me your wife has things running so smoothly that there is little for her to do."

"Helen is gulling you again," Kenric said between bites. "The duties she assumed should keep her busy all day."

"Well, perhaps I exaggerated a bit," he admitted. "The fact is, Helen was hoping she would be allowed to visit Lady Tess. The request seemed reasonable and I told her I would ask your permission."

"Nay."

"None in the fortress have laid eyes on the lady for nearly a week." Fitz Alan knew he was wading in dangerous waters but continued anyway. "Only Miriam has seen Lady Tess, and her reports have Helen worried. According to Miriam, she eats barely enough to keep herself sustained and she hasn't spoken a word to anyone since she's been in there."

" 'Tis not Helen's place to concern herself with my wife. Tess is feeling sorry for herself. She will eat when she is hungry enough."

"She is—"

"I will not discuss this subject further."

Fitz Alan scowled, abandoning the conversation. It was a pointless one. Kenric wasn't ready to listen to reason. He might not ever be. Whatever Lady Tess had done, the damage was serious and it went beyond a harebrained attempt to escape. Fitz Alan made a mental note to have Miriam report the baroness's condition to him each day. He would take matters into his own hands if her condition seemed to worsen. If Kenric refused to act sensibly, he would do it for him. Someday he might even be thanked, assuming he lived long enough for such praise.

Kenric was determined to ignore Fitz Alan's warning. If Tess was suffering, she deserved every minute of it. Starving herself was probably a deliberate ploy, knowing he would eventually learn of her "pitiful" state. He hoped the gossip reached her intact. He wanted her to know that he'd been told of her fast and remained unmoved. She would likely eat like a horse the moment she knew her trick wouldn't work.

Tess had been in his thoughts constantly the past week, even though he'd tried to banish her from his mind as completely as he'd banished her from his life. He knew other men who kept unwanted wives in virtual imprisonment. But Tess wasn't like any other wife. She was a gift from his king, and Edward had made it clear that he wanted a male heir for Remmington by the time they were called to court. Tess had shown no signs that she would follow his orders so easily. That forced Kenric to reconsider his relationship with his wife, although in the end his decision differed little from what he planned the day he sent her to the solar. To keep his bargain with the king, he would be forced to visit her occasionally until she conceived. The visits would continue if she failed to produce a boy.

The prospect of bedding his wife wrenched at his guts. There would always be the worry that he would weaken again and perform his duty as something more than just that. Already he wondered if he could manage it. Tess deserved nothing more than his contempt. He tried to console himself with the hope that she might have conceived the last time they were together. It would be a fitting reward for the hell she was putting him through.

That was his thought as he climbed the tower steps and entered his bedchamber that night. It was the time of day he dreaded most, knowing the long days he put in on the practice field were never long enough for a restful night. Nothing of Tess remained, yet the memories of her lingered everywhere, especially here. Images of her haunted him with the deceitfulness of soft smiles and innocent looks, memories he had no control over. He would glance at the table and recall the way she used to rest her chin in her hands while she listened to his stories, her eyes shining with what he'd thought was admiration as he recounted some of his more noble deeds. Other times it was an image as simple as the way she'd turned and smiled at him while brushing her hair. She was in his bed, at his bath, drying her hair before the fire, pushing open the shutters in the morning sunlight, her every curve outlined through a near transparent chemise.

Yet the memories were beginning to fade. Each day they cluttered his thoughts less often. In a few more weeks they would be gone entirely. By then he'd know if he would be forced to visit his wife and stir them all to life again. Settling into his empty bed for the night, he tried to fill his head with plans for the next day, of every exercise that would hone his skills for the battles that lay ahead, hoping tomorrow they would be exhausting enough to let him sleep undisturbed. Yet every night he awoke at least once, reaching for Tess in his sleep. Her punishment had become his own.

Kenric's suffering would have surprised Tess greatly. She was sure he'd simply resumed his life as if she'd never been in it. He probably wore that foolish grin of his all day, happy at last to be free of her. Foolish, endearing grin. She missed him more than she'd known possible, the loss settling into a dull ache in her chest.

The nights were not so bad, for then she could dream of him. In her dreams he held her close again, whispered softly in her ear, kept her safe from the world until the cold light of reality peeked through the windows. Seven days after being banished to the solar, it was not only the sunlight that woke her, but a vague sense of unease. Despite the sameness of her solitary day, she couldn't shake the feeling that something was wrong. Or about to be. It was a sense of dread that kept her brow furrowed as she bent over Helen's tapestry, a task she'd been forced to through sheer, desperate boredom. The oppressive feel of a coming storm filled the air, despite the sunny day.

The tapestry was nearing completion and Tess wondered already what would fill her days after that. Perhaps Miriam would be allowed to bring her supplies for another. Unless her guards wanted a madwoman on their hands, they would surely allow that much.

It was only mid-morning, yet she couldn't seem to contain the yawns as she pressed her needle endlessly into the tapestry. One yawn caused her to drop a stitch when her attention wandered for a moment and she gave the needle an irritated tug, accidentally pricking her finger. She stared down at the bright drop of blood, knowing it was only a pinprick, watching in horror as it flowed into a river, over her hand, across her lap, flooding the floor around her in a bright sea of red. She squeezed her eyes shut, terrified by the sight of what she knew could not be. The vision began the second her eyes closed. It lasted only a few minutes, but they seemed the longest of her life. When she opened her eyes again, she was screaming.

Tess's two guards rushed into the room, both with drawn swords. They startled her back to reality, dragging her senses away from the awful vision. Thinking quickly, she pointed to a section of the mullioned window that she'd propped open earlier that day.

"A—a man dropped down from the battlements and entered through the window!" She turned toward the garderobe. "He fled in there when I screamed!"

The guards moved cautiously toward the garderobe, too intent on their prey to notice the baroness edging her way behind their backs toward the door. She was on the tower steps before they even opened the garderobe door and found the small chamber empty.

Tess raced down the tower steps, through the small door to the gardens and down the path that led to the lower bailey, as if reaching the training grounds were a matter of life or death. From the shouts behind her, Tess knew her guards were gaining on her. The vision had shown her exactly where to find Kenric. She just didn't know if she could reach him in time.

20

The baron's mood was dangerous. Another restless night was not the only reason he wore a scowl. The conversation he'd overheard between one of his soldiers and a serving wench in the gardens was the cause. He'd taken a shortcut to the training grounds that morning and was passing the long line of tall arbors that separated the path from the herb plots when a voice from the other side made him pause.

"Do you think he will release her soon?"

Kenric gave the bushes an odd look, for it certainly sounded as if they'd spoken. A moment later he realized there was a couple trysting on the other side.

"Aye," the soldier answered. "I have been with the baron many years. He is a hard man, but a fair one. He will free her when his temper cools."

" 'Tis said they had a fierce argument," the wench confided. "Jane believes the baroness tried to run away because she feared her husband's anger. *I* would not want to be anywhere near the baron when he is in a rage."

Kenric could almost picture the girl's shudder. He was about to leave the couple to their gossip but was stopped by her next revelation.

"Everyone in the castle has continued the duties she assigned them. The steward says it is the only way we can show the baroness our loyalty. When she is allowed to return, Lady Tess will realize that we did not turn against her as the baron has."

"We are doing much the same," the soldier admitted. "Though 'tis no great task to scrape our boots and eat like civilized men. I think most of my comrades are enjoying the novelty of behaving as mere mortals."

Kenric eyed the bushes and contemplated the direction of the soldier's voice. Revealing himself at this point would be humiliating so he settled for another form of revenge. He poked his sword through the brambly growth, and was rewarded with a startled yowl. Having had his fill of eavesdropping for the day, he stalked away, grinding his teeth over his newfound knowledge. By the time he reached the training grounds, the fury that had simmered all week was back at a rolling boil.

The soldiers avoided the baron, recognizing a foul mood when they saw it. Robbed of sparring partners, Kenric went to work on a row of tall posts that had been driven into the ground. He used his long battle sword to hack away at the posts, swinging the weapon high overhead to strike one side then the other until the wood splintered apart. The gossip ate at him like an acid. None within the fortress knew the true treachery behind his wife's attempt to escape. Everyone thought they'd had a lover's quarrel and he was simply sulking over her means of retaliation. No wonder Simon could not look him in the eye without the trace of a defiant glare. They were all on *her* side. He wasn't about to make a fool of himself with the truth. Let them think her abused. Let them think him cruel beyond reason. What else should they expect from the Butcher?

"Milord?"

Kenric spun on one heel, startling Fitz Alan with the reflexive move that brought the tip of his sword to rest against Fitz Alan's neck. Fitz Alan took a prudent step backward.

"You know better than to walk up behind me. What do you want?"

"The joust," Fitz Alan reminded, aware that Kenric's thoughts were elsewhere. "The Italian is eager to test his mettle and you did agree to ride against him today."

"Tell Roberto his wish is granted." Kenric picked up the linen shirt he'd discarded earlier and wiped his brow before tossing the garment aside again. He stalked off toward his warhorse, muttering under his breath, "Best he prepare for a sore backside."

The joust was an unusual event for Kenric's men while they were in training. Such a knightly skill was unnecessary for the siege of Remmington and their days were spent practicing with the weapons of war. Yet the young knight from Italy was new to Kenric's army and anxious to prove himself against such a legend. Some of the men tried to dissuade Roberto from his foolish determination, though most waited patiently for the arrogant young knight to be put in his place.

Kenric took the reins of his warhorse from Thomas and led the animal to the end of the practice field. It didn't take long to prepare for the match. Blunted ends were placed over the tips of the deadly lances, which eliminated the need for heavy armor. The blunting allowed knights to practice the joust without serious injury. Shields were the only protection necessary to deflect the blows, though everyone knew Kenric wouldn't use a shield with blunted lances. He preferred the punishment of the jolt to remind him of a rare mistake. He also knew his lack of armor intimidated his opponent.

The two contestants were just taking their positions on opposite ends of the practice grounds when a commotion arose near the gates that led to the gardens. At first Kenric thought his eyes deceived him. Tess could not be running toward him as if her skirts were afire, the expression on her face one of sheer terror. He believed it when he saw first one soldier then another tear through the gates in pursuit. The one in the lead finally overtook his prey, grabbing her arm and yanking Tess backward, nearly pulling them both off their feet in an effort to stop her. Kenric had the ridiculous urge to run the man into the ground for daring to touch her. It didn't matter. He was a dead man already for allowing her to escape in the first place, as was the second man who'd come to a stop a few paces away, his hands resting on his knees to catch his breath.

Tess was indeed several pounds thinner than the last time he saw her, almost gaunt. Kenric was amazed when she summoned enough strength from her frail body to break free again and continue the flight toward her husband, as if she expected to find safety there. He dismounted, crossed his arms, and waited. She skidded to a halt before him, about to speak when the soldier caught up to her.

The soldier grabbed the long end of her braid and gave her a vicious jerk backward, trying to avoid being clawed again by her nails. He never saw the blow from his overlord coming.

Kenric's grip on Tess's arm was painful, but less so than the soldier's grip had been on her hair. Noticing at last that he was naked from the waist up, she bowed her head and remained silent as he issued a curt order and the fallen man was dragged away. She was thankful for a few moments to catch the breath that had been robbed by her flight. The rest of his men backed away to a respectful distance, though every pair of eyes watched them.

"Thank God, I'm in time," she panted, still winded by her run.

Kenric grabbed her arms and gave her one hard shake, then lowered his head to within inches of her face. "You have just condemned your two guards to death. Tell me, Tess. Was your brief bid for freedom worth the price?"

"Nay, milord! I was not fleeing. My guards were tricked, for I could not take the time to explain the danger. There was not time."

"What danger?"

"You are in danger." She nodded toward the other end of the field, toward Kenric's opponent. "He means to kill you."

"Roberto?" He'd expected a tale, but this one was fanciful, indeed. "You think the Italian intends murder?"

"I was working on a tapestry and closed my eyes for just a moment, but I saw everything in my vision. The blunting on his lance will break away when it strikes your shoulder and the poison used on the tip is potent enough to kill anyone within a day. I know this sounds—"

"I've heard enough." His gaze found Simon and he motioned him forward with a jerk of his head.

"You do not believe me," she stated flatly.

"I believe you made a very stupid attempt to escape the solar and cooked up this story when it was obvious you were going to be caught. I believe you came to me when you were cut off from whatever escape route you'd planned this time, thinking I would be fool enough to believe your lies. That is what I believe, Tess."

"You must be right, milord." She bowed her head and stared at the ground. "I am sorry that I disturbed you."

Sorry that she disturbed him? He couldn't believe how easily she dismissed two deaths. She was colder than he'd suspected. Watching her twist her braid, he realized the trait did not necessarily manifest itself each time she perverted the truth and made note to remember that fact. But she was lying now. She wasn't the least bit sorry. He resisted the urge to slap the mouth that lied so blatantly, knowing he'd probably snap her neck.

"Milord?" Simon drew to a halt at the baron's side.

"Take her back to the solar. I will deal with her later."

Kenric turned and walked away without a backward glance. Simon held one arm forward, indicating that Tess should proceed him from the grounds. He didn't haul her away or even take her arm to escort her. With a field full of men and her husband's wrath to prod her, no one would think that she would do anything but return quietly to the solar to avoid further trouble.

Tess waited until Kenric was a good distance away then turned and started walking slowly toward the gates, glancing once over her shoulder to judge Simon's distance. She breathed a sigh of relief, realizing he was several yards away. It was all the head start she needed. Her hands fisted in her skirts and she lifted them past her knees, bolting toward the Italian. She wondered if she could reach the end of the field and snatch away the assassin's lance before anyone knew her intent. Men began shouting and she heard Simon's angry bellow, but she kept running, knowing they would never catch her in time.

So caught up in her determination to reach the end of the field, she wasn't immediately aware of the implications when Roberto lowered his lance and crouched down to position himself for the attack. Only when the Italian spurred his horse forward did she realize what was about to happen.

Tess skidded to a halt, confronting her peril head on as the great warhorse tore up the turf between them. The deceptively blunted lance lowered to eye level and her blood froze at the sight of the man's ghastly smile. She heard Kenric shouting her name but couldn't move. She stood as still and silent as a cornered rabbit, too terrified to take a step in any direction.

There was no longer a doubt in Kenric's mind about the truth of Tess's story. He tossed aside his useless sword as he rushed forward. There was no doubt in anyone's mind about the fact that he would never reach her in time. Even Simon was too far away. Watching the mounted warrior bear down on the small, defenseless figure, Kenric was certain his heart was being ripped from his chest. He shouted at Tess to run but she wouldn't or couldn't move. She was going to die before his eyes and he was powerless to prevent her murder!

The arrow appeared from nowhere.

One moment the Italian was smiling, the next, an arrow shaft protruded grotesquely from his left eye. The sight so shocked Tess that she was shaken from her stupor. She turned to run toward Kenric and safety. Roberto toppled backward and the lance fell uselessly to the ground. But the warhorse hesitated only slightly before galloping on. To a horse trained for war as well as tourneys, anything running on foot was an enemy and he changed direction to pursue Tess, intent on trampling anything in his path. Another rapid volley of arrows struck the animal's head and neck, slowing but not stopping his charge.

Tess ran past Simon toward Kenric, sure she could feel the animal breathing on her neck. A nudge on her back propelled her forward, right into Kenric's outstretched arms. He lifted her effortlessly and kept running.

Tess heard the agonized, inhuman scream just as the massive bulk of the horse flew by them. Simon had somehow grabbed the reins and brought the horse's head down, sending the animal's body careening over its broken neck. Kenric didn't dare stop until he knew they were out of the animal's path. He finally slowed to a walk then dropped to his knees when he was certain they were safe. His arms were wrapped around Tess so tightly that they squeezed out what breath she had left. Loosening his grip, he cupped her face then slid his hand lower across her throat until the palm rested against her chest, needing the reassurance of the frantic heartbeat he found there.

"You are not hurt?"

Kenric knew his voice betrayed his lingering fear. He'd never been so terrified in his life. Another moment and she would have been dead. He couldn't even begin to fathom the fact that she'd just risked her life to save his. It defied logic. Kenric wouldn't allow himself to consider the possibilities. Not now, anyway. He would wait for a quiet moment alone to torment himself with such musings. Right now there was a traitor in Montague and his possible accomplices to deal with. Just as soon as he felt able to walk again. God, he'd almost lost her!

"I'm just a bit winded." Her voice was soft yet uncertain when she questioned him. "You believe me now?"

Kenric glared down at her, unreasonably angry that she'd risked her life so foolishly to prove her point. Then he realized he'd be dead if she hadn't done just that. He settled on a disgruntled frown.

"Aye." That simple answer opened a whole new kettle of fish, but he didn't want to deal with the startling accuracy of his wife's vision right now. "You are certain you were not harmed?"

"I am fine," she assured him with a smile. Kenric was amazed by her composure, her ability to smile so soon after her brush with death. It occurred to him that he would never know how her mind worked. "It is over now?"

"Aye, but I will have the head of the archer who denied me the pleasure of killing that traitor myself." Kenric frowned again. "Nay, I will give the man who saved your life whatever reward he names."

"I believe I will go check the Italian's injuries," Fitz Alan said mildly. He was standing just behind Kenric with a longbow still clutched in one hand. "At least until you decide if I am to lose my head or be showered with gold." He smiled then at Tess. "You will let me know the outcome, Lady Tess? I should like to make myself scarce if the decision is not in my favor."

Tess tried to contain a startled giggle but Kenric's scowl remained fierce. He rose on unsteady legs with Tess held securely in his arms and walked toward Simon. The old soldier was still lying on the ground, others standing nearby with drawn swords, all clearly appalled by their lady's close call. Simon lifted one hand when he saw Kenric approach but it fell limply to the ground, his arm hanging at an odd angle.

"I just wanted a short rest, milord." Simon's voice was teasing, but pained. "That damned horse jarred my shoulder."

Tess immediately began squirming in Kenric's arms. "I can ease his pain, if you will let me."

He hesitated a moment before setting her on the ground. Tess welcomed the distraction of examining the injured man. It took her mind off the crowd gathering around them and the group of soldiers farther up the field, surrounding Roberto. A short time later she knew the cause of Simon's pain; a dislocated shoulder. The agony Simon must endure to right such an injury was necessary, hopefully accomplished before the man could figure out what was going to happen. Kenric barely had Simon propped up when Tess moved in from behind and applied the required pressure. She frowned over Simon's sudden howl but knew he would feel immediate relief. She was busy instructing Simon on his recovery when Fitz Alan returned to Kenric's side.

"He is alive," Fitz Alan murmured. "Though I cannot say for how long."

"I can." Kenric was ready to kill with his bare hands. But he was torn between the need to give the traitor his due punishment and reluctance to leave Tess. His arm tightened around her shoulders, pulling her closer to his side. He needed her there to help calm the raw fury still coursing through his blood.

"I will stay with Lady Tess," Fitz Alan volunteered. Kenric nodded and began to loosen his grip on her shoulders.

"Nay. I would go with you," Tess stated calmly. "I

have seen wounds of all sorts, milord. Do not worry that the sight will disturb me. I know where the arrow struck."

Kenric's expression remained grim, but he put his arm around her waist and led her toward the group of soldiers who were clustered around the fallen Italian. The men parted instantly to allow them near Roberto then closed in again to form a tight circle.

The sight was indeed gruesome. Tess took several deep breaths, determined not to seem squeamish in front of Kenric's men. She tried to eye the Italian dispassionately, to view him as any other wounded man. He wouldn't live. In his agony, Roberto had ripped the arrow from his face, leaving a grisly, gaping wound. The man would slowly bleed to death. Tess was amazed that Roberto was still conscious. His good eye was glazed with pain but he looked around the gathering with alert wariness.

"Get his lance," Kenric ordered. Thomas ran to do his bidding, returning with the weapon. Kenric took the lance and rested the long, blunted end on Roberto's neck. He waited a moment then lowered the tip to the ground just above Roberto's shoulder, suddenly thrusting the lance forward. The razor-sharp blade emerged from the dirt, the blunting shattered to reveal its false end. "Who are your accomplices and where are they? Name them swiftly, or defy me and die slowly, in a way that is guaranteed to take your mind off your present injury."

Roberto closed his good eye and remained silent. Kenric started forward then stopped abruptly. He motioned to Fitz Alan. "Take her someplace where she cannot see or hear this."

"I understand your need to hurt him," Tess whispered, so the injured man would not hear. "But he will not last the day. Let me try reason once more before you try torture."

It would be hours before Roberto died of his injury or by the means Kenric would use to extract the information he wanted. Kenric ordered his men to pin Roberto to the ground then allowed Tess to kneel down beside the man.

"I have seen a wound like this before," she told him in a sympathetic voice. "Nothing can be done to save you, but your death will not come swiftly. My husband will have long hours, perhaps as much as a day or more to punish you for your treachery. He spent many years in the Holy Lands where he learned from the infidels how to inflict great pain without killing his victim." Tess didn't know if this was true or not, but thought it sounded wicked enough to be believable. "The tortures you will endure are hard for a gentle lady to imagine, but you must know what Baron Montague is capable of doing to his enemy."

Roberto's eye was open again and Tess could see his growing fear. She drew her dagger so fast that none of Kenric's men had a chance to object, though she heard their startled gasps. None but Tess would dare deny Baron Montague his prisoner. The small, jeweled dagger that she'd been allowed for use with her meals now rested against the Italian's neck. She tried to push away the memory of another man at her mercy in just such a fashion.

"Tell my husband what he wants to know and I will kill you myself. One swift cut and you will be spared the torture."

There was nothing to gain by remaining silent, but much to suffer. Having no loyalties to anyone but himself, Roberto wisely chose to divulge his plan. His voice was a hoarse whisper as he revealed his secrets, the pain and his growing weakness evident.

Just as suspected, MacLeith was behind the Italian's plot. The knight was a mercenary, approached by MacLeith almost two months ago in the Scottish king's court where Roberto was employed to rid that ruler of a troublesome in-law. MacLeith knew his stepdaughter was at Montague and wed to Kenric, the information coming from

Montague's own bailiff. MacLeith feared Kenric's army. Without their leader, he felt certain Kenric's men would not attack Remmington. Roberto was to kill the baron then escape from the fortress by his own means. The bailiff had fresh horses and men waiting along the road to Scotland, where they would meet up again with MacLeith for final payment.

"'Tis the . . . whole . . . of it, lady." Roberto struggled to get the words past the swelling in his throat.

"Why didn't you try to kill me first?" Tess asked, puzzled that Kenric was the intended target.

"Remmington belongs to the baron . . . by your marriage. You were to die only for spite if . . . I could not kill your . . . husband." Roberto took several deep breaths then his voice rallied and became stronger. "Keep your promise, demoiselle. Kill me . . . now, lady."

"Is there anything more you wish to ask, milord?" Tess questioned Kenric without looking up, unable to tear her eyes from the morbid sight of Roberto's disfigured face.

"Nay. 'Tis all I need to know."

She could tell by his tone of voice that he was giving her permission to end Roberto's life. Her gaze dropped to the tip of her dagger, still resting against the Italian's neck. She'd done this once before. It would be an act of kindness to end Roberto's misery and spare him Kenric's retribution. Even if Kenric left him alone, Roberto would suffer a long time before finally dying. Already the man begged for death.

"I must keep my promise," she whispered, admitting the truth in her next breath. "Yet I cannot do it." Kenric's hand closed over hers and gently pried the knife away.

"You should not have to."

Tess didn't resist being pulled to her feet and handed over to Fitz Alan.

"Turn around, Tess."

She turned her back to Roberto, barely aware of Fitz Alan holding her against his chest to insure she would be spared the sight. She heard Kenric murmur something to Roberto but could not make out the words. No more than a moment passed before Kenric lifted her into his arms and carried her from the field. She didn't trust her voice until they were nearly to the great hall.

"Is it over?"

"Roberto is dead, but it is not over. Fitz Alan will take a patrol out to find Roberto's men and my bailiff. I will have them brought before me tomorrow. Today I would kill them all, before they might be convinced to reveal more secrets." He looked down at her pale face and frowned. "I still might."

21 🌸

Tess felt light as a feather as Kenric carried her up the steps to the great hall. He wondered if she'd truly intended to starve herself. The scent of spring flowers made his nostrils flare, knowing it was the scent she used in her soap. He breathed deeply, trying to trap the heady scent inside him. Now that the immediate danger had passed, the feel of her in his arms was also arousing his starved senses. Her arms were wrapped around his neck and he wanted to press her whole body against the length of his. Her hands were tangled in his hair, almost caressing the nape of his neck, and he wanted to yank out the small ribbon that held her braid in place and spread her hair across his chest. They were ridiculous thoughts. She was still too shaken by her ordeal to realize what she was doing.

Mounting the tower steps, he hesitated only a moment at the top before taking the passage that led to the solar. If he took her to his chamber, there wasn't a doubt in his mind that he'd make love to her. After coming so close to losing her, there was a deep, burning need to confirm his possession of her in the most elemental way possible. Forcing her to his bed was not the answer. He'd only wonder later if she'd enjoyed the experience, or if she'd simply played along again in hopes of buying her freedom with her body.

He noticed the changes in the solar right away. The room looked cozier now, a table and chair by the fireplace, a small bed he wouldn't fit into if he tried, a chest in one corner and a tub propped up in another. It was a warm, cheerful place. She should be happy here.

He laid her down on the bed and saw her wipe away tears. Giving her a moment to compose herself, he poured a mug of cider from the pitcher left on the table. "Drink this."

Tess took the mug and he watched her take a few small sips. The color that had been in her face earlier from all her running was gone now, emphasizing the new leanness he saw in her. Loose tendrils of hair swirled around her face in disarray and the gown she wore would look better on a London street urchin. Aye, she looked a mess. She was still the most beautiful woman he could imagine. He turned away and tried to find something in the room that would be distracting, knowing nothing in the world was more distracting to him than his wife. He hated her. She was a treacherous, plotting female who would have unmanned him, if he gave her enough of a chance. He wanted to see her suffer. He wanted to climb into that small bed and hold her for days, sate himself with her body until he could be sated no more. She would probably laugh at him the whole time.

"Is the food Miriam brings not to your liking?" He tossed a fresh log into the fire, then picked up the poker and began stirring the coals to keep himself busy.

"The food is fine. I've not been very hungry of late."

"You will tell your guards if there is anything in particular you would like for your meals."

Tess wiped away fresh tears. "Will the soldiers who guarded me today still be punished? They had no way of knowing I intended to flee. I told them an intruder had climbed into the room and they were trying to do their duty and protect me. It seems wrong for them to be . . . to be—"

"They will live," Kenric said shortly. "Simon and Evard will be at your door from now on. You will go to Simon if anything else . . . unusual occurs."

He trusted those two more than any others to keep her safe. The MacLeiths wanted her dead now but none would be able to harm her here. He was actually doing Tess a favor by keeping her confined to the safety of the solar. If she expected freedom as payment for his life, she wasn't going to get it. Still, affording her a few rewards for her actions today would not be unreasonable. "Helen has been asking to visit you. I will see that she does."

He glanced toward the bed to gauge her gratitude, but Tess seemed unmoved by the boon. She quickly lowered her gaze and took another sip from the mug. Setting the poker aside, he began examining the other objects in the room, lingering over the tapestry as if it held great interest.

Tess knew he didn't want to be in the room with her, wondered why he was still there when his restlessness was so obvious. She wanted him to leave so she could cry in peace. She wanted him to stay, not knowing how long it would be before she saw him again.

"You will tell Simon if there is anything you need or want," he said at last, turning away from the tapestry.

Tess nodded, swallowing the lump in her throat. She thought he meant to leave, but instead he sat down in the chair nearby, looking uncomfortable. He cleared his throat once, then turned his hand over to examine the nails.

"Why did you save my life?"

Tess was dumbfounded by the unexpected question. It hadn't occurred to her that he would need a reason. "You were in danger."

"My death would have accomplished the same as an annulment. You would have been free of me without the bothersome legal entanglements."

"I *never* wanted your death!"

A silent moment passed, then Kenric leaned back in the chair and crossed his arms. "Tell me about your vision."

Tess paled slightly and shook her head. "I don't want to think about it."

"That gruesome?"

"Very!" Tess nodded several times to emphasize the fact, her eyes dark with lingering fear.

"You've had these visions before." It wasn't a question, but he was demanding an answer.

Tess's gaze dropped to her hands and she nodded again. "Nothing like this one, but glimpses here and there of events I don't recall until they happen and seem familiar."

"Are you a witch?"

Kenric thought it a reasonable question. Tess looked insulted. She crossed her arms against her chest, her eyes changing to dark sapphires as her expression turned indignant.

" 'Tis a gift," she claimed stoutly. "Uncle Ian says it tends to appear in the women of our family, though it often skips several generations. My grandmother was the last. I doubt anyone accused her of witchcraft if she saved their life." She gave him a pointed look, her eyes narrowing even more. "And I daresay those who knew her well would not doubt her warnings."

He deserved that, he supposed, wanting to smile over the flash of fire in her eyes. Aye, she was highly insulted. If Tess told him the sky was falling, she would doubtless expect him to line up his men to witness the event. "Tell me about some of the things you have sensed in the past, perhaps events less grisly than today's."

Tess eyed him warily, suspicious of his motives. A man who would contemplate bringing his wife before the church with charges of witchcraft would need evidence. "Why?"

"I'm curious. Humor me."

"I can't recall anything," she said quickly, shaking her head. "Aye, everything has faded."

Kenric eyed her braid, frowning. "I would still like to thank you for saving my life. I would not have you risk your own again to do it. A warning will suffice."

"You are welcome," she said quietly.

"Simon and Evard are doubtless at your door already. I will make sure they remain there." Kenric stood up and stretched his arms out in front of him, an unconscious habit that indicated he was nearing the end of this discussion. One hand went to the center of his chest to scratch a nonexistent itch. "Fitz Alan will have a patrol out already to search for the bailiff. I intend to join them to make sure the traitor does not escape the noose this time."

Tess stared intently at his chest and Kenric's gaze followed to his hand. He'd forgotten that he was bare-chested. It struck him suddenly that he was half naked and Tess was no more than a pace or two away, a misleading look in her eyes as she stared at him. His hand dropped to his side as if he'd burned it. He wouldn't allow himself to read his own weakness into her expression. It was time to leave, while his control was still tightly leashed.

"You have been through an ordeal this morn and I will not keep you from your rest. Helen will visit you tomorrow." Kenric turned and walked to the door, suddenly anxious to be away. His hand hesitated on the latch when she called his name. He remembered hearing it many times before in other circumstances, usually when her lips were very close to his ear. He responded without turning to look at her. "Aye?"

"Will you visit me again?"

He closed his eyes, telling himself it was not longing in her soft voice, but simple curiosity. His answer was strained. "Perhaps."

22

The unusually warm weather soon changed the winter-dulled
countryside from drab gray to the bright colors of spring.
An entire week had passed since the joust, yet Tess was
certain it had been at least a year. The sudden change in
seasons only made the time she'd been in the solar seem
longer. Each day she waited in hopes that Kenric might
visit her, yet each day she waited in vain. His "perhaps"
had been a polite way of saying no. Helen and Miriam
were the only two who came to her door, but sometimes
Tess propped it open when Simon and Evard were in talkative moods.

Although she'd been apprehensive about Helen's first
few visits, they were now something she looked forward to
each day. The long afternoons nearly flew by while her
sister-in-law related all that was happening in the castle.

She learned that the bailiff and Roberto's men were captured only a few hours after the joust, but Helen knew nothing more of the traitors' fates. It took two days before Helen would speak a word of Fitz Alan, then she explained all, in a seemingly endless torrent of words. Helen was embarrassed by the abruptness of her betrothal, and she was still furious that Fitz Alan and her brother had placed wagers to decide whether he would marry her or not. Then she announced that she'd fallen in love with the man.

Tess was certain her jaw was on the floor that day. It took a lot of convincing on Helen's part before Tess even began to believe her, wary of another time she'd been duped by Helen's mooning. On the other hand, it was no secret that Fitz Alan was a ladies' man. Helen would complain of Fitz Alan in one breath, then sigh over him in the next. Tess could hardly believe this was the same cold woman she'd met the day she arrived at Montague.

Today Helen was unusually quiet on the subject of Fitz Alan. Nearly an hour of their daily visit had passed and Tess still hadn't heard his name mentioned.

"When are you going to do something about those awful gowns?" Helen asked, drawing a needle through her tapestry. Their needlework frames were placed in the middle of the room where the sunlight was best, facing each other to make conversation easier. Helen leaned around her frame and eyed Tess's linen dress with disapproval.

Tess gazed down at her worn garment, knowing its best days were long gone. "There seemed so much to do when I first arrived here that new gowns seemed far less important. They would have been ruined with all the cleaning we were doing. I thought to wait until spring when the cloth merchants returned with the traveling fairs."

She'd also waited for Kenric to take some notice of her wardrobe and offer the coin required to replace it. In her stubborn refusal to point out his oversight or wheedle him for the money, she'd ended up spiting herself. She eyed Helen's gown wistfully, though it was just a simple moss-green daygown. Tess could hardly remember what it was like to have a gown so spotless and no more than a year old. It was unlikely she would know the feeling anytime soon. There would be no spring fairs for Tess this year.

"I'd give you some of my fabrics but they were all made up into gowns last fall," Helen told her, frowning slightly. "But a few of my gowns could be easily altered to your size."

Tess was tempted. Any one of Helen's gowns would be a great treat, yet she was still stubbornly set on the matter of clothing. She'd not take castoffs from another. It was bad luck. Tess shook her head, refusing the offer.

"Kenric thinks you dress that way apurpose," Helen said evenly. "Last night he asked if you were still wearing that gown with the yellow bodice. When I said that you were, he scowled and called you colorblind."

Tess frowned. "Did you point out to his high and mightiness that I have no colors at all to choose from? That his great wealth might eventually recover from the staggering debt incurred by a bolt of fabric?"

Helen smiled at Tess's show of spirit. "I intend to point that out at dinner tonight. He caught me off guard, or I would have said something very similar at the time.

"Do you know anything about the particulars of betrothals?" Helen asked suddenly.

"A little."

"When you were betrothed to your stepbrother, did you and he . . . That is, were you . . . intimate?"

"Nay, never," Tess answered surely. "Gordon had no interest in me. In fact, women in general hold no interest for Gordon MacLeith, if you know what I mean."

Helen stared blankly.

"Never mind," Tess mumbled. "Why do you ask?"

Helen blushed furiously and bowed her head over the tapestry. "No reason."

"Are you and Fitz Alan becoming intimate?" Tess ventured, trying to keep her voice casual.

"He would have me believe it common for betrothed couples to . . . well, do certain things together." Helen still refused to look up from her work.

Tess smiled, almost picturing Fitz Alan wooing and coaxing the reluctant Helen. "Actually, I believe it is quite common for many betrothed couples to become as intimate before the marriage as they will be after. Indeed, 'tis the reason Fitz Alan was born at all."

"What do you mean?"

"Kenric told me that Fitz Alan's parents were betrothed, but his father was killed in a battle just days before the wedding. Though a betrothal is as binding as any marriage, Fitz Alan's father was the heir to a great estate and his uncles made haste to destroy any legal evidence of the betrothal. His mother's family was outraged and the two houses waged wars for many years, yet neither side could win and they finally declared a truce. Unfortunately, that left Fitz Alan unable to claim his estates, though he seems to have done fine on his own."

"Why, that lying cur!" Helen's hands turned into fists. "He told me his mother was a common tavern wench! That *she* wasn't sure if his father was the village fish monger or a swineherd." The sound of Tess's laughter only made Helen angrier. "He made me think the circumstances of his birth were more base than a serf's!"

"It seems he would have you accept him no matter who he is," Tess said quietly, though she was still smiling. Helen's mouth opened to object then snapped shut again. "You've made it no great secret that you resent your brother because he is a bastard. Why would Fitz Alan think you hold him in any higher regard?"

"Nay, he tries to sink my regard to new depths with his lies," she retorted, her eyes narrowing. "Fitz Alan would have me think him born of sin when in fact the church blessed his parents' union by betrothal."

"Is the difference so great?" Tess asked reasonably. "Whether the union was blessed or unblessed, the same child resulted. It does not make the man who grew from that union any better or worse. The world sees that Fitz Alan can prove no legal claim to his father's name or estates, so he is called a bastard. That does not make it right, and it should not make him any less worthy of respect."

"He should not be made to bear the foul name," Helen said forcefully, growing frustrated with the tangled mess. " 'Tis not fair!"

"I agree," Tess said slowly. "Yet you would have Kenric bear that name, even though your father agreed to accept him as his own by marrying your mother. Aye, that seems very unfair, Helen."

"The two are nothing alike. Kenric was not denied estates that were rightfully his!"

"You think not?" Tess asked mildly, remaining calm in the face of Helen's mounting anger. "Has it never crossed your mind that Kenric is at least ten years older than Edward's son by the queen? Do you realize what would have been Kenric's had the church recognized *his* parents' union?" Tess remained silent a moment to let the thought flourish, for Helen's expression said she'd never considered the possibility. "Do you truly believe that thought has never crossed Kenric's mind? Montague and Remmington together pale in significance."

"Their union was *not* blessed," Helen muttered, stubbornly trying to cling to her beliefs.

Tess shrugged. "God saw fit to bless them with a child."

"Ooh, you are trying to confuse me." Helen picked up her needle and began poking at the tapestry again. "The three of you are like to drive me mad."

Tess was silent for a moment, drawing her own needle through her tapestry several more times as she waited for

Helen's temper to cool. When Helen's stitches became less driven, Tess began speaking quietly, her head bowed to hide her expression.

"I have listened for days to the way you talk about the man you will marry. You seem to hold some affection for him, yet you will let yourself be swayed by what others would call him, see nothing in him but what you think you should see. You are my friend, Helen, and I would not want to see you make the same mistakes in your marriage that I made in mine. Bastard or not, Fitz Alan has as much pride as my husband. If you do not judge him fairly, he will turn against you. When that happens . . ." Tess couldn't continue. She'd revealed too much of her pain.

"I'm sorry," Helen whispered, watching tears glide down Tess's cheeks and onto her tapestry. Tess's nod was barely perceptible as she acknowledged the useless sympathy. Helen shifted uncomfortably. "Would you like me to leave?"

Tess shook her head, wiping her eyes with her cuff. "Nay, 'tis I who should apologize. I'm a woman grown and have no business weeping like a child." She sniffed a few more times then managed to give Helen a weak smile. "I will have you believing marriage is an awful thing when it can truly be quite wonderful. Have you discussed the date of the ceremony?"

"Nay," Helen replied, visibly struggling to adjust to the change in the conversation. "Fitz Alan tells me he is in no hurry."

"It sounds as if he is in a great hurry indeed, if he is anxious already for the more intimate aspects of marriage. I believe I would make him wait until he could be bothered to set a date for the nuptials."

"Wait for what?" Helen asked innocently.

Tess rolled her eyes, certain that Helen would drive Fitz Alan crazy.

23

"*Well?*"

Kenric glared at Helen, wishing she'd stop fidgeting. Days ago he'd stopped pretending idle curiosity about her visits with Tess and started demanding a full report, with strict orders that she not repeat a word of his interest to Tess. These nightly interviews in his chamber before evening meals were becoming tortuous. Helen invariably spent a good five minutes being stubborn, blushing and stammering as she stood before him, finally prodded into a sketchy account of her afternoon.

"Well, she'd like a few new gowns," Helen blurted out. "There is no cloth left from last year's supply to make them. I thought—"

Kenric waved his hand in a quick motion meant to silence her. "You will have two of your gowns cut down to her size."

"But she—"

"Don't you dare object. You have enough gowns for ten women." Helen's mouth opened slightly as if she meant to defy his order, then she changed her mind and gave him a slow nod. "What else?"

"We talked of the fine weather we've been having. She noticed how much sun I'd taken yesterday and advised I wear a wimple or risk freckles."

Kenric wondered if Tess still looked as pale as the last time he saw her. Some fresh air and sunshine would probably do her good. Perhaps he would allow her to walk in the gardens for an hour each day. Perhaps that was an incredibly stupid idea. "Is she eating well?"

"I shared midday meal with her again today and her appetite seems healthy." Helen knew that was an understatement. Tess had done all but scrape up the crumbs. She found it amazing that the slight woman found a place to put it all.

"Did she speak of me today?"

Helen hesitated a moment too long.

"What did she say?"

"She does not complain of you, milord." Helen knew he had a purpose for extracting this report each night, but she still wasn't sure of its purpose. If he meant to gloat over Tess's misery, she would tell him nothing to please him. Yet if he was waiting for some sign that Tess had suffered enough, she didn't want to withhold that, either. Remaining vague was becoming increasingly difficult as his questions became more pointed each night. The first day she visited the solar, Tess had looked awful. In the days since then, Tess's appearance had improved steadily while Kenric's became haggard. He looked as if he hadn't slept for days, certainly hadn't shaved for a number of them, and his mood had become more volatile. It was telling, but telling of what? "I believe she mentioned that Fitz Alan has as much pride as you do."

There. That was surely vague. A comment that could be taken as a compliment or an insult, or neither.

"You talked about Fitz Alan?"

"Well, um, there were a few remarks here and there about our betrothal. Let me see. Aye, she asked if I knew the date of the nuptials and I told her I did not, and *she* said that I should ask Roger what date he would like and *I* said that Roger did not seem interested in any particular date and maybe I would suggest that myself. Milord."

Kenric's eyes narrowed dangerously. "And what did Tess say in response to all that blathering?"

"She said that sounded like a fine plan."

His glare turned menacing. "Exactly where in this conversation did Tess mention that Fitz Alan had a surplus of pride?"

Helen thought hard on that question. Her brows drew together over her eyes and she chewed on her lip. Kenric gritted his teeth when she started fidgeting again.

"If you can't think up anything believable, why not try the truth?" Kenric crossed his arms against his chest, waiting.

Helen stopped moving, nearly stopped breathing. "She warned me not to abuse Fitz Alan's pride. She said if I did, he would turn against me."

Kenric mulled that over, trying to decide if he should read anything more into Tess's remark than a friendly warning. His wife was right. Fitz Alan *would* turn against Helen if she tried to humiliate him. Aye, he supposed Tess was a veritable font of knowledge concerning a man's pride. She'd certainly given his a bath.

Tess must be turning bitter. She thought she should be forgiven since she'd saved his life. The warning she gave Helen today meant she knew that would not happen. His mind conjured up an image of Tess in one of her pitiful gowns, not the one that made him dizzy, he decided, shifting the mental image of her to a gown that lacked color entirely. Yes, that was it, this picture was much clearer.

She was sitting on the small bed in the solar, growing thinner, growing paler, everything he'd liked about her fading with the image.

" 'Tis all we talked about today, milord."

Helen's voice trembled noticeably. Kenric knew without a doubt that she was lying. He didn't want to hear any more of what she would tell him. Rubbing his brow with one hand, he dismissed her in curt silence with the other.

He didn't go down to dinner at all that night, didn't eat, didn't drink, simply thought of his wife, trying to decide what to do with her. He'd wanted her to suffer, and she'd suffered. He'd wanted her to pay for her deceits, and she'd saved his life. He'd wanted to torment her with the knowledge that she would never see him again and had instead created his own private hell. He wanted her to come to him again, giving herself to him as she had that night before her attempted escape, and he wanted to hear words she would never speak. He'd even started lying to himself as he lay sleepless in his bed, reliving each moment of their last night together, telling himself it was real, that she'd meant every word. He was going mad.

He leaned back in his chair and flipped open the lid of the trunk behind him, searching only a moment before pulling out Tess's mirror. He'd retrieved the bag of her hidden belongings from the garden the day she'd tried to escape, thinking he'd enjoy knowing that she was doing without these meager comforts. Now he was morbidly attached to them. They represented the woman he thought she'd been. He turned the mirror over and stared at the image reflected back at him. It was not a pretty sight. Could he really blame her for trying to flee it? The image frowned.

Questioning his sister each night was becoming odious. He needed to see for himself how she fared. Tess would not consider his visit all that odd or even promising. In a moment of weakness he'd said that he might visit her. He'd thought it a lie at the time. Now he would make it truth. He rubbed his chin, examining the rough growth of beard in the mirror. This face would frighten her. With a new purpose to his step, he found a pitcher of water, the blade he used for shaving, and scraped away the stubble. He considered his clothing then decided the breeches and simple linen shirt he wore would be sufficient, otherwise she might think he'd dressed specially for their visit. Then he began wondering what they would talk about.

Before he sent her to the solar, there had never been a lack of words between them. Well, perhaps occasionally, but even the silences had been comfortable. Silence between them tonight would not be comfortable. He pulled his chair up to the table and rested his elbows there, propping his chin in his hands, trying to find some topic he could keep on neutral ground. He knew nothing of tapestries or sewing, the task that seemed to consume the lion's share of her day. A handful of words and he'd be done for. Asking about her day would only point out that he'd taken away all the tasks she used to tell him about so proudly, even with a hint of boasting. And why on earth would she want to know about his day? She would no longer feel a part of it. Lord, would Tess be wrong in that assumption. She was fast possessing every hour and every minute of his days. Even the training grounds could no longer distract him. Every time he looked onto the field, he pictured Roberto trying to run her into the ground.

Perhaps it was time to talk about their marriage, how he would visit her occasionally until she conceived. That was bound to be a jolly conversation. No, he would visit her once or twice before imparting that bit of news. Staring into the dying embers of the fire, Kenric finally realized the hour had grown late, probably well past midnight. She wouldn't even be awake. Knowing how soundly she slept, he thought it doubtful she'd rouse to a conversation that would probably consist of five words; "greetings," "how fare you," and "good-bye." No, she would sleep right through that. She could sleep through . . . almost . . .

anything. There was a shadow of a smile around his mouth as he rose from the table and left his chamber.

Three soldiers were at her door. The flickering light of rush torches revealed Simon and Evard fast asleep on the bedrolls they'd spread out in the hallway. Bertram had been assigned to stand guard while they slept, although he was actually sitting, whiling away the night hours with a solitary game of dice. He leaped to his feet the moment he spied the baron, ready to bellow a greeting that would wake the other two.

Kenric held a finger to his lips and quickly shook his head, relieved when Bertram nodded. The soldier reached for the latch to open the door but Kenric slapped his hand away, easing the door open with a fraction of the force Bertram would have used in his eagerness. He stepped silently into the room and waited for his eyes to adjust to the darkness. The barely discernible glow from the hearth was the only source of light, any moonlight that might have shed its weak light through the windows obscured by a clouded sky. He wanted to see her.

Tess could sleep through almost anything, he told himself again, finding several logs in the pile of kindling laid out for the morning fire. The weather might be warm outside, but the thick stone walls would hold the cold of winter for another month. He stirred the coals until they came to life again, flickering a little higher as the logs fed the tiny flames. He made his way across the room, crouching down on one knee when he reached the side of the bed. She was lying on her side, her face toward the fire, one hand tucked beneath her cheek. The lines of her face were vague in the dim light but he studied her intently, searching for signs of illness or distress. He could barely see her.

One of the logs burst into flames just as he leaned closer, the flickering lights bathing Tess's face in a brilliant glow of gold. Kenric's breath caught in his throat and he sat back abruptly on his heels, startled by the sudden radiance of her beauty. The memories did not come close to this vision. He reached out with one hand and trailed his finger along the soft curve of her cheek. Her lips turned up slightly in a smile and she rubbed her other cheek against her pillow, the same way she used to rub against the middle of his chest. Kenric used his free hand to massage away the ache there, where she should be, becoming motionless when she murmured his name in her sleep. It was a sweet sound, one he'd taken so much for granted that he'd forgotten how often she did it until now.

Afraid of disturbing her, he drew his hand away from her face, down her bare shoulder and arm to the hand resting against the covers. Her hands were not as soft as the rest of her skin, but they were much softer and considerably more delicate than his. He pressed a tender kiss in the palm then turned his face to nuzzle against it, the same way she'd just rubbed against her pillow. She mumbled something unintelligible then scooted to the edge of the bed, closer to him. Slowly, inch by inch, Kenric moved first one arm beneath her then the other until he'd eased her into his arms and himself onto the bed, sitting cross-legged in the center. Holding her sleep-warmed body was an exquisite torment. She curled up trustingly against his chest, shifting occasionally in her sleep to snuggle closer. He bent to press his lips against her forehead, turned to lay his head against the crown of her hair and stroked the satiny surface with his cheek, lifting his head to treat the other side of his face to the softness. His hand found her braid tucked over one of her shoulders and he eased the knotted ribbon from the end, loosening her hair one plait at a time, knowing he'd find hours of pleasure just sifting the silky strands through his fingers.

The solar door opened again an hour before dawn and Kenric slipped quietly into the hallway. All three soldiers were awake now, obviously waiting for the baron to emerge, their heads bowed to hide wolfish grins. Kenric ignored them and stalked off toward his own chamber.

"I told you he'd give in eventually," Evard boasted after Kenric left, elbowing Simon's ribs. Simon gazed thoughtfully in the direction of the baron's bedchamber. "Now that he has succumbed to temptation, he will have her moved back to his chamber by nightfall. Our hallway duty will come to an end. We can spend our nights in our own beds at last, or in the company of a lively wench," he added with a lewd wink.

"We shall see," Simon murmured doubtfully.

Tess awoke remarkably refreshed, feeling more rested than she had for weeks. There was something different about the morning but she couldn't quite put a finger on what it might be. Leaning up on one elbow in her bed, she realized her hair had come undone in the night, but that wasn't it. Tossing the covers back, she rose from the bed and headed to the garderobe. It wasn't until she was pulling her gown on for the day that she perceived what made this day different from others. The sickness that still troubled her in the mornings had disappeared entirely. At last!

Smiling over her reprieve, she finished dressing then propped her door open for the day. Simon and Evard were outside the door as usual, both looking at her rather expectantly. She bade them her usual good morning then enjoyed her breakfast a short time later.

"She acts as if nothing has happened," Evard whispered to Simon while the baroness was distracted by Miriam's company. His brow furrowed into a puzzled frown. "Nor has she started packing. Do you think it possible she doesn't realize that he will release her today?"

Simon nodded. "'Tis possible he made no promises last night. The baron does not give in easily. In fact, he's never conceded anything that I know of. It might take him time to come to terms with this concession. We will know by evening meal if he intends to end this."

By the time Tess finished her dinner that night, her guards were looking downright bleak. They'd been unusually quiet all day, silent, alert, as if waiting for something.

Tess shrugged over the oddity. She closed the door behind the servants who filled her tub then lingered a good hour over her bath. The servants returned to haul the water away as she sat before the fire, brushing her hair dry and thinking over her day.

Helen had been quiet, too, though she ventured a few more questions about her betrothal that became embarrassing for both women. It didn't take long for Tess to realize that her own maidenly knowledge of marital relations had been vast compared to Helen's. Montague doubtless had plenty of trysting nooks the ladies of the castle were unlikely to stumble across, as Tess had stumbled across them at Langston Keep. Tess's healing skills with people as well as animals took her to birthings and exposed her to other more basic facts of life. Helen had yet to guess they existed. Aye, Fitz Alan was in for a time of it.

Helen's questions forced Tess to recall her own marriage, the kisses and caresses Kenric had given her carelessly. Pining for them only made it worse. She tossed and turned restlessly on her bed for an hour or two before finally drifting off into an exhausted slumber.

Bertram nudged Simon nonchalantly with his foot late that night as he rose to greet the baron. None of the men were grinning when the baron emerged again hours later without a word. Their expressions reflected puzzled curiosity. The baroness greeted them as usual that morning, going about her day as if nothing out of the ordinary was transpiring at night. At dawn on the fourth day of this new routine, it finally occurred to Simon that Lady Tess might not be aware of her husband's visits.

"I noticed that you've been using more wood on your fire during the nights," he remarked, after she'd finished her breakfast that morning. "I can have the fire stoked with more logs before you retire each evening to save you the trouble of tending it yourself when the room grows too cold for . . . sleeping."

"I haven't been the least bit cold during the nights,

Simon." Tess looked genuinely puzzled by his concern. "And I certainly haven't been tending my hearth at night."

"There is wood missing each morning from the stack I left the night before," he said reasonably, nodding toward the fireplace.

"I'm sure you're mistaken. The wood you lay in the fireplace at night has been quite enough to last until morning."

Simon nodded, his curiosity satisfied. Lady Tess had no idea that the baron had found a new torment for himself.

24

The king's herald and his escort were quite a sight to behold.
Crowds gathered at the wayside of every village and ham-
let they passed through on the road to Montague. Two
pages led the parade of thirty soldiers, each holding a long,
slender pole with an enormous banner stretched between
the two. Everyone recognized the banner with three lions
stitched in gold thread on a background of crimson silk. It
was the king's coat of arms. Gold tassels fringed the impressive banner, their ends sparkling and fluttering in the
breeze to draw attention.

The king's herald, a tall, dignified man named Vin-
cent de Guille, rode at the center of the procession, his
beard as long and snowy white as his hair. He wore the
official robes of his station, the crimson and gold embroidered cloak pinned at one shoulder by three broaches,

each in the shape of a lion. In his arms he carried a sturdy, banded chest. The king's missive rested safely inside, the scroll sealed and stamped with red wax against prying eyes.

Kenric knew of the herald's approach almost two full days before his arrival. News of such an important person traveled much faster than the traveler. Kenric made the necessary preparations, but he used the time to decide much more than what supplies would be necessary for the long journey to court. By the time the herald's entourage rode through the gates of Montague, he'd made his decision. After four nightly trips stealing into Tess's room under the cover of darkness, he knew those trips had to stop. Aye, it was time to put a stop to it all.

The herald was welcomed in the great hall, Kenric dispersing quickly with the pleasantries. After handing over the chest entrusted to him by the king, the herald looked surprised when Kenric tucked the chest under his arm and stood up to leave.

"Milord, you've no need to fetch a priest to read the king's word. I was sent along for that purpose."

"I've no need of a priest," Kenric said shortly. "I will read the message myself."

"Your pardon, baron," the herald said stubbornly. "But many men would have trouble deciphering these noble words. My duty is to ensure that the king's message is delivered in its entirety."

Kenric glanced down at the chest, eyeing the words that were engraved on the metal bands. Holding up the chest to eye level, he recited them for the herald without hesitation. "I will uphold the word of my sovereign, King Edward. Only God's word is higher." Kenric gave the herald an impatient glare. "Does that assure you that I am capable of reading the king's message?"

"Aye, milord." The herald bowed as the baron turned and left the hall.

Kenric retreated to his chamber to read Edward's message in private. Spreading the parchment out on the table, he began picking his way through the courtly rhetoric and flourishing scripts of the scribe who was entrusted to write the king's messages. The elaborate seal at the bottom assured him the document was genuine, but part of the message surprised Kenric. He read it twice before he understood why the king would make any mention of an annulment. They both knew the MacLeiths would demand it, so there was little reason to remark upon the fact. The king was warning Kenric. MacLeith must be using the church to pressure Edward into annulling the marriage because of Tess's pledge to MacLeith's son, Gordon. If the church took a strong stand in the matter, the situation could become serious. Aye, he was being warned to expect the worst. He wanted to laugh at the irony.

Rolling the parchment and tucking it under his arm, Kenric left his chamber and walked purposefully toward the solar. Tess's door was standing open, Simon and Evard hanging halfway into the room at the doorway, Helen and Miriam already inside. Tess was seated before her tapestry, wearing the same colorless dress he'd hoped would be burned by now.

"Out."

The single word emptied the solar of all but Tess and Kenric. The door closed and they were left alone. Tess hadn't seen Kenric since the joust. She stared at him openly as he gazed silently out her window. He looked as if he'd lost weight, his dark leather breeches and tunic not as snug as they usually were. Dark circles shadowed his eyes as if he'd been a long time without sleep. She could sense his tension and a disquieting difference in his solemn expression. Something was wrong. Something serious. He wasn't angry, but he was a man troubled. The feeling of dread that settled in the pit of her stomach said she didn't want to hear whatever it was he'd come to tell her. She was right.

"This marriage was a mistake," he said finally, in a voice that was not complaining but stating a simple fact.

"None will profit by its existence now or in the future. An annulment is the only solution."

Tess had longed to hear those very words weeks ago, prayed for them in the first days of her marriage. Her prayers had been answered. She vowed to never pray again in her life. She felt as if he was driving a knife into her heart. In a flicker of curiosity, she wondered if he'd felt any portion of this awful pain the day she'd told him she wanted an annulment. Nay, it was his pride that was injured that day, not his heart.

"The king's herald arrived with orders that we are to appear in court within two fortnights." He looked down at the parchment as if he'd forgotten its existence. He held up the scroll to show her the king's seal, the proof it was genuine, then he tossed it onto the mantle above the fireplace and clasped his hands behind his back. "You were right from the beginning. The king suggests an annulment as a way to take Remmington intact. The MacLeiths are also demanding an annulment, but I will turn you over to the king instead. After the abuse you have suffered from Gordon is made known, the king will break the betrothal agreement with the MacLeiths. You will be allowed to retire to a convent. Helen and Miriam will be allowed to accompany you to court. We leave on the morrow."

Without another word or even a glance, Kenric turned and left the room. Tess stared silently at the door, trying to absorb the news. He was letting her go. She had somehow won. There was never a greater feeling of loss. Her gaze moved around the room, knowing she'd not be locked in there much longer. That should make her very happy. Her days of imprisonment would end tomorrow.

Tess shook her head, knowing her days of misery were just beginning. She'd thought Kenric would forgive her in time, that the child she carried might sway him somehow, enough to allow her another chance to regain his trust. He didn't even know the child existed. It would be a month or more before her condition became obvious. If she remained silent, he might not even guess she was carrying until the marriage was over. Would it make a difference if he knew?

Tess wrapped her arms around her waist, as if protecting the slight bulge there. An annulment would be best. She'd known that from the moment the marriage began. Even the king agreed. Now Kenric did, too. The marriage would end, the MacLeiths would be forced to leave Remmington, and everyone could go about their lives as if this time had never been. Yet the proof of their time together would become obvious enough in the next few months. For the first time, she allowed herself to think beyond what would happen in the weeks after the annulment.

She would retire to a convent, probably the one near Kelso Abbey. Her child would be born there, allowed to stay with its mother should it be a girl, sent to the father if a boy. No matter how hard she'd prayed for a girl, Tess felt instinctively that it would not be. She would be robbed of even that part of Kenric. He would have his heir and Remmington, and she would have nothing. With a son, Kenric would surely see that Remmington prospered. He would keep her people safe and the lands protected. In a few years, no one would even remember she was alive. She would never see her child grow and she would never see her husband again. That would be the price she paid to spare Remmington a siege.

Tess stood up with her hands fisted at her sides. The price was too high! She was not that noble, could not sacrifice so much. Did she deserve nothing in life? What if the MacLeiths decided to keep Remmington, no matter what the church said? Her sacrifice would be worthless, lives ruined and none spared. Tess began to wring her hands, growing frantic.

If Kenric knew of the babe, he might be talked out of the annulment. Would he truly go through with it, knowing he was agreeing to make his child a bastard? Would he destroy all of Remmington in a siege, knowing he wielded his sword over his child's future? She began to pace, contemplating other effects of upholding her marriage.

If Kenric kept her at Remmington, she might be permitted to know her child, perhaps to raise him the first few years. If allowed the freedom of the fortress, she could tend the ills and injuries of her people, assure them that they'd never been forgotten in her heart. She might even be allowed the duties of the household that would give purpose to her days. What reason would Kenric have to keep her locked away and idle at Remmington? Aye, the confines of marriage looked much more appealing than the veil of a convent. In time, Kenric might even forgive her.

There was little doubt in her mind that Kenric despised the name bastard. He would not knowingly give his child the same name. She was sure of it. Her argument against the annulment would be a strong one. But what of the king? She tried to rub that worry away from her brow, but knew it would not be dismissed that easily. If Edward insisted on an annulment, would Kenric go against the wishes of his sovereign to make his child legitimate? To keep an unwanted wife? There would be too many arguments against her. Not only would Kenric have an heir and Remmington, he would be rid of his wife and could keep his pledge to Guy. Their child would have no claim to Montague. That argument would be much stronger. Tess felt her hopes slipping already.

The parchment above the mantle caught her eye and she realized Kenric must have forgotten it in his haste to be away from her. There was little reason for him to be mindful of the document now that he'd read its message, and he would never suspect that she could make any sense of it. The carefully delivered scroll was useless after the contents were known and the parchment would likely end up in the kitchens to line the bottoms of bread pans, a common end to most documents. Thinking it might contain something useful to her cause, Tess spread the parchment on the table. The entire first paragraph consisted of an inane greeting, but the second paragraph got down to business, relating charges of kidnapping that had been brought against Kenric and the immediate annulment demanded by her family. It was the third paragraph that made Tess's mouth drop open in surprise. She read the first sentence three times. *Your king would find it grievous to see the marriage of his baron at Montague annulled.*

She read the remainder of the document carefully, yet there was no more mention of an annulment. The king did not want the marriage annulled. Kenric had lied to her. He intended to go *against* the wishes of his king. On the other hand, he could be lying about his intent to see the marriage annulled, simply to get her to court without argument. She stood up abruptly, her expression as firm as her will to know the truth. He was going to get an argument whether he wanted one or not. Determined to hear the truth from Kenric, Tess rolled the message and headed to her door. Simon and Evard were on the other side to stop her.

"Milady," Simon said pleadingly, holding on to her arm. "You cannot leave here."

"Remove your hand from my arm," Tess said, gazing down at Simon's hand. Simon was so surprised by the uncharacteristic coldness in her voice that he complied. "Move aside."

Simon moved to the center of the doorway to block her path more completely. "I cannot do that, milady."

"You will move aside, or I will move you myself."

Simon smiled down at the delicate baroness, as if picturing her forcibly moving him. When Tess drew the small knife she wore at her waist, he quit smiling. "Baroness, be reasonable."

"Aye, milady. We cannot allow you to leave," Evard piped in, eyeing the dagger nervously. "The baron would have our heads."

Tess's gaze moved slowly from Evard to Simon, knowing there was more than one way to get what she wanted.

"Your baron's life is in danger," she lied, satisfied when Simon's eyes grew wider. "Do you keep me from him now, he will die."

Simon hesitated. He was looking at Tess's hand, the one nervously twisting her braid. He stepped aside. "The baron is in his chamber, milady."

"But—" Evard stepped forward to protest. Simon planted his elbow in Evard's mid-section. "Ooof!"

"Stand aside, Evard. We shall escort the baroness to her husband."

The nearer they came to the bedchamber door, the less certain Tess grew of the wisdom in confronting Kenric. Aye, this was foolish. But it was too late to turn back. Simon had already rapped on the door. She put her hand on the latch but Simon shook his head and pushed her behind his back. He rapped on the door then waited for Kenric's order to enter.

The sight of Simon in his doorway made Kenric bolt upright from his chair, his sword already in hand. Simon held up his hand to stop him. "The baroness is safe, milord. She believes you are in danger and has reason to fear for your life." Simon pulled Tess to his side. "We felt it necessary to bring her here in all haste."

Kenric sheathed his sword, his eyes never leaving his wife. "Close the door behind you, Simon."

Tess's gaze swept slowly around the bedchamber, noting that little had changed. She heard the door close and finally allowed herself to look at Kenric. His arms were crossed against his chest and his feet braced, waiting for her to explain what urgency brought her here.

"You forgot this in the solar," she said weakly, holding out the parchment. He made no move to take the scroll and she walked forward to lay it on the table. There was a menacing feel in the air that she tried to ignore.

"What did you see?" He gazed so intently into her eyes that Tess had to look away, bowing her head as she grasped the tassel of her braid and began to worry at the ends with her fingers.

"Just a warning that you might be in danger."

"You're lying."

Tess nodded her head without looking up. "I read the king's message."

"You did what?" His tone said Kenric didn't believe that, either.

" 'Tis truth. Friar Bennet taught me the skill." Tess finally met Kenric's dark gaze and saw that he thought that another lie. She picked up the scroll and unrolled a portion to read the king's greeting. "From Edward, King of England, defender of God's word on earth, wise in his benevolence and awful in his vengeance, his words as told to Alfred of Carlys on this twenty-fourth day of—"

Kenric snatched the scroll from her hands and tossed it into the fire. "The message was not yours to read. You will have your annulment, Tess. I did not lie to you about that. The king will grant me as much for taking you from the MacLeiths. I have conceded that you are right about our marriage and will convince Edward as well."

Kenric turned away, wondering what she would do next to make his decision more difficult, more painful. Simply saying the words was bad enough. How many times did she want him to repeat them? The scent of flowers came to him. With his back to Tess, he was left staring at the bed. He closed his eyes, knowing her presence was too much of a strain for his starved senses. "Return to the solar, Tess. You should not have come here."

"Nay, I would spend my last night at Montague in your bed."

Kenric turned slowly to face her, his incredulous expression fading to anger and suspicion. "What is your game, Tess?"

"If you truly intend to annul our marriage, then this will likely be the last night we will have any privacy, the last night I can hope to change your mind."

"You've wanted an annulment since the moment we were married," he said evenly. "Do not think to convince me that you have changed your mind at this late date."

"I was wrong," she said quietly. Kenric shook his head, refusing to believe her. Tess nodded. "In the time we have been parted, I have given much thought to our marriage, what it would truly mean to have it ended. The price is too high, milord. I thought to sacrifice myself to spare Remmington, yet there is every possibility that the MacLeiths will ignore even the law of the church. They have disregarded every other. I promised before God to honor and obey my husband, yet I have done neither in great quantity. Remmington has been yours since the day we married. It will be yours even if our marriage is annulled. I blinded myself to the fact that you are lord of Remmington, that you are capable of judging what is best for those estates and that it is indeed your right alone. I would plead against needless slaughter should you lay siege to my home, but I will honor any decision you make. I would remain your wife willingly, milord."

Kenric closed the distance between them in two easy strides. He wrapped one hand firmly around her throat, pulling her forward none too gently until their foreheads were almost touching. Tess's eyes grew round with fright, but she did not struggle against his hold.

"Do you think I am fool enough to believe any of those lies?" He shook her once, his eyes narrowing. "What do you hope to gain by them? Tell me the truth, Tess!"

Tears formed in her eyes and the words poured out painfully. "I would do anything to stay with you, even if it means being no closer than the solar. I would forsake Remmington to cling to the hope that I might see you occasionally. I would betray my king if I thought it would buy your forgiveness."

He relaxed his grip on her throat slightly then he released her, pushing her back a step. "You are a better liar than I gave you credit for."

"Please," she whispered, her tears flowing unchecked. "Tell me what to say and I will say it gladly. If I have hurt your pride then take mine. I have no use for it without you."

"Very pretty words," he drawled, without revealing a trace of his inner turmoil. She'd already told him more than he'd ever dreamt she would say, words he would be ten times a fool to believe. He crossed his arms again and looked down at Tess as if he found her worthless. "There is nothing you can say. If you want to stay here tonight, do so and I will use you thoroughly. It will make no difference on the morrow."

That should make her turn tail and run. Whatever her reasons for this ridiculous game, she would never share her precious body, knowing his decision would not change. He didn't believe for a minute that she didn't want the annulment she'd plotted for months. There was some devious reason behind her lies that he couldn't perceive with his thoughts so muddled by her tempting words. She would retreat to the solar and design some new scheme to get what she wanted. She would plan new lies to torment him. She was undoing her bodice.

"What the hell do you think you're doing?" he demanded, staring at her hands as they fumbled at the laces.

"I would have one more memory. If you will have me this night, then I am yours."

Kenric grabbed her arms and pulled her closer, shaking her once. "I've told you it will make no difference! Why are you doing this?"

"Because I love you," she whispered brokenly.

Those were the words. Of any she could have said to him, those were the only ones that could crumble his defenses. He'd heard them too often in his mind, certain she would never think to use them as a weapon. They sliced through him as cleanly as the sharpest knife. He dragged her forward until she was pressed against his chest, his body reacting instantly to the feel of her, lowering his face to within a breath of hers. "Again! Tell me again."

"I love you. Even knowing that people I have known all my life will die because of it, I love you still."

Kenric gazed into the depths of her violet eyes, trying to discern the lie, finding nothing but her soul laid bare. A soul as wounded as his own. "God help you if you are lying, Tess."

His mouth crushed hers with all the pent-up emotions of too many nights without her, of too many days spent dreading those nights. His arms wrapped around her shoulders and hips, lifting her from the floor and pressing her tightly against his body until he could get her no closer. She was returning his kiss, returning his assault. Her arms were wrapped around his neck, her hands fisted so tightly in his hair that his scalp burned. He didn't care. She loved him.

How many nights had he dreamt that she would come to him? Kept prisoner in the solar, she'd still managed to accomplish it. He'd wished impossible wishes that she would have some affection for him. She had told him three times that she loved him. He was afraid to end the kiss, afraid he would wake up in another sweat and discover this was but another feverish dream. Fear was taking hold that she would gaze up at him and say she'd been mistaken, that she didn't mean a word of what she'd just said. He had to know, had to be sure. He drew away from her mouth reluctantly, intending to separate them, but buried his face against her neck instead, his lips parted against the smooth column, stroking the silky skin while he waited for his heart to stop slamming against his chest. That wasn't going to happen. He murmured the question that plagued him against her ear.

"Can you overlook the fact that I am a bastard?" He felt her stiffen in his arms and the pounding in his chest turned painful. He finally drew away and gazed down into her face.

"I can overlook the fact that you are a warlord who has likely killed more people than I will ever know. The circumstances of your birth bear no comparison." Her hand brushed upward to stroke the lines of his face with her fingertips, her expression intent. "I have never lied to you about that, Kenric. 'Tis said bastards have no souls, yet the man who raised you was the one who lacked a soul, for he tried to rob yours. I do not fear the name 'bastard.' 'Tis what that name has made you that I fear. From the time I could walk I have been taught to nurture life, to protect it at all costs. You were taught to destroy it."

Tess eased her hand over his forehead, smoothing away the scowl. "Nay, I do not judge you, husband. 'Tis fact and you know it. Have you never wondered if we were meant to be together because of our differences? To balance them against each other?"

Kenric shook his head. Her reasoning was astounding, fanciful at the very least, but he would not challenge it. If this was not the truth, they were the most beautiful lies ever spoken. He was a warlord and women feared him because he was a bastard. He was a bastard and Tess feared him because he was a warlord. She made no sense. He didn't care.

The lies between them were lies he'd told himself. That night before her escape had been truth. Every word he'd tormented himself with had been spoken from her heart. Tess was so obsessed with trying to spare the lives of a few serfs and retainers that she'd intended to sacrifice her own. He reasoned that she'd deserved to be punished for thinking her life any less valuable. He prayed she'd learned her lesson. Another would surely kill him.

"You will not change me," he warned. "I cannot ride into a battle with any worry of where my sword will fall."

"I know," she murmured, framing his face with her hands. "It has taken me a long time to accept that fact."

The kiss he gave her was long and lingering, savoring her sweetness. He lifted her into his arms and carried her to the bed, startling a gasp out of Tess when he took a steep, swift step into the center and turned to sit in the middle with his legs crossed, cradling her in his lap. Smiling down at her, he picked up her braid and slipped the ribbon from the end, deftly unplaiting her hair.

"I just want to hold you for a little while," he explained, brushing his fingers through her hair to spread it across her shoulders. "Have you never wondered why your hair is undone each morning?"

Tess gazed up at him with a puzzled frown. He delighted in the mixture of disbelief and understanding that pushed away the troubled expression.

"Aye, you sleep sounder than anyone I've ever known." He leaned down for the kiss he'd wanted each night in her bed. When it was finished, her eyes looked far from sleep. He lowered his head again, intending to banish her thoughts entirely. "I've often wondered if the one time was coincidence, or if I can truly make you faint with pleasure."

25

"When did you eat last?"

Tess's stomach growled again at the very mention of food. It was nearly time for evening meal and she was starved. The babe was responsible for her hunger these days. The time was right to tell Kenric of his child. They'd made love an hour ago with a fury she still found astonishing. In the sated aftermath that followed, they were using their hands to leisurely reacquaint their bodies, elbows propped on their pillows, lying face-to-face on the bed to gaze hypnotically upon the nudity of the other. The caresses ranged from gentle curiosity to frank intimacy. Tess continued to explore the planes of Kenric's hip while his fingertips abandoned the pattern he'd been tracing on her ribs and outlined the curve of her breast.

"I ate this morning," she answered, groaning softly

when Kenric circled his palm against her. "There is something I would like to tell you."

Kenric kissed a path to her mouth, murmuring against her lips. "Tell me again that you love me."

Kenric made her speak the words around his kiss. His mouth trailed off for a leisurely exploration of her neck and Tess stroked her fingers through his hair. Making her repeat the vow so often probably meant he felt the same, even if he hadn't actually said the words aloud just yet. She still wasn't quite certain how he would take the news of his impending fatherhood. Surely he would be happy, yet there was Guy to consider as well. Now that she thought about it, he hadn't exactly said that he intended to keep her. Nay, his last specific words on the subject were that lovemaking would not change his decision.

"Oh, all right," he murmured, kissing the downward curve of her lips. He rolled off the bed, then smiled down at her. "I will see that you are fed. Your strength must be maintained if we are to keep at this all night."

Tess smiled back, glad of a few more minutes to gather her courage. He was going to be angry with her for keeping the secret so long. She was sure of it.

Kenric found the discarded coverlet and made sure his wife's exquisite body was hidden beneath it before opening the door to his chamber. He was surprised to find Fitz Alan waiting on the other side with Simon and Evard.

"Fetch our evening meal," he told Evard in a clipped voice, turning to Fitz Alan when the young soldier scurried away. He stretched one arm above his head to drape his hand over the top corner of the open door and leaned his shoulder against the doorjamb, the stance deceptively relaxed, really meant to conceal the delightful view of Tess in his bed. He wouldn't share that sight with others. "What do you want?"

"Your lack of modesty still astounds me at times, Baron." Fitz Alan rolled his eyes, keeping them conspicuously averted. Simon was gazing at the ceiling as well.

Kenric glanced down and remembered he was naked. His tone turned surly. "I've no time to pander to your delicate sensibilities, Fitz Alan. What are you doing here?"

"The baggage carts are being lined up in the bailey," Fitz Alan answered in a stilted voice. "Do we leave for London on the morrow?"

Kenric shifted his elbow on the doorjamb and rubbed his chin. "Nay, we leave three days from the morrow. That will still get us to London within the time Edward allotted."

"What about the herald?" Fitz Alan asked. "He awaits the company of his host in the great hall."

Kenric scowled. He'd forgotten all about the king's envoy. He didn't have time for that nuisance, either. "My wife and I must have eaten tainted fish for evening meal last night. Tell the herald we are ill and will be unable to leave our bed before the journey. Convey our apologies."

"Aye, milord."

Kenric wanted to smack the impudent grin from Fitz Alan's face then noticed that Simon wore the same. Fish hadn't appeared on a Montague trencher for nearly a fortnight. They were both trying his patience.

"Simon, you will see that meals are delivered to our door during this 'illness,' but no one is to enter this room without first gaining permission. Leave the tray outside the door if there is no response. See that a bath is delivered each night as well. Nay, the baths will be delivered in the mornings." Kenric decided he wanted to enjoy that particular ritual in full daylight. Another thought made him scowl and he spared a quick glance over his shoulder, knowing Tess was too far away to hear this conversation but lowering his voice just the same. "Under no circumstances will my wife be allowed outside this door. Do we understand each other?"

Simon rubbed his mouth and stared down at the tips of his boots to hide his grin. "Aye, milord."

"Good." He took a step back and slammed the door

with enough force to satisfy his irritation. He was smiling again by the time he turned around to walk back to the bed. "Now, where were we?"

He pulled the covers away to admire the curves of Tess's naked bottom and trim back. He'd grown accustomed to the traces of scars on her back long ago and noticed them no more than he did his own. He kissed a path from the back of her knee, across her hip and waist, then up over her shoulder to nuzzle playfully at her neck. "I think we were about to work on our appetites."

He eased onto the bed behind Tess and fit his body against hers, reaching down to sweep his hand from one trim ankle to her slender neck, lingering occasionally in between. She caught his hand between hers and pressed an urgent kiss in the palm. He shifted closer, pleased by the effect of that kiss, but she eased away and turned to face him.

"There is something I must tell you."

Kenric's fingertip drew an outline around the serious look in her eyes, knowing it had nothing to do with her appetite for food or her husband.

"What is it?" he asked quietly.

Tess caught his hand for another kiss, this one pressed against the back. When she lifted her eyes to meet his gaze, they were pale with fear and he shifted uneasily.

"You will be made a father before this year is done, milord."

Kenric's smile grew slowly until his whole face was transformed by the exuberant expression. But the smile faded just as slowly and his hand drew away from her. "How long have you known?"

"A few days." She caught a stray lock of her hair with her fingers to twist the ends.

"How long have you known?" His voice was quietly menacing now. His hand covered hers and pushed it onto the bed. "Tell me."

"I suspected when the morning sickness started the

day after you sent me to the solar." She didn't mention that it had lasted day and night. It was at an end and no longer mattered. What mattered now was Kenric's expression, growing more remote by the second.

"Was that the reason you came here today?"

"Nay! I did not know if you would welcome the news. Knowing your pledge to Guy, I had no idea which way it would sway your mind about our marriage. I—I still don't know if you intend to keep me!"

Tess turned her face into the pillow to hide her tears, but they subsided abruptly when she felt his hand stroke her hair.

"You have to ask?" He brushed her hair away from her face and she risked meeting his intense gaze. "No man alive could take you from me."

"You believe me?"

Once before he'd fooled himself into thinking he couldn't tell her lies from truth. He would never doubt his instincts again. "How could you think I would be anything but overjoyed?"

"The child will be the heir to Montague, as well as Remmington. Your pledge to Guy—"

He placed a finger over Tess's lips to silence her. "Our child will have no claim to Montague."

"But—"

Kenric pressed his hand over her mouth. "I will be stripped of my title to Montague and any claim to these estates as my punishment for kidnapping you and marrying without my king's permission, taking as my own a woman betrothed to another."

Tess bit his hand. He eased it aside and she propped herself up on one elbow to glare down at him. "That is outrageous! The king, himself, ordered you to do all of that! Against your wishes! You are to be *punished* for your loyalty?"

"Tis the 'punishment' I requested, Tess."

"But why would . . ."

Kenric nodded, encouraging the flicker of understanding. "Aye, Tess. The title will fall to Guy. 'Tis nothing I ever wanted. My army and what I have earned on campaigns will still be mine. And you," he added with a teasing smile, flicking his fingertip down the slope of her nose. " 'Tis possible the king will someday bestow your father's titles on me as payment for past services, but the title will fall to my son regardless. Still, I would find it irksome to bow my head to my own child, simply because he outranked me."

"I cannot picture it," Tess said honestly, settling her head against the pillows again. Kenric frowned at his wife, hesitating a moment before he forced her to look up at him. "I shall manage to survive the indignity," he assured her, wrapping her in his arms.

"I thought you would be angry because I didn't tell you sooner."

"I am not overly pleased." His thoughtful expression grew darker. "You knew you carried my child the day you risked your life on the training grounds."

Tess nodded guiltily, lowering her lashes.

"You will *never* do anything so foolish *ever* again!"

Tess winced from the sheer volume of his bellow. "Aye, milord."

"Let me look at you," he ordered. He gazed at her intently as he skimmed his hand over her belly, his frown skeptical. "Are you sure of this, Tess? I can see no difference in your body. Your breasts are fuller, perhaps, yet—"

"Are you blind?" Tess rose up on her elbows to give him an exasperated look, then placed his hand firmly over her stomach. " 'Tis at least two months since your seed flourished. I thought surely you would guess before I had a chance to tell you."

The slight changes that seemed so glaringly obvious to Tess were barely discernible. Yet she pressed his hand against her belly with more force than he'd dare use himself and he felt the firmness that had not been there before.

"That's it?" he asked, still looking doubtful.

"Your lack of appreciation is displeasing."

He insulted her further by laughing.

"Ah, sweetheart, I am dumbstruck," he said, half teasing. He straddled her legs and began planting kisses where their child rested within her. "I cannot wait to see you swell with my seed."

"That has begun already. I shall grow so fat that I will disgust you."

Kenric cupped her face between his hands. "You will be the most beautiful sight in the world, Tess."

He lowered his head for a kiss, teasing her with his tongue until she opened her mouth, allowing him to plunder her completely. His hands left her face to begin caressing her. He deepened the kiss with every intention of ignoring the soft knock on their door.

"Someone is at the door," she murmured, turning her head to one side. He began kissing her neck.

" 'Tis our dinner," he said impatiently, anxious to sate another appetite. Tess's stomach growled. He drew away. "Would you like to wait just a little while to eat?" he asked hopefully.

Her stomach answered the question. Tess's apology didn't help much, but he managed to give her a wry smile as he shifted from the bed. This time he decided a robe would be in order and took a few moments to dig one out of his clothes chest. Making certain Tess was covered again, he shrugged into the dark blue robe and cracked open the door, his eyes widening at the size of the tray Evard held. There was more food on the platter than two men could eat in one sitting.

"We are not like to starve before morning," he remarked dryly, eyeing the variety and sizes of the dishes.

"Milady's dinner," Evard announced solemnly. "And

yours, Baron," he added, nodding toward a normal-sized trencher of stew placed next to a much larger one.

Kenric gave the soldier a disgusted look then took the tray inside, slamming the door with his foot. Tess had also found one of his robes, a rich burgundy that made her hair shimmer enticingly. She was hovering over the table before he reached it, looking the dishes over greedily as she helped him unload a hearty five-course meal. Kenric stared at her in stunned amazement, watching her eat as much in one sitting as he would eat after a hard day on the practice fields. He began gulping down his own meal, half afraid it would disappear with everything else she was eating.

"Have they not been feeding you?"

"We missed midday meal," she said between bites of buttered beets, as if that could explain her appetite.

Before tonight, he'd not seen her eat this much food at three meals. A normal dinner for Tess might consist of a ladleful of stew and a slice of bread. He was fairly certain she'd downed that much as tonight's appetizer.

"Your child needs nourishment, milord. We are making up for the week I was too ill to face more than bread and thin soups." Tess pointed the dagger she was using to carve her food in his general direction. "Are you going to eat those spiced apples?"

"You will make yourself sick," he predicted, sliding the bowl of apples within the range of her carnage.

"It seems to digest quite quickly. Ofttimes I find myself hungry again only an hour or two after such a meal."

Kenric's jaw dropped in amazement. "The pantries will be bare by the time this child is born."

"You need have no worries." Tess looked over the table of empty trenchers and platters, searching for something she might have missed. Her gaze lingered on the sweet syrup at the bottom of the spiced-apple bowl, but Kenric pulled it away before she decided to lap that up, too. " 'Tis not uncommon for a woman's appetite to grow less hardy as a babe fills more of her stomach. There will not be much room for food."

Tess patted her own small but full stomach, her smile suddenly fading. Soon nothing would fit in or on her. Only three gowns remained of those she brought with her from Langston, and they were dreadful.

"I have no gowns fit for court, milord. Helen has graciously offered the use of her wardrobe and perhaps if I rode in one of the baggage carts I could alter a few during the—"

"There is no need to alter my sister's gowns."

"But she is much taller than I am. Her gowns will drag—"

"You will not wear borrowed clothes to court."

"Aye, milord." She bowed her head, trying not to feel sorry for herself or to think about the embarrassment she would surely endure in London. She would look like a beggar.

"I have a small surprise for you, wife."

Tess looked puzzled as Kenric stood up and extended his hand. He led her across the room to one of his chests, the one that was always locked. He pulled an ornate key from a hiding place behind the trunk and crooked his finger at her. She stepped hesitantly to his side, questioning him with her eyes when he placed the key in her hand.

"Open it." He urged her hand toward the trunk.

Tess opened the lock but needed Kenric's assistance to lift the heavy lid. The first thing she noticed was a girdle made of finely wrought gold set with row upon row of sapphires and amethysts. He lifted it from the trunk so she could see the way the hem fell to chevron points, each ending with a sapphire or amethyst suspended from a short gold chain. Next came a matching necklace, bracelets, earrings, and a headband so crusted with the jewels that she could see the gold setting only by looking on the inside of the band.

"This should go well with those pieces," he said, removing a gown from the trunk and draping it over her arm. The fabric was like none she had ever seen, made of whisper-thin threads of purple and black so finely woven that the colors blended to become the color of the sky just before nightfall.

"Don't you recognize the colors? The amethysts are the color of your eyes when you smile, and the sapphires are the color of your eyes when they flash with anger. And the gown?" Kenric wrapped her in his arms, lowering his head until their lips just touched. In that moment, his expression went from tender and amused to fiercely serious. "The gown is the color of your eyes when you burn with desire for me."

He captured her lips in a searing kiss. His mouth moved over hers insistently, yet he drew back frequently to look at her eyes, to assure himself that he was right about the gown's color. It wasn't long before Kenric forgot about the color of her eyes. The sweet taste of her mouth held his full attention. He released her so quickly that Tess had to put one hand on the trunk to steady herself. His hands trembled as he laid the gown and headband on the bed then turned again to the trunk, reminding himself that there would be plenty of time for lovemaking later. At the moment, he wanted to see her laugh in delight when he showed her all his gifts.

"I must admit that those are my favorite," he said, pulling more jewels and gowns from the chest. "You may find another outfit more to your liking. There are twelve gowns altogether, with jewelry, slippers, and undergarments to match."

Tess watched him unload the trunk in silence. The room soon looked like a jewel-encrusted rainbow, with gowns, stockings, slippers, and bliauts of every color scattered about the furniture, a myriad of precious gems winking from the folds of the beautiful fabrics.

"I had the devil's own time keeping you out of the east tower," he told her, puzzled by his wife's reaction to his gifts. Any other woman would be dancing around the room in delight. Tess looked horrified. " 'Tis the reason Simon told you there were criminals kept in that tower and you were forbidden entry there. I sent to London for seamstresses and goldsmiths soon after our marriage and Simon kept them hidden away in the east tower to work in secret. They used the measurements from a gown of yours that I lent them. I thought sure you would notice it missing before I could have it returned."

"I wanted to surprise you," he went on, trying to fill the awkward silence. Did he do something wrong? What was the matter with her? "Many of the jewels and fabrics came from the Holy Land, rewards of the Crusade. Others were given as prizes at tourneys and contests."

Tess looked around the room as he spoke, but remained silent. Her face betrayed none of her emotions, which was a true oddity for Tess. He had a sinking feeling she was about to cry again. Why she would remain dry-eyed over the prospect of departing for court then cry over a trunk full of new gowns was beyond his understanding.

"The jewels can be reset if the designs displease you." He sighed in exasperation, certain she was unhappy with his choices. "The gowns were cut loosely enough to allow final alterations, although I doubt they can be completely undone."

The disappointment in his voice finally shook Tess from her stupor. "How could I wish to change perfection? I have never seen such beauty in my life." Amazement filled her eyes. "Your gifts are overwhelming, milord. I do not feel worthy of such riches. This is a fortune, perhaps your entire fortune. How can I accept so much when I have given you nothing? Even my holdings you must war for."

"My child is nothing?" he asked. Kenric's smile was tender but inside his heart tightened. Of course she would be overwhelmed. The clothing she brought from Langston was scarcely better than that of a servant and he'd never noticed so much as a bracelet in the way of adornments.

Even her hair ribbons were threadbare. Yet she'd never complained. "In case you have not noticed, this is not my entire fortune." He pulled several leather pouches from the trunk and busied himself by repacking the jewelry. "You have yet to see *my* court wardrobe, wife. The men at court are as vain about their clothing as the women, but we shall outshine them all." He took Tess's hands in his own, lifting first one then the other to place a soft kiss in each palm. "And I can think of no finer setting for such jewels. Your beauty outshines the brightest gem. *You* are my greatest treasure. There isn't . . . Tess?" He drew his crying wife into his arms, trying to soothe her tears. He should have known he'd be no good at tender words. His heartfelt vow sounded idiotic. "What is the matter, sweet? Have I said something wrong?"

Tess shook her head, still too emotional to respond. Her tears finally subsided but she kept her head buried against his chest. Her voice shook with uncertainty. "You . . . you have truly come to care for me?"

"I love you, Tess."

Her eyes flew up to meet his, large violet pools filled with shock and disbelief, but most of all, sparked with hope. Kenric tried to cover the tightness in his throat as he smiled down at her. "I think I began loving you the moment you started arguing with your uncle at the abbey. You became more precious to me with each passing day until I could not imagine a day without you."

"How can this be true? I caused such trouble. Damn, Kenric. I will soon cause a war! How can you possibly love me?" Her gaze turned suspicious. "You said those things because you feel sorry for me."

"I speak nothing but the truth." Kenric's frown deepened and he grunted in aggravation, knowing he should have expected this. Only Tess would be so stubborn.

"You cannot take it back." She was crying again and her voice was muffled against his chest.

"I have never told another woman that I love her," he

informed her indignantly, though he placed her hand gently on his chest. "Those are not words I give away lightly, wife. You have my heart until it ceases to beat."

Kenric frowned over the renewed round of tears. He comforted her the only way he knew how. Carrying her to the bed, he laid her gently amidst the jewel-colored gowns, then pushed the costly garments to the floor, far more concerned with a greater treasure.

Tess kept her face turned away, but he parted her robe to kiss and caress her trembling body. He lingered over the small swell in her stomach with a smile, thinking she would have been happiest if he'd gaped at the tiny bulge as if it were the size of a pumpkin. It doubtless would be in a few months. That thought made him frown with worry about the size of the child he'd put inside her. He spread his hand, realizing that just one part of him covered her womb completely, his fingers stretching across her from hip to hip.

"Is your belly supposed to be so round this soon?" His shoulders stiffened and he used both hands to explore her stomach, overlooking the fact that the swelling hadn't even been noticeable until she pointed it out. "You are so small, Tess. How will you be able to carry my child if he takes after his father?"

"He?" Tess asked with a smile. "You are hoping for a son?"

"I would be happy with a son or a daughter," he answered truthfully. " 'Tis only that I know this and the next two babes shall be boys. You told me yourself when you were fevered." He nodded at her look of disbelief. "Another vision, I believe, like the one you had of Roberto."

The sudden realization that Tess would fare this pregnancy well enough to bear at least two more children brought a wave of relief. "My son would not dare grow too large for his mother," he declared. He ran his hand over Tess's belly again. "I forbid it."

His expression was so serious that Tess laughed. Disgruntled, he turned his attention to completing what was interrupted earlier. Tess was no longer laughing the next time she met his gaze. The dark look in his eyes said there would be no more interruptions this night.

"We will have three nights together," he said, his voice roughened by the unbanked fire of desire in his eyes. He shook his head when her eyes widened fearfully. "Nay, Tess. You, I will have forever, but we will leave for London in three days' time. There will be men there who would tell any lie to touch you the way I am touching you now."

He squeezed her breast in a fiercely tender caress.

"There are others who would face death to know what is mine alone to know."

She felt his hand move lower and her breath caught in her throat.

"I know you will not willingly give yourself to another, but know there are men who will try anything to possess you. Others will soon realize what you mean to me, enemies who have never before found a weapon to use against me. While we are at court, you must never stray far from my side." He covered her mouth for another searing kiss before she could answer, using his mouth to impress his will on her. He didn't lift his head again until he was certain she would remain silent.

"You belong to *me*," he told her fiercely, his voice hard with desire. His eyes burned with the ominous fire of complete, uncompromising possessiveness. "While I breathe, no other man will ever touch you the way I touch you. No other man will know the taste of you on his lips."

He tenderly stroked the curve of her cheek, his fingertips lightly tracing the outline of her lips. The affectionate gesture was at complete odds with his harsh expression. The hard, set lines of his face lacked any trace of tenderness.

"And no man will raise a hand against you and live to tell of it. You are mine, and I protect what is mine. If you ever place your life in jeopardy as you did with Roberto, I shall beat you myself." Kenric took her chin firmly between his hands. "Do you doubt what I say?"

Tess shook her head as much as his grip would allow, torn between fear, desire, and an insane urge to smile over his threat. She didn't actually believe he would beat her, but at this point she wouldn't dare disagree with anything he said. She turned her head and rubbed her cheek against his open palm, telling him without words that she accepted his command unconditionally.

That small caress, such a simple show of affection, unleashed something coiled deep within Kenric. In that moment he finally understood what drove men to wage wars over a woman, why a man would give almost anything to possess the woman he wanted above all others. No amount of gold, fame, or glory could come close to arousing the emotions she stirred in him. Nothing else in the world.

26

The trip to London was made longer by wet, muddy roads that bogged down carts and sucked at the horses' hooves. Kenric had originally intended Tess to ride her own palfrey, but now she rode before him on his warhorse, for he would trust her condition to nothing but the safety of his arms. He felt vaguely uneasy if she was even a pace or two from his side while they set up camp each afternoon. He hadn't allowed her from his sight during their last three days at Montague, except for occasional visits to the garderobe. The first night he didn't even sleep, half afraid he would wake up in an empty bed with the realization that nothing of the day before had transpired. His arms still tightened around her more securely at night when she simply stirred in her sleep.

It was at night that doubts began to plague Kenric's

mind, the suspicion that his wishes had been granted too easily. Not just granted, but lavished on him tenfold. Tess loved him with an intensity that left him shaken. It was too perfect, his treasure gained too easily. Each morning he expected the god who had kept himself entertained by giving him these gifts would tire of the amusement and take them all away again. Tess would wake up despising her bastard husband and demand an annulment. Watching her violet eyes open and her mouth curve into a sleepy smile when she spied him was the sweetest sight imaginable. He'd been granted one more day.

Kenric knew already that he would deny God himself to keep Tess at his side, in matrimony or in sin. He'd do what he could to ensure their marriage remained valid, to defend his right to call Tess his wife, yet there was one threat that would render him defenseless. Tess could betray him at court.

She knew he intended to invalidate any claim the MacLeiths had to her. Once that was accomplished, she could turn on him too, with the protection of the church at her back. It was the reason he'd finally agreed to the annulment, thinking that was her intent anyway. If there was any vengeance in her at all, she would have him stand before England a love-besotted fool and do what no man had ever accomplished. She would drive a sword straight through his heart.

In the light of day he couldn't even consider his suspicions. When Tess gazed up at him with her heart in her eyes, they seemed obscene. But at night, the suspicions came back to haunt him. He finally accepted the fact that he would not be free of the vile thoughts until Tess stood willingly by his side before the king and remained silent when the church declared them lawfully wed. Until then, he would do everything within his power to make sure she did just that.

The travelers finally passed through the gates of London, winding their way through narrow streets past more

people than Tess had seen in her lifetime. From the lowli-
est begger to rich merchants, the streets were alive with
the wondrous variety of life. At last the outer walls of the
palace came into sight. The Tower of London was not the
impressive sight Tess had expected. Almost all she could
see of the walls were scaffolds and building materials, for
Edward was in the midst of adding a second outer wall and
several new towers. They passed through the gates and
entered an enclosed inner courtyard where they were met
by the captain of the guard. After the group dismounted,
he led them through a doorway into a maze of hallways so
vast that Tess was certain she'd never find her way out
again. Helen explained that they would normally pass
through the courtyards and gardens, but they were taking
the inner passages because of the weather, which had
turned again to a steady downpour.

They stopped before two large oak doors that were
thrown open to reveal a room nearly the size of Montague's great hall. Mullioned floor-to-ceiling windows along
the far wall looked out over a garden that was lush even in
the rain, brightening the gray weather with splashes of vi-
brant red and soft white roses. Tall oaks swayed gracefully
over paths that spread through the gardens as intricately as
a spider's web, as much a maze as the hallways they were
just led through. Although Tess remembered climbing just
a few sets of steps, they were now at least one or two
stories above the ground, which made the room seem as if
it nestled among the treetops. It would have been a very
romantic spot if not for the racket of Kenric's men filing
into the room behind them. Tess and Helen found a quiet
corner while Kenric and Fitz Alan supervised the steady
stream of trunks and baggage the soldiers carried in. There
were three doors on each end of the room and, much to
Tess's relief, Helen was familiar with this hall and explained that the doors led to sleeping chambers. Visiting
nobility usually found themselves quartered in rooms suspiciously similar to dormitories, but Kenric and a few other

high-ranking nobles were given their own apartments. Tess and Kenric would have their own chamber, and Helen would share a room with Miriam, while the other rooms would accommodate Kenric's knights. The remaining soldiers and servants would sleep on benches in the main hall. The arrangement also provided extra security, as any intruder would have a hall full of soldiers to pass through and six doors to choose from if they sought to harm a lord or his lady.

A full hour passed before Kenric found a moment to speak with his wife. He couldn't help but smile over the pitiful picture she and Helen presented. Both looked as if they'd been drowned. He wrapped an arm around Tess's shoulders and led her to their room. Though not nearly as big or nice as their chamber at Montague, there was a large canopied bed and the mullioned windows overlooked the same garden as the main hall. A small fire blazed in the hearth to chase away the constant dampness of castle walls and buckets of water stood ready to bathe the travel-worn guests.

"I want you out of those wet clothes," he told her, already unlacing her gown. Tess was so tired that she simply stood there, not offering to help. He loosened her ties, then started to rummage through a trunk. "Have you an idea where I would find a sleeping gown?"

" 'Tis far too early for bed," she protested.

"Aye, but a nap would do you good." He found a nightgown and looped it over one arm, waiting while she struggled out of her clothing. He crossed his arms and leaned back against the trunk, allowing himself to enjoy the sight of her body. The last weeks had seen them without a dry bed even at night, and he'd used that excuse to avoid tiring his wife any more than the trip had already accomplished. He'd been truly content just to hold her. Now the outline of her soft curves beneath the damp, clinging chemise reminded him of how long it had been since they made love. He was seeing full measure what he'd glimpsed in the dimness of his tent and discovered with his hands at night. His son might have gotten off to a slow start, but he was making up for lost time at an amazing rate. Without the cover of her cloak and high-waisted gowns, Tess's condition was more than apparent. It was alarming.

"Kenric?"

It took a while before he realized she was waiting for him to hand her the gown. He was so fascinated by her body and the changes it was undergoing that for a moment he'd forgotten why he'd asked her to undress. She held out her hand for the gown but he shook his head, wagging his finger to call her closer. She crossed the room until she stood less than an arm's length away, yet he still didn't touch her. He smiled at her serious expression. "I will give you the gown for a kiss."

She looked surprised for a moment, then laughter entered her eyes for the first time in days. She stepped between his legs and wrapped her arms around his neck. The kiss she gave him said she'd missed their intimacies as well. Her mouth found its way to his ear and she whispered to him, her voice deep and sensual. "I want *you* out of those wet clothes, milord."

Kenric recognized his own words and smiled. His humor faded as he carried her to the bed, the need to possess her taking hold. He meant to be gentle, to be considerate of her condition and deny the urgency he felt, but Tess demanded his passion. She forced him to let go of his control completely until he could no longer think, but could only feel.

He wasn't given time to ponder his lack of restraint until they lay wrapped in each other's arms, reveling in the warm aftermath of their lovemaking. Some things would never change, he decided with a yawn, gently stroking her back. Tess had the ability to stir some new emotion each time they made love. When he voiced concerns about his roughness, she merely smiled at his worried frown and traced the outline of his lips with one finger.

"Surely the same feat that made our babe could not harm him," she reasoned, looking innocently concerned, even though her eyes told a much different story. The things he found to worry over in her pregnancy provided her with a near constant source of entertainment.

He considered her words then decided she was probably right. Not that it would take much reasoning to convince him. He would deny himself when the time came, but he wanted to enjoy her just as often as possible until then. He kissed her forehead then began to stroke her back again. " 'Tis time to sleep now, sweet. In a few hours I will send Miriam in to help you dress for dinner."

"I do not think I shall be able to sleep, knowing what lies ahead of us this eve," she said. Kenric frowned at the fear in her eyes. She pressed a kiss against his chest. "I trust you to see us safely through this ordeal, still I cannot help but dread facing Dunmore MacLeith again. He has frightened me for as long as I have known him."

"Shh," he whispered, pressing a finger against her lips. "Do not think of that now. I would have your head filled with thoughts of your husband."

His words were light, but Kenric couldn't wait until the man and his son were no longer a threat to his wife's peace of mind. By rights he should be with his king at this moment, learning more of the situation before they faced everyone at the evening meal. Yet he couldn't leave her until she fell asleep, warm and safe in his arms. He knew it might very well be the last time he held her this way, his marriage intact, his heart cradled gently in her hands.

Five minutes later, she was so soundly asleep that he had little trouble slipping the nightgown on over her head without waking her. He spent a few minutes just holding her as she slept, every doubt in his mind making the feel of her in his arms nearly painful. He pressed a gentle kiss good-bye on her sleeping lips then dressed and slipped quietly from the room. Nearly two hours had passed since their arrival and he knew the king would be waiting, probably most impatiently by now. Kenric smiled grimly on his way to the king's quarters, knowing the MacLeiths' time on earth was drawing to an end, wondering if he was hastening his own.

The meeting with Edward did not go well. As usual, his father was reserved, nothing in his behavior revealing any parental feelings he might harbor for his bastard son. Plantaganets were not known for being particularly fond of their legal heirs. As a bastard, Kenric had never expected recognition and he'd never received it. Any favor the king showed him had been earned on the battlefield, the bond of fealty more binding than blood. Edward was pleased that Kenric's part of the plan was proceeding without incident, relieved to learn that Tess had conceived. A babe would ease their difficulties. An unplanned threat had arisen in the months since Kenric's marriage and the church now had its hand in their scheme. Cardinal Jerome would be attending tonight's dinner to offer God's guidance in deciding the validity of the marriage.

With Cardinal Jerome's Scottish heritage and the likely promise of a good portion of Remmington land from the Scottish king, both Edward and Kenric were certain of the real reason for the cardinal's sudden interest. There was every possibility the cardinal would not decide what was best for Scotland or England, MacLeith or Kenric, but what was best for the church.

Edward tried to weigh the odds in their favor and had arranged for three English bishops to attend the meeting as well, but a ruling by the cardinal in MacLeith's favor would override the bishops' combined objections. Opposing Cardinal Jerome's judgment of the marriage could also jeopardize Edward's standing with the church, which already stood on shaky ground because of his past criticism of the church's greed.

It was a tangled mess and one Kenric had no liking

for. Strategy on the battlefield was a simple affair. Yet no matter how he racked his brain, a sound strategy for this situation remained elusive. The only good news was that Dunmore MacLeith sent his son in his stead, claiming a broken leg left him unable to travel. Kenric suspected that Dunmore MacLeith was remaining entrenched at Remmington should the decision not be in his favor. Appearing at court would render him far too vulnerable.

Kenric was so lost in thought that he didn't immediately notice the strange silence when he entered the main hall of his apartments. The odd way each of the thirty or so men in the hall watched his sister's door finally penetrated his concentration. Only Simon and Fitz Alan seemed oblivious to whatever seemed so fascinating about Helen's door. The two men were engaged in a rather quiet game of dice that ended when Kenric took the seat next to Fitz Alan.

"What goes?" Kenric asked, perplexed by his men's strange behavior.

Simon leaned back in his seat and laced his fingers together behind his head, his smile smug. "You will know soon enough, Baron."

" 'Tis your wife," Fitz Alan explained, putting one hand on Kenric's shoulder to discourage him from standing up. Kenric was already half out of his seat. "She just went into Helen's room wearing one of those new gowns you gave her."

Fitz Alan smiled over Kenric's confused expression. "Do you recall our reaction the first time we saw Lady Tess in the abbey?" When Kenric nodded, Fitz Alan's smile became as broad and smug as Simon's. "You are seeing a like reaction among your men. They are waiting for another glimpse of your angel."

Kenric looked the room over again, seeing a dumbfounded expression on more than one face. His men had seen Tess on numerous occasions. Why would a new gown suddenly cause them to lose their wits at this late date? He lifted his fist and brought it down with a crash on the table, causing the dice to dance off the edge. He brought it down twice more before he had the attention of every man in the room. His voice dripped with barely veiled sarcasm. "Did anyone happen to notice that we have just been joined by Dunmore MacLeith?"

The room erupted in chaos. Chairs and benches over-turned as men reached for their swords and searched the room for their enemy. One by one they turned, each expression sheepish as they faced their baron. He stood up and crossed his arms, frowning at them all. "And you call yourselves—"

The sight of his wife stopped him in mid-sentence. The doorway to Helen's chamber framed Tess perfectly, a painting come to life. She looked like a princess in her deep purple gown, with the sparkling jewels that matched her eyes. He understood immediately why his men were acting like idiots. Tearing his eyes away from the vision, he gave his men a stern rebuke even as he crossed the room to take Tess's arm. He pulled her into their chamber before he allowed himself to look at her again. He positioned her in front of the fire and stepped back until his heels touched a trunk. He sat down without thinking, his voice a harsh whisper. "Good God!"

Tess looked down at her gown then behind her. "You do not like it?"

"The gown?" His gaze traveled from her slippers to the top of her head, then back down again. The dark, rich color of the amethyst gown made her skin glow as pale and delicate as the white roses blooming in the gardens below them, the natural coloring in her lips and cheeks more perfect than any artist's brush could imagine. Her eyes out-shone the gems that sparkled with her every movement, and her hair was a cloak of rich, lustrous gold. Even though the clinging gold mesh of her girdle revealed more of Tess's swollen stomach than it hid, the jewel-trimmed bliaut she wore over the gown effectively concealed her condition. Kenric scowled, wishing the presence of his child was more obvious, that the court wouldn't have to look so closely before seeing the proof that she was his. "Lord, Tess, you look like an ancient pagan queen come to life. Give me a minute to accustom myself to it."

Tess waited patiently as he continued his perusal. "I look foolish, don't I?"

He shook his head, his eyes glued on her bodice. The neckline was cut no lower than the gowns of other ladies he'd passed in the halls on his way to see the king, yet he didn't remember seeing quite so much of them. "Give me a minute, Tess." He suddenly had the insane desire to take her straight back to Montague and lock her in their chamber where no one else but he would ever be allowed to see her. She was sure to cause a sensation tonight. More than one would likely consider the story about kidnapping his bride a fine idea. Perhaps one would even entertain the notion of using a similar tactic to take her from him.

"*You* look very handsome," she said shyly, walking closer to brush her hand across the shoulder of his white surcoat. Montague's coat of arms was stitched in midnight blue and gold thread on his chest and he wore a deep blue tunic, matching leggings, and boots dyed the same shade. Blue leather armbands tooled with gold covered his wrists up to his elbows and an ornate sword hung from each hip, the blades resting in jewel-encrusted gold sheaths. Kenric looked every inch the mighty warlord and Tess said another silent prayer of thanks that he was hers. Just the sight of Kenric would give the MacLeiths something to worry about. She brushed the hair back from his forehead and placed a gentle kiss there. "I do love you dearly, Kenric, but you begin to worry me. Should I change my gown? Is it not to your taste after all?"

Kenric finally shook himself from his stupor although he didn't take his gaze from his wife.

"Your gown is exactly to my taste, wife. I am troubled only by the other appetites it will whet. I forbid you to

step farther than a pace from my side tonight. Or any
other time we are outside these apartments," he added,
just for good measure. It was a foolish demand and one he
knew must be broken on occasion, but he felt better for
making it just the same.

Tess leaned down to kiss his cheek. "I am glad you
like it."

"Like it or not, I still need more time to accustom
myself to the thing." He couldn't tear his eyes away from
her. At this rate, he'd probably shame them both by walking into a wall on their way to evening meal, too busy
watching his wife to watch his step.

"Unfortunately, there is no more time. We shall probably be the last ones in the great hall as it is." He wrapped
Tess in his arms and gave her a sweet, lingering kiss. Before it could turn serious, he stood up and again wrapped
her firmly in his arms, resting his chin on the top of her
head. "I will tell you of my meeting with the king, then
'tis time to face our judgment."

Kenric told her of Cardinal Jerome and the threat he
represented, relieved yet somehow suspicious when Tess
took the news so calmly. She kept repeating that she
trusted him to keep his family safe, unconsciously reminding him that it was not only Tess who was at stake.
Kenric didn't consider what would happen if the Mac-
Leiths got their hands on his wife and child. It simply
would not happen. Ever. He'd already decided that nothing would separate him from his wife, not even Tess herself. If the MacLeiths somehow managed to have the
betrothal upheld, or if Tess herself renounced her husband,
he would use any means necessary to keep her. If that
meant fighting his way through the king's men and fleeing
England, he would do it. He'd brought enough of his army
along on this journey to ensure as much. Kenric had more
than thirty men within the castle walls, yet only a handful
of those soldiers realized that the rest of his army was already camped just a few miles outside London. Tonight

would decide whether they marched on Remmington, or fought their way to the sea.

Later, as they walked toward the king's hall, Tess began to notice a change come over her husband. His shoulders became stiff, his back as straight and unyielding as a spear. The lines etched around his eyes and mouth seemed deeper, his eyes gradually becoming dark and fathomless. She could almost feel him growing distant from her, as if several feet separated them instead of inches. He still held her hand on his arm, but she felt no more a part of him than the swords that hung at his side. His steps no longer took her smaller ones into consideration and she hurried to match his pace. By the time they reached the great hall, Kenric looked exactly like the stranger she had married. Gazing across a sea of unfamiliar, decidedly *un*friendly faces, Tess suddenly realized what he'd done.

Kenric had prepared himself for battle.

27

*Dining with a king was rather like attending a fair, Tess de-*cided, midway through dinner. The entertainment during the meal was quite spectacular. Brightly dressed jugglers, minstrels, and acrobats all vied for the attention of the audience, but Tess couldn't shake the feeling that she and Kenric were the main attraction.

At first she was too fascinated by King Edward to notice the attention she herself drew. There was no question where Kenric got his size, although Edward's piercing blue eyes clearly marked him a Plantaganet. The king's profile was also similar to Kenric's, but it was their mannerisms that were almost identical. The king's orders were given with the slightest movement of his hands. She understood the wealth of meaning behind the king's arched brow, or the tightening of his mouth as he looked around the room.

She followed the king's gaze and soon discovered that nearly everyone else in the massive hall was looking at her.

It didn't seem to matter where her gaze happened to fall, there were eyes on her constantly. Most of the women would glance away nervously when Tess caught them staring, but then they would put their heads together and whisper. The men were worse. Often as not, they weren't polite enough to turn away. One young blade even had the nerve to wink at her! She wondered what to do about that outrageous act until she felt Kenric stiffen beside her and start to rise from his seat. Although she didn't look at her husband, she sensed he'd also observed the suggestive wink and intended to warn off her would-be suitor.

The poor man's reaction was almost comical. In an instant he'd dropped his knife and turned over a goblet of wine onto the lady sitting at his side. He didn't pause to apologize for his clumsiness, but bolted from the hall. Tess turned to give her husband a thankful smile but he was already busy glaring at some other man. She sighed and tried to concentrate on her food.

The dinner came in seven courses, each deliciously prepared, but the little amount she was able to eat seemed tasteless. Even the pageantry of the court and the enormous hall, filled to capacity with colorful characters, paled next to Tess's fear of what lay ahead of them that evening.

Gordon MacLeith and three other MacLeith men were seated far across the hall and she felt Gordon's cold eyes on her more than once. She kept her hand on Kenric's leg much of the time, needing to touch him, to assure herself of his protection.

The meal finally ended and the tables and chairs were cleared away by unobtrusive servants. The king's throne was brought in and placed on a large dais at one end of the hall. The king took his seat and was soon surrounded by his advisers and the bishops Kenric had told her about. In the space of a few minutes, the hall changed from a dining room to a royal court.

She watched in fascination as the courtiers vied for the best spots to view the unfolding drama, many assuming exaggerated poses to show off their clothing and finery. The noise in the hall faded away to near silence as the king motioned to Gordon.

The ladies of the court inched their way forward to get a better view of the young MacLeith, for he was indeed pleasing to look upon. The jewel-green tunic he wore was expertly cut to emphasize his lean body, his leather breeches molded snugly to long legs. There were no battle scars to detract from the smooth, classical lines of his face, a face saved from being too beautiful by slightly overstated male features. He had a way of negligently tossing his head that brought attention to his startling white-blond hair, and his deep blue eyes seemed to hold many untold secrets. No matter where a lady's taste might fall, none could deny his physical perfection, or help but compare him against the rough, massive darkness of Baron Montague. Tess thought Gordon the ugliest man alive.

While Gordon made his way through the crowd, Edward held his goblet out and a squire rushed to his side to fill the chalice with wine. The king seemed in no hurry to get started and made Gordon wait awkwardly until the squire finished the duty.

"You have Our permission to address your king and state your business."

"Gordon MacLeith, at your service, Your Highness." He bowed low then straightened again, his gaze guarded, his manner challenging. "This eve I represent myself and my father, Dunmore MacLeith, and would petition our king on a most grievous matter, the kidnapping of my bride by one Kenric of Montague."

Gordon paused to let the impact of his charge ripple through the audience in waves of murmured comments. He did not turn to look at the crowd, but Tess could almost sense the way he listened for their approval. Then he pointed at Kenric. "Not only did this man deny Tess Remmington her home and loving family, he worsened his crime by wedding her, knowing she was betrothed to another, betrothed to me by your very hand, Your Highness." A more startled murmur went through the crowd, indicating many were not aware of the betrothal. Tess tried to ignore the queasy feeling in her stomach as she wondered how Gordon could say the words "loving family" without choking on them. She prayed the bishops would recognize such blatant lies and was thankful for Edward's disgusted expression.

"For many long weeks we grieved for our Tess, knowing not her fate until we learned by chance from a visitor that she had fallen into Baron Montague's vile clutches. He told us the baroness at Montague was terrified of her husband, that he beat her constantly. We sent messengers to Montague, hoping the baron would see reason and release the woman he held so cruelly into the arms of her loving family and to me, the man to whom she is rightfully betrothed. Our messengers returned empty-handed, Your Highness, turned away without an audience." Gordon sounded so defeated that several ladies in the audience sighed sympathetically. " 'Tis why I stand before you today, my king. To plead the cause of justice, knowing you will return Tess Remmington to my side and punish those who stole her from me. Although she has doubtless been sorely used, we are anxious to have her safely home again where she can forget the terrors of the last few months."

Edward was silent for several moments, continuing to stare at Gordon as if judging his words. Gordon didn't flinch once under the scrutiny and boldly returned the king's stare. Edward took a slow sip of wine then looked across the room to Kenric. His deep voice carried easily over the whispered words of his courtiers. "Kenric of Montague, you are charged with serious crimes. Do you respond to these charges?"

"Aye," Kenric replied, already making his way forward. He glanced back to make sure Tess was securely flanked by Fitz Alan, Simon, and Evard, then continued until he stood before the king. Although Gordon turned to face his adversary, Kenric didn't acknowledge the Scot's presence with so much as a flickering glance. He bowed low to the king, nodded his head to acknowledge the advisers and holy men, then waited for the king's permission to speak.

" 'Tis a strange tale you have heard this eve, Your Highness." Kenric spoke to the king, but he looked meaningfully at Gordon. "And bound to get stranger still, I warrant. You may as well know now that the charges of kidnapping are simply not true."

Kenric waited for the crowd's reaction to die down to hushed whispers. "Aye, 'tis more than possible the incident appeared a kidnapping to this boy and his father. Yet kidnapping cannot be charged when a knight chances upon a lady fleeing for her life.

"Best you explain this story," the king advised.

"By your order, I did escort Father Olwen to Kelso Abbey in the first month of this year," he began. "After seeing the priest safely to his new home, my man and I decided to hunt for game in the area that night to replenish our supplies for the return trip to Montague. The abbot at Kelso gave his permission to hunt the surrounding forests and it was there we happened upon Lady Remmington. Though the lady was disguised, we recognized her as a woman of some importance from the cut of her clothing. Knowing the forests are no place for any lady, we took her immediately to the safety of Kelso Abbey. It was there we learned her true identity and received our first glimpse of the prize we held when she shed her disguise. I think you will agree, Your Highness, that one need but look at my wife to realize why I decided to wed the lady that very eve and give her the protection of my name."

Kenric didn't turn to look at Tess, but knew everyone

else in the hall did. The murmurs of agreement didn't grate on him half as much as the appreciative chuckles.

"Your point is taken." The king's smile revealed none of his knowledge of the affair. "But did the lady not tell you of her prior betrothal?"

"She did. Yet when the full circumstances of her situation become known, I believe you will reconsider her betrothal to Gordon MacLeith."

"A king's betrothal cannot be broken simply because a baron is smitten with lust," Gordon sneered at his side.

"Silence!" the king commanded, glaring at Gordon. "You have presented your charge without interruption and will give Baron Montague the same consideration." He waved one hand toward Kenric. "Continue."

"Lady Remmington was kept prisoner at Langston Keep since her mother's death nearly five years ago. During that time she was beaten regularly by her stepbrother, the man who stands before you now. Although it is well within a family's rights to punish a woman in any manner they see fit, my wife was punished not for wrongdoing, but simply for spite. The last beating she received from Gordon MacLeith was so severe that it drove her from the safety of her home to the treacherous wilds of the forest."

" 'Tis a lie!" Gordon stared at Kenric with such appalled shock that Kenric himself might have questioned the story if he hadn't seen the proof.

Kenric ignored Gordon. " 'Tis the sorry truth, Your Highness. My wife fell unconscious soon after our wedding and 'twas then I discovered the extent of the damage done her. Her back showed proof of no less than fifty lashes delivered by a stout whip. A whip held by Gordon MacLeith. My men can attest to the marks and to the fact that she lay abed with a fever for nearly a week as a result, so ill we knew not if she would live."

"He is lying," Gordon told the king. "If there was any such beating, he did it himself to provide an excuse for his wrongful actions. Aye, I trow he beat Lady Tess many times since so she will lie to protect him, too afraid to speak the truth for fear of his reprisals."

" 'Tis a fact I have never beat my wife and never will. She has pledged herself to me freely and endeavors to please me in all things. A baron does not abuse those under his protection who are loyal and faithful to their lord."

The audience voiced its approval of Kenric's logic and Gordon began to look worried.

"With your permission, King Edward?" Everyone's eyes turned to Cardinal Jerome as he rose from his seat, leaning heavily on his curved staff. The king nodded and the cardinal stepped forward to address the two men. "The matter of the lady's beatings is disturbing, but it is not clearly relevant to the fact of her betrothal. You, Kenric of Montague, have admitted to taking a woman to wife who was legally betrothed to another. Such a binding contract cannot be set aside because of such trivial matters. Gordon MacLeith has a prior claim to the lady and she must be returned to her rightful place unless something was done to invalidate God's contract. If you lack evidence of such wrongdoing, Baron Montague, your marriage will be set aside by the church."

This time there was no answering murmur in the crowd to echo the cardinal's words. Everyone waited in tense silence for Kenric's response.

"I do possess such evidence, Your Eminence." Kenric didn't turn around, but motioned Fitz Alan forward and took the scroll his vassal held. Kenric handed the document to the cardinal. "In this scroll you will find the sworn statements of four men, duly witnessed by Father Olwen and Abbot Samuels of Kelso Abbey. Two of these men are former MacLeith soldiers stationed at Langston Keep, one is a merchant who called often on Remmington Castle, the other, a former companion of Gordon MacLeith's. My wife has no knowledge of this document, but over the past few months she confirmed much of what you will find inside. 'Tis sworn by these four men that Gordon MacLeith had no intention of taking Tess Remmington to wife in more than name. He did on numerous occasions promise his bride's favors to soldiers in his company for the purpose of getting her with child."

Kenric paused, waiting for the crowd's noisy response to die down before presenting the most damaging argument against MacLeith. "The reason Gordon MacLeith made such promises is that he is incapable of fulfilling a husband's duties himself. 'Tis common knowledge in the MacLeith household that Gordon has never lain with a woman but has maintained a steady string of unholy alliances with young men and boys. He was so repulsed by the thought of being legally bound to a woman that he swore to murder his bride as soon as an heir to Remmington was safely delivered."

The hall erupted into a chorus of startled gasps. The court had never been witness to such open scandal and this time no one bothered to whisper their responses to the sensational disclosure. Gordon paled. Even Cardinal Jerome looked stunned by the announcement and began to quickly scan the parchment to confirm the charges. Kenric didn't wait for things to quiet down but announced his final argument over the noise of the crowd.

"I hereby ask that my wife's betrothal be set aside in light of these facts. Unlike an alliance with Gordon MacLeith, her marriage to me is true to God's word and He has seen fit to doubly bless our union. My wife will deliver me of a son this fall and she does now carry an heir to the baronies of Remmington and Montague."

If anything, the noise in the hall grew louder, mostly because those who could hear the latest announcement had to relate it to those who could not. A few remarked on the fact that the baron seemed certain his unborn child would be male, but others pointed out that Lady Tess would certainly do her best to produce the boy the Butcher of Wales expected. The king finally held his hand up for silence but had to wait several minutes before anyone took notice. Even then the level of noise only dropped to a low hum. Cardinal Jerome returned to his place behind the king and the four holy men put their heads together, whispering furiously. Edward's gaze bored into Gordon, the corners of his mouth turned downward as if he'd found something repulsive under his shoe. "The charges brought against you are serious, young man. Do you have an answer to these charges?"

"Aye, Your Highness." Gordon didn't have to work hard at affecting the stance of a man bitterly betrayed. "I know not where Baron Montague found men to tell such lies and can only wonder if they are truly who he says they are, for I have three healthy bastards residing this moment at Remmington Castle. Never, *never* in my life have I committed the atrocious acts I find myself accused of." He glanced at Tess and gave her a sickly, apologetic smile. "Forgive me for my indiscretion, sweet, but you must understand what is at stake here." He turned again toward the king. "I do not wish to embarrass my betrothed, yet it is surely my fourth babe that rests now in Lady Tess's belly, if she is indeed with child."

Fitz Alan caught Kenric's arm the instant he reached for his sword. Several of the king's guards rushed forward even as Gordon made sure everyone saw him take several cautious steps toward the safety of the king.

Kenric couldn't look at his enemy in that moment or he would kill him. He kept his attention focused on the king. "My wife was a virgin when we wed, Your Highness, and I swear by all that is holy, she has never known another man in her bed."

" 'Tis time to hear from the lady herself," Edward announced, looking troubled.

He motioned to Tess and the crowd parted to let her through. She didn't hesitate but walked straight to Kenric's side, the side away from Gordon. Many heads nodded their approval at her show of support for her husband. Fitz Alan stepped away and moved to Kenric's left to stand as a buffer between the two enemies.

"We are sorry to subject you to this, Lady Tess, but We would hear whether or not your child could be fathered by Gordon MacLeith."

Cardinal Jerome cleared his throat and the king inclined his head, giving him permission to speak.

"Do not fret, my dear," Cardinal Jerome began, giving Tess a fatherly smile. " 'Tis not a serious sin in the eyes of the church to become intimate with your betrothed before the wedding. He is, after all, the man pledged to you by your king and God. You must also know that you are now under the king's and God's protection. The man who calls himself your husband does not have the power to punish you, should you speak the truth. You must tell us with complete honesty if you have ever been intimate with Gordon MacLeith."

"Nay, never," Tess answered, her voice a mere whisper. The king looked satisfied but the cardinal's expression remained doubtful. Tess took a deep breath, knowing her future depended on her courage at this moment. Her next words carried clearly, her voice firm. "I do swear the only time Gordon MacLeith touched me was with a raised fist or a whip. He beat me last because I dared to stand between him and the eight-year-old boy he was attempting to rape. I knew—"

"*Lies!* Vicious lies," Gordon cut in, acting the outraged innocent. "Only a man such as Montague would pollute a fair lady's head with such vile slander." He turned to Tess, his arms spread in a helpless gesture. "My Lady? What have they done to you? Has he threatened you? Now is the time to renounce him and he will never be able to harm or threaten you again."

Tess moved closer against Kenric's side, unaware she was holding his hand until she felt him give hers an encouraging squeeze. She looked up and found the comfort she needed in his eyes. He wasn't ashamed of her or the awful horrors that were her life with the MacLeiths. Nay, she could see only pride in his eyes and it bolstered her courage.

"I knew he would beat me," she continued, as if Gordon hadn't interrupted. "But until that day I never truly feared for my life with his abuse. Even so, I knew he would kill me eventually and did make my own escape from Langston Keep to be spared MacLeith's monstrous plans. The charges my husband makes against Gordon MacLeith are true. Gordon swore never to share my bed in marriage and did promise I would die painfully after delivering an heir by one of his soldiers. Baron Montague saved me that fate and I entered freely into this marriage. Though I knew 'twas a sin to wed one man while betrothed to another, I was sure my king and church would not recognize a man so ungodly as Gordon MacLeith."

"He's cowed her into lying," Gordon declared. "A woman can be trained to say anything, and Baron Montague has had many months to turn her against me. You can see by the gown and jewels she wears that he has given her the finery women appreciate so she will support his claim. I am only saddened that she has forgotten the tender moments we shared and the promises made between us. Yet I will surely forgive her, for these charges are too vile to come from this sweet lady's lips. They were placed there by another. Every man here knows how savagely the Butcher deals with his enemies. I did not realize 'ere this night the depths this man would sink to. He produces a lie for every truth I speak and lays vile crimes at my door. I can defend myself only with the truth."

"The church is not convinced in this matter," Cardinal Jerome announced, inclining his head toward Gordon to show his preference. Gordon relaxed visibly.

Kenric's blood ran cold. "Your Highness, I would beg a private word with Cardinal Jerome and yourself."

"The man you accuse has the right to hear any addi-

tional charges you would bring against him," Edward
warned. Cardinal Jerome nodded in agreement.

" 'Tis my wife who needs be spared these words."

"Do you agree to this condition?" Edward asked Cardinal Jerome. Perplexed by the strange request, the cardinal nodded. Tess was just as confused and looked up at
Kenric with questioning eyes. He patted her hand, a puny
comfort, but the only way he knew to tell her without
words that everything would be fine. He prayed he was
right.

Kenric had been certain the charges against Gordon
would convince the church to set aside his betrothal.
He had but one weapon left in his arsenal. If that failed,
he would be forced to fight for Tess, not with words, but
with his sword. He almost hoped it came to that, even
though it would mean excommunication and exile for
them both.

Edward ordered Fitz Alan to take Tess a few paces
away and motioned to Gordon to back up several paces.
Kenric stepped up to the dais. The two men leaned close
to listen to Kenric's whispered words, every ear in the hall
also straining to hear. The crowd grew restless as the minutes dragged by. When they finally broke apart, both king
and cardinal looked amused by whatever they had learned,
Baron Montague appeared uncertain, while Gordon
MacLeith looked downright uncomfortable.

Edward motioned Tess forward again with a wave of
his hand, but stayed Kenric when he moved toward his
wife. "You will stay here, Kenric, by my side, where all can
see that you do not interfere with your wife's answers." To
Gordon, he said, "Cardinal Jerome and I have decided
that Kenric's words will remain private for the time being,
but you will be made aware of them before any decision is
made.

"There are a few more questions you must answer,
Lady Tess, in light of what your husband has just re-

vealed," Edward told her. Tess nodded anxiously, looking
to Kenric for support. He gave her an encouraging smile
that didn't fool Tess for a minute. He was worried about
whatever was afoot. "First, your husband has said that he
was anxious to wed you from the moment you met. Did
you readily agree to wed Baron Montague when you first
learned of his desire to marry you?"

Tess frowned, trying to puzzle out why the king would
ask such a question. She could only assume the correct
answer was "yes," but could not quite bring herself to lie
outright to her king. Her eyes shifted nervously as she
sought an honest answer that would not damn her husband. "I became aware of the wisdom of such an alliance
very quickly, Your Highness."

"But did you agree to the marriage from the very start,
when the wedding was first suggested?"

Tess paused a moment, long enough to catch a fat
strand of hair and begin twisting it in her fingers. "Aye,
Your Highness, I agreed right from the start."

Cardinal Jerome looked startled by her answer, the
king very pleased. Tess couldn't help but smile over the
approval she saw in Kenric's eyes. But the elation she felt
was short-lived and soon turned to cold dread.

"Your husband says differently. Are you telling me the
full truth, Lady Tess?" Edward questioned gently.

Her hands fell from her hair and she bowed her head
in shame. "Nay."

Edward tried to give her an honorable means of excus-
ing the lie. "Did you object at first because of your betrothal to Gordon MacLeith?"

"In part," she replied, still unable to meet her leader's
eyes. She was certain she'd never be able to look another person in the eye for the rest of her days, for she
would be branded a liar. A liar who lied to a king, no
less! She mumbled the full reason for objecting to her marriage, yet so quietly that Edward made her repeat the ex-

cuse. Her voice was louder, yet just as pitiful. "I thought he ate little babies for his dinner and drank the blood of his enemies. I did not think he would make the best husband."

Smothered giggles came from several corners but laughter didn't erupt in the hall until Edward's face creased into a smile. But he didn't stop there. Nay, the king laughed outright at her heartfelt confession until tears ran down his cheeks.

"My first impression was quite wrong, Your Highness. My lord Kenric is a very fine husband." She turned to glare at several courtiers who were still laughing. "Kenric of Montague is the very *best* of husbands! He is the kindest, gentlest man I have ever known." For some reason, everyone thought this was almost as funny. Tess didn't understand that reaction until she realized she'd just called the Butcher of Wales a "kind" and "gentle" man. "Of course, he is also a warrior and can be ruthless and bloodthirsty when the occasion warrants."

This time no one waited for the king to start laughing. Courtiers who stood perfectly posed just moments before now leaned on each other for support. The staid bishops tried to cover their faces with one or both hands but everyone could see their shoulders shaking. Even Cardinal Jerome was smiling and his round belly jiggled suspiciously. Only two people other than Tess found little humor in her remarks. Gordon and her husband. She didn't care what Gordon thought, but she was good and worried by Kenric's glare. She bowed her head and prayed for the floor to open up and swallow her whole.

"I am relieved to learn my kind and gentle baron can be ruthless and bloodthirsty when need be," Edward said at last, though he immediately fell into another round of chuckles that took several more minutes to contain. He finally sighed long and hard, his expression growing serious again. "Now, Lady Tess, you must tell us if your husband has ever beat you."

"Nay, never," she said firmly, hoping the king's other questions would be so easy. She folded her hands and started to relax, answering just as truthfully when he asked the same question about Gordon. "Aye, Gordon raised his fist against me many times, Your Highness."

"She continues to lie," Gordon interrupted, waving his hand through the air as if to dismiss her answer. " 'Tis obvious from the lie she was just caught in that she will say anything to protect Baron Montague."

Edward ignored Gordon's outburst and kept his attention on Tess. "On the night of your escape, Lady Tess, did you meet with anyone other than your husband or his man in the forests outside Langston Keep?"

Tess's eyes flew to the king then to Kenric, frantically searching for an answer. She didn't care why the question was asked, or what sin of purgatory she would burn in for lying. Her uncle's life depended on the secret being kept. She shook her head but twisted her hair feverishly. "Nay, no one else. Only my husband and Roger Fitz Alan were in the woods that eve."

Gordon gaped at Tess, his mouth open in surprise. One finger pointed accusingly toward her. "She is lying! She had an accomplice."

"You will remain silent or be taken from the hall," Edward warned quietly.

Gordon scowled and lowered his head to sulk. The king asked six more questions before Gordon's head jerked up again, his startled gaze meeting Kenric's in a moment of understanding. Kenric smiled.

The king held up the document with the four signed confessions. "Are the charges made tonight against Gordon MacLeith true to your knowledge, Lady Tess?"

Tess nodded and opened her mouth to reply when she saw a quick movement from the corner of her eye.

The hall suddenly erupted into chaos. Very few were certain what caused the blood-curdling screams to ring out across the vast room. Royal guards moved forward to surround the king and protect him from danger. More guards surrounded the petitioners, their spears and swords ready to deliver a deathblow to any or all at a word from the king.

28

The king started out of his seat and took a step forward, holding up one hand to wave his guards away. The soldiers surrounding the king parted slowly, standing close to their ruler in case they were still needed. The ones standing guard over Fitz Alan, Gordon, Kenric, and Tess also backed away, using their bodies now as barriers to hold back the courtiers who peered over the soldiers' shoulders. Many of the ladies turned away in revulsion at what was revealed.

Gordon lay on the floor, his face drained of color, his left hand cradling the stump that used to be his right arm. The cleanly severed limb lay a few feet away on the floor, a long dirk still clutched in the lifeless fingers. The injured man moaned low and steady, an eerie, crooning sound sometimes heard in the aftermath of battle when men lay wounded or dying on the battlefield. He didn't appear aware of Kenric's bloody sword at his throat, too shocked by his loss to be aware of anything else at that moment. Kenric loomed over his enemy like a dark, avenging angel, his right arm extended to hold the sword in place, his left arm wrapped securely around his wife. She was pressed tightly against his side, his body turned slightly to hold her away from danger. Fitz Alan stood behind Kenric, his sword also drawn to protect his lord's back from any over-zealous royal guards.

Edward stepped from the dais and walked a semicircle around Gordon. He reached down and pulled the weapon free, then held the dirk aloft.

"Assassin!" Edward announced to the crowd. He walked slowly in front of his soldiers so all would see the weapon, then turned and pointed the dirk toward Kenric. "But for my loyal baron, this traitor would have killed his king."

The king's guards relaxed and lowered their weapons, but Kenric's sword remained steady at Gordon's neck. Edward returned to his throne and threw the weapon at his feet, looking down at the fallen man in disgust. "I do hereby break the betrothal set forth between Gordon MacLeith and Tess of Remmington on the grounds of deceit and treachery. You have also forfeited your life to Baron Montague this eve, Gordon MacLeith. He may do with you as he will."

"It was Tess I was after," Gordon cried out, roused from his stupor by the king's words. He looked into Kenric's eyes and cringed. "Please, Your Highness. My father . . . Allow me to live and I will make a full confession."

"Aye, you are the type of traitor who would betray his own father," Edward sneered. "I have no doubt you will make your full confession long before Baron Montague is done with you. Take this man to the dungeons." Edward waved his hand away with sharp finality, sealing Gordon's doom. "Bind his wound and keep watch that he does not hasten his own end. There he will await my baron's judgment."

Kenric backed away as Gordon was pulled to his feet by the king's men. Knowing his fate, Gordon began struggling against the two men who dragged him from the hall, screams of pain and protest mingling in his terror. The stunned court parted to allow the prisoner through their ranks and remained silent until the screams faded away down unseen corridors.

The ladies were the first to notice the way Baron Montague held his wife, wrapped securely now in his arms. They sighed when he cupped her cheek with one hand, the love between the two obvious as they gazed into each other's eyes. Everyone waited in breathless anticipation as the baron slowly lowered his head to kiss his beautiful bride. When their lips finally met in a sweet, lingering kiss, the women sighed again over the beauty of the moment while the men called out their encouragement. The king finally interrupted the spectacle by calling for silence, even though his face was also broken by a grin.

"Kenric of Montague, you do indeed have my blessings to kiss this lady, who is your wife in the eyes of God and your king."

The court erupted into cheers. Kenric watched Tess carefully, oblivious to the shouts of well-wishers. Tess smiled up at him, but her brows drew together to form a silent, puzzled question. The smiles and cheers faded when the king continued to speak, his face suddenly grave. "However, the matter of your marriage is not completely settled."

Now she will speak, Kenric thought wildly, his hold on Tess's arm tightening as they turned to face the king again. Tess remained silent as she laid her hand against his, indicating that he was hurting her. He relaxed his grip immediately and she bowed her head to listen to the king's words. After all that had transpired, Kenric could no longer stand the suspense. He leaned down to whisper in her ear.

"This is your last chance to be free of me, Tess."

Kenric wasn't sure she heard him. She didn't move for a moment or even glance up at him. Instead she edged closer until the hem of her gown brushed against his leg, casually straightening the skirt until it covered the toe of the boot closest to her, then he felt Tess's slippered heel grind all her weight into his foot. She actually managed to make it painful.

The king gave Kenric a quelling glare, telling him without words that he should have enough sense to look serious and contrite at a time like this. Kenric knew he was smiling like an idiot. Edward cleared his throat and continued.

"Although We are pleased this lady's holdings did not fall into the hands of a scoundrel such as Gordon Mac-Leith, Remmington needs a baron in constant attendance to see to its proper protection. Lady Tess needs a husband who will dedicate himself to her lands, yet Montague's holdings are just as vast with the same need for a strong overlord. And we cannot overlook the fact that you married without your king's permission, to a woman legally betrothed to another at the time. The church does not view such matters lightly and I am sure Cardinal Jerome will agree that some punishment is in order."

"Aye," Cardinal Jerome said, nodding his head thoughtfully. "Yet considering the circumstances, I am of the opinion that God had a hand in bringing these two young people together. The church does not ask for a severe punishment in this case, Your Highness."

"I will take your opinion into consideration when making my judgment." Edward paused a moment to rub his beard, then he leaned forward from his throne, staring intently at Kenric. "Before I bring judgment upon this man, be it known that he will retain any goods, services, armies, or rewards collected in his capacity as knight and soldier."

Edward leaned back and eyed his court as the suspense mounted.

"As punishment for the actions that resulted in the marriage between Kenric of Montague and Lady Tess of Remmington, these two people are hereby stripped of the titles Baron and Baroness of Montague, and will forfeit all Montague titles, lands, wardships, revenues, and entailments in favor of Kenric's younger brother, Guy of Montague."

The cries of outrage from the courtiers seemed to surprise even the king. "Do you believe I will not also reward a man so loyal to his king?" Edward asked the court, his exasperation obvious. The protests died down and Edward nodded, turning again to Kenric. "Considering that you have surely saved Remmington and a vast stretch of English border from a traitor, I do hereby bestow upon you, Kenric, the title of Baron Remmington, and restore to you, Tess, the title of Baroness Remmington. All titles, lands, revenues, wardships, and entailments attached to Remmington are yours, and will pass to your heir upon Kenric's death, in accordance with the rules of all other baronies of this land."

Kenric bowed and Tess dropped into a deep curtsy to thank their king. The court cheered once again for the couple.

"Thus it is done," the king said, smiling once again. "Rise, Baron Remmington."

Kenric straightened for a moment, took a few steps forward then bowed again over the king's hand to kiss his overlord's ring. This show of fealty done, Kenric backed away slowly to stand beside Tess. He felt her small hand slip into his and he squeezed it tightly.

The hour was late when Kenric's group returned to their apartments. The congratulations of well-wishers and toasts

to their marriage went on long into the evening until
Kenric finally noticed how tired his wife looked. Yet he'd
been in no hurry to leave the court that evening, wanting
everyone to know that his wife stood by his side willingly.

They retired quickly to their bedchamber when they
reached their apartments. Tess couldn't wait to be held in
Kenric's arms without a hundred eyes upon them. At last
there was no longer any need to worry over their marriage,
or fear that her husband would be taken from her. The
years of facing the MacLeiths alone were at a blessed end.

She leaned back against the pillows and wrapped her
arms around her knees, watching Kenric undress. Her eyes
grew soft and thoughtful. Tonight he'd thought she would
want to be rid of him. She'd had to settle for grinding her
heel into his foot rather than giving him the good kick he
deserved.

"How is your foot?" she asked politely, not looking a
bit contrite.

" 'Tis sure to be sore a week," he said, smiling as he
slid into bed. "I am turning you into a violent little thing.
Next you will be poking me with that sharp dagger of
yours when I displease you."

"I had not thought of that," Tess mused, as if considering the idea. "Do not think yourself above punishment
the next time you say something so foolish and insulting."

"I tremble in fear of your retribution, Lady." Kenric
rolled his head back with an exaggerated look of pained
remorse.

Tess nodded sharply. "As well you should. How could
you ask me such a question, especially after everything
that happened tonight? Have you never trusted anything I
told you these past weeks?"

Kenric's grin evaporated. His expression became
downright fierce. "I have not lived this long by placing my
trust foolishly, Tess." He shook his head when he saw the
hurt in her eyes. "Nay, sweet. You I trust completely. To-

night you could have used it against me. Any other woman would have."

"Any other woman would have coshed you over the head." She still didn't understand how he could trust her yet expect that she would turn against him.

"Ah, Tess, you are delightfully blind. You call me handsome, when none other on this earth would second your opinion. You stare at me with a look that borders on drooling while every other woman turns away in revulsion." He took her fingertip and traced the scar that ran the length of his cheek. "Have you never noticed that my face and body were scarred beyond handsome long ago?"

"Your face is beautiful," she declared, sweeping her hand from his forehead to his jaw. "Any lady with eyes can see it." Her eyes narrowed as her hand brushed across his chest. "I will scratch out the eyes of any lady who dares look at your body to see these scars you have become so vain about."

"You see?" he asked, smiling again. "No matter how farfetched, I can do nothing but trust you. If you say I am handsome, then handsome I am."

"Why, you arrogant man," she sputtered, pushing against his shoulder. "Had I known you were wheedling flattery, I would have lied and compared you to a toad."

"I would have known you were lying," he declared smugly.

Tess sighed, defeated. "Everyone knows when I lie. Is it something in my expression that makes it so blatant?"

"Aye," he chuckled. "You have a look of guilt about you that none could miss for a mile. I suggest you give up the sinful habit before it lands you in serious trouble someday."

She changed the subject entirely. "Do you think my stepfather will leave Remmington willingly?"

"Nay," Kenric replied, his eyes serious now. " 'Tis why I always considered your scheme to run from me so foolish." He smoothed away her worried frown with his fingertips. "You will never hear me tell you it was a sound plan, Tess, but I no longer condemn you for trying. 'Tis a measure of your loyalty that you were willing to risk your life for what you thought was your duty. You understand now that it is my duty as your husband to take those risks." He gave her a hard look until she nodded her understanding. "MacLeith is like me in one respect; he will not willingly give up what he has made his own. The fact that the church has turned against him will not matter. He is preparing for a siege as we speak."

"I should have trusted you sooner," Tess murmured.

"Aye, you should have," he agreed, softening the rebuke with a gentle kiss to her forehead. "I cannot guarantee that your people will be spared, Tess. But I will not slaughter them needlessly. Those who flee before my army will not be chased down unless they show signs of gathering arms to stand against me. 'Tis unlikely those within the walls will be so fortunate."

Tess nodded, knowing there was no other way.

"You have had enough of serious thoughts for one night," he murmured, pressing a line of kisses across her forehead as if to chase them away. "I would send you to slumber with more pleasant thoughts on your mind."

His lips captured hers for a kiss that left Tess breathless, her thoughts far from sleep. She was surprised when he ended the kiss by tucking her head against his shoulder, lying back against the pillows.

"You need your rest," he told her, answering the unspoken question. He reached down to stroke her swollen belly. "As does my babe."

"We are not sleepy," she said with a mischievous grin. Kenric lay on his back with one knee bent and she moved her hand in a tantalizing motion along his inner thigh.

"You looked ready to sleep on your feet in the hall," he countered, capturing her hand and returning it to his chest. "I have heard such is possible, but have never actually seen anyone sleep that way. I was tempted to stay, knowing you of all people would be able to show me how this was done."

"I am much too excited to sleep just yet. So much has happened this eve!"

"Aye, true enough," he admitted, staring up at the canopy of their bed. "My brother should return to court by tomorrow night to collect his title. Edward kept him at Windsor, so as not to arouse suspicion. I am curious to see his greeting. 'Tis been several years since I saw Guy last, though I have been kept informed of his activities."

Tess gasped, propping herself up on one elbow. "I forgot all about Guy. This shall be a family reunion, of sorts. Helen must be very excited."

"Helen is probably quaking in her boots," Kenric snorted. He shook his head and his expression grew serious. "She is under the impression that her dowry includes Montague wealth and lands that Guy now has the right to reclaim. Without a dowry, Fitz Alan could break the betrothal."

"He would not do that, would he?"

"Nay, but he is sure to torment Helen with the possibility. Then again, 'tis within Guy's rights to break the betrothal himself, as I gave my approval after we were wed. Though my punishment was received this eve, legally it will be viewed as being in effect the moment we were married. It was not my right to name Helen's husband."

"Guy is certain to approve of Fitz Alan," Tess said firmly, though her brows rose in question. "Is he not?"

" 'Tis no certainty. I have been told Guy harbors me no ill will, but what is said and what is truly felt can be quite different. In any event," he added, kissing the tip of his wife's nose. "I am sure you will make Guy see the wisdom of such a match. Doubtless you have a few plagues yet to use as a means of persuasion, should he dare disagree."

"I am no witch," Tess said indignantly. She fell back against the pillows and crossed her arms over her chest. "What a horrid thing to say."

"I do but tease, sweetling." He leaned over to nuzzle her neck. "You are the best of all women, a veritable saint among mere mortals."

"Now you mock me," she said crossly, though she turned her head to expose more of her neck to his kisses.

"Hmm, I do not think so," he murmured, nipping at her ear. He reached down and grasped the hem of her nightgown, sweeping it over her head in one smooth movement. "If it is mocking I do, then I wish to mock all of you."

Before he could carry out the threat, Tess asked a question that made his hands still, his body go rigid. "What will you do to Gordon?"

"He will live. For now," he amended. "Gordon will journey with me to Remmington when I call upon his father. We shall see how dearly the Devil holds his child."

Tess shook her head. "Dunmore MacLeith will not give up Remmington for his son. Your plan will not succeed if you think to lure Dunmore out with Gordon."

"Nay, 'tis not my plan." Kenric stretched out beside her and propped himself up on one elbow. He captured her hands and held them together, his lips placing measured kisses along her fingertips. His eyes watched hers intently over their hands. "Dunmore will see his son suffer as much as you have been made to suffer under their care. 'Tis part of the punishment for their sins."

"You are indeed ruthless," she whispered.

"You are the one who has suffered, Tess. Do you plead for them, I shall promise to slay the MacLeiths swiftly. But do not ask me to spare their lives. Enemies such as the MacLeiths will be a threat to my family as long as they live."

Tess's brows drew together in a frown. "The MacLeiths have done nothing to warrant my plea now, but they have done everything to warrant the justice you would mete out." She loosened her hands from his grip and reached up to stroke his face. "You are a fair man, husband. You have my love and respect in all things. Nothing you say or do will be loathsome or repulsive in my eyes. In this case, I can think of no punishment that could match their crimes, though I have the feeling you can and will."

Kenric pulled her away from his chest, his eyes intense. "I have passed judgments on many men and slain many more in battles. But I gain no pleasure from the death or punishment of others. It is not sport to me, Tess. But God help me, on this occasion I fear I will find true pleasure in meting out justice."

"How can you accomplish it?" she asked quietly. "The other holdings may fall, but Remmington Castle has food and water inside the walls to last years. How long will your army survive the winter, living off the sparseness of the countryside?"

He shrugged, unconcerned. "MacLeith is no longer lord of Remmington. I will do whatever is necessary to claim our son's birthright. 'Tis my hope that Dunmore MacLeith and his spawn will be deep in their graves before my son draws his first breath. I must trust that God will show me the way."

"You are most confident of God's interest in this matter," she said skeptically.

"I am confident in my own abilities and God's justice. 'Tis a certainty I have God's support, for many barons have already pledged their men and arms to my cause, barons who would have laughed in my face, had I asked their assistance six months ago. I have asked for nothing, yet am now offered an army larger than my own."

He gave her a roguish grin, his serious mood lightening as he cupped her chin in one hand. " 'Tis surely God's hand or yours, sweetheart. 'Tis a fact, most men cannot resist the idea of a demoiselle in distress. Given Gordon's attack on you this eve, everyone at court believes you a tragic heroine of epic proportions. That you embrace my name and protection so readily assures them you are, indeed, a desperate woman."

"I am desperate only for your love," Tess answered surely. Her eyes grew softer, more luminous in the flickering candlelight. She leaned back in his arms and stroked his chest seductively. "After making that vile statement that earned you nothing more than a sore foot, perhaps you could make amends by assuring me of your love."

Kenric gave her all the reassurance she needed and more.

29

*Remmington Castle was nestled in the deep valley like a cold,
priceless jewel,* her manors and keeps scattered across vast
miles of England's northern border in an unbroken chain.
Kenric drew to a halt at the crest of the last hill and gazed
down into the fertile valley, the lush land that was domi-
nated by his future home. He had little appreciation of
Remmington's cool, indomitable beauty, his eyes assessing
only its potential flaws. Tomorrow he would ride the perimeter of the curtain walls, but setting up his camp would
occupy the remainder of this day and evening. From his
vantage point, Kenric could only see four of the great towers and the tips of the other four behind them. Two of the
six smaller towers that flanked the barbican were also visible, as were the twin gatehouse towers.

A thin ribbon of smoke rose from the south end of the

walls, surely the ramp to the postern gate being burned away, for MacLeith could not help but know of his arrival. From this height, Kenric could see small dots he knew to be soldiers lining the battlements of the fortress, but they would disappear from sight and bow range when his army entered the valley. Kenric smiled, picturing his wife on one of the tower walls, a long, colorful scarf fluttering in the wind to welcome her husband home. But Tess was at Kelso Abby, in Father Olwen's safekeeping until Kenric regained control of Remmington. She'd foolishly assumed he would allow her to accompany him to Remmington, had argued mightily when she realized he intended to leave her at the abbey. Even her tearful pleas could not sway his decision. Aside from the fact that her condition was hardly suited to a battle camp, he would not allow his wife within sight of a MacLeith ever again. He'd left Helen at Kelso as well, hoping she would be of some comfort to Tess during the weeks they would be separated. Although he didn't yet know how he was going to keep his word, he'd made Tess a solemn vow that their babe would be born at Remmington. He lifted his hand and motioned his army forward into the valley.

Kenric's battle camp spread across much of the countryside, eclipsing the village outside the castle. His first surprise came early the following day when the residents of the village returned from their hiding places in the surrounding forest. Their blacksmith, the official leader, explained the reason for this strange behavior to a succession of Kenric's soldiers until he was finally allowed to speak to the warlord himself. Normally the villeins of a besieged castle stayed as far out of the way as possible, knowing the knights on both sides of the castle walls valued the lives of peasants far less than their warhorses or swords. Yet the villagers at Remmington were more than willing to share their meager stores and lend aid in any way possible to Kenric's army. They had known only misery and starvation under MacLeith. The villagers also held to the slim hope that their homes would not be razed by this army if they offered their support. It didn't matter to the villagers who Kenric was or his reasons for laying siege, yet the smith was moved to tears when he learned the fierce warrior was the husband of Lady Tess. She was remembered with great affection by the villagers, for many owed their lives to cures or care provided by her or her mother. Kenric thanked the smith for his offer and promised to spare the peasants' homes, knowing he would have burned the village to the ground had he laid siege to this castle before his marriage.

A tall post was driven into place at noon of that day, well within sight of the soldiers on the battlement walls. Gordon MacLeith was brought forward, his good arm tied behind his back, a long tether tied round his neck. Kenric picked up the end of the tether and mounted his warhorse, ignoring Gordon's screamed insults as he kicked the horse forward, keeping the pace just fast enough to make Gordon scramble to keep up. Kenric slowed the pace as he rode the perimeter of the wall, just out of bow range, though he heard the insults and jeers called down from the walls. As he neared the camp again at the end of his journey, Kenric knew the deep bellow of fury came from his captive's father. He released the tether when Gordon stood in front of the post then ordered his captive tied there. There was only silence now, from his camp and from the walls. Gordon was too winded to say anything. Kenric's voice rang out clearly, his words raising the hair on many a man's head.

"You have until nightfall to claim your son's life, Dunmore MacLeith. Open the gates and I will promise your men safe passage to Scotland. If the gates remain closed at nightfall, your son hangs. Until your surrender or his death, he receives a score of lashes each hour."

Kenric kicked his horse away from the post, closer to the gates of the fortress. He gazed up at the wall where he knew Dunmore MacLeith stood, knowing MacLeith would think Kenric was looking directly at him.

"You know of me, MacLeith. You know I carry the title of Butcher for good reason. Do these gates remain closed at daybreak, I will raze these walls until no two stones stand atop each other and destroy whatever I find within. The fact that Remmington Castle is my property will not make my sword fall any lighter. The gold weighs heavy in my chests from many campaigns and I can well afford to build another. If you remain behind those walls at daybreak, gaze well at the hills beyond you, MacLeith, for you will never walk them again."

Kenric's warhorse backed away from the gates in measured steps. He finally turned the animal and slowly circled the post where Gordon was tied. Gordon remained silent, knowing there was no possibility of mercy in the warlord's eyes.

The night fell so quietly that crickets could be heard in the surrounding fields and the occasional hoot of an owl in the nearby forest. But the peaceful sounds of the night were shattered by Gordon's pleas and shrieks of fear as he was dragged to a tall, graceful oak tree. Silence fell abruptly and one by one, the crickets began to chirp again.

Later that night, Kenric lay on his cot with a drained flask of wine at his side. He felt no remorse for his actions that day. Such was the responsibility of his rank. If anything, he'd given Gordon an easy death, a much more merciful death than the man deserved. He'd just ended the life of a man who inflicted more pain than could possibly be received in one day as retribution. What mattered most was the fact that his wife was safe forever from Gordon. Only the father remained.

Tess rolled to her side and punched the straw pillow again, longing for the comfort of her own bed. Kenric's bed. How could she have forgotten so quickly what it was like to live with only the meanest comforts? She looked across the small monk's cell to see Helen sleeping soundly on her own straw pallet, surprised that the tiny window allowed enough moonlight to see anything.

"Close your eyes, Tess."

Tess sat up on her pallet and searched the shadowy corners of the room. The thought was her own, but the words seemed to be spoken aloud in a deep male voice. Nerves, Tess decided, lying back down. She closed her eyes and tried to imagine what her husband would be doing at that moment. It was late and he would doubtless be asleep in his tent. She pictured him lying on his cot, one arm resting across his forehead, the other on his chest. Tess sighed and drifted into sleep.

In her dream she joined Kenric on the cot, smiling when he opened his arms in his sleep to wrap her safely within them. She lay there contentedly for a time until the flap of Kenric's tent opened and a man stepped through. She didn't feel fear or surprise when she recognized her father, but a strong sense of contentment tinged by sadness. The lines of his face, blurred by memory, came into sharp focus with the flood of a thousand memories. She'd forgotten what a big man her father was. He smiled down at her, then his gaze traveled to the sleeping form of her husband and he nodded his approval. Tess returned the smile and rose from the cot, taking the hand he extended to her. They walked through the flap of the tent to the camp outside, making their way around several dying campfires until they stood beneath the walls of Remmington. Her father gazed up at the walls for a long time and Tess could sense an overwhelming sadness that he should be standing outside his own walls, the enemy safely within.

"Look closely, my child." Tess didn't see his lips move but heard his voice just the same. Her father pointed up at a long, narrow drainage pipe that descended from one tower, the tower housing the kitchens. "My castle has but one flaw."

As Tess watched, shadowy figures of soldiers emerged from the night, creeping stealthily toward the drainpipe. They were not soldiers at all, merely the dark shadows men would cast against the wall. The black outline of a phantom ladder was leaned against the wall and the men began to climb, a slight man first, to test the pipe's strength. One by one they climbed until more than a score of soldiers were inside the walls.

"You know the layout of the castle," her father said, looking over his shoulder, but not at Tess. " 'Tis your skill from there that will carry you to victory or defeat."

Tess glanced over her shoulder, surprised to see Kenric standing there. He nodded solemnly at her father's words.

"Return to your dreams, daughter." Tess's father laid a gentle hand across her eyes.

Tess felt rested and completely at peace, as if something important had been accomplished. The memory of a misty dream floated across her senses and she struggled awake, thinking she would better remember the dream without sleep dulling her thoughts. The first thing she saw upon opening her eyes was Helen's empty pallet. She searched the dark room until she spied her sister-in-law, her back flattened against the wall in one corner of their room, her eyes wide with fright.

"You saw him, too?" Tess whispered, the memory of the dream rushing forward to greet her. Helen jerked her head forward to nod.

"Milord?"

Kenric tore his gaze from the drainpipe, surprised that Tess and her father no longer stood before him. His eyes were glazed, not quite focused when he turned to stare at Fitz Alan.

"Kenric, are you awake?" Fitz Alan asked, his voice a low whisper so the MacLeith soldiers on the wall above them wouldn't hear. They were easy targets and within close range of the enemy's archers. He'd noticed Kenric leaving his tent and followed him here to the foot of the south tower. Something in Kenric's manner made Fitz Alan hesitate to call out to him or even place a restraining hand on his arm until now. It was as if the baron moved in a daze, walking as a man does in his sleep, with his eyes wide open but unseeing. Though the night was warm, the blank look in Kenric's eyes sent a shiver down Fitz Alan's spine. "We must be away from here, milord. The moon is too bright to stand this close to the enemy."

Fitz Alan waited a moment then took Kenric by the arm when the man made no move on his own. He led Kenric as quietly as possible back to his tent, relieved when they passed none of their soldiers who would question their lord's strange manner. Kenric seemed to rouse from his strange state the moment they entered his tent.

"I have found the flaw, Fitz Alan," Kenric said quietly. He lit the tall candle near his cot then opened a small trunk. The layout of Remmington Castle that he'd drawn with his wife's assistance was unrolled and Kenric motioned to Fitz Alan to sit next to him so they could study the map.

Fitz Alan listened in amazement as Kenric laid out his plan for taking the castle. The next night, while the castle slept, twenty men would scale the drainpipe that led to a window above the kitchens. There they would subdue the servants within, or lock them in one of the storage bins if they seemed unlikely to raise a warning. From there the men would make their way to the walks of the curtain wall. With luck, the few guards standing watch there could be silenced quietly and they would reach the gatehouse with little or no fighting.

The plan went better than Kenric expected. Not only did he and his men reach the gatehouse without a warning being sounded, they found most of the guards within the strategic point sound asleep. The chains holding the drawbridge in place were easily struck and the portcullises raised, allowing Kenric's army to pour into the castle before the enemy was fully awake. His soldiers moved quickly to the donjon, taking the great tower before the MacLeiths could move to that last haven of safety.

The sounds of battle rang within the walls of Remmington for no more than three hours. It was almost too easy. Those who did not die in battle were herded into the dungeons. Kenric released the poor souls he found incarcerated there and ordered them from the fortress, certain their crimes could not be so great as their captors'. Then it was time to search for Dunmore MacLeith. Though each prisoner was questioned, none knew or would tell where the lord could be found. Kenric began to worry that MacLeith had found a way out of the castle through some secret passage.

To his great pleasure, it was Kenric who finally flushed his enemy from cover. He was searching the highest floor of the north tower when a garderobe door sprang open, its occupant bursting from the interior with a flash of deadly blades. Kenric recognized his foe immediately from his wife's descriptions and his smile was cold and unforgiving as he drew his own sword.

"Ye'd best say your prayers," the old man warned, finding his own smile when Kenric ordered his men to back away. MacLeith crouched down to assume his battle stance, circling in slow, measured steps around his enemy. "I'll no turn o'er this fortress to the likes o' you, Montague. 'Tis said Death guides your sword, but the Devil guides mine."

Kenric tracked MacLeith's movements with the tip of his sword, content to wait for the attack. "Before this day is out, you will convey my respects personally to whoever you meet on the other side."

"It comes down to the two of us," MacLeith said, drawing small circles in the air with the claymore he held in his right hand. His left held an equally deadly dirk. "I'll be having your word that your men will honor my victory when I slit your gullet."

Kenric shook his head. "You will not leave here alive. If lightning strikes me dead this moment, you'll have to fight every one of my men between here and your grave."

The older man shrugged almost imperceptibly, as if he'd already known the answer. "Then I'd best get started."

The words weren't even out of his mouth before his claymore struck steel, lunging forward to meet the Butcher's sword head-on. MacLeith was a skilled warrior, but not so skilled as Kenric. Their swords rang out in the fierce song of battle, but no more than half an hour passed before MacLeith knew his defeat lay moments away. Worst of all, it was obvious the Butcher of Wales meant to take him alive. Blows that should have brought his death were turned at the last moment to deal deep, vicious slashes to his arms and chest, his armor no match for the strength behind the sword that sliced into his body. Backing toward the door, Dunmore moved onto the battlements.

The wind blew fiercely at this height and MacLeith swayed against it, backing away from the man who stalked him. There was no hope of escape, not even the hope of a quick death at the hands of the victor. Recognizing the fire that burned deep in his enemy's eyes, Dunmore knew he would be punished long and dearly for his crimes. He spared one last glance at the walls of Remmington Castle, sorry he'd wielded the power that came with such a fortress for only five short years. He backed away again to put a few more feet between them, thankful the Butcher was certain enough of his victory to provide the opening he needed.

Kenric didn't realize MacLeith's intent until it was too late. One moment the grizzled warrior looked old and defeated, the next, a flash of defiant life sprang to his eyes and he leaped agilely to the ledge of the parapets. Even as Kenric rushed forward, MacLeith swung his claymore high overhead and let loose a fierce battle cry as he vaulted over the walls to his death.

Kenric leaned over the battlements, gazing down at the broken body far below. It wasn't supposed to end this quickly, but end it had. The long, bloody reign of Dunmore MacLeith was over.

30

Tess wasn't smiling when she entered the gates of her home for the first time in five years. Nay, she felt like crying. So much death and destruction since her father had ridden through these gates. So much misery, so much bloodshed. MacLeith had left his mark in many ways on Remmington, though the Scottish soldiers who once lined the walls were gone, those who survived stripped of their horses and weapons before being escorted to the border. Uncle Ian was on the other side, making sure they passed quickly through his lands. She learned from Simon that many other powerful lairds north of her uncle waited to provide the same quick escort. No one would offer refuge to MacLeith's fallen army.

Tess was thankful that so few of Kenric's men were injured in the fighting and amazed that not one of his men had died. Everything had happened so quickly that few of her people were injured and only one dead from a fall. The rumors of his soldiers' skills were certainly well-founded, for more than a hundred of MacLeith's men lost their lives that bloody day. She and Helen heard the story of Kenric's victory over MacLeith many times from Simon, Evard, and Fitz Alan. The long trip from Kelso, made slower by her advancing pregnancy, gave the men ample time to tell the tale over and over again. The first time Tess heard the story she could not hide her shock, remembering well the dream of her father. She dared not speak of the dream with anyone but Kenric, yet her husband did not ride with his men to collect her. Nay, she tried to be understanding when Fitz Alan explained that Kenric rode out with his brother to secure Remmington's other holdings and would not be at Remmington Castle when she arrived. She tried very hard not to feel sorry for herself. Tess did not want to face what MacLeith had done to the inside of her home, not without Kenric by her side. It was sure to be devastating and she needed his support. Why would he send for her, knowing she would not want to face this homecoming alone?

They passed through the gates without much notice, Tess so caught up in her thoughts that at first she didn't notice the crowd gathered inside the lower bailey. She could not help but heed their roar of welcome.

The entire castle was gathered there, Kenric's knights and soldiers, and to her great joy, many old, familiar faces of villagers and castle folk who had survived MacLeith. But the face that caused hers to light up was that of her husband, standing with crossed arms and braced legs atop the steps to the great hall.

He descended the steps slowly as she rode forward, meeting her at the base of the stairs. He caught the reins of her palfrey then swept her carefully into his arms. Tess laced her arms around Kenric's neck, unable to believe he was here to greet her. "Simon and Evard said you would not return—"

"The other keeps fell easily, once MacLeith's vassals learned of his death," Kenric said, explaining his presence. Without relinquishing his hold on her, he turned to face their people. "Your lady is restored, Remmington, and she carries with her the next heir."

Although gossip had carried this news well ahead of Kenric's announcement, the crowd reacted joyously. Waiting until the shouts and clatter of sword banging against shields died down some, Kenric gave them another reason to cheer. " 'Tis to be a day of celebration and feasting. The stores have been opened and you will enjoy the bounty of Remmington this day with your lord and lady's blessings."

Kenric didn't linger to enjoy the crowd's shouts of delight. Unable to tear her gaze from her husband's well-loved face, Tess was vaguely aware of passing through the hall and mounting the steps that led to her parents' old chamber. She raised her lips and tried to capture his mouth for a kiss. He lifted his chin, avoiding her lips even as he shook his head. "Nay, sweet. Do you kiss me now, we will make love in this stairwell. 'Tis unsafe and I wish to take you in the comfort of a bed."

Tess nodded, smiling, even though she began to dread entering her parents' chamber. It held too many memories and she feared the evidence of Dunmore MacLeith there would make the place repulsive. Kenric kicked the door open and she released the breath she'd been holding in a huge sigh of relief. Not a trace of MacLeith remained in the chamber. In fact, it didn't look much like her parents' old chamber, either. Instead it looked exactly like Kenric's bedchamber at Montague. Every piece of his furniture, from the massive bed, to rugs, chests, and trophies, were in place exactly as she remembered. That was the last thought she gave to the room as his lips descended upon hers for a long, soul-stirring kiss.

He hadn't teased her on the steps. There was no controlling him when his lips touched hers. Her mantle, bliaut, chainse, and chemise sailed across the room along with Kenric's clothes, like leaves in a strong fall wind. He wasn't satisfied until she was naked, then he lay siege to her body with his hands and mouth.

"You will be the death of me yet," Kenric declared, when they both lay sated. He rolled to his back and sprawled his big body out on the bed, one arm holding Tess to his side. "I am amazed each time I survive your passion."

"Mmm," she murmured, rubbing her cheek against his chest. " 'Tis rather unnerving, is it not?"

"You have doubtless been told how we retook Remmington," he said abruptly.

Tess nodded. "How did you know about the drainpipe?"

"A dream." He lay back on the bed and propped one hand behind his head, staring up at the canopy. "At least, I think it was a dream. Four days after I made camp at Remmington, I was asleep in my tent, having a most pleasant dream that my wife joined me in bed. Just when I thought to start kissing her, a man entered the tent, a stranger, yet his features were vaguely familiar. Somehow I knew this man was my father-in-law. He led you from the tent, turning as he held the flap aside to call me forward as well. I followed to the battlement walls where he revealed how the castle could be breached. I could see shadowy images of my own men as I gazed up at the wall. When I looked down again, you and your father were gone."

"I had the same dream." She caught her lower lip between her teeth, her gaze searching his face. "Do you truly think me a witch?"

"You are my wife," he murmured, enfolding her in a gentle embrace. "You are also the mother of my child and the woman I love more than anything on this earth. Beyond that, I care not what others would call you for your strange abilities. I have always thought you special, Tess.

What you have is a gift from God, for surely the Devil could find no welcome in a soul as gentle as yours. Men have often sought to destroy what they do not understand, so 'tis best to keep this knowledge to ourselves. Yet there is nothing that could make me think less of you, sweetheart. Should any man seek to persecute my wife, I would protect your life with my own."

"You truly do not care?" she asked anxiously. He kissed her brow and gazed tenderly into her eyes.

"I care only that you love me."

She smiled and snuggled closer against his chest. After five long years of impossible dreams and tarnished hopes, Tess had finally come home.

Epilogue

Five Years Later

"*Trevor, Tristan, you will not play pranks on Agnes,*" Tess warned, shaking her finger at the identical twin boys. She received two solemn little nods for her effort, or at least as solemn as the four-year-old boys could manage. "Your brother, Phillip, has just had his dinner and I want all my boys asleep now."

"Phillip would like to hear one more story, Mama." Trevor pointed to the cradle where his new brother cooed happily.

"Aye, the story of the naughty fox," Tristan piped in.

"You've had your story for the night, young men. Now off to bed. Your mother needs her rest as well."

Tess tucked the children into their beds and kissed each one good night, smiling as she closed the door to their bedchamber. Her children slept in the room she used as a child, next to the chamber she now shared with her husband. Miriam's daughter, Agnes, slept in the children's room as well, helping Tess care for the children.

Anxious for a bit of sleep, Tess hurried to her own bed. Phillip might be full and happy at the moment, but Agnes would bring the babe to her again in three or four hours for his next feeding.

It was amazing how easy one babe seemed after the surprise of the twins' birth. Even Kenric took her latest pregnancy in stride, not worrying overly much about the outcome as he had with the twins. Tess could still remember the funny expressions on Kenric's face when she grew so fat with the twins. He would stare at her belly in horror, certain she would give birth to a full-grown man. Aye, the twins were a pleasant surprise, for even Tess began to worry about her size long before she went into labor. Yet she'd been doubly rewarded for her worries. Both boys were the image of their father, with dark hair and smoky gray eyes. Phillip too favored his father's dark looks, but Tess secretly hoped he would keep the blue eyes that turned more violet each day, looking very close in shade to his mother's. She couldn't wait to boast over the trait to her husband.

She was certain Kenric would return any day from his journey to Montague. Although Guy had proved a wise and able ruler for his young age, he'd recently gotten himself into trouble that required his brother's counsel and his brother's famous army as well.

Word arrived shortly before Phillip's birth that Guy required his older brother's assistance, yet Kenric had delayed the trip to Montague until his son was safely delivered. He'd nearly refused to make the trip at all when Tess tried to resume her duties with the twins too quickly and was forced back to bed until her strength returned. Although he professed great reluctance to make the trip, Tess suspected he looked forward to fighting at his brother's side again, if Guy's foolish challenge had indeed come down to a battle. He'd even taken Roger Fitz Alan along on the trip, a sure sign he expected his sword would be put to use. Poor Helen. She was probably cursing her husband this moment for leaving her with two young daughters and another child on the way.

Tess sank wearily onto her bed and closed her eyes, but the smile that played around her mouth was a happy one, the joy and contentment of her life reflected in her face. Another week at the most and her life would be complete again, for Kenric would be at her side once more. She awoke several hours later. A quick peek at the window said the night was well under way, yet she could hear the echoed sounds of many horses in the inner bailey. She sat up in bed, her heart beating faster as she realized the commotion was probably caused by her husband's return to Remmington.

Kenric stepped into his chamber a short time later, the hairs at the nape of his neck standing on end at the sight that greeted him. Tess was sitting up in bed and smiling quite prettily. The light from two tall, fat candles left burning on either side of the bed cast a golden sheen to her hair and the warm glow beckoned him forward from the dark shadows of the room. It was an exact picture of an image he remembered from many years past. His greeting was murmured in such a low voice that his wife probably didn't hear it. "I knew I would find you this way."

"Kenric!" Tess's smile was nearly blinding. She held out her arms, hugging him fiercely when he came forward to sit on the bed. "I have missed you so!"

"You are feeling better?" he asked, gathering her close to his chest. He knew for a fact that his wife was in perfect health, for he'd sent messengers back and forth from Remmington to Montague throughout his absence, for the sole purpose of assuring himself of his family's well-being.

"I feel wonderful now that you have returned." She sighed, satisfied now that his arms were around her. "It seems as if a year has passed instead of a month. What think you of your new son?"

Kenric rubbed his cheek against her hair, much more interested in the sweet scents and silkiness of his wife's body at the moment. "Hmm?"

"Your son," she chided, playfully nudging his arm as she drew back in his arms. She mistakenly believed he'd checked on the children as he did as a habit before retiring to their chamber each night. "You left only a week after his birth. Surely you have not forgotten the babe already? Or are you still pouting that I have yet to produce a daughter?"

"I seem to recall having had this conversation before," he replied, smiling over her serious expression. This wasn't the first incident he'd "relived." He recalled well the eve just after they were married and Tess lay abed with a fever, looking exactly as she did now and speaking nearly the same words. The first few experiences of this sort had unnerved him, ringing so true to his wife's visions of the future. Yet he'd gradually accustomed himself to her unusual abilities and the exceedingly odd experience of actually living out one of her visions rarely bothered him these days.

"You should say you are happy to have three fine boys," she instructed, missing the meaning behind his words.

"Wait," he said, quickly setting her from his lap to shed his shirt and tunic. That done, he gathered her in his arms again and presented his bared chest, smiling wickedly. "Now you may rub against my chest, wife."

"How did you know my intent?" she asked suspiciously, refusing his order. She couldn't resist tracing a line from the nape of his neck to the waistband of his breeches. She loved the feel of that solid wall of muscles and shivered in anticipation.

"This is an old vision, sweetheart. Do you remember the fever you had the first week of our marriage?" He shrugged when she shook her head and claimed she remembered little of that illness. " 'Tis much the same, though we must change one part. We did not make love that night so long ago, but nothing could keep you from me this eve."

Desire sparked to life in Kenric's eyes just before he claimed her mouth for a long, deep kiss that left them both wanting more. He pulled his boots off, hearing them hit the floor at the same time he unlaced the neck of her gown to nuzzle her shoulders.

"I missed you greatly, love. We need to make up for lost time."

" 'Tis been long enough since the birthing to start working on your girl," she purred seductively, baring her neck to his mouth. Tess drew away finally to take her turn, tracing little kisses along his throat as her fingertips drew light patterns along his leather-encased thigh, drawing ever closer to his heat.

One moment Kenric was well on his way to being seduced by his wife, the next he dumped Tess unceremoniously on the bed before he leaped toward the door, his sword already in hand. A second later, the tip of his weapon rested at the throat of the silent intruder in their room. Poor Agnes screamed in terror, frightened nearly to the point of dropping her precious bundle. Phillip began protesting the commotion quite loudly.

"Damnation, woman!" Kenric bellowed, sighing impatiently when Agnes jumped again at the sound of his voice. He slammed his sword back into its sheath and took his fussing son from the terrified woman's arms. "A knock at your lord's door would not be misplaced at this time of night. Or any other," he warned darkly, clearly picturing the scene Agnes might have walked in on. He was about to order the woman from their room when Tess's voice stopped him.

"Kenric, you have frightened Agnes half to death. She was merely being thoughtful, trying not to disturb me any sooner than necessary. She's brought our babe to me each evening for his feeding, ofttimes laying him on the bed so quietly that I am scarcely awakened before he's well fed and returned safely to his cradle." She ended up shouting to be heard over the baby's wails. "You did not know of your baron's return, did you, Agnes?"

"Nay, milady," Agnes answered just as loudly, bobbing a quick, nervous curtsy to her overlord. "Welcome home, milord."

"My apologies, Agnes, if I frightened you," he told the maid, surprising her with the concession. "You have served my lady well and deserve my thanks. Return to your bed now. I will bring the babe back to his cradle when his dinner is finished."

Agnes left the room as quickly as she could. Kenric stared down at his little son's face, pinched and red now from wailing. He smiled over the lusty bellows, though they did make his ears ring. The smile turned to a grimace when one fat little fist caught hold of the hairs on his father's chest and promptly ripped several free.

"Yeow!" Kenric rubbed the stinging spot on his chest. His expression appeared puzzled when he looked to his wife. "I do not think he likes me."

"He seeks something other than hair on a chest," she answered with a giggle, holding her arms out for the babe.

The babe quieted the moment Tess took him in her arms. Kenric settled next to his wife and son on the bed, thinking there was nothing quite so perfect as the picture of a mother feeding her child. He cupped the baby's soft head with his hand and kissed the crown of his son's head, knowing the fragile babe they had created would grow as strong and healthy as his brothers.

" 'Tis odd to see just one child at your breast," he murmured, watching Tess switch the babe to her other arm. He remembered a time, a lifetime ago, when he swore never to marry, to deny himself a wife and children. He appreciated now what that vow nearly cost him. The ache that stirred his loins just moments ago returned to his chest. Once he had kept that feeling locked from his body, allowing nothing to touch his heart. Had he ever truly believed that allowing himself to love Tess would make him weak and vulnerable?

Tess met his gaze at that moment and gave him a soft smile, the answer, as always, there in her eyes. Nay, their love did not make him weaker, but made them both stronger.

"Your son is finished with his meal," she said quietly, nodding at the sleeping babe in her arms. She looked puzzled by the intensity of her husband's expression.

"Do not move," Kenric said, taking the baby as he rose from the bed.

When he rejoined her on the bed, he murmured his greeting in her ear. "I love you, wife."

His hot breath filled her senses and brought her body instantly alive again from the short slumber of motherhood. The hard proof of his arousal pressed against her belly, proving his next words true. "And I need you now, God help me."

"You've yet to tell me how well your trip went," Tess murmured, her voice roughened by desire. She arched her hips, not really caring about the answer. "Does Guy intend to wed that woman he kidnapped?"

Kenric kissed his way back to her mouth, penetrating his wife's sweetness as he whispered the answer against her lips. Tess didn't remember a word.

About the Author

ELIZABETH ELLIOTT took a turn off the corporate fast track to write romances on the shores of a lake not far from Woebegone. In her spare time, she works as a free-lance writer/consultant in the software industry. At home with her husband and sons, she is currently writing her next novel.